'Taut, terse, thrilling and brutal, this
— Neil Broadfoot, author of *No M*

'A real firecracker. *No Way to Die* is
thriller.'
— Adam Hamdy, author of *Red Wolves*

'*Killer Intent, Power Play* and *Marked For Death* are fantastic thrillers.
No Way to Die is on another level, a masterpiece in plotting, scene
setting, building tension, the writing is sublime, I loved it.'
— AMW Books

Praise for *Power Play*

'Twist after twist... It builds to a brilliant finale.'
— *Daily Mirror*

'A high-octane conspiracy yarn.'
— *The Times*

'An intricate, twisty minefield of geopolitics and absolute power gone
rogue. Kent has outdone himself with this one.'
— David Baldacci

'A gripping conspiracy thriller.'
— Ian Rankin

'Reads like Baldacci at his best. Really intelligent, bang-up-to-date
thriller.'
— Steve Cavanagh, author of *Thirteen*

'Scarily credible, and so pacy and well-written that I forgot where I
was, who I was, and indeed that I was reading a book at all. Gripping,
absorbing, a page-turner with characters you commit to 100%.'
— Judith O'Reilly, author of *Killing State*

'The kind of fast-paced action thriller that keeps you hooked until the very end. I loved it.'
— Simon Kernick, author of *The Bone Field* series

Praise for *Marked for Death*

'Fast-paced, tightly plotted, utterly brutal in all the right places . . . *Marked For Death* ratchets up the tension and releases it like a final gunshot.'
— Jack Grimwood, author of *Nightfall Berlin*

'Another tour de force through the legal world in a tense and atmospheric hunt for a serial killer. With this second instalment in Michael Devlin's journey Tony Kent cements himself as a shining star in crime writing.'
— Angela Clarke, author of the *Social Media Murder* series

Praise for *Killer Intent*

'A compelling combination of political drama and lethal action. There are echoes of Michael Dobbs's *House of Cards* but there is more derring-do in Kent's twisty tale, which has all the makings of a bestseller.'
— *Daily Mail*

'An astute, cleverly plotted and scarily plausible conspiracy thriller with plenty of twists.'
— *The Daily Express*

NO WAY TO DIE

TONY KENT

Elliott&Thompson

First published 2021 by
Elliott and Thompson Limited
2 John Street
London WC1N 2ES
www.eandtbooks.com

This paperback edition published in 2022

ISBN: 978-1-78396-553-3

9 8 7 6 5 4 3 2 1

A catalogue record for this book is available from
the British Library.

Cover design by Stephen Mulcahey
Cover images © Shutterstock
Typesetting: Marie Doherty
Printed by CPI Group (UK) Ltd,
Croydon, CR0 4YY

For my sister Kate

Yes, the next one is coming . . .

12 JULY
2021

ONE

4.57 a.m.
Eastern Daylight Time

The cheap polyester shirt sucked against Ricardo Garcia's skin like wet cling film. After so long, it had become a familiar feeling, but no less of an irritation. Twenty-one years ago, Garcia would not have ignored it. He would have questioned why his comfort was not worth the few cents extra for cotton.

Not any more.

Now he was used to the feeling of slick man-made fibre. To literally peeling his patrolman's uniform from his body at the end of every humid night shift. It was the price he paid for steady employment.

He looked over at the newbie beside him as they turned right from Mallory Square and on to Duval Street, nearing the end of their closing-time round. The conditions had hit Clinton Dewitt just as hard, Garcia could see; his chest and stomach muscles were almost visible through the sweat-soaked khaki. The younger man's movement seemed affected by the constriction of his uniform. Not by much, but enough for Garcia to recognise discomfort.

'Still not used to the heat?'

The question was no criticism. Dewitt was from the north

and had been in Key West for only a month. To acclimatise in four weeks was a big ask. But when those four weeks were in July? No chance.

'The heat I can take.' Dewitt's tone matched his expression. The discomfort was making him ill-tempered. 'It's the damn wet in the air that's bothering me. Is it always like this?'

'You promise you won't quit if I tell you it gets worse?' Garcia chuckled as he answered, keeping his tone light. The humidity *was* much higher in the winter months, but he did not want to add to his colleague's already bad mood.

Low pay and antisocial hours made it hard to attract good candidates to the City Commission's Area Patrol Group. The lack of any route to promotion made it even harder to keep them. So when they managed to find someone like Dewitt? Early thirties, fit and strong, even willing to give up his rest night for a chance to learn the ropes with an old hand like Garcia?

They ain't gonna want to lose him.

Neither man said another word as they turned left, off Duval and on to Front Street. Garcia had been walking the same route since he had started the job. Twelve times a night between 10 p.m. and 5 a.m. He could follow it with his eyes closed. This was only Dewitt's seventh night but – physical discomfort aside – he already seemed a veteran.

'You see that?' Dewitt asked, breaking the silence.

'Uh-huh,' Garcia grunted in response. He had noticed the same movement.

The northernmost section of Front Street was short, even by Key West standards. And so the corner it shared with Duval allowed both men a view of North Bay Marina at its far end. The start and the end point of the circular patrol route, at 5 a.m.

the marina was always the last inspection of the night. And thanks to Key West's bars closing around thirty minutes earlier, it was rarely a quiet one.

Tonight looked to be no exception.

'What do you think?' Dewitt increased his pace as he spoke, causing Garcia to do the same.

'Same as always,' Garcia replied. His eyes had fixed on shapes he could barely make out in the darkness. '*Pendejos* have too much to drink, those boats become a homing beacon.'

Dewitt seemed to agree. Or at least he didn't argue. He maintained his pace, and with the edge of the marina barely four hundred yards from Duval, they covered the distance in under two minutes.

But sunrise was still two hours away, so being closer did little to assist their view in the darkness. Not that light was usually necessary; beer and vodka jello shots tended to have a noise-amplifying effect. It made locating drunken tourists in the early hours more an aural task than a visual one.

And it was that very fact that made the current silence so unusual.

As they reached the entrance to the marina, Garcia could read none of his own apprehension on the younger man's face.

He hasn't noticed the lack of sound, Garcia thought. *Why would he? He doesn't know how rare it is yet.*

Garcia strained his eyes as he attempted to count the figures who were now just about visible at the end of the marina's third jetty. It was no use; at this distance it was just too dark. The marina was not wide, but the jetties themselves – four of them – each ran a length of around one hundred yards.

'Are we gonna go deal with this?'

At the hissed question, Garcia turned his head to face

Dewitt. Unlike the darkened smudges that he could barely make out inside the marina, he could see the younger man's face clearly.

Still no fear. No concern. Garcia shook his head.

Well, he did say he wanted to learn.

'You know how many there are, do you?' Garcia asked. He was attempting to make his tone instructive, but it was difficult to achieve at the low volume. 'Or even *who* they are?'

'It's what you said, ain't it? It's drunks looking for something to do after closing?'

'Maybe,' Garcia replied. 'Maybe not. But tell me this: when did you last hear drunks that quiet?'

Dewitt gave no answer. Didn't have one, Garcia figured. Instead he, too, squinted into the distance. But Garcia doubted that the younger man could make out any more detail than he was able.

'Well, if it's not drunks then who is it?' Dewitt finally asked. His confident tone was unchanged by the unknown.

'Who knows,' Garcia replied. 'Could just be boat residents. Could be someone looking for something to steal, or some other sort of trouble. Worse trouble.'

'Or it could just be quiet drunks.'

Garcia shook his head. 'No such thing.'

There was silence for a moment.

'Well, we ain't gonna find out standing here, are we?' Dewitt stood up from their crouch, his tone now impatient. 'Let's go ask *them* who they are.'

Dewitt took one step forward. Garcia reached out and grasped his forearm before he could take another.

'You really wanna take that risk, Clint?' he asked, his voice suddenly a whisper. 'I've been doing this a long time, man. And people creeping about in the dark, all silent-like . . . that ain't usual. It ain't good. We're not cops; we don't have to do this.'

'Like hell we don't,' Dewitt replied. There was a streak of disgust in his voice that Garcia could not ignore. 'We're paid to patrol these roads and these ports and . . . all this. If we start avoiding places because of what, a few shadows? How's that doing our job?'

Garcia hesitated. He knew Dewitt was wrong. That there was no need to put themselves at risk. And his gut was telling him that this *was* a risk. But in the same instant, he felt shame. Shame that, after over two decades as a patrolman, he was not willing to do his duty as readily as a man who had only just started. Worse, a man who was not even officially on duty tonight.

'Look,' he finally said, 'I . . . I just don't see what we have to lose by calling this in. By letting the cops deal with this.'

'What about our credibility, Ricardo? And our pride, man? You really want to call other men down here, to do something because we can't? What the hell does that make us?'

'It's just . . .'

'And what if this *is* nothing? What if they *are* just a bunch of drunks?'

'They're not drunks. I've been doing this long enough. We'd hear them, we'd—'

'OK, residents, then. Boat owners. What if we call the cops and it's just the damn boat owners? How do we look then? I need this job, Ricardo. I'm not risking it. I'm going down there.'

Dewitt pulled his arm from Garcia's grip and took another two steps forward before turning to face the older man.

'You coming or you staying?'

Garcia hesitated again. His instincts were telling him one

thing. But his shame was saying something else. And Dewitt's words had hit home. *I need this job, Ricardo.*

Dewitt had three kids and another on the way. That, he had told Garcia, was why he had taken a job for which he was overqualified. And why he was so determined to do it well. Dewitt needed the money. He needed the work. And Garcia wasn't going to put that at risk. He wasn't going to see those kids go hungry,

'Dammit. Yeah.' He reached for his sidearm, a Smith & Wesson M&P 9. Pulling it from its holster, he fixed his gaze on Dewitt. 'Yeah. I'm coming. But we do this armed and ready, understood?'

'Understood,' Dewitt replied, unholstering his own identical weapon as he spoke. 'You gonna lead the way?'

Garcia stepped forward in answer, past the younger man. The same mixed emotions that had forced his agreement were now compelling him to take the lead. He was, after all, the senior patrolman.

These were *his* docks.

He covered the first fifty yards of the jetty slowly, his firearm raised. His steps were silent, at least as far as he could tell. He hoped his heart was too; in his own head, it was beating like a snare drum.

Dewitt's steps seemed louder – clear enough to tell Garcia that the younger man was just a few feet behind – but hopefully not enough to attract attention.

The patches of light thrown by the tall lamps that intermittently illuminated the jetty gave him cause for concern, but they managed to pass under the first two unnoticed.

That left just one more, perhaps seventy-five yards along the walkway. It was close enough to announce their presence once Garcia stepped into the light. More importantly, it was close enough to finally see their targets.

'I'll stop under the last light,' Garcia whispered over his shoulder. 'You come up beside me, weapon raised. Understood?'

'Got it.'

Two more steps to go. Somehow Garcia's heart rate increased even further.

He took a deep breath. He had intended it to be calming but it had no such effect. It did nothing to slow his racing pulse.

But still Garcia stepped forward again. Slowly. Deliberately. Into the light.

He focused on his raised weapon, his hands shaking.

He could see the shadows now. Not their faces. Not their features. But he could see what they were doing, and in that moment he knew that he had been right.

There was nothing innocent happening here.

'STAY EXACTLY WHERE YOU ARE.'

Garcia's voice was loud and firm. It sounded calmer than he had thought he could manage. Filled with more authority. Enough to stop the shadows moving at least; each one turned to face Garcia where he stood, now visible in full uniform under the jetty's final light.

'DON'T MOVE A GODDAMN MUSCLE.'

He felt a surge of confidence as the shadowy figures obeyed his orders. It calmed him where the deep breath had failed. With his hand steadied and his eyes fixed on the shadows, he called out behind.

'Newbie, you joining me up here or—'

The final words never left Garcia's lips. The feeling of a dull, heavy blow to his back distracted him from finishing the sentence, but, even without it, the eight-inch blade that plunged into and then across his back, expertly puncturing both lungs in one strike, would have made any further sound impossible.

Garcia tried to turn. Tried to see who had struck him from behind. But now his legs would not obey him. He felt his knees give way as he slowly crumpled down to the damp wooden planks beneath his feet.

For just a moment, he wondered what had happened.

It was a fleeting confusion, instantly replaced by an agony beyond anything he could have imagined as the knife was torn from his back. He looked up and in that moment his unknowing eyes locked with his killer's, just as the blade bit into the side of his neck and was drawn slowly across his throat.

TWO

5.35 a.m. EDT

Joe Dempsey leaned against the guard rail of his thirty-fifth-floor balcony, took a first sip of tea and watched the early red-gold hints of sunlight reflect off the glass frontage of the building ahead.

The Manhattan air was already warm, suggesting another blistering day ahead. By now Dempsey expected nothing else; the past weeks had been an uninterrupted run of glorious summer. He had been cautioned about New York's intense seasons before moving here. Told that half the city's population would go elsewhere between June and September, to escape the unbearable heat.

That warning had come almost four years ago and yet since then the mercury had rarely hit those fabled heights. Dempsey's first few summers as an adopted New Yorker had been unusually mild. No bad thing, he realised now. The previous summer had been hard enough on the city, thanks to the Covid-19 lockdown.

The addition of a heatwave would have made it unbearable.

But that was then. It was 2021 now and though the world was still in recovery, there was freedom enough to make the soaring daily temperatures manageable. Shops were open. Bars and restaurants. Even the parks. After fourteen months of strict limits on their liberty, Manhattan's one point six million residents could now leave their homes, the city and even the state.

This renewed freedom made Dempsey smile as he watched the streets below. For far too long he'd been looking out on an eerie mix of stillness and silence, the life of the city seemingly extinguished by an invisible enemy. But now? It was alive. And while still far from its normal self, it was recovering fast.

A true testament to human resilience.

Or maybe it's just New Yorkers?

The question flashed through his mind as he registered an angry exchange of words and car horns at the intersection of 74th Street and 1st Avenue. Loud enough for the sound to reach Dempsey a block away and four hundred and fifty feet up, he quickly spotted its source: a yellow cab turning right and into the path of an oncoming garbage truck, neither driver willing to give an inch. Only the crunch of metal on metal would have made the scene more quintessentially 'New York'.

And all before 6 a.m.

Dempsey dismissed the thought as soon as it had arrived. As typical as the scene was to Manhattan life as he had grown to know it, Dempsey had seen enough of the world to know that neither his adopted city nor its residents were unique. Not before Covid. Not during it. And certainly not after.

The virus had hit the entire world and it had hit hard. Dempsey had seen *that* first hand. The International Security Bureau had been unaffected by the shutdowns that had blighted economies across the globe. There had been no reduction in existing threats, worldwide *or* domestic. If anything, the overall danger level had increased, with rising tensions between the US and China over the impact of the virus.

And that had made Dempsey and his team as essential as they ever were. Maybe even more.

For almost a year, the threat of conflict between the USA and its only realistic global rival had preoccupied the United Nations as much as the sickness itself. That meant that it had preoccupied Dempsey too, resulting in him spending less time in New York in 2020 than he had in either of the two years before it. While everyone else stayed home, Dempsey and his ISB team had travelled an eerily quiet planet, pursuing the source of the misinformation that had put the two giant nations at odds.

But that was then. It had been months now since they had uncovered the truth. And so months since the USA and China had put their rivalry aside and focused solely on beating the virus. The mass vaccination programmes that were now in place had almost achieved that.

For now he could put those thoughts out of his mind and just watch the sun rising over Manhattan, awakening the city that supposedly never sleeps.

Apartment 35D of the Stratford Building – 1385 York Avenue – faces west. A fact that should have made its balcony better positioned to enjoy a sunset than a sunrise. That had been Dempsey's expectation when he had signed the lease three years earlier, but it had taken just one morning for him to be corrected. Rarely asleep beyond dawn, he discovered on that first day that the three blocks between The Stratford and its nearest high-rise neighbour was the perfect distance for the sunrise to be reflected back towards him.

At the height of the morning, it would provide a sheer wall of light. But now, as the sun barely crept over the rear horizon, the first few beams turned those opposing windows into small portals of gold, allowing the New York skyline to break through the darkness of the night.

For Dempsey, *this* was when the city was at its most magical.

The sound of multiple sirens reached his ears from the distance. One was close. Just three blocks away, by his reckoning. The surest sound of city life. It almost brought his smile back, as he took another sip of hot tea, but Dempsey forced the reaction down.

As welcome as it was to hear life in Manhattan again, those sirens meant bad news for someone.

He reached for his smartphone. In just seconds he had connected to the live departures board at New York JFK airport. An instant more and his fingers were moving again, locating British Airways Flight 1594 from New York JFK to London Heathrow.

10.30 a.m., the display told him. *Departing on time*.

Dempsey allowed himself that smile. He was happy. In less than five hours, and for the first time in two years, he was going home.

THREE

5.40 a.m. EDT

'Is that the last crate?'

Cam Arnold pointed to the sealed plastic container that Scott Turner was holding. Arnold stepped forward as he spoke, careful to avoid contact with the pool of congealing blood that had spilled out of the still-warm corpse lying between them.

'All but the smaller box,' Turner replied. 'That's back ... that's along the jetty, up by the boat. Just like you said.'

Turner's voice was quiet, naturally muffled by the ski mask that concealed his face. But was that the only cause?

Arnold couldn't be sure. Every one of his men had been trained to kill, Scott Turner included. But, until this morning, Turner at least had never seen real death. Not violent death, anyway. And sure as hell not up close and personal. That had now changed.

And Arnold had to wonder what effect it was having.

It's his first time, he reassured himself, *that's all. Shit like this, it can affect the best of us.*

For now, Arnold would keep things simple. No complex orders. No discussion. He would give the boy time and space to get his head straight. Turner was uniquely important to what they were here to achieve, Arnold believed, and he knew the kid would need a clear mind for what lay ahead.

He pointed again to the crate in Turner's hands.

'Take that one to the back of the van and load it, then wait for me there with the others.'

Turner nodded his head without a word, stepping aside as he did so to give the older man space to pass him on the jetty. A little more space than was necessary, Arnold noticed.

The unforced distance clinched it: Turner *was* spooked.

Maybe I should have warned him.

Arnold forced the doubt from his mind.

What's done is done. Plus he's motivated. It'll kick in.

Arnold walked away without another word, into the darkness and towards the small boat he knew to be moored at the far end of the jetty. Turner did the same, but in the opposite direction. Back to North Bay Marina's entrance and to the deserted Front Street.

The shape of a vessel gradually emerged out of the shroud of darkness as Arnold moved closer. It was far smaller than the luxury sailboat he had passed towards the front of the marina; if anything, it was closer in size to a local tourist fishing boat than to the yachts that were more common in this particular marina. The difference, though, was not as noticeable without other boats close by for comparison. Unlike the other jetties, this one was mostly unoccupied. Arnold had seen to that.

He continued to walk, the dimmest of lights from the boat now just about illuminating his path. A few more steps and he was parallel with the bow, and, for the first time, he could make out the small box that Turner had mentioned. Placed in the very centre of the walkway, it had been hidden from sight by the same darkness that had protected the boat itself.

Arnold placed a hand on the body of the vessel and leaned in.

'You ready to go?'

A single outlined figure was just about visible from where Arnold stood. The boat's only occupant, Arnold knew.

'As soon as you say the word.'

'Perfect. Give it ten minutes from now, then get moving.'

'OK.'

'In the meantime, stay alert. You hear anything that worries you before the time's up, you cut and you run. Got it?'

'Got it, Cam.'

'Good. See you back at the camp.'

'You too. Good luck.'

Arnold did not acknowledge the man's final words. Why would he? He had planned this thing to perfection and so luck had nothing to do with it. Instead he crouched down, carefully picked up the small box and slowly walked back towards the lights of the marina.

A minute later and he was on Front Street, by the open back doors of a long, grey Dodge Sprinter van. Four men were waiting, all now visible under the street lighting, their masks removed.

It was the first time Arnold had seen the faces of his team in weeks. He had deemed it too risky to have them all in a location as small as Key West while he made the arrangements for tonight, so he had stationed himself here alone. All recent contact between them had been via the usual discreet channels.

That stage of the operation was now over. With his preparations having gone perfectly and his isolation no longer necessary, Cam Arnold was back where he belonged.

He was back in command.

He carefully placed the small box into the rear of the open van, then repositioned three of the larger plastic containers that had already been loaded so that they pinned that box in place. Satisfied it could not move during the journey ahead, he stepped back, closed the van doors and turned to his men.

'Is the Jeep parked where I told you?' Arnold directed his question to Turner.

'Exactly where you said,' Turner replied.

'And you took the route I told you, right? From there to here?'

'To the letter.'

The answer sounded strange to Arnold's ear but then so did a lot of the language Turner tended to use, especially with his British accent thrown into the mix. Arnold skipped past the thought as quickly as it arrived, his mind instead focusing on one far more important.

The kid's voice, he told himself. *It's more certain than on the jetty. He sounds like himself again.*

Arnold studied Turner's face even as he assessed his tone. He looked intently at the younger man's eyes, looking for any sign of doubt. To his relief, he found none.

Just a wobble, Arnold told himself. *Same thing could happen to anyone. But he's back.*

'OK. OK, good. Then you know what has to happen now. You take the exact same route back to the Jeep and you get moving. And you make damn sure you follow the road directions I gave you to get off the island. Understood?'

Turner nodded his head. Two of the others grunted their understanding. And the fourth man – Paul Holly – stayed silent.

The lack of questions reassured Arnold. Every one of them knew the plan – or at least enough of it to perform their own role within it. And every one of them, he was sure, would do their duty.

He turned to Paul Holly.

'You're with me, like we agreed.'

Arnold gestured towards the Sprinter's passenger side as he spoke and Holly moved towards it without a word or even a glance towards the other men. Another unquestioning soldier.

Arnold glanced to his left while Holly moved, his eyes drifting back towards the marina's entrance as he took a final moment of reflection on 'Phase One'. So far his plan had run perfectly, but there was no time for celebration. There was a hell of a lot still to do and a hell of a lot that could still go wrong. But still he could not suppress his satisfaction.

He had hand-picked his men for this task. Four of them, selected from the fast-growing patriot militia known as Liberation. Once a force to be reckoned with, it had taken Arnold ten years to return the group to its former strength. For most of that time, tonight's success had seemed an impossible dream. A fantasy. But not any more. Arnold had seen to that, with the unknowing, ironic assistance of a government of traitors.

The corrupt, self-serving bastards in Washington had gone too far, Arnold knew. And finally people were beginning to wake up. To understand. Not everyone. That would be too much to hope for. But enough that he now had an army to choose from, made up of followers who would act without question.

And now Liberation had struck its first blow. It would be the first of many.

Arnold forced himself to shake the thought and returned his attention to the remaining three men on his team. For what was ahead to play out as he intended, it was key that they all did their part.

'You know what has to happen now, guys.' It was a statement rather than a question.

'We do.'

'Just make sure you stay under the radar. Do nothing to draw attention to yourselves, you got that?'

'We've got it, Cam.'

'And don't dawdle.' Arnold turned his attention back on Turner as he was speaking. 'You get back there as fast as you can and you make sure they're ready.'

'They'll be ready, Cam. We all will.'

Arnold stepped forward, thrusting out his hand. First towards Turner, who took it and shook it firmly. The other two men did the same and then stepped back, ready to go do as Arnold had instructed.

'We've got one shot at this.' Arnold stayed close as he spoke. 'We've got one chance to show these fuckers in Washington that they don't own us. One chance to show them whose country this really is. So let's make that count.'

FOUR

6.40 a.m. EDT

The tiniest vibration of Brian Spence's phone was enough to wake him, just as it was most mornings. Brian had always been a light sleeper and an early riser. The opposite of his husband, Andrew, who had yet to find a storm that could rouse him. Brian's sunrise alarm could have been set at full volume and it still would not have woken the man next to him.

Not that Brian was going to take that risk. His sunrise ritual was his alone. His moment of peace and contemplation. Brian wasn't giving that up, and especially not today. Not now they were finally in port.

The journey from Teichman Point in Galveston to Key West – just over one thousand nautical miles – had taken eleven days by sail. And of all the places he and Andrew had visited in their years together – and there had been many – none meant as much to them both as Key West.

Pulling on a thin white robe, Brian slipped quietly from the shared main cabin and made his way to the galley. Three minutes more and he was climbing the steps to the deck, a steaming mug of black coffee in one hand and a double-cupped bowl containing two halves of a pink grapefruit in the other.

The sun had been going down when they'd arrived at North Bay Marina the previous evening but it had been light enough to notice that the place was quieter than usual. Normally it took some serious skill to manoeuvre into their regular mooring on the third jetty, but even with the rest of the marina being busy, the third pier had been deserted. It had made the task of docking almost effortless.

Now, as the sky began to streak with orange and as the darkness began to break, Brian was grateful for that desertion.

He settled himself onto his regular cushioned seat. It faced east, with no sight nor sound of other boats either side, and – just as he had for the past ten mornings – Brian felt in that moment as if he were the only man on Earth.

He looked at his new watch – like this trip itself, a birthday present from Andrew. 6.51 a.m. Two minutes to sunrise. The colours of the sky were changing by the second as the sun prepared to make an appearance.

He placed his coffee on the surface next to him and climbed to his feet, just as the tip of the sun finally broke on the horizon. His timing by now perfected, he raised his hands high above his head as he took in a deep breath. Three seconds in as his arms went up. Five seconds out as they came back down.

He took another. And then another. His morning ritual, played out in his favourite place on Earth. A reminder, if he ever needed one, of just how lucky he was to have this life. Confirmation that . . .

The object on the jetty caught Brian's attention and broke his contemplation. He slowly lowered his arms as he focused his eyes, trying to make out some detail.

What the hell is that?

He could not see enough to answer his own question.

Whatever it was, it was at the far end of the wooden walkway. Maybe seventy yards distant. From what little he could see, it was motionless.

He squinted, trying to focus as the dawn slowly lit up the dock. It looked like an animal of some sort. Or the body of one.

Is it . . . is it a seal?

The size seemed right, as did the way it was crumpled on the floor.

Or maybe it's just a pile of clothes?

He willed it to be this more attractive possibility. A dead animal, rotting on the walkway, was not how he wanted himself and Andrew to begin their time here. That was not a good omen, and they were a couple who took such things seriously.

A pile of clothes, then. That's what it is.

He climbed down from the yacht and onto the jetty, moving carefully; the last thing he wanted was to make that night's headlines.

'Texas socialite drowns in deserted Key West marina'? No, that's not how this trip's ending.

Brian walked slowly, careful that his cotton slippers did not slide on the damp wood. The details of the object became clearer with every step.

Twenty yards and Brian already knew his guess was wrong.

Forty yards and he no longer thought he was looking at an animal.

And sixty yards was as far as he got before he turned, kicked off his footwear and sprinted back towards the boat.

FIVE

8.10 a.m. EDT

Sergio Vega wiped a sheen of morning sweat from the back of his neck as he slammed the car door hard. The lack of air conditioning inside the vehicle had left him dripping, even on the short ride here. It had taken his already sour mood and dialled it up to ten.

A/C was an extra cost in a squad car. Vega knew that. And he knew that the bean-counters back at the sheriff's office would never authorise that expense on a fleet vehicle they would never see, let alone drive.

Sonsofbitches never miss a chance to save a dime, he thought irritably. *Just so long as the saving doesn't affect them.*

He wiped his palm across his brow and flicked off the perspiration. For just a moment, he felt like kicking the car. He might even have done it if only he'd been somewhere else. Somewhere other than a crime scene. But he wasn't and so he would do what he did every day.

He would suck it up and he would get on with his job.

Vega took a deep breath as he approached the loose yellow tape separating North Bay Marina from the rest of the world. The air was already hot and the feeling of it as it filled his lungs did little to change his mood, but it was better than the stuffy interior of his car. Another two breaths and he had reached the tape. One more and he was under the cordon and inside the marina, his mind now fully focused on what lay ahead.

Whoever he was here to see, they deserved his full attention.

Vega had joined the Monroe County Sheriff's Office ten years earlier, at the age of just twenty-five. It had been his first real job after graduating college and in the decade since then he had dedicated himself to it, to an extent unmatched by any of his colleagues. Vega's focus had cost him much – while his brothers and sister had built families, he'd managed not one relationship that had gone beyond its first month – but it had been worth it. At least as far as he was concerned.

Vega had made sergeant within six years and had been the local homicide investigator for the past three, working out of Major Crimes. With career progression that fast, his ultimate ambition – to be the first Cuban-born county sheriff – had evolved from a snowball's chance in hell into a near sure thing.

Even so, his specific role within the department did not account for much of his working day. Suspicious death was relatively rare in the Florida Keys and so, like many of the specialist officers under Monroe's sheriff, Vega doubled up on that duty with more regular responsibilities. Everything from routine patrol to standard investigation work. Even – when manpower was stretched – the curse of Key West night duty.

Unfortunately for Vega, manpower was *often* stretched. Last night had been no exception.

The night shift had ended at 7 a.m. and Vega had reached his small apartment less than ten minutes later. The short time span between clocking out and falling into bed was, Vega always told himself, one of the few positives of living so close to the centre of town. A positive that had been denied him today.

Vega had caught no more than twenty minutes of sleep before being called back to work. As the only homicide investigator in the district, the body at North Bay Marina was his responsibility.

Immediately after the call he had showered, pulled on a fresh set of clothes and headed straight to the sheriff's office's local headquarters on College Road, where he had picked up his crime scene kit and his sweatbox ride. From there he had rushed to Front Street. Door to door to door, all within forty minutes of the call-out.

Pretty damn efficient, he thought. *Even if I do say so myself.*

It took barely five steps for Vega's satisfaction in his own efficiency to fade as he spotted his deputy.

Lucas Willis was a new addition to the sheriff's office. The latest in a long line of young deputies, all appointed to Key West with misjudged ideas of how life in party central would be. As a rule, each lasted as long as it took for those illusions to be shattered. Willis had hit five months so far and Vega had seen his smile dampen with each passing pay cheque.

What he had also seen – an even surer sign of the deputy's discontent – was his weight gain. Willis had hardly been slim on recruitment, but he was twenty pounds heavier now than he had been in January. With the extra lumber he looked unhealthy even on his best day. And this was *not* that day.

A painful combination of stress and exertion dominated his sweating face as he 'jogged' towards Vega.

'Jeez, Luc. We've already got one dead body this morning. Don't go adding another.' Vega stepped forward as he spoke, half expecting that he would need to catch the deputy as he fell.

'I'm sorry, Sarge,' Willis panted, already out of breath. 'It's just . . . it's . . . the Key West PD. They're here.'

'What?' The detective made no attempt to hide his irritation. 'What the hell—'

'And . . .' Willis tried to push on through pained breaths. He had more to say. 'Sarge, they're not . . . they're not alone.'

The statement halted Vega's train of thought, his flash of anger replaced by confusion.

Not alone?

'Who else is here?'

'No clue, boss. But they ain't local.'

Vega had more questions, but what was the point? Willis's last answer was plainly the extent of his knowledge. He focused on the practicalities.

'Where's the body?'

Vega looked around as he spoke, looking to answer his own question. He did so almost instantly. As large an area as North Bay Marina covered, there were only four jetties that stuck out from the dockside and so only eight lines of moored boats. And only one of those jetties had a cluster of sheriff's office deputies.

'It's over there, Sarge.'

Both Willis's reply and his pointed finger were unnecessary; Vega was already moving.

'Who did PD send?'

'Lieutenant Smart.'

Willis was breathing hard as he answered, struggling to keep up as Vega increased the pace. The difference in physical condition between the two men – Willis's borderline obesity against Vega's naturally slim, gym-honed fitness – could not have been more evident.

'He say why he was here? The report was pretty clear that this one's a homicide.'

'I didn't . . . I didn't speak to him, Sarge,' Willis replied. 'Susie did. They just . . . they . . . they told her to . . . clear the scene.'

'Clear the scene?' Vega felt his internal temperature rise. 'They told her to clear *my* scene?'

His pace increased even more. It left Willis trailing behind, breathless and unable to reply. Vega hardly noticed; Willis had exhausted his usefulness.

The detective's attention was already elsewhere.

For a location as easily cordoned as the marina, Vega would expect no more than four deputies; the sheriff's office could just about spare that minimum. Willis was one and the other three were now directly ahead, all of them just feet from the third jetty. In front of them, blocking their access to the wooden walkway, was a yellow cordon. It was an expected detail but, Vega quickly realised, it was not one of their own.

That's PD tape. He felt his heart rate rise, his earlier irritation turning to anger. *Those sonsofbitches have ejected my team from my own goddamned crime scene. Just who the hell do think they are?*

'Sarge. Did you know these guys were gonna be here?'

The question came from one of the deputies, half-shouted as Vega approached. He did not answer. He did not even glance over. Instead his eyes remained fixed on the three figures he could see through the morning haze, all standing together near the far end of the jetty.

He passed the deputies without a word, ducked under the yellow tape and covered the seventy or so yards of the walkway at speed. His focus was now absolute as the details of the group ahead became visible.

Vega recognised one. The only man and the person Willis had told him to expect: Lieutenant Frank Smart of the Key West Police Department. The two women he had never seen before. Which, in a community this small, could mean only one thing.

They're federal.

The realisation slowed him. He was close enough now to see the two strangers clearly, but both were facing out towards the sea and so his view of them was limited. One – the taller of the two by more than a head – seemed to be dressed consistently with Vega's conclusion. A black jacket over a black skirt, with a hint of a white collar visible against her long blonde ponytail. The other was dressed for comfort in the summer heat: sandals, knee-length khaki shorts and a loose white blouse. The more informal dress suggested that she was the senior of the two.

None of which tells me anything I need to know, such as just who the hell . . .

The sound of his approach must have been louder than Vega realised and so he found his thoughts interrupted as all three turned to face him. For the first time he could see the faces of the women. The sight confirmed what he already knew: he had met neither of them before.

'Sergeant Vega.'

Lieutenant Frank Smart stepped forward as the detective came close. His formality was unusual; Vega could not remember the last time Smart had addressed him by his rank. It took barely a moment to deduce why Smart had come over all official.

A show for the feds.

'We've been expecting you,' Smart continued.

'Well, I sure as hell wasn't expecting you, Frank.' Vega had no intention of engaging in Smart's display. Feds or no feds, he was here to work. 'The call I took said this was a murder. That makes it my jurisdiction, not yours. So why's the PD here?'

'There's no need to turn this into a conflict, Sergeant.' Smart's tone was reasonable. His repeated use of Vega's rank instead of his name was not. 'We're only here to help.'

'You're here to help? Help, as in "assist", you mean? So were you *assisting* me when you threw my team off my crime scene, huh?'

'That's on me, Sergeant Vega. I'm the one who ordered your team to stand by.'

Vega turned his head at the interruption, to face the shorter of the two women. Her intervention suggested that he had been right; she *was* the boss.

'I apologise if I crossed a line there, son. Be assured, all I was trying was to preserve a crime scene. *Your* crime scene.'

The words were carefully chosen and delivered with a melodious accent that, to Vega's ear, hailed from somewhere in the Mississippi Delta. It was not the voice he expected from a fed – too soothing, for one thing – and yet it carried its own subtle authority.

The combination was disarming but Vega was determined to stay focused.

'And who were you preserving it from, exactly?'

'Well, since you ask, it was from *your* people. A few of them, son, seemed they were fixin' to trample all over the place, given half a chance. I didn't reckon you'd want that.'

Vega wanted to answer, to think of something smart to fire back, but instead he said nothing. The 'people' she had referred to? He looked back towards the marina, towards a group of deputies that included Lucas Willis. The metaphorical bull in a china shop.

With Willis factored in, there could be no good answer to what she had said.

'No,' he finally replied, turning back to face the woman he already thought of as 'The Boss'. 'No, I wouldn't want that.'

'I didn't think so.'

The Boss smiled as she spoke. A warm, genuine smile. Vega felt himself return the gesture – it was somehow impossible not to – and, as he did, her earlier words came back to him. Words he had overlooked.

Your crime scene.

'Wait, you called it my crime scene?'

'Who else's crime scene is it gonna be? This is Monroe County jurisdiction. And you're the sheriff's homicide investigator. We ain't here to change that.'

They were exactly the words Vega wanted to hear and yet not for one moment did he believe them. It was just not how the feds worked. Not now. Not ever.

'All due respect, Agent . . .' He left a long pause, expecting it to be filled with an introduction. When the Boss did not accept the invitation, he continued. 'You're down here throwing around orders and making things happen. And so I've got to ask: just who the hell are you?'

The Boss's smile widened. An irritating reaction, whether intended or not. Vega looked towards her colleague for an answer. The taller agent was, he now realised, unusually striking, with a cold, perfect symmetry and near-porcelain skin. She was also all business, her expressionless face giving nothing away.

Having received no response from her either, he turned back to face the Boss.

'Look, it's pretty damn clear that you're about a hundred

pay grades ahead of *this* guy—' he pointed his finger at Smart as he spoke '—so I know you're not police. And you sure as hell ain't dressed for the FBI. So I'm gonna ask you again: who the hell are you?'

Smart stepped forward, as if to answer. Judging by the angry look on his face, Vega's insult had bothered him. Just as Vega had intended. He half-turned to face Smart before they were stopped by the Boss's raised hand.

It was a clear, unspoken message. She would answer for herself.

Smart stepped back.

'I ain't dressed for the FBI, Sergeant, because I ain't with the FBI. And I ain't from no other branch of local or state law enforcement with which you might be familiar. My . . . interests, they go a little beyond that. I'm Special Agent O'Rourke and all you need to know is that I'm with Homeland Security.'

O'Rourke indicated to the woman next to her.

'And this here, Sergeant Vega, is Agent Nicki May. Department of Justice.'

Vega followed O'Rourke's gesture and his eyes met May's for the first time. Her previously stern expression broke in turn, replaced with a polite, one-sided smile and a nod of her head. The slight grin brought some character to a face that was otherwise too perfect, with the improvement only increased by the spark he believed he now saw in her eyes.

A moment more and Vega would have been holding Nicki May's gaze for too long, but he stopped himself in time. He gave her a quick smile and turned his attention back to O'Rourke.

'Homeland Security? What does any of this have to do with you guys?'

'Officially, nothing. As far as anyone knows, we're not even here. Not yet, anyhow. Like I said, this is still *your* crime scene. I intend for it to stay that way.'

At first Vega said nothing, all too aware that it was a lot to take in. The mere fact of a Homeland agent at the site of a random Key West murder would have been enough; just why the hell *was* she there, he still wanted to know. But then that same agent not pulling rank? That was unheard of.

He looked wordlessly from O'Rourke to May and then to Smart, then back along the jetty to his own small, insignificant team. Four of them, all behind a cordon they were not considered important enough to pass. That fact had angered Vega just minutes earlier. But not any more.

Now it just gave him the clarity he needed.

Because they are insignificant. And so am I.

He turned back to O'Rourke.

'You mean for now.'

'What?'

'You mean it'll stay my crime scene *for now*. Right up until I find something that makes it *your* crime scene.'

O'Rourke did not reply, but then she didn't need to. Vega was right and every one of them knew it.

SIX

8.30 a.m. EDT

The blood from Ricardo Garcia's throat had congealed into a sticky, viscous pool that spread a full three feet out from his body. To the untrained eye, it would have resembled nothing more than thick, red corn syrup. Lots of it.

To Vega, it was a potential mine of information.

The relative sparsity of arterial spray told him that Garcia had died quickly. Perhaps from the deep wound to the back that was visible through his torn patrol shirt; even without the addition of a slit throat, that wound would have been fatal. Whatever the ultimate cause, the manner of blood loss suggested that the patrolman's heart had stopped just moments after the final wound was inflicted.

What blood had left his body from that point onwards, while still substantial, was a result of both pressure and gravity.

Vega could tell all of this from blood placement alone. Unluckily for him, the timing of Garcia's death was much less clear-cut.

The average July temperature in Key West was enough to accelerate rigor mortis far beyond its usual speed. As a result, the rigidity of Garcia's corpse meant little. The temperature of the body itself was equally unhelpful. With the surrounding environment so warm, Garcia's remains would never cool to the same level as would happen elsewhere.

Both factors made Vega's job more difficult. Or, to be more accurate, they made it slower. The medical examiner would be able to settle time of death at autopsy. But Vega took pride in never having to wait that long. Today, he realised, he would have little choice.

The body, then, had told him all it could for now and so he rose from his crouched stance, gently replacing the sheet he had pulled from the corpse as he did so. He moved slowly, careful to give the fallen patrolman the respect he deserved. Ricardo Garcia was a victim now. His body was evidence. But until last night he had been a living, breathing human being.

More than that, he had been someone Vega knew.

Stepping back, Vega turned and faced the group of three people – O'Rourke, May and Smart – who were still behind him on the jetty. They had stayed ten yards back, both a respectful distance and one that maintained the integrity of the scene. O'Rourke had already assured Vega that none of them had approached the body prior to his arrival, adding credibility to her claim that this remained *his* case.

As welcome as that reassurance was, it still begged the question:

So just why the hell are they here?

The thought continued to bother Vega as he walked back towards them, noting as he did so what a mismatched grouping they appeared from a distance.

Frank Smart, a senior Key West police officer who always wore a black suit totally unsuited to Key West weather, was the dictionary definition of a WASP. Put him in any lawyer's office in any major city and he would be indistinguishable from ninety per cent of the men around him. Physically *and* intellectually. But down here? Down here he stood out like a . . . well, like a WASP in Key West.

Agent O'Rourke, conversely, was no one's impression of any kind of federal agent, which was what most intrigued Vega about her. Aged in her mid-fifties, he would guess, and both short and overweight, O'Rourke was wearing the uniform of a middle-aged holidaymaker – she could have passed for any one of a thousand tourists who would be frequenting Duval Street later today – and yet it did nothing to diminish her presence. As a black woman representing the pinnacle of the intelligence community, she was impressive, and an automatic role model to someone like Vega, who knew better than most the challenges faced by minority agents and officers in law enforcement.

Then there was Agent Nicki May, the physical ying to O'Rourke's yang. Nine or ten inches taller – more in her heels, which gave her an inch on even Smart – May was naturally pale and likely rail-thin beneath her black suit. She also seemed to lack the easy authority of her Homeland counterpart. That was possibly an unfair conclusion, Vega realised, no doubt based on her younger age and her deferment to O'Rourke as lead agent. But it was still the conclusion he had reached and so far he'd seen no cause to reassess it.

He fixed his eyes on Smart as he drew closer.

'This one's gonna hurt the guys at the Patrol Group, Frank.' Vega's earlier animosity towards Smart had lessened. After what he had just seen, he regretted that he had succumbed to a petty rivalry. 'That's no way for a good man to go.'

'I know.' Smart had not seen the full crime scene up close, but he had seen enough. 'I know.'

'What's the Patrol Group?'

Vega turned towards O'Rourke. He had assumed that Smart would have explained this already.

'It's one of our key resources in a place like this,' he began. 'We're tourist-heavy with lots of minor crime. The Patrol Group sends out lone patrolmen to handle the small stuff, the kind of things that would usually be a distraction for the sheriff's office or the PD.'

Vega gestured towards Garcia's covered corpse before continuing.

'This ... this doesn't really happen to cops down here. Not often, anyway. But it *never* happens to patrolmen. They're gonna take this hard.'

'And this particular patrolman. Mr Garcia. You knew him?'

'Every cop knew Ricardo,' Smart answered. 'He'd been on patrol so long he'd become an institution.'

'In that case, I'm sorry for your loss.' O'Rourke reached out to touch Smart's arm in consolation. It was an instinctive reaction. Informal and fleeting, and quickly turned into a gesture towards May. 'We both are.'

'It's neither of us who need condolences.' Vega stepped forward as he spoke. 'We're not here to grieve for Ricardo. We're here to catch the bastard who killed him.'

'Good to hear, Sergeant Vega.'

O'Rourke's lyrical voice made every positive comment feel like a reward. The effect was no doubt intentional and Vega knew that he had to ignore it. He needed a clear head. Not easy in the presence of two agents who were both, for very different reasons, unusually intriguing.

He made a decision.

'Special Agent O'Rourke. Agent May. I think I need to speak to Frank – to Lieutenant Smart – alone. Do you mind?'

'You go for it,' O'Rourke replied. She glanced towards May. 'We can keep each other company right here.'

Vega smiled his thanks, indicating for Smart to follow, and then walked him a short distance along the jetty, in the direction of the marina. When he spoke again, Vega kept his voice low.

'Have you spoken to anyone from the Patrol Group yet?'

'Only real quick. I didn't pass on any details or anything. Didn't think it was my place.'

'What did they tell you?'

'Not much. They were in shock at the news, even without knowing the full picture.'

'Anything we can use?'

'Hard to say,' Smart replied. 'Though what they did say, it confirmed to me that Ricardo was killed while on patrol. And that the marina was the last stop on his round, which ended at five a.m. So I figure that gives us a pretty clear time of death.'

'Not necessarily,' Vega replied. 'Did you get any idea when his last call in to the Patrol Group hub was?'

'The last time Ricardo checked in was twelve past one. Two drunk girls needing help home. They passed it on to your office.'

'Yeah, I remember the call. I was on duty last night, I almost took it myself but one of the deputies was closer. They picked them up, delivered them back to their hotel.'

Smart said nothing, and so Vega continued.

'If that was Ricardo's last call in, then that means he died sometime between twelve past one and five a.m. That's the best we can say for now.'

'But his patrol ends here, and he's dead here,' Smart

observed. 'And we can tell from the level of blood on the walkway that he wasn't killed somewhere else and dumped here, right? He's lying where he fell.'

'That's right, but his patrol route is twelve rounds over seven hours. So after he last called in, Ricardo could have passed through this marina what? Four times at least? Poor guy could have bought it on any one of them.'

'Shit.'

'What about witnesses?' Vega shared Smart's frustration, but it was not the time to show it. 'Anyone report anything out of the ordinary?'

'Not really. The man who found the body – guy called Brian Spence, from the sailboat further up the jetty – he said he heard a few noises outside the boat last night. But nothing worth getting out of bed to investigate. So he thought, anyway.'

Vega shook his head; there was nothing to be said, and so instead he looked back along the jetty. Back towards the white sheet that covered Ricardo's corpse. From this distance he had a wider view, and so for the first time he could see not just what was on the walkway, but what was in the water next to it.

He took a step to the side of the jetty for a clearer view and focused on the water nearest to the body. It took just a moment to confirm what he thought he had seen in his peripheral vision.

Fins. Lots and lots of fins.

Vega turned back to Smart. His mind was now racing.

'Could there have been a second vic?'

'A second? No.'

'You're sure about that? No reason that Ricardo might've had another patrolman with him?'

'None I know of. Those guys patrol alone, Sergio. You know that.'

'Then what about marina security? Did anyone turn up missing since last night? Employees? Boat owners, even?'

'No. Why?'

'Because that's a whole shitload of sharks in the water over there.' Vega pointed to the jetty's edge as he spoke. He counted at least ten visible fins. 'There's got to be something that's attracting them.'

Smart followed Vega's outstretched finger. He was silent for a few moments. Considering the possibilities. Finally he turned back to Vega.

'You think there's another body in there?'

'It's a possibility, isn't it? Because we sure as hell don't know what happened here last night.'

'It could just be the blood from Ricardo.'

'"Could" doesn't cut it, Frank. We need to be sure. We need to clear those sharks and we need to get someone beneath the surface to find out if anyone else is down there. Agreed?'

Smart slowly nodded his head.

'Agreed.'

Vega turned away and took a deep breath, tasting the warm saltiness of the air. He hoped he was wrong; one dead man was bad enough. But if there *was* another body, at least that might tell them a little more about what had happened here.

He turned back to Smart.

'And that's it, is it? There's nothing else?'

'Nothing yet. But come on, man. It's only been an hour.'

It was the answer Vega had expected rather than the answer he wanted, but the lieutenant was right. It *had* only been an hour. Vega had to be realistic on what could be achieved and how quickly. But that sense of realism did not make the truth any more palatable.

A peacekeeper was dead. Killed in the most violent way imaginable. That hit Vega where he lived. Area patrol. Police department. Sheriff's office. When all was said and done, they were all the same.

They were all lawmen.

'Garcia was one of our own.' Vega's tone was low as he spoke, his voice firm. 'We'll find who did this. Whatever it takes.'

'You gentlemen mind if I make an observation?'

Both men turned at the sound of O'Rourke's voice. Her approach had been silent and so her intervention was unexpected.

'Depends what it is.'

Vega's reply was sharp. Aggressive, even. The presence of Homeland Security still concerned him and, after just a minute or two free from O'Rourke's honeyed influence, that made him defensive. He still had no idea why Homeland or the DOJ were here, or even how. How had Homeland heard about Ricardo Garcia's death fast enough to have an agent here before a local cop?

And why the hell do they even care?

'It's nothing sinister, Sergeant Vega.' O'Rourke's tone was as disarming as ever. As if she could read Vega's thoughts and knew reassurance was needed. 'It's just, well, look up there. Directly above Mr Garcia's corpse.'

Vega did as suggested.

'What?'

'The jetty light. He was killed directly beneath one of just three lights on the whole one hundred yards of this walkway. Now we know that this murder happened in the dark, between twelve past one and sunrise. And yet for some reason the killer chose to off Mr Garcia in one of only three spots on this jetty where the crime could have been seen.'

'But it *wasn't* seen,' Vega replied. 'There are no witnesses. Even the guy who found the body . . .'

'Not what I'm driving at, Sergeant,' O'Rourke continued. 'Point is, for whatever reason, Mr Garcia was murdered in a spot where that murder was visible. And if it was visible, it could have been recorded.'

O'Rourke turned to Smart.

'Lieutenant, this is a major marina for this island, ain't it? Key to the local economy?'

'Yes. Yes, it is,' Smart replied. 'It's not the biggest, but it is one of the most popular for pleasure trips.'

'That's what I thought. And those there boats, they ain't cheap, are they?'

'No. The typical client of North Bay Marina, they wouldn't . . . they wouldn't have to settle for cheap. This is where the rich tend to moor.'

'OK. So we can assume, then, that the City Commission has security cameras here? For taking good care of the rich folk.'

'They've got a closed-circuit system at points around the island, yeah,' Smart confirmed. 'Stands to reason that it might cover some of the marina. But it'd be a very limited number. There's a balance between security and the visitor's . . . privacy. And with it being so dark, it's unlikely they'd have captured much.'

'Absolutely, Lieutenant. But if most of this place is pitch-black, it'd make sense for the cameras they *do* have to be aimed at the few places where things *can* be seen.'

'Well, yeah. I guess. Yeah.'

'Which makes it a good bet,' Vega offered, irritated that Smart was not living up to his name, 'that there's one covering the area under the jetty light. The exact spot where Garcia fell.'

SEVEN

8.36 a.m. EDT

Cam Arnold let out a relieved breath as his van hurtled past the US Route One milepost. The sign marked the end of the Overseas Highway. It was the point of transition where the Keys ended and mainland Florida began.

For Arnold, it marked something much more.

Mission accomplished.

He glanced at the dashboard clock.

Two hours and sixteen minutes to drive the full one-hundred-and-thirteen-mile distance. It seemed slow, but he had needed to avoid attention and so he had been forced to stick to the Route One speed limits. That obedience was unusual in itself – following what he saw as yet another ridiculous law would have been counter-intuitive to a man like Arnold on law any normal day – but this morning it had been especially difficult. After what he had done back at the marina, his every instinct was to put as much distance as possible between himself and Key West.

He had fought that urge, that desire to flee. For the mission to succeed, he had to reach Orlando. A simple enough task that would be made more difficult, he was sure, by the attention his earlier action was about to attract. So for now he needed to be invisible; even a citation for speeding was too big a risk.

He had stayed on the island until 6.20 a.m., over an hour after the patrolman had bled out on the jetty. That wait, too, had gone against his survival instincts; if anything it had been harder even than obeying the Florida State traffic laws. But for all the risk that it had carried, Arnold knew his delayed departure was necessary. It was vital that Scott Turner made it back to camp safely. And so he had waited sufficient time that no one could connect the two vehicles that departed for the mainland an hour apart.

The success of everything might just depend on Scott Turner, Arnold believed. And Cam Arnold had not dragged the Liberation movement from its lowest point to where it was today – on the brink of striking a devastating blow against the US establishment and its so-called government – in order to fail now.

A smile threatened the corner of his mouth as he considered what he had in mind for Turner. Of the role the kid might have to play in what was, to Arnold, the greatest act of patriotism in his nation's history. For decades – for centuries – the likes of Arnold and his Liberation recruits had been under a jackboot. The country that had been established *for* them had turned *against* them.

The combination of corrupting foreign interests, prioritised minority rights, the immigration flood and the sheer, unbridled perversions of the Washington elite had combined to crush real Americans. To grind them under a heel of lies and deceit and what was, he believed, nothing short of a war against true citizens.

And if it's a war they want . . .

The thought made him smirk. They truly believed that they had won. That they had broken the spirit of resistance amongst the American people. Well, they had not broken Arnold. And thanks to him – and despite their best efforts – they had not broken Liberation.

And so they would soon find out just how wrong they were.

It was this belief that now drove Arnold on and which convinced him of what had to follow. The plan had to play out. It was the only way. And while he trusted his men – he had chosen them carefully – he also knew their limitations. Almost all of them believed as fanatically as Arnold himself, but would any of them be able to see this through? Could any of them deal with what Arnold would soon have to endure?

He could not be sure. And that was why, for this, he could count on only himself.

It has to be me.

He looked to his right. Paul Holly was asleep with his head against the passenger-side window. Had been for well over an hour. That rest, when it came, had been as welcome a relief for Arnold as it was for his companion. Holly seemed to have a frustratingly basic understanding of their movement's ideology and so Arnold found it a chore to discuss it with him. Add in Arnold's general intolerance for small talk and it was no surprise that he preferred to drive in silence.

If he could have completed the full mission without support, he would have done so. But there were some tasks that took more than a single pair of hands and they were about to reach the first of them.

'Paul.' Arnold reached out and placed a hand on Holly's shoulder as he spoke, shaking the sleeping man awake. 'We're here.'

Holly opened his eyes. For just a moment he seemed disorientated. An instant later and he was fully focused. The speed impressed Arnold, and he congratulated himself for it; as he had with all of his team, Arnold had hand-picked and trained Holly.

Another job well done.

The thought was still in Arnold's mind as he indicated right, changed lanes and slowed, ready to take the narrow roadway that led off the highway and towards the swamps of the surrounding Everglades.

He had no idea how far the road would run. Nor did he intend to find out. The further they drove along it, the closer they would come to the swamps that dominated this part of Florida. That would mean reptiles, Arnold knew. Or at least a risk of them. And if there was anything that could put him off his game . . .

He brought the van to a stop barely two hundred yards along the road, with the highway still visible in his mirrors. Not as far as he had intended to go, but far enough; he was sure they could not be seen.

'Come on. I want to do this quick.'

Holly climbed out of the van without a word and opened the sliding side door just behind his own. There was little space between the plastic crates that filled up most of the Sprinter's fifteen and a half feet of cargo space and the wall that separated the cab from the hold, and what there was had been filled with a series of plastic rolls and a number of very specific tools.

Arnold had climbed out too, but he had stayed on the left-hand driver's side. From here he could detect the sound of movement in the back of the vehicle, as Holly pulled together what was needed.

Moments later and Holly had joined him. He was carrying one of the tall rolls of plastic that had been stored in the back. Arnold had not seen the item before, but he knew exactly what it was; he had ordered it, after all. He gripped the loose end of the plastic by both its top and bottom corner and remained in place as Holly stepped backwards, unrolling the sheet as he went and revealing the fresh signage displayed upon it. Once fully opened, Arnold carefully applied the loose end to the driver's side of the van, flattened it against the metal and, with Holly's help, slowly moved the rest of the decal into position.

It took just minutes. Quicker, even, than Arnold had anticipated. And it looked good. The full blank-faced left side of the grey Dodge Sprinter had been converted into the colourful display of a Florida-registered parcel delivery company, the name and details of which Arnold had invented just weeks before.

It took less than ten minutes for Arnold and Holly to apply the same process to both the passenger's side of the van, and to its front and its rear. Five minutes more and the licence plates were changed, too. From the original Ohio to Florida.

It made for an impressive transformation. On even careful inspection, the van that now rejoined the north side of US Route One with Paul Holly at the wheel looked a different vehicle entirely from the Dodge that had left Front Street less than three hours earlier.

'You think it's enough?' Holly turned the wheel right, guiding the van back onto the highway, and pressed hard on the gas. 'You think it'll fool them?'

'It has to.' Arnold adjusted the direction of the air conditioning and made himself comfortable as he spoke. 'If it doesn't, we won't make it north of Miami.'

EIGHT

Key West City Hall had been open for business for over an hour, but Sergio Vega was unsurprised to find the building almost empty. Key West was a late-night town. Latin hours. It would be a cliche to say that most of the population were still sleeping off the previous night, but Vega knew his city. And besides, cliches had to start somewhere.

Frank Smart held the door of the main entrance open, allowing Vega to pass him and enter. O'Rourke and May followed, all walking into the cold relief of the air-conditioned lobby.

The sound of May's heeled footwear on the lobby's marble floor echoed off the white walls. The noise would not have travelled so effectively in a busier room, but it was loud enough here to announce their presence to the lobby's sole security guard.

'Can I help you?' The guard rose stiffly to his feet as he spoke.

Vega raised his hand to reach for his badge; the light linen trousers and short-sleeved shirt he had chosen for the heat did not announce him as an obvious police officer. It was unnecessary. Smart intervened before he reached his shield.

'It's OK, Bruce,' Smart said, striding ahead of Vega. 'They're with me.'

The guard seemed to recognise Smart. Inevitably, Vega concluded. The Key West PD was much more heavily involved in the day-to-day running of the island than his own office. It made sense that a senior officer like Smart was a regular inside the building.

'You're here about Ricardo?' The guard's voice was low, his tone sad.

'Yeah. Yeah, we are.' Smart spoke quietly. A show of respect for what those inside the building had lost. 'We need to speak to Cesar about what happened.'

The guard shook his head.

'It's a terrible thing, Lieutenant.'

'I know, Bruce. Can you call through?'

'No one to call through to. Cesar benched the Patrol Group for the rest of the day. He wanted everyone to have time to get over what happened.'

'You mean there's no one back there?'

'No one but Cesar.'

'In that case, you mind if we make our own way inside?'

'Sure thing.' The guard ushered Smart past with a wave of his hand. 'And Lieutenant?'

'Yeah?'

'You get the sonofabitch who did this. You get him. Whatever it takes.'

The offices of the City Patrol Group were small, little more than a space near the very back of City Hall. An afterthought was how they had been described to Vega and he now saw why.

Just a front desk for the public and behind that a communal working area with two closed doors at its rear.

The detective had spent most of his life on the island and yet he had visited City Hall on perhaps ten occasions. And on none of those had he been to this forgotten corner of the building. It left him with no idea what was behind either of the back doors.

Smart had no such doubts. He passed the unmanned public counter, crossed the empty space behind it and headed straight for the right-hand door, sure of where he was going. He knocked once and stepped back, while Vega, O'Rourke and May slowly followed to stand just behind him.

It was half a minute before the door was opened. Long enough that Smart might have knocked again, Vega figured, if it were not for the sound of movement from inside. The reason for the delay was apparent as soon as the handle turned and Vega saw the face of Cesar Montoya, the director of the Area Patrol Group.

Montoya was a mess. The cheap purple shirt that formed the top half of his uniform looked dishevelled. His usually slicked-back hair was gel-free. His face – obviously just washed – bore the swell and the reddening that comes only from tears. He had tried to make himself presentable, Vega realised. But he had failed utterly.

The expression on Montoya's face changed as his eyes moved from the local lawmen and on to the two strangers.

'Cesar, this is Special Agent O'Rourke and Agent May. They're here to help me . . .' Vega stopped himself, then indicated to Smart, 'to help *us* with, with . . . what happened last night.'

'You mean with what happened to Ricardo.' Montoya pulled himself up to his full height as he spoke. At five foot ten, it brought him eye to eye with Vega. His voice wavered slightly as he spoke, but otherwise he seemed strong. 'You can say his name, Sergio. I'm hurt, but I'm not broken.'

Vega dipped his head in apology. He realised how his delicacy could be perceived by a man like the director. The detective and Montoya shared a background if not a generation – both Cuban refugees; Montoya as a young man, Vega when no more than an infant – and so Vega of all people should have been aware of the director's culture.

To cry for a lost friend is no shame. Tears are not weakness.
Only weakness is weakness.

'Of course, Cesar. I understand. We *are* here for Ricardo. And we need your help.'

'Anything I can give, it's yours. What do you need?'

'The Patrol Group's camera system. You have anything that covers the North Bay Marina?'

Montoya's eyes widened at the question.

'Is that . . . is that where it happened?'

'You didn't know?'

'We're not police, Sergio. We know only what we've been told. And all *I've* been told is that Ricardo was killed during his patrol.'

Vega glanced towards Smart. It was the PD who had checked in with Montoya and so it was the PD who had failed to give him even the barest detail of his patrolman's – of his friend's – death. It was wrong. And Smart seemed to agree. The lieutenant averted his eyes from Vega's withering look.

Vega turned back to Montoya.

'I am so sorry that you were not fully informed, Cesar. You deserve better than that.'

'I have no interest in apologies. There are more important

things here than my pride. You asked about North Bay Marina. The answer is yes, we have cameras that cover the location.'

'How many?'

'Only three. It used to be more, but over time we have lost most of them. The usual weather damage, mostly. The marina has always requested that they are not replaced. Seems that their guests prefer that they are not . . . overlooked.'

'But you still have three?'

'Two inside the marina. And one outside. Technically this is a Front Street camera, but it covers the entrance to the marina. Which means they could not object to our maintenance of that one.'

'And the others? The ones inside?'

'The others each cover a point on a jetty. Not the whole thing, as it takes three to cover the full distance. But it is better than nothing, no?'

'That depends,' Vega replied, 'on which jetties we're talking about.'

'From memory I don't know which points. But I do know that we have a camera on Jetty One, and a camera on Jetty Three.'

Vega glanced at O'Rourke. Their eyes met, but neither said a word. He assumed they were already thinking the same thing: *That* is *better than nothing*.

He turned back to Montoya.

'We're going to need to see that footage, Cesar.'

'Of course. I will make arrangements immediately.'

Montoya turned, as if to head back into his office. As he did, a thought occurred to Vega.

'And Cesar, one more thing. Ricardo. Are you sure he was working alone last night?'

Montoya stopped himself mid-turn.

'Why do you ask that question?'

'Just . . . just a hunch, that's all.'

Vega did not want to mention the sharks he had noticed in the water. Not until he had to, anyway. Montoya has just lost a friend. He did not need to be concerned with more lurid details.

'He should have been on patrol alone, yes. Our insurance and our regulations, they only provide for single-man patrols.' Montoya's tone sounded less certain than his words. 'But in the last few weeks, there have been occasions . . .'

Montoya trailed off.

'Occasions of what?'

The question came from O'Rourke. The first words she had spoken since they had been here.

Montoya took a breath.

'The training we can provide to our patrolmen, it is . . . it is limited. The Patrol Group is not well-funded. And so there are times where a new patrolman will join a more experienced member of the team. Accompany him for a few hours of the patrol. It is not supposed to happen. It's against regulations because it is unpaid and so it's uninsured, so it's not logged or discussed. But it is the best way to prepare them for their own patrols. I know that, in the last two weeks, Ricardo has been accompanied by our new recruit on two occasions.'

'And last night?'

'Last night I do not know. It was always informal. But the recruit, Clinton Dewitt, I called him this morning. To break the bad news and to tell him that I was standing the group down for today and tonight. There was no answer. And he has not returned my call.'

Vega felt a chill run down his spine.

'You need to have someone call him again, Cesar. And if there's no answer, you need to have someone sent out to his address.'

'You don't think . . .'

'It's too early to think anything for sure.' Vega could picture the fins in the water as he spoke. 'But we need to play it safe. We need to make sure you only lost one man last night and not two.'

NINE

9.26 a.m. EDT

'Are you sure you want to see what this might show?'

Smart's question was directed at Cesar Montoya, just as the still image from the third jetty's camera appeared on-screen. The lieutenant sounded genuinely concerned. Like Vega, he knew that Montoya and Ricardo had been friends. The only members of the Area Patrol Group to have seen anything like their years in service.

The three men were in the video monitoring room, behind the second of the two doors that Vega had observed from the public desk. Like everything else connected to Patrol Group, the space was small and seemed to have been thrown together on the cheap. Large, near-obsolete video monitors and control equipment took up three quarters of the room's square footage.

With every spare inch taken, O'Rourke and May had no choice but to remain outside. Vega suspected they would prefer it that way and when it came to May he felt the same; as strictly professional as he was, her presence distracted him. He was relieved, then, that she and O'Rourke remained beyond the open doorway while he focused on Montoya and on the screens that bore down from the room's back wall.

This was footage that Vega *had* to watch. As the lead investigator in the homicide, it was not a matter of choice. But Montoya did not. Murder, even on one of the marinas covered by his Patrol Group, was well outside of his remit. And if the camera had caught anything of Ricardo Garcia's murder, then what they would soon witness on the monitors would be graphic.

Cesar can skip this one, Vega thought to himself. *And if Ricardo's corpse is any indication of what happened, he probably should.*

But when he had suggested that earlier, Montoya had disagreed. And while it was Vega's investigation, this was the director's kingdom.

'I'm sure I want to see it.'

Montoya's reply was directed at Smart, his voice now stronger than it had been when they arrived.

'It can be no worse than my imagination,' he continued.

'Even so. It won't be easy viewing.'

'I need to see it.'

'But—'

'He was my friend, Lieutenant Smart. And my colleague. Would you expect less of yourself?'

Smart said nothing. It was a question that carried no easy answer. And so Vega, guessing that the moment of silence might drag, stepped in.

'Play it, Frank. Let's get this over with. For all of us.'

Smart nodded in reply and turned his attention to the monitor control. The console was oversized but simple enough to use. Intuitive, as technology could be even back then, before the simplicity of gigabytes and 5G. The lieutenant was no computer whizz, but his age – he was in his late forties, some way beyond a decade older than Vega – put him in the same generation as the equipment. Both he and Vega guessed that this made Smart the best bet to operate it.

Eight fifteen-inch screens above the console had come to life as one. All showed the same image: a single patch of light on an otherwise pitch-black jetty. Vega was fairly sure he recognised it, but still he turned to Smart for confirmation.

'That where I think it is?'

'It is.'

The answer did not come from Smart, or even from Montoya. Vega turned towards the door and saw that May had found a clear view of the screens across their three heads.

'How can you know that?' he asked.

'There are no boats nearby,' May replied. Her tone was abrupt. The voice of someone with absolute confidence in their own conclusions and little patience for explanation. 'The other three jetties were full, left and right. If this is North Bay Marina last night, this is the third jetty.'

'Good point. But just because it's the third jetty doesn't mean it's the spot where Ricardo Garcia was killed, does it?' Vega took pleasure in the correction. May's answer had seemed a little too self-satisfied for his liking. It was not the first real exchange he had hoped to have with her and it bugged him. 'There were three lights across the length of the walkway. He was killed under one of them. How do we know this is the right one?'

'I suppose we don't.' May seemed unfazed by the rebuke. Maybe even amused. She still seemed certain of her own correctness but her tone was now a little more charming. 'So let's watch this through and find out shall we, Sergeant?'

Vega smiled slightly at what sounded like a friendly

challenge. A moment later and he realised how inappropriate that reaction was. Remembering why they were here and what they might be about to see, he forced the expression from his face and returned his attention to the screens and to the flickering darkness that they displayed.

'Fast-forward to twelve past one, Frank. Then we can use the speed play to run through from there.'

'Already did that while you were flirting,' Smart replied, his voice almost a whisper. He pointed to a timer at the top right of the main screen. 'See?'

'Yeah, sorry. You're ahead of me.'

'Ready to run through?'

'Let's do it.'

The on-screen speed play was one of the few video facilities that more advanced technologies had not yet bettered. It allowed every detail caught on camera to be displayed, but at a massively accelerated pace. Each minute of real-time footage took less than ten seconds, with no detail missed.

The perfect tool for the exercise, Vega thought and settled into his chair, his eyes fixed intently on the screens ahead.

TEN

Joe Dempsey let out a long, frustrated sigh as he found British Airways Flight 1594 on the JFK departure board. The time column displayed the scheduled take-off – 10.30 a.m. – but the status column was just a little more accurate.

Delayed.

Dempsey glanced down at the smartphone he was holding in his right hand.

Bloody thing's not so clever, after all, he thought, as he slipped the handset back into his jacket pocket.

He had arrived at New York JFK Terminal 7 fifteen minutes earlier, and already he was checked in and through security. One of the advantages of his status at the International Security Bureau was a United Nations arrangement with its member states' national carriers. Dempsey was entitled to use the check-in and priority security facilities at any airport, as well as being automatically upgraded on any international or domestic flight that could accommodate him.

It was a necessary perk of the job, intended to make his frequent on-duty air travel more comfortable and to make it easier for him to pass through an airport – and to board a plane

– while heavily armed; something he was required to do a lot more often than other passengers would comfortably realise.

But, for all that, it was also a hell of an upside for those rare occasions, like today, when he travelled for pleasure.

The devastation that the pandemic had inflicted on air travel was still being felt, even months after the roll-out of the vaccine. The usually bustling airport was almost eerily quiet.

He put the thought out of his mind as he approached the Concorde Room – the British Airways First Class Lounge – and showed his ticket to a single member of staff at the desk. The receptionist was young, aged in her twenties Dempsey guessed. It was difficult to be certain with half her face covered by an on-brand British Airways face mask.

The hostess tapped a few buttons on the keyboard ahead of her, scanned the screen for the results and then looked up.

'Looks like your take-off has been delayed to one p.m., Mr Dempsey.'

'A two-and-a-half-hour delay?' Dempsey did the maths in his head. With flight duration and time difference taken into account, a 1 p.m. departure equated to a 1.30 a.m. arrival. It was not welcome news, but he hid his irritation. It was no more the receptionist's fault than it was his. 'Any idea what's caused it?'

'I'm afraid it doesn't say, sir. Sorry.'

'Nothing for you to apologise for. You're not flying the thing.'

Dempsey smiled and walked away from the desk, towards the long corridor that led to the main area of the lounge. The place where, he now realised, he would be spending at least the next two hours.

The delay was an inconvenience, but it could have been worse. The lounge itself was comfortable enough for a short wait and was downright luxurious compared to what Dempsey had endured in the British Army. More importantly, the reason behind his trip was still days away.

It had been close to four years since Dempsey had any kind of significant personal time. He had moved from London to New York towards the end of 2017, when he had joined the ISB. And, although he had been home again once or twice since then, he had not set foot in the UK since the summer of 2019.

His absence had not been a choice. His work at the Bureau had kept him busier than he had ever been, an achievement for a man whose personal life had always come a distant second to his professional one. But this time there could be no excuses. What was happening in London in five days' time was not something Dempsey could miss.

Nor did he intend to.

Dempsey had met Michael Devlin and Sarah Truman just a few months before he had left London and yet in that short time they had grown close. The circumstances behind their first encounter had been both traumatic and tragic. All three had lost close friends – and, in Michael's case, family – over the course of just a few violent days. But they had come through it together, with that combination of mutual loss and survival forming a bond that distance had been unable to break.

The bond between Michael and Sarah had been greater still, of course. Which was why they would soon be christening their eight-month-old twin sons – Liam and Daniel – in London. And they would do that with Dempsey beside them, acting as godfather for two boys he had yet to meet.

He had been surprised to be his friends' choice. Liam and Daniel had been born the previous October, within weeks of the US election and at the height of the pandemic. All of which had conspired to keep Dempsey away from the UK, away from Michael and Sarah, and away from the children.

He would have understood, then, if his friends had opted for a more constant presence to watch over their children. Someone the boys might see from month to month, rather than from year to year. And if he was being honest with himself, Dempsey might have even preferred that himself.

What does a man like me even know about kids? How will I know where to start?

Those doubts could not change the facts. Acutely aware of how unpredictable his life would always be, Michael and Sarah had still chosen to place their trust in Dempsey. And as daunting as that was, it was as great an honour and as great a responsibility as any he had ever been given.

So a two-and-a-half-hour delay? That was nothing.

It would take a whole hell of a lot more than *that* to keep Dempsey from the church.

ELEVEN

8.28 a.m.
Central Daylight Time

The Ghost sat at the far end of the long metal bench, his back pressed against a wall of whitewashed concrete blocks. He was looking down at the lunch tray on the table ahead of him. It seemed to hold his interest completely. He paid no attention to the one man who was permitted to sit with him, nor did the deafening noise or the constant movement of the room seem any distraction.

Corporal Deontay Bush looked away, towards the other tables. The sight made him shake his head as he suppressed a smile. As ever, the contrast between the Ghost's small oasis of calm and the insanity of the room around it was impossible to ignore.

The Facility Mess was not a huge space. Barely eighty feet long, it was just wide enough for four rows of tables of about half that length, each with two rows of bench-seating on either side. With a single exception, every table was overcrowded; the orange-suited inmates were tightly packed in, side by side and taking up every last inch of every bench.

The exception, as always, was the Ghost.

He had a name, Bush knew. Hell, he had two. But neither

of them fit the way the young soldier saw him. For Bush, names were for men. And the Ghost was something other than that. He was something more.

A force of nature.

The Facility was no ordinary prison. Built in what had once been a top-secret military installation and still staffed by the United States Army, it held a maximum of two hundred and fifty inmates. All of them men. All of them dangerous. And all of them erased from existence.

Today the population stood at two hundred and twelve. All deemed to be enemies of the state, locked up without trial or due process, and with no prospect of release. And all of them – between the hours of 8 and 9.30 each morning, then again twice more for lunch and for dinner – were herded into a single room, with just twenty armed military personnel to oversee them.

It was a recipe for disaster every single day. And yet, every single day, that disaster was somehow avoided.

Bush was in his second year of guard duty. It was an unusual tour. Most of his colleagues were here a year and then done, released on to other assignments with their time at the Facility classified. But the colonel had asked Bush to stay on. The reason was obvious. Bush's size alone made him stand out. Six foot six, two hundred and fifty pounds, almost all of it solid muscle. Plus he was a fighter, with an Olympic bronze as a super-heavyweight to prove it.

The combination made him one of the few guards who was a match for the men imprisoned here. Guys like Bush, they were rare. He knew that. But he also knew his limits. And so, it seemed, did most of the inmates. At least when it came to one man.

Those unspoken but universally understood limits were

why the Ghost enjoyed his own space within the Mess. They were why he was kept company only by his cellmate, with at least fifteen feet between them and the men seated closest to their bench. And they were why an unarmed Englishman in his late forties, who weighed barely one hundred and eighty pounds, was the most respected prisoner in the place.

Bush had heard the Ghost's name on his first day. It was just one word, spoken with reverence by the guards. In any normal prison that would have been a strange sight: an inmate inspiring awe in his jailers. In the Facility it was damned near unique. These were no ordinary prison guards. They were trained killers in their own right. Infantrymen, special forces, military police. Every one of them a veteran of war.

And yet still the Ghost's infamous name was whispered.

He had been a prisoner here since 2017. Two years before Bush's first tour. Like every inmate, the crimes the Ghost had committed were irrelevant. It was his status that mattered. He had been considered too dangerous to stand public trial and too dangerous to ever again see the light of day. The same was true of every prisoner here. They were the reason the Facility existed.

But with most, there was at least some doubt. Some question of whether they were as bad as their sentence suggested.

With most . . .

Bush's thoughts were interrupted by a movement caught in his peripheral vision. The movement itself was not unusual. The time was approaching 1 p.m. and lunch was not yet halfway done, so it was inevitable that there would be inmates moving back and forth between their seats and the depository. A heaving body of hungry men. Almost all of them loud, energetic and naturally aggressive.

Perhaps it was that which caught Bush's eye. The calm of

the man. The steady, focused way in which he rose from the bench a whole half a hall downwind from the Ghost. The easy movement with which he closed the near forty-foot distance between them, all the while seemingly free of malicious intent.

Innocence was rare in the Facility. And so feigned innocence stood out.

Still unsure of what he was seeing, Bush switched his gaze back to the Ghost. He was still seated. Still focused on his lunch. If trouble was on its way – and Bush could not be sure that it was – then the Ghost was unaware.

The inmate grew closer by the second, and Bush became more convinced that something was wrong. His hand moved instinctively for his nightstick. Not the most lethal weapon he carried, but the one best suited to what *could* be coming.

Comforted by its feel in his grip, he began to move. One slow step. Two.

And then he broke into a run as he realised what was about to happen.

The second and third attackers had been sitting much closer to the Ghost. Level with him at the end of their own bench, they had been seated with their backs towards him, on the next table along. While Bush had been distracted by the first man, both of them had leapt from his seat and turned in an instant, perfectly timed to attack the Ghost together.

Bush needed to reach the Ghost first. He needed to stop this.

He needed to save three lives.

Whether it was reflex or instinct or training or who-knows-what else, Bush would never understand how the Ghost could react as quickly as he did. For Bush, there was only one explanation.

Force of nature.

The Ghost did not look up as, with one hand beneath it, he threw the table into the air, while at the same moment his other hand grabbed something from the tray. The table peaked and, as it dropped, he kicked it hard towards inmates two and three.

They had managed barely four steps before the table hit them, breaking their stride and forcing them backwards.

'GET BACK!!!' Bush screamed as he accelerated. Other guards – closer guards – were moving too. But none were as near as they needed to be.

The Ghost moved fast. His foot was barely back on the ground as he twisted round to face the inmate who had moved first, now coming at him from his right. Bush saw the Ghost switch whatever he had snatched from his tray to his left hand, just in time to use his right to block a blow from his attacker. At least it looked like a blow. The sound of metal hitting the floor told him otherwise; Bush realised then that the first man had been armed with a knife.

It explained the confidence with which he had moved. But with this target, that confidence was entirely misplaced. The Ghost had used his right to deflect the knife strike by hooking his hand around the guy's wrist and twisting it to breaking point, all in the blink of an eye. An instant later and whatever the Ghost had lifted from his tray was thrust deep into his attacker's neck.

Expertly placed, Bush did not doubt, as the man fell to the floor, and the Ghost picked up the dropped knife.

Whatever he had used to kill his first attacker had been makeshift. Most likely a piece of plastic cutlery, roughly snapped for the job.

The next two men? They would face nothing so rudimentary.

A second more and the Ghost had closed the distance between them, just as his two would-be killers were composing themselves.

By now the other prisoners were all on their feet. Bush could not help but notice their silence. Violence usually caused uproar. A near riot of sound. It was testament to the Ghost's reputation, then, that none so much as raised their voice.

When *he* fought, no one was there to support or cajole. They just wanted to see what he did next.

It was not a long wait.

The attack had begun mere seconds ago. Bush and the other guards were moving fast but they were still not close enough. They could do nothing to stop the Ghost and he knew it. Bush had noticed the glance. In that one sweep, the Ghost had calculated exactly how long he had. Three seconds, Bush guessed, before the first guard reached him. Maybe five before he was engulfed by them all.

It was more than enough time.

Inmate two went down fast. The table had hit him head on and so he had been forced to clamber over it to move forward. He need not have bothered. His 'victim' was coming to him.

The man had barely found his footing when the Ghost reached him, the dropped knife now held tight and blade-down in his right hand. One forward thrust – almost a punch into nothing – and the blade had crossed the second inmate's throat. The wound was fatal but still the Ghost pulled his arm backwards and drove the blade into his heart.

It left two seconds and one attacker. Bush did not like the third man's odds.

And neither did the third man.

The Ghost had not stopped moving, a tornado of fatal

forward motion. It left the third man no time to think. All he had was instinct, and that instinct screamed 'run'.

He did exactly that, turning and bursting into a sprint towards guards who were now just yards away. Guards who, had the third inmate thought ahead and stayed where he was, might have saved him. But they could do nothing as the Ghost raised the knife and threw it with precision and exact weight into the nape of the third man's neck.

Bush was just feet away as the man fell. He stopped running. It was already too late. Less than ten seconds had passed since he had noticed the first man's movement. Less than five since the Ghost had bothered to stand.

In that time, and in the space of just a few feet, three men were dead. While their killer had shed hardly a bead of sweat.

Bush did not move as the Ghost stepped back, placed his hands behind his head and lowered himself back onto his bench. He glanced to his left as he pushed his back against the wall. Towards his cellmate. A man who, Bush now realised, had been frozen to the spot in the attack.

With the room paralysed by the same silent shock, Bush lifted his radio to his mouth, pressed the mic and spoke.

'We need a restraint team in the Mess. Incident over so no immediate threat, but we've lost three inmates.'

There was a beat before the reply. As if the speaker was trying to understand what she had just been told.

'What do . . . what do you mean you've lost three inmates?'

'I mean we've lost them. They're dead.'

'I . . . what . . . what do I tell the colonel?'

Bush exhaled deeply, his eyes fixed on the Ghost.

'Tell him it was Joshua.'

TWELVE

9.30 a.m. EDT

Eden Grace flashed her ID as she approached the security point in the lobby in the United Nations Secretariat Building. It was an unnecessary habit. Grace was a full one-year veteran of the International Security Bureau. Fieldwork aside, she had been based on the building's nineteenth floor for that entire time. By now the security detail knew exactly who she was. And Grace being Grace, she knew each of them in turn.

'Morning, Eden.' Grace was greeted by Tommy Hobbs. One of the senior guards. 'Didn't you just leave?'

'Feels like it,' Grace replied. She stopped moving as she spoke and picked up a newly disinfected plastic container from a stack next to Hobbs' desk. 'Your shift not done yet, Tommy?'

'Finished an hour ago. Somehow I'm still here.'

'Anything to skip morning traffic in midtown, huh?'

'I'd rather the traffic than this.'

Hobbs indicated behind Grace with a tilt of his head, but she did not need to look around to understand. It seemed that of anywhere in New York City, the United Nations Plaza had reverted to its previous self with the least delay. And so, just as it had at this time of day pre-lockdown, the lobby of the

Secretariat Building was being hit by a tidal wave of suits. Men and women from every corner of the globe, arriving to work in their Manhattan hub as one unified mass.

Grace had beaten the crowd just as she always did, but only by moments this time.

'You've only got yourself to blame, Mr Hobbs.' Grace smiled as she spoke and began to walk forward. 'You should know to be gone by now.'

'You've got me there, ma'am. Have a great day.'

'You too. Now go home.'

A line of magnetometer arches separated the building's public lobby from the restricted areas behind and above. An entirely penetrable, mainly plastic wall, it would offer no resistance to a full-frontal assault on the security of the Secretariat. But short of such a declaration of war, it was more than enough.

Grace approached the third arch from the left, just as she did every morning. It was a habit she had picked up on her first day and one which she could not explain. Grace was not superstitious. Not even a little. And yet she would happily join a line to pass through *this* security point, even if the arch to its left or its right were free.

That commitment was unnecessary right now. In a few moments those lines would surely form, but until then every archway was free.

Grace placed her ID, her wallet, phone, two pistols and two spare magazines into the plastic container she was holding, then passed it to the guard at the left-hand side. Now metal-free, she walked through and waited for a beat as the detector confirmed that fact.

A moment later and the guard nodded her head.

'How's little Lauren?' Grace collected her belongings from the tray as she spoke.

'Summer camp,' the guard replied, her voice muffled by the face-mask that she still chose to wear.

'And you're here?' Grace paused as she bent down to holster her second pistol against her ankle. 'Jeez, Connie. When's *your* vacation?'

'I got three weeks' break from cooking for a vegan teen, Eden. That's all the vacation I need.'

'Different world when you have kids, I guess.'

Grace took the last item from the container – her phone – and turned towards the elevator bank. Connie called after her as she walked away.

'You'll find out for yourself one day.'

Grace had already reached her elevator as she heard the guard's words. She turned her head and forced a smile. It was not a welcome subject, but Connie could not know that. And nor did Grace want her to.

'We'll see.'

The Secretariat Building's elevators were fast. Enough that Grace felt the sudden change in altitude in her inner ear, even at just nineteen floors. It was only a moment's discomfort, one she had grown used to, and it was already clearing as she stepped through the doors and turned left.

The International Security Bureau had been based in the building for over a decade but for much of that time it had been an irrelevance. A concept born from one iteration of the United Nations Security Council and then disregarded by the next.

Grace knew the ISB's history. She had researched it back

when she had applied for her posting here. Hell, she had even lived through some of it.

As the threat of Islamic extremism had grown in the late 2000s, the Security Council had experienced a rare moment of unity. Agreeing that some formal cooperation in international intelligence was needed, they had voted to form the ISB. An agency without borders, with agents able to act without prior authority in any territory on the planet. It had been a revolutionary step.

Or at least it should have been.

International relations can change fast, and within weeks of the formal formation of the Bureau, relations between the US, China and Russia – three of the five permanent members of the Security Council – had hit rock bottom. And with the three global powers at odds, the spirit of cooperation needed for the ISB to succeed was absent.

For the next six years, the Bureau had existed in only the barest of forms. With minimal budget and non-existent political will, it had occupied a small three-room suite on the building's third floor. An afterthought of an agency, it comprised the minimum personnel its mandate would allow: a director, an assistant to the director and a single agent. None of whom had applied for their positions and none of whom wanted to be there.

The ISB had become a graveyard, where careers go to die.

It would have stayed that way, but for the election of US President John Knowles.

It was this part of the history that Grace knew best. The part that she had been involved in.

John Knowles was now in his second term as president and for the past eighteen months had proved himself one of the most effective men to ever hold that office. A welcome change from four years earlier when he had been under the thumb of a dangerous man with a terrible agenda. That time had been particularly hard for Grace, thanks to her personal relationship with the president.

She had known Knowles since childhood, first as commanding officer to her Navy SEAL father and later as something of a surrogate, with Knowles having stepped in after his death. It was with his attention, encouragement and financial support that Grace had thrived through adversity, and he was the reason she had joined the Secret Service. It had devastated her, then, to watch Knowles become a man she barely knew. A man who broke his election promises, who backtracked on so many of his aims, and who seemed to completely turn on the beliefs she knew he held.

It was only when Grace met Agent Dempsey at the ISB that she finally uncovered the truth of how Knowles had lost control of his own presidency. And of the identity of his puppet masters.

Grace and Dempsey had worked together to break that hold over the White House but it had been far from painless. For all the good they had done, a double murder inside the Oval Office, an elaborate cover-up and Grace's own brush with death in the Afghan snow had been enough to end her time with Presidential Protection.

So much had happened back then. Much more than even Grace would ever knew, she was sure. But all of it had led her here. Away from the Secret Service and into the ISB.

Into Joe Dempsey's Alpha Team.

Exactly where Eden Grace knew she was meant to be.

THIRTEEN

10.10 a.m. EDT

A little over forty minutes of staring at a lone patch of light on eight otherwise black CCTV monitors had dampened Vega's earlier enthusiasm for the Patrol Group's outdated video system. Even with a frame rate that meant ten seconds on-screen for each sixty of footage captured, it had still taken a full ten minutes to cover every hour.

With no idea of what the footage would show and no way to know when Ricardo Garcia was killed within a near four-hour window between 1.12 a.m. and 5 a.m., they had been able to risk no shortcuts. But that necessity did not make the exercise more tolerable.

The combination of the room's heat and a lack of sleep were threatening to overwhelm Vega as he watched the timer approach 4.40 a.m. Most of the others were doing no better. O'Rourke had already quit – she had taken a seat at the Patrol Group's public desk and was busy emailing from her phone – while Smart was increasingly bleary eyed. As for Montoya, he had not said a word since the tape had started. It seemed to Vega as if the director had retreated back into his own world.

Only May seemed unaffected. Still standing, still focused,

her eyes were studying the screen with the intensity of a predator seeking its prey. Her poise had begun to make Vega question himself. Was *that* the difference between the DOJ and a local cop? That kind of readiness? That kind of—

He did not conclude the thought, interrupted by a flicker of movement on-screen. It was fleeting, almost enough to miss, but still sufficient to fire his mind awake.

'Stop.'

Smart did as instructed. He seemed to have missed whatever Vega had seen. May's silence suggested that she had too. The second possibility made the detective feel a little smug, even as he kept his attention on the task ahead.

'Go back,' he instructed. 'Just a few seconds.'

The timer began to move backwards. The progress was slow compared to what they had grown used to, one second of real time for every second of footage. And so it was a full eight seconds later that they saw what the movement had been. A figure – a man, based on the height and build – dressed head-to-toe in black and walking in a strange reverse motion along the jetty. A moment later and there was another. Then another. Then a fourth.

Four of them in total. Every one of them in what looked to be identical dark clothing. Each one visible for little more than a second as they passed beneath the jetty light.

'OK. Stop, then play it forward.'

Vega turned to Montoya as Smart worked.

'Cesar, from the location of that camera, are those men walking towards the marina end or the sea end of the walkway?'

Montoya thought for a moment.

'Towards the sea.'

'Yeah. That's what I thought.'

Vega noticed O'Rourke move back into the doorway as he turned his attention back to the screens. The four figures were there again. Walking one at a time along the jetty, this time forward. Vega surmised that they were all heading towards an unregistered boat; the marina logs had no record of a second vessel on the third jetty but Vega had no doubt in his mind. Without a boat at the end of that walkway, there was no reason for anyone to be there.

No one spoke as the timer moved on.

4.41 a.m.

4.42 a.m.

4.43 a.m.

No more figures. No more movement. Not even a return journey.

Finally O'Rourke broke the silence.

'How about we skip forward,' she suggested. 'We know that if we're gonna see Mr Garcia, it's gotta be in the next seventeen minutes or so. Ain't like we'll miss it.'

Vega nodded to Smart and all five sets of eyes stayed fixed to the screen as the footage scanned on at speed, back to ten seconds for every sixty in real time.

A minute passed. Then another. Still nothing; no more movement from the four figures who had headed off to the end of the jetty and no sign of Ricardo Garcia. Vega watched with disappointment as the timer passed 5 a.m.

It can't be a bust, he reassured himself. *Ricardo died on that jetty. He has to at least walk by*.

The thought was hardly complete when he noticed another flicker of movement on-screen. A new figure had walked into the small patch of light. And this one – unlike the earlier four – had stayed where he could be seen.

'Stop.'

Vega hit Smart's shoulder with his open hand as he spoke. It was unnecessary. Smart had seen it too and was already manipulating the console controls. The footage paused and for the first time the image was clear.

It showed Ricardo Garcia, standing alone under the light with his pistol pointed directly ahead.

'Cesar, are you sure you want to see this? No one will think less of you—'

Montoya raised his hand before Vega could finish. An indication to stop. He raised himself up in his seat and took a deep calming breath.

'Enough, Sergio. I need to see this. If there is even the smallest detail that I can see that will help you find these men, I need to see.' He turned to face Smart. 'Lieutenant. Please. Play.'

Smart did as he was asked. With the press of a button, the timer began to tick forward and Vega felt the sensation of nerves deep in his stomach.

We're about to see Garcia die, he thought. *And if I'm right, it's not just him.*

Smart stopped the time jump the instant Garcia appeared on-screen.

Garcia stood in the centre of a pool of light, his pistol held out and aimed into the darkness. He seemed to be shouting something.

'Does the CCTV have audio?' May asked.

'Doesn't seem to,' Smart replied.

The footage continued. Garcia seemed to shout again. And then again, the last time with his head tilted a little to the side. As if he were calling out behind . . .

An unseen figure appeared from nowhere in the light behind Garcia and plunged a knife into the patrolman's back.

'Jesus fuck!'

Vega felt himself physically jump, shocked by the suddenness of what had happened. He watched with his eyes wide as Garcia sank to his knees. For a moment it did not seem real; as if it were something out of a slasher movie.

Garcia's fall gave them a better view of his murderer. A man wearing a uniform identical to Garcia's own. In that moment, Vega knew that his instinct had been both right and wrong.

Right because Garcia had *not* been on patrol alone. And wrong, because there would be no second corpse.

With Garcia on his knees, the second patrolman stepped around him, bringing his face in full view of the camera. Vega knew what was coming next. He had seen Garcia's wounds back at the marina and so he knew that his murderer did not stop here.

A moment more and it was done. Garcia was dead, his throat slit from ear to ear. And yet his killer did not move. He stood over Garcia's corpse for at least five seconds. Maybe more. The whole time unknowingly giving the camera the clearest possible view of his face.

The small room was silent as the footage continued.

It was seconds more before the killer finally moved out of frame, heading towards the jetty's end. In the direction of the four unseen men whose presence must have first brought Garcia into the marina. Only once he was out of shot did Smart hit the pause button.

Vega and Smart both turned to Montoya for confirmation of what they had just witnessed, and it was then that Vega noticed the effect the footage had had on the older man. Montoya's mouth was wide open, his naturally brown skin now almost white with emotion. Tears once again filled his eyes.

The Area Patrol Group director was visibly shaking and he seemed unable to look away from the screen. He just continued to stare, his face a mask of pure horror and . . . something else.

'You know who he is, Cesar,' Smart said. 'You know who that sonofabitch is.'

'Of course he does,' Vega replied. 'It's—'

'Clinton Dewitt,' Montoya interrupted. It was almost a whisper, but it was enough to silence Vega. 'That's Clinton Dewitt.'

The name was no surprise but Vega was happy to have the confirmation. What they had seen on-screen was harrowing but it was also a gift. How often did a murder investigation wrap itself up so neatly?

'Call your office, Frank, and I'll call mine. We need an APB put out on Clinton Dewitt right now.'

He turned to Montoya. The director's eyes had still not left the screen. But for all the sympathy Vega felt, he could no longer afford the gentle approach.

'Cesar, I need Dewitt's file.' No request. No apology. Just an expectation that Montoya would comply. 'Any information you have that will make him easier to find.'

He turned back to Smart, ready to direct their next steps, but before he could get further another voice spoke over his own.

'Forget the file. And forget the APB on Dewitt.'

Vega had almost forgotten that O'Rourke and May were in the doorway. The sound of the Homeland agent's heavy accent changed that in an instant. O'Rourke's actions in the last hour or so had persuaded Vega that she had meant it when assuring him that this was still his case.

Now, just from the tone of her voice alone, he felt that rug being pulled.

With those two instructions, the feel of the room had changed. Up to now O'Rourke had been a shadow. A tagalong. Occasionally helpful, but always in the background. That, Vega now realised, was at an end.

'Why "forget the file"?' he asked, as if the answer would make any difference to what would follow.

'Forget the file, Sergeant, because that file's gonna be as accurate as my grandmother at a gun range. There ain't no truth in no file named Clinton Dewitt. And that's because there ain't no Clinton Dewitt.'

'What?' This time it was Smart who spoke. 'What does that mean? How can you—'

'Don't waste your time, Frank.' Vega rose to his feet as he spoke, his eyes never leaving O'Rourke. 'I take it, Special Agent O'Rourke, that we've hit that moment when *my* crime scene becomes *your* crime scene.'

O'Rourke nodded slowly.

'I'm afraid we have, Sergeant. This is now a federal investigation.'

'Any chance you'll tell us why?'

'Very little chance at all, son. That information's on a need-to-know basis.'

'And is there anything we *do* need to know?'

'Just one thing right now. For the purposes of the APB.'

'And what's that?'

'The guy we're looking for? The so-called "Clinton Dewitt". His real name is Campbell Arnold. And right now he's just about the most dangerous man in America.'

FOURTEEN

10.20 a.m. EDT

Scott Turner had been driving for around four and a half hours. A little over two of those had been on the Overseas Highway, between Key West and the Florida Mainland. Another thirty minutes or so on US Route One towards Florida City, then on to the Ronald Reagan Turnpike and north to the I-95.

Two hundred and forty-six miles, point to point. On two thirds of the Jeep's tank.

Turner did the maths.

One thousand, one hundred and fifty miles left to go. Last part without a highway.

Two days for the whole thing. Well within schedule.

He glanced right, to the seat next to his own.

Cliff Clemons was asleep. Deeper than Turner would have expected in the cramped passenger seat. But then Clemons had taken the final four-hour driving shift through the Keys last night, hadn't he? And he seemed to be the first awake this morning.

No wonder he's bushed.

Turner's eyes moved upwards, towards the rear-view mirror and the sight of an unconscious Kenny Brooks. Brooks was as out of it as Clemons, half-stretched out across the Jeep's tight back seat. But unlike Clemons, he had done little so far to earn his rest.

Turner shook his head as he refocused on the road ahead. This section of the I-95 was a typical American toll road. Wider than necessary, Turner had thought yesterday, as they were travelling in the other direction. It had not seemed then to carry near enough traffic for its obvious capacity. He thought no different now, as it took them back north.

But in every way other than size, the I-95 was unremarkable. A big, empty road with nothing to look at and nothing to break the monotony. Just the same sight – the same identical highway fence – passing again and again and again, like the backdrop of a kid's cartoon.

Freeway hypnosis, Turner heard himself think. *I can see how it could happen*.

He reached out, tapped the Jeep's built in satnav and located the next gas station.

Three miles.

This time the maths did itself.

Three minutes.

He glanced again at the mirror. Brooks was still out, unaware that he was three minutes away from taking the next four-hour stint at the wheel. Turner considered waking him, to give Brooks a chance to rouse himself properly before he had to take over. A moment's thought and he had changed his mind.

If Cliff Clemons had been next to drive it would have been different. Turner would have woken him a few miles early. He actually liked Clemons. As much as he liked any of the men in Liberation, anyway. They were *all* fanatics; they had to be, to believe the things they did. But compared to most of them, Clemons was pretty reasonable. He could even be good company.

Those were descriptions that could never be applied to Brooks. Brooks was, Turner had concluded, a born and bred extremist. One who seemed to speak of nothing but the many obsessions that drove him. Over the course of almost two years, Turner had learned to tune out most of the bizarre rantings of the men who surrounded Cam Arnold. But sometimes that was impossible. Sometimes it just became a wall of sound and – over the three days they had spent together on the journey to Key West – Brooks had hit that height.

But it was not just Brooks' beliefs. Not just his paranoia. Those were par for the course amongst Cam's followers. No, it was the sadistic relish that Brooks seemed to apply to even the thought of violence. Turner could not be sure, of course, but he got the distinct impression that blood, pain – even death – aroused him.

And then there was this morning. When Cam had killed that man on the jetty, Turner had been horrified. He hoped that Clemons had felt the same. But Brooks?

Even through the ski mask, he could tell that Brooks had enjoyed it.

The thought brought the image crashing back into Turner's mind. He had tried to banish it. Unsuccessfully at first; as hard as he tried for the first few hours, he just could not shift the horror of what he had seen. It had only been the hypnotic effect of the featureless highway that had ultimately put it out of his mind.

And now it's back.

He felt his blood turn cold as those few seconds played out in his mind once more. The man on his knees, helpless from the wound Cam had inflicted on him from behind. Then the sight of the knife, pulled silently across his throat like the ritual slaughter of some dumb animal.

And then perhaps the worst part of all: the almost casual aftermath. A human being, slumped on the jetty with his blood seeping through the cracks between the wooden planks. All but ignored as the last few moments of his life slipped away.

Turner was not sure what horrified him more: the fact that a man had been murdered to further their plan or that he had been murdered by Cam Arnold. As much as he hated to admit it, it might just be the latter.

For all the extremes of his ideology, Arnold and Turner had grown close. Closer, Turner believed, than Arnold was to either Brooks or to Clemons, or to almost anyone else in Liberation. And while the fanaticism that drove him prevented Arnold from ever truly being his friend, Turner had come to trust him. To respect him, even. Which was why he had been horrified to see Cam kill a man with such . . . such calm.

Whatever Turner had come to expect from Cam Arnold, it had not been *that*. It was not in the man's nature, he had believed. And it sure as hell was not in the plan. A plan that Turner knew back to front.

Cam had mapped it out for him months ago. From beginning to end and with meticulous attention to detail. But the death of the patrolman? There had been no suggestion of that.

There wasn't even supposed to be a patrolman. Not a real one, anyway. That was the whole point of Cam 'becoming' Clinton Dewitt, wasn't it?

Turner had already spent hours rationalising what Cam had done. Things must have changed at the last minute, he had told himself. Maybe the patrolman had insisted on joining Cam for his rounds? Maybe it was too late for Cam to contact them with an update?

Whatever it was, Cam would have his reasons. Murder would have been his absolute last resort. Turner believed that.

Turner *had* to believe that.

The sign for the upcoming rest-stop and gas station caught his eye, interrupting his thoughts.

One mile.

Turner changed lanes, glancing towards the satnav for confirmation. A strange need for reassurance. The road sign was hardly going to lie.

First I'm doubting Cam, he thought to himself. *And now it's the bloody mile markers.*

The realisation almost made him laugh out loud. He was questioning everything. And his underlying scientific mind told him why: it was a combination of stress, anxiety and tiredness. A killer threesome at the best of times, it was inevitable that it would hit him as the mission – years in the making – neared completion.

The thought improved his mood. He was sure of two things.

Cam only did what he had to. And I need to sleep.

FIFTEEN

11.40 a.m. EDT

The operational suite of the International Security Bureau had come a long way from the three-room afterthought it had been just a decade ago. As the world's premier internationally mandated intelligence agency and the frontline arm of the Security Council itself, the ISB now took up a third of a floor of Manhattan's UN Secretariat Building.

The private offices within the suite were reserved for the senior staff. Director Elizabeth Kirk's was the largest. A working space built more to impress than for practicality. Next to Kirk's was the smaller, busier workspace of Henry Garrett, her logistical assistant and the central nervous system of the entire Bureau.

The deputy-director's office was situated on the opposite side of the suite to Kirk's, and lining one wall between them were the offices of the ISB's twelve principal agents, each facing out through the building's curtain wall and over New York's East River. An equal mix of men and women, each hailing from a different member nation, every principal agent headed his or her own team of five agent-operatives.

Or, as Eden Grace preferred to think of them, the worker bees.

After a year as one of them, it was a nickname that Grace was well qualified to bestow. Assigned to Joe Dempsey's Alpha Team, her appointment had taken Alpha's agent total to six, all working under the man himself. It was a unique set-up that recognised Dempsey's status as the ISB's lead principal, permitted by Director Kirk herself to extend his team at Grace's recruitment.

Dempsey was currently absent – away on personal leave, the first Grace had ever known him take – but there was no fear that this would affect Alpha's operation. These days the team needed little direction even from him. Exactly as Dempsey preferred it.

Each of the team's six agents had been hand-picked from their respective countries' security services. Once recruited, Dempsey had divided them into pairs: Kentucky's Dylan Wrixon with Italy's Salvatore Gallo, California's Kate Silver with Ethiopia's Adama Jabari, and, for the past year, Grace herself with Beijing's Shui Dai.

Each pair was routinely left to handle their own caseloads. A rare holiday for their boss was no reason to change that.

Like the rest of 'the bees', Grace's desk was in the large communal space that took up most of the ISB's suite. Alpha Team were concentrated in the spot closest to Dempsey's office, across three sets of two adjourning desks. From where she sat Grace had a direct line of sight to Dai, based at the workstation closest to her own. It was a practical set-up; as ever, the two agents were working together on an investigation. One which had already occupied them late into the previous night.

Grace tapped her index finger on a notepad as she listened to the melody of Dai's voice. Her focus should have been on the words she had written down – the result of a call of her own, finished moments ago – but the sound from across the table was an enjoyable distraction. Grace had always found language fascinating. She could speak three fluently – English, Spanish and Italian – and had a passing command of French and Arabic. But Mandarin? Even after a year of working so closely with Dai, it remained a poetic mystery.

Dai ended the diversion by replacing her telephone's handset into its cradle. She did so gently, giving no hint of whether the call had been good, bad or indifferent.

'So who's going first?' Grace asked.

A pointless question. Grace had worked with Dai long enough to know the answer.

'Tell me,' Dai replied.

It was an instruction unburdened by pleasantries, exactly as Grace had come to expect. She had found Dai's way of speaking a little rude when they had first met. A year later and she knew it for what it was: a combination of cultural difference and absolute focus.

By now, any other reaction would just feel wrong.

'I have an update on the bank accounts . . .'

Grace paused as a member of the ISB's admin team approached Dai's desk. A skinny young man, he was at least twenty-five, the minimum age for a job on the nineteenth floor. Yet he looked barely out of his teens.

'Agent Dai, this just came through the system.' He handed Dai a single sheet of A4 paper, folded over. 'It's marked for Alpha Team's attention.'

Grace sat a little more upright in her chair. The same thing had happened twice yesterday and each time it had been a system alert relating to their key suspect. Grace expected this time to be no different.

Dai read the notice to herself and gave nothing away.

'Third time's the charm?' Grace asked. 'Any hint in this one why he's here?'

'It is not about him.' Dai replied without looking up. 'It is something else. Something . . . different.'

'What?'

Dai did not answer. At least not immediately. And Grace did not push. Instead she watched in silence as Dai processed whatever she had just been handed. As she ran through the decisions she now had to make and the implications of each.

Finally Dai stood up, the paper alert still clutched in her hand. She looked to the nearest two-table set-up, a match for the one she shared with Grace. Her movement attracted the attention of its occupants, Kate Silver and Adama Jabari.

'Agent Silver, I need to brief you on our investigation,' she began, taking no time to explain anything to Grace. 'I need you to replace Agent Grace and work alongside me.'

'Replace me?' This was *not* what Grace was expecting. 'What? Since . . . what was in that notice?'

'A priority,' Dai replied. 'You can return to the case once you are back.'

'Back? Back from where?'

'Back from Florida.'

'Florida? What the . . . Why am I going to Florida?'

Dai handed her the note.

'For this.' Dai's answer gave Grace time for just a glance. 'We can discuss shortly, but first I suggest you call Dempsey. You need to catch him before he boards the plane to London.'

SIXTEEN

12.26 p.m. EDT

Despite its name, Naval Air Station Key West was situated on Boca Chica Key, around a mile east of its more famous neighbour. Like every island that collectively made up the Florida Keys, Boca Chica was technically within the jurisdiction of Monroe County Sheriff's Office. And yet – to the surprise of Special Agent O'Rourke – Sergeant Sergio Vega had never set foot there.

The island had been home to a US Navy presence since the earliest days of the nineteenth century. Established to combat the area's piracy epidemic, the base had only grown bigger in the two centuries that had followed. It was now South Florida's largest Air Force facility. Almost a city of its own.

But unlike civilian cities, this one did not welcome outside interference. Even when it came with a badge.

O'Rourke glanced at her watch, then back towards the horizon. Even with the deep-blue sky rolling out for miles ahead, there was no sign of the Homeland Security team she had summoned to join her.

They're twenty-six minutes late.

She looked across to Vega. Like her, Vega had been out of

91

the sheriff's office patrol car for almost forty minutes. And like her, he had spent that time on the exposed airfield under the intense July sun. Somehow, though, the heat did not seem to be affecting him in the way it had quickly hit her.

O'Rourke knew why. Vega was used to the weather down here. Born in Cuba just ninety-four miles south of where they now stood, he had spent his life first there and then in Key West. It made him as suited to the local climate as any person could be.

The same could not be said for O'Rourke. Her weight was far from ideal – the negative effects of her BMI had been dropped into conversation by Homeland medics a whole lot more than once – but the blame really rested on her less visible conditions. Issues she had so far kept to herself.

She lifted a near dripping-wet handkerchief to her brow and dabbed at the sheen of sweat that covered it. It did little, she knew. Just moved the beads of salty liquid around. But it was better than nothing.

'Struggling?'

Vega's question did not seem loaded. Just a genuine enquiry, from one colleague to another. It would have been negligent if he *hadn't* asked, O'Rourke realised, and one thing she had recognised in Sergio Vega was his professionalism. He was unusually competent, which was the main reason she had decided to keep him around now she had taken over the case.

Plus some local knowledge ain't gonna hurt, she had told herself.

'I'm fine.' O'Rourke kept her discomfort from her voice. 'You?'

'You're thinking I'm made for this weather, right?'

'I don't reckon there's a man alive made for *this* weather, son.'

Vega smiled.

'You're not wrong. Still, it looks like it's hitting you hard. You sure you should be out here?'

'It ain't ideal and I ain't denying it; back home we'd say this was hotter than two rabbits screwing in a wool sack. But I'll live.'

Vega's smile widened in reply. O'Rourke was used to the reaction. She had been with Homeland Security long enough to know how it affected people. It was a big, faceless and ultimately powerful organisation, and that scared people. Whereas what *didn't* scare people was a short, older lady speaking in Mississippi whimsey.

O'Rourke's personality and turn of phrase always put people at their ease. She had learned that early on and she had quickly used it to her advantage. The O'Rourke that Vega was experiencing, she was no act. But she just might be an exaggeration.

'Any idea how long we'll be out here?'

O'Rourke glanced at her phone, checking for an update. She found what she was looking for and turned towards Vega.

'They're telling me wheels down in four minutes.'

Vega nodded his head. He seemed to think for a moment, his mouth opening then shutting twice without a word. As if he were concerned that he would overstep a mark.

'Are your people always this late?' he finally asked.

'Not usually.' The question was a reasonable one, O'Rourke thought. 'It's a specialist team flying in.'

'I thought you said we were waiting for your investigators?'

'We are. But my people ain't coming alone. Not on this one.'

Vega's eyes narrowed at O'Rourke's answer. Her answer

had been deliberately vague, yet it still suggested far more than she had offered since the name Campbell Arnold. O'Rourke could see that she had piqued his interest.

'And this team takes longer why?'

O'Rourke studied Vega before she answered. She had a decision to make. An instant later and she had done so.

'You get that everything that happens here is classified, right?'

'Do I look like I'm new at this?'

'You're so new at this, Sergeant Vega, that right now you don't know whether to check your ass or scratch your watch.'

The answer was a carefully chosen slap-down. It would take too long to decipher to cause immediate offence, O'Rourke knew. Which would give her time to continue before Vega could respond.

'There's a good chance that I'll need local knowledge on this one, so I need to trust someone from hereabouts. And of the folks I've met down here today, my gut tells me that someone should be you. Take that whatever way you want, but it's intended as a compliment.'

O'Rourke paused. When Vega did not attempt to fill the silence, she continued.

'So I guess here's what you need to know. It's been bothering you all day how Nicki and I were at that marina before you this morning. The answer to that one's simple: we were already en route to Key West from Key Largo when Mr Garcia was found.'

'But the call came in near seven a.m. Why were you—'

'We'd been in Key Largo for the previous thirty-six hours, following up on intelligence. We had reason to believe that Key Largo was due to be point of delivery for a consignment of . . .

material. Something we didn't want finding its way into the United States.'

'Material?' Vega seemed engaged. Even more than before. 'What does that mean? If it was drugs you'd just say drugs. So what was it?'

'Classified, remember? This goes no further.'

'I get that, yeah.'

'It was caesium-137. We were tipped off that a shipment was heading for one of the marinas in Key Largo. And we were told it was coming this weekend. It was expected any time in the day and a half just gone, or at some point today. That's as much as we knew.'

'Caesium-137?' Vega looked confused. 'I don't want to sound ignorant here but I've never even heard that term before. So I don't know what you're referring to.'

'Sorry.' O'Rourke's apology was sincere. 'Sometimes I forget not everyone lives this life.'

'No problem, I get that. I make a lot of bad assumptions about what civilians know and what they don't know. Makes for some awkward date chat. But this stuff? This caesium? What is it?'

'Caesium-137. It's radioactive material. A by-product of nuclear fission.'

'Nuclear fission? You mean like atom bombs?' Vega's voice was raised and his delivery fast. Not an unusual reaction, in O'Rourke's experience. 'You mean you're here chasing atom bombs?'

'No. No, nothing like that.' O'Rourke paused as she rethought her answer. 'Well, maybe *something* like that. But not atom bombs. My department at Homeland, Sergeant, it's the Domestic Nuclear Detection Office. The DNDO. We specialise in this stuff. Which is why I know that caesium-137, it's a *by-product* of fission. Which means the bomb part – or, much more likely, the power station part – which is when the fission actually occurs, well, that's already done with. What's left after that process, that's the caesium.'

'OK. And what's its use? It's still got to be something bad, right? If you're interested in it? It can't exactly be harmless.'

'Oh, it's very far from harmless. It's got some legitimate uses, sure. There's some medical applications, where it's used inside certain specialist equipment. And it's used to calibrate detection meters like Geiger counters, so they can go looking for the big-boy stuff like uranium and plutonium. But when it's used for any of that stuff then it's used carefully. In lab conditions and in sealed equipment. Outside of those conditions, it's damned dangerous.'

'In what way?'

'In the nuclear fallout way, son. Anyone properly exposed to that stuff, they're not dying pleasant. Cancer's a cert, but if there's enough of it? Radiation sickness. The kind of thing they use to scare us all shitless in the movies.'

At first Vega said nothing. Again, it was not an unexpected reaction. What O'Rourke was telling him, she knew it was hard to take in; even after all her time in the job, it still scared her. She was impressed, then, that it took just a few seconds for him to take on the information and come back with a practical question.

'If this is all correct, are you seriously telling me that they sent, what, one agent from the . . . what was it? The DNDO? And one from the Department of Justice. And that's it?'

'It wasn't that solid a tip,' O'Rourke replied. 'You got to understand, we get endless intelligence like this. Once a tip comes in, it gets assessed and resources get deployed based on that assessment. This one didn't come with much information. Even the whole caesium element was sketchy. All the encouragement we had was an ID on the terrorist group our source said it was going to. So resources were allocated accordingly.'

'OK, I get that. But still, one agent from Homeland? Plus Agent May? And, no offence, but neither one of you looks like a field agent.'

O'Rourke smiled.

'You'd be surprised on maybe half of that one, son. I wasn't always a fat old lady.'

'I wasn't—'

'But I get it. Which is why they sent one special agent, plus Agent May, plus four other field agents from the DNDO and a whole specialist scientific unit in support, just in case. Weak-ass intelligence or not, we're still Homeland Security. The rest of the team stayed in Key Largo, liaising with the coastguard and surveilling the probable importation points.'

'But something pulled you away?'

'It was a six a.m. tip. Different source this time, and not to us. This one came via the DOJ. We had no time to carry out a proper assessment. The info referred to the same shipment and the same group, so we couldn't ignore it. But we also couldn't let it pull our full team away from their posts. Lucky for us the second tip named a particular point of delivery – North Bay Marina – which meant it could be covered by a smaller team.'

'But just two of you?'

'We were in the air by six forty-five, here by seven twenty. The tip hadn't included a delivery time and so we didn't know if we had time to pull in more of our own men from up in Miami. The whole thing was a last-minute plan, out of necessity. To be truthful with you, in the end we opted to second in some units from your office and from the police department. We were making that call from the chopper – arranging to have a squad waiting for us here on this very tarmac – when we learned about Mr Garcia.'

Vega nodded his head. O'Rourke was sure that she could follow his thinking. Her explanation had answered many of the questions that had bothered him since this morning. Problem was, it also raised a whole lot more.

And it was no surprise to her which one most concerned the murder investigator.

'Campbell Arnold. You knew him on sight. How?'

'The organisation that was due to receive the shipment. It's a group called Liberation. Cam Arnold heads them up. Has done for near on ten years.'

'Ten years? He didn't look that old?'

'He's not. He's thirty-seven. But he's been part of Liberation since the beginning. We smashed the bastards back in 2012. Left them in tatters. Arnold ended up leading what was left of them. Which, up until last year, wasn't a whole lot.'

'And what's their thing?' Vega asked.

'The usual redneck shit,' O'Rourke replied. 'Anti-government, anti-federalism, anti-regulation. Anti-anything that doesn't let them do whatever the hell they want, pretty much.'

Vega nodded again. He seemed to have more questions, but the growing sound of engines and rotors were now impossible for either of them to ignore.

O'Rourke looked upwards towards the sound. Two large

black helicopters were heading towards them, the only features visible in the clear blue sky.

'The team?' Vega asked.

'The team.'

'And when they get here? Is that me gone?'

'If it was, I wouldn't have told you what I just told you. Like I said, you know the island. You know the community. I'm going to need that, Sergeant.'

Vega nodded a final time, seemingly grateful for O'Rourke's decision.

'It's Sergio, by the way.'

'What?'

'My name. It's Sergio. Not Sergeant.'

'Nice to meet you, Sergio. And since we're getting familiar, I'm Bambi O'Rourke. Which means you can call me O'Rourke. Or Agent O'Rourke. Or even Boss, for as long as you're part of the team. All your choice. But just make sure of one thing.'

'What's that?'

O'Rourke lifted her arm and pointed a short, thick index finger towards Vega.

'Whatever you do, you never, ever call me Bambi.'

SEVENTEEN

1.30 p.m. EDT

The private waiting area at LaGuardia Airport was as deserted now as JFK's Terminal 7 had been just four hours earlier.

The lack of other passengers was less surprising here. At JFK, Dempsey had been waiting to board a three-hundred seat British Airways Boeing 787. This room held no more than thirty, while the Learjet 75 being prepped outside maxed out at ten.

Today it would carry just four: two pilots, Dempsey and Grace.

LaGuardia and JFK were ten miles apart. A little further than the smaller airport was from United Nations Plaza in Midtown Manhattan but with a much lighter flow of traffic in between. It had taken Dempsey barely thirty minutes from the time of Grace's call to exit Terminal 7, hail a cab and make the journey.

Had he known it would take Grace almost two hours to travel the same distance in the opposite direction, he would have spared the time to wait and collect the checked-in luggage that had no doubt been removed from the waiting plane. But with no reason to expect the delay, Dempsey had left JFK within minutes of the call and so for now his personal effects stretched to his phone, a notebook, a barely used computer tablet and a single Glock 19.

Plus the clothes he had on.

'Dressed for comfort I see, Boss.'

Dempsey looked up when he heard Grace's voice. The worn carpet of the waiting room had disguised the sound of her footsteps and so she was just feet away. Close enough that he could see her amusement as she inspected his appearance.

'I didn't expect to be on duty so soon into a ten-day leave.'

Dempsey stood up as he spoke and gestured down to his travelling clothes: light-coloured deck shoes, loose-fitting khaki cargo pants and a battered white T-shirt he had owned for longer than he could remember.

'Weird seeing you in anything other than black,' Grace commented, her smile wide. She indicated her own regulation ISB outfit. The usual dark suit and white blouse. 'You want me in something a little more casual too?'

'You might wish you were once you get there.' Dempsey held up his phone. 'I checked the weather app on this thing. It's over a hundred degrees.'

'Phew. You sure you really want to go? I hear the A/C's better in Vegas.'

As she spoke, she placed a large leather holdall on the seat next to the one Dempsey had just vacated.

'I've brought everything you asked for, including the intelligence files. You want them now?'

'No. Let's do that on the flight. Did you bring the clothes?'

'As much as I could throw together.' Grace held out a bulging plastic bag as she spoke. 'Jeans, boots and a polo shirt.

Smart casual's as good as it gets today, but at least the shirt's black.'

'Where we're going, smart casual's pretty much formal wear.' Dempsey pulled out the polo shirt. 'I wear this in the Keys, I'm basically James Bond.'

'Aren't you anyway?'

Dempsey ignored the comment as he held the shirt up against himself. He could already see how tight it would be on his frame. He was six foot two with a forty-eight-inch chest and a thirty-three-inch waist. Those were ratios from which even the most ambitious mannequin manufacturers tended to shy away and so he found it difficult to find clothes. But this?

'Who'd this come from?' he asked.

'Dylan Wrixon. He was the only one with a top to hand.'

'Dyl's half my size.'

'I was in a hurry, Boss.'

'And the jeans and boots?'

'Those are yours. Got them from your office.'

Dempsey nodded his head. He looked again at the top. It was not ideal but even undersized it was more appropriate than what he was wearing right now. Besides, there wasn't much he could do about it now. Grace had done her best.

He pushed the clothes back into the bag.

'Thanks for these. I'll change once we're on the jet.'

'Any idea when that might be?' Grace took a step back and looked around the room as she spoke. She seemed perturbed by the lack of activity that surrounded them.

'Not too long, I think. The plane's already on the tarmac.' Dempsey retook his seat and gestured towards another that was directly across from him. 'But I wouldn't tempt fate by staying standing if I were you.'

Grace lowered herself into the seat. Dempsey waited, aware of what would come once she was comfortable. He already knew most of what was in the intelligence files and he had no doubt that Grace would have read them before leaving the ISB offices. And so he could anticipate the questions that Grace would have.

The first, then, came as no surprise.

'Boss, I've got to ask, why are we even interested in these Liberation guys?'

Dempsey thought for a moment. The answer was a complicated one, with far more information than Grace needed to know, at least for now. He did not enjoy deceit – even deceit by omission – but there were some details he just did not want to share. Not while he had a choice.

'They're a resurgent terrorist organisation,' Dempsey replied. 'They were a real danger about a decade ago, when they were led by a guy called Peyton Travis. Back then there were hundreds of them. Maybe as many as a thousand, depending on what intelligence you believe. And they were well-funded. Peyton Travis was a defence contractor. An advanced weapons specialist; a real-life Tony Stark type. But as much as he made billions from selling weapons to the US military, he was – unknown to them – also a massive believer in the patriot movement. Anti-government, anti-federalist, all of that stupid shit. The guy was a fanatic. And so he founded, funded and led Liberation, which set them apart from the groups like them. There's a hell of a lot more damage you can do when you've got a bottomless bank account behind you.

'By 2012, they were posing a substantial terrorist threat. Enough for Homeland Security to take an interest. When that happened, they stumbled on a plot to attack the Capitol that was already in full swing. Homeland hit them hard to prevent it. They ended up taking out a good number of the key people in the movement. Scores of them put away, Travis and a bunch of others killed. What was left of the movement, without Travis, petered out. Followers drifted away. A small core remained but nothing that warranted further attention. With the messiah gone, they were just a little band of unfunded, under-resourced cranks.'

Grace was listening carefully, Dempsey could tell, but she was also hearing nothing new.

'That's all in the intelligence files, Boss. As is the fact that Cam Arnold just about kept them alive over the last decade. And that the president's shutdown led to a small rebirth. I know all that already.'

Dempsey nodded. President John Knowles *was* partly responsible for Liberation's recent resurgence. He had acted fast and he had acted hard at the outset of the pandemic the previous year. He had gambled his own popularity ahead of an imminent presidential election by locking down practically the entire country. A gamble that had paid off: it had kept both the infection and death rates well below the global average, success that had helped Knowles achieve a landslide re-election in November 2020.

But not everyone was happy. Some were simply unwilling to accept the level of intervention the federal government had taken. They saw Knowles' lockdown as an ideological declaration of war and so Liberation had seen its membership swell, as the anti-government feeling grew. But the same was true of other so-called patriot groups, too. And there was nothing in the files to suggest a risk of imminent action from *any* of them.

In fact, there was nothing in there to suggest a threat from Liberation, either. Which meant that Grace's question remained unanswered.

'What I don't understand is what sets these Liberation guys apart. Why have we got them flagged?'

'Why does that matter?' Dempsey asked. 'Whatever the reason, it seems justified now, doesn't it?'

'Only if what Cam Arnold did was for Liberation. We don't even know that it was. He could have been acting on his own account.'

'Everything Cam Arnold has done for a decade has been done on Liberation's account. The man's a one hundred per cent extremist. He lives and breathes the movement.'

Grace took a breath, as if steeling herself for what she wanted to ask next. And in that moment, Dempsey knew that she had done more than merely read the intelligence file.

She had discovered its originator.

'And how do you know that, Boss?' she asked. 'Because that's very specific knowledge for someone who hasn't had sight of the file yet.'

Dempsey smiled. His faith in Eden Grace's ability had never faltered from her first day beside him. Still, the occasional reminder was always welcome.

'If I wanted to spend the next few days being cross-examined by a lawyer, Eden, I'd have got on that plane to London.'

'Then why didn't you, Joe?'

Dempsey sat back. Grace rarely used his first name. That she did so now was a sign that she was no longer speaking as just a member of his team. What was about to follow was being asked as his friend.

'Why aren't you on that plane?' Grace's voice was soft. Her question gentle. 'There's nothing in the Liberation file that identifies them as a viable threat, either imminently or in the long term. And there's nothing in there that should make them of interest to the ISB. But they're of interest to *you*, aren't they? Enough for you to walk away from your godfather duties in London.'

'I haven't walked away. I still have time—'

'Don't change the subject.' Grace smiled as she scolded him. 'Just tell me the truth. What the hell has made Liberation so important to you?'

Dempsey did not answer immediately. Instead he took a moment to consider his options.

He could easily pull rank. Grace would have no choice but to accept silence as an answer, if that was what Dempsey chose to do. It would be disrespectful, sure. But Grace would live with it.

Dempsey, though, would not. At least not easily. He respected Eden Grace as much as he respected anyone alive. Both as an intelligence agent and as his friend. And if she was to be a part of what might be coming then she was entitled to the whole truth.

He took a long breath and looked her in the eye.

'When you read the file, did you see the name Scott Turner?'

EIGHTEEN

2.10 p.m. EDT

The mid-afternoon sun was at its peak as Sergio Vega approached Front Street, its heat searing the asphalt underfoot. But thanks to what he could now see up ahead, Monroe County's homicide investigator hardly noticed.

The detective had been on-site twice today already. His first trip to the crime scene, when he had been introduced to O'Rourke and May and had examined Ricardo Garcia's corpse. And then back again later, after O'Rourke had identified Cam Arnold at City Hall.

On both occasions, the scene had been controlled by his own team.

Not any more. Now it's Homeland's ballgame.

Vega approached on foot, his patrol car now back at headquarters. He no longer needed his forensic crime kit – the state-of-the-art equipment offloaded at the Naval Air Station had left his own obsolete – and so he preferred to walk the short distance to North Bay Marina. As hot as the sun was, he'd take the heat of the street over the oven of an A/C-free car any day.

At O'Rourke's suggestion, Vega had headed straight home from Boca Chica, to shower and freshen up before the real work began. That had been just over an hour ago. It could have been longer, but he had refused O'Rourke's advice to catch up on the sleep he had missed after his early call-out.

Vega wanted to be here. He was part of the team now, however temporary, and so he wanted to be on hand. He wanted to offer whatever help he could. And, if he was honest, he wanted to see for himself how Homeland operated.

The immediate answer to which, he now discovered, was 'in isolation'.

The northmost section of Front Street had not been busy at 8 a.m., but at least it had been accessible. Now, as Vega approached the right turn that would take him off Duval and towards North Bay Marina, he saw that this had changed. A yellow police cordon was visible from at least a hundred yards in every direction.

Vega reached for his sheriff's office ID and flashed it to a black-suited agent as he reached the cordon. He paid no attention as the man examined his credentials. Instead he looked beyond him, at a Front Street that now seemed so unfamiliar.

The road was deserted. Not a person or a vehicle in sight.

Which means there's no one there to witness a thing, Vega thought to himself. *I guess that's how spies work.*

'I'm sorry, Deputy. I can't let you in.' The agent's tone invited neither discussion nor dissent. 'You'll need to move away.'

The response interrupted Vega's thoughts. It was *not* what he had been expecting. When he did not react the agent spoke again.

'You'll need to move on, sir.'

'I'm expected,' Vega replied. The response had unsettled him. 'I'm expected by your boss.'

'And who would that be?'

'O'Rourke.'

The agent raised an eyebrow.

'You mean *Special Agent* O'Rourke. And what's your business?'

The agent emphasised O'Rourke's title. And, Vega noticed, omitted her Christian name.

I guess she was serious about that, he thought.

'Deputy, your business with Special Agent O'Rourke, please?'

The agent was all business and no courtesy. And now that Vega was over his own initial surprise, he found that attitude . . . irritating.

'Whatever it is, it's with *her*. Now, how about we stop wasting all of our time and you put in a call, Agent . . .?'

Vega deliberately left the question of the man's name in the air. He only half-expected an answer and so he was unsurprised when he did not get one. Instead, the agent stepped back – far enough that Vega could not hear what was said – and put his phone to his ear.

It was a short conversation. Moments later and the agent was back, his expression unchanged.

'Step through.' He lifted the cordon high as he spoke; enough for Vega to crouch underneath. 'Head up to the marina but don't cross the threshold there. Someone will meet you.'

Vega did as he was instructed without a glance or a thank you. The agent's attitude had been unwelcoming, even after Vega's status had been confirmed. It left the detective in no mood to be civil.

So this is my new team? Vega shook his head as he set course for the marina. *Pajero.*

It took just a few steps for Vega's irritation to melt away; with the agent now behind him, his attention was fully on the road ahead. He now noticed a large, black, square-backed van, parked a few hundred yards ahead, across the entrance to the marina. It was his first sight of the vehicle; it had not arrived with the rest of O'Rourke's team and their equipment at Boca Chica.

Hell, there was no aircraft that could have carried something that size, he told himself. *It must have come in by road.*

As he grew closer, he saw that the van dominated the view, almost entirely blocking visibility of the marina beyond – no doubt the intention, he guessed – but there were a still few lines of sight available. From these Vega could make out the activity beyond.

The marina seemed busy, but the number of operatives within it was small. From the limited amount he could see, Vega counted four figures in distinct yellow hazmat suits as they moved in and out of his view, from one visible spot to the next. They appeared to be focusing on the area that separated the jetties from the entrance.

Vega could only guess at what the figures were doing, an exercise more likely to be wrong than right; he had no idea of how these teams worked outside of what he had seen in movies. And even if he did have some expertise in the field, how would he bring that to bear when he could see less than ten per cent of what was going on?

He forced himself to stop the speculation. It was unhelpful and no doubt inaccurate. And besides, O'Rourke would soon tell him anything he actually needed to know.

Instead, he focused on his immediate surroundings. Front Street. In contrast to the marina – and uniquely in Vega's own experience – it was completely empty.

The final stretch of Front Street was rarely a destination for anyone; it lacked the mass of restaurants, bars and shops that filled the roads around it. But it was still a part of the most popular district on the island. It was close to both Mallory Square and to Duval Street, and it acted as a connecting route to other destinations in and around the Old Town.

So to see it now, looking like some B-movie's deserted ghost town? It just seemed . . . alien.

Before that feeling of unfamiliarity could sink in, Vega's attention was caught by movement ahead. He shifted his focus immediately, dismissing the strangeness of his surroundings and concentrating on Nicki May, who was now walking towards him.

May was in her mid-thirties, Vega guessed. The same as himself. Her black trouser suit was near identical to the one worn by the agent at the cordon and her long blonde hair was pulled tightly back and pinned up in a practical, no-nonsense style. It complimented her naturally pale skin, which was already reddened by the Florida sun. And it gave the fullest possible view of the face that had been distracting him all morning.

'Sergeant Vega.'

May smiled as she greeted him. She seemed genuinely happy to see him again. Or at least Vega hoped that she did.

He nodded his head in response, his preferred alternative to the now frowned-upon handshake. As he did so Vega found himself considering the spark he had detected between them earlier. Distracted by his thoughts, he moved more slowly and lower with the gesture than intended, accidentally turning it into a half-bow.

'You going to crane kick me next, Sergeant Vega-san?'

The smile was still there as May spoke. She seemed much more comfortable now than she had earlier. Enough to tease. The lightness suited her, Vega thought. He returned the smile.

'Only if you sweep the leg,' he replied. 'Otherwise we can call it a draw and put the All Valley on hold.'

'Yeah, let's do that. There's enough happening here already without us dragging a dojo feud into it.'

May paused for a moment, her eyes still locked on Vega's. If they had been elsewhere – if the circumstances were different – he would have thought that May was flirting. Maybe she was. But now was not the time to find out.

Like she said, there's enough happening here already.

'O'Rourke's ready to brief us on the developments of the last few hours,' May continued. 'She's waiting for you in the on-site operational centre.'

'The oper . . . the what?'

'The van. I mean the van.'

'Ah,' Vega laughed. 'That's federal language right there. Don't worry, I'll get used to it.'

'I wouldn't if I were you. Your human language is so much nicer.'

Definitely flirting, Vega thought, his smile widening.

May indicated towards the North Bay Marina entrance, where the big, black 'on-site operational centre' was parked.

'Shall we, Sergeant?'

They both began to walk towards the van.

'Sergio,' Vega offered. 'Not Sergeant.'

'Nicki, then,' May replied.

'But not Bambi, apparently.' Vega smiled again. 'I've been warned off that one already.'

'Yeah, she's not a fan of that name. Thinks it makes her

sound unprofessional,' May replied. 'I get special dispensation since we go back a long way. But even I have to stick to O'Rourke when we're working.'

'You're old friends?'

'Mentor and mentee, really. It was Bambi who recruited me to Homeland straight out of law school. We've been close ever since.'

'You were with Homeland?'

'For ten years, almost. Until last year.'

'What did she make of you switching teams?'

'The DOJ? She was fine. She wanted me to do whatever was best for me. Plus Justice is hardly a rival to Homeland. If it was I wouldn't have brought them the tip about the caesium, would I?'

'That came from you?'

'It came from one of my sources, yeah. But one look and I could see it was in Bambi's wheelhouse. Not mine.'

Vega smiled at the answer. May noticed and smiled back.

'What?' May asked with a laugh.

'Just that name. It's so . . . well, it's so not her.'

'Trust me, it could be worse. Her maiden name was Moon.'

'Bambi Moon?'

'Yep.'

'You can't be serious.'

'Oh, I'm serious. Hippy parents, apparently. Peace, love and harmony and all that stuff.'

'Not her kind of thing?'

'Not her kind of thing at all. Hence her six-week marriage to an Irishman, years before I met her. Get her drunk and she'll tell you she only married him for the name.'

Vega smiled. He did not know O'Rourke well. He probably

never would. And yet what May had told him, it made sense. And it made him like both the Homeland agent *and* May even more.

They walked the final few yards in silence, his eyes repeatedly shifting to the DOJ agent. He found his smile widen with every glance.

The day was not turning out as the detective had expected.

NINETEEN

2.17 p.m. EDT

'How sure are you that it was the caesium?'

O'Rourke was seated in a large fixed chair in front of the back wall of the van. Ahead of her were Vega and May. Both were standing. They were a similar height – Vega about five ten, May closer to six feet in her heels – but neither needed to crouch under the van's high roof.

'We won't be one hundred per cent on that till we lay hands on the stuff. But the team, they've covered just about every inch of this place so far. There's a clear radiation signature from the third jetty right down to the top of Front Street. It starts about twenty yards on from where Mr Garcia was lying, it heads directly on past where we are now, and ain't no trace of a signature nowhere else. Only one conclusion I can draw from that.'

'So what does that mean?' Vega asked. 'For the marina and for Front Street. Do we need to evacuate? We'll need to bring in the PD for that sort of an operation.'

'Whoa, slow down, you're off like a scalded haint.'

The interruption brought Vega up short, exactly as O'Rourke had intended. She continued without missing a beat.

'We've already evacuated as far as we need. That's why that street out there's got no one on it, son. Caesium-137, you see, it needs direct contact to do any damage worth a damn. The signature itself, it's no worse than having an X-ray. It won't hurt anyone. But if they find any of the caesium itself, well, that's a different story. That shit burns to the touch, even in tiny amounts. Any more than that, it's death. That's why we got the team sweeping the place now. Inside the marina first, then out to the street. They're gonna make sure there's nothing physically there.'

'What's this stuff look like?' Vega asked.

'What does that matter?' O'Rourke replied. 'I've got a team of nuclear specialists out there, son. What do you think's gonna happen? You're gonna stick on a hazmat and go help out? Don't be making yourself look foolish, OK?'

Vega went visibly red. Noticeable even with his sun-darkened Cuban skin. O'Rourke immediately regretted the flippant comment that had caused the reaction.

'I . . . I wasn't suggesting . . .'

'I know that, Sergio. I wasn't serious. Now both of you, take a look at the TV.'

O'Rourke indicated to the largest of five screens. It sat just behind her own chair, in the centre of four smaller monitors all set together at the cab end of the van. She aimed the remote control as she spoke and pressed play.

The central screen came to life, but only barely; the image was mainly black, with just a single light illuminating a spot in the otherwise complete darkness. O'Rourke kept her eyes on Vega. She could tell that he recognised it immediately. Just as he recognised the slumped body that lay directly beneath the light source.

Ricardo Garcia.

'Is this the same footage we saw in City Hall?'

'This part is, yes,' O'Rourke replied. 'What comes after it ain't. But stay with me on this.'

Vega nodded, his attention plainly fixed on the single detail anyone could make out: Garcia, motionless on the jetty.

For the first minute there was nothing else. Just Cam Arnold – or Clinton Dewitt, as he had called himself then – standing motionless over the body, before disappearing off-screen in the direction of the sea end of the jetty.

'Why did he stand there like that for so long?' Vega asked. He was, O'Rourke observed, the first person besides her who had wondered about Cam Arnold's prolonged time under the light.

'What do you mean?' asked O'Rourke, interested to see if the detective's mind really was working like her own.

'He just stands over the body,' Vega explained. 'For how long? Three, four seconds? Why?'

'No way of telling without audio,' O'Rourke replied. 'My assumption is he was being told something by the guys off-screen. But it intrigued me too.'

'What guys off-screen?' May asked.

'Same guys we saw earlier who passed the camera at four forty-five. Take a look.'

She indicated back to the screen. The activity was about to begin.

The spotlit circle containing Garcia's corpse was still the only visible feature on the footage, but an instant later and it was no longer an empty frame. O'Rourke watched as Vega and May saw the detail for the first time. She knew what was coming – she had seen it at least ten times already – and so her interest was now focused on the detective's reaction.

Vega could have barely adjusted his focus to the screen when the first figure appeared.

A man, masked and dressed in black, carrying a large, featureless and seemingly sealed container, stepped into the light. Unlike Cam Arnold, he neither looked towards the camera nor stopped moving. He just walked forward, eyes straight ahead and avoiding Garcia's pooling blood as he headed towards the land end of the jetty.

The figure was visible for perhaps two seconds, maybe less; just as long as it took to cover the illuminated patch of light. But as he left the screen, another man – identically dressed and carrying an identical container – entered from the direction he had come. Then another. And another.

And finally Cam Arnold himself.

Five men. One after the other, each no more than two seconds apart. Exactly the same routine as they had seen earlier, only in the opposite direction and now with the addition of Arnold.

Vega turned to O'Rourke.

'Where did they go from there? And are they carrying what I think they're carrying?'

O'Rourke ignored the second question. Instead she manipulated the console controls and brought the surrounding monitors to life. Each one showed the same image. The front end of a large Dodge Sprinter van. Light-coloured, it seemed. Although it was hard to be exact with the black-and-white footage.

What was clear, though, was the van's Ohio plate. O'Rourke watched as Vega reached for his pen and began to note the detail. He stopped halfway through, glanced up from his pad and met O'Rourke's eye.

'I'm guessing you guys have taken the licence plates already, right?'

'Taken 'em and run 'em,' O'Rourke replied. 'But don't worry. You get no criticism from me for being thorough. Since we're against the clock, though, you can take it from me they're fake.'

Vega nodded and closed his pad, just as a figure – identical to the first of the five men from the main screen – appeared in shot once more. It was only the briefest glimpse, but it was enough to see that he was heading for the Sprinter.

'The way the van's parked, we can see the back doors are open but we can't see what's going on in there. Is there another camera angle?'

'No. This is the only lens that covers any part of the street that's useful,' O'Rourke replied. 'But taken together with the jetty footage, it's enough. The containers these guys are carrying, they've got to have landed them from a boat further on up. Then they've carried them down to Front Street and loaded them into the back of the Dodge.'

'Where's that guy going now?' May this time, pointing at the first figure. He was moving back into shot on the smaller screens, as if he were headed back towards the marina.

'He's going back along the jetty,' O'Rourke explained. She pressed a button as she spoke, switching the main screen to the same view of the van. 'They all do. Four times each, each time with an identical container. Then a fifth for Cam Arnold, who comes back with a final, smaller box.'

O'Rourke hit the 'skip' function on the remote, taking the footage to its end. All three then watched as the van's back doors were closed, and two men – Cam Arnold and one of the other four – climbed into the cab.

Moments later and the van pulled away, out of frame.

'Where'd the other three go?' May asked.

'In the back with the load,' O'Rourke replied. 'Either that or thin air.'

'Is there an APB out on the van?' Vega this time.

'Has been for the last forty minutes. And we're having all other public camera footage checked as we speak. I need to see if we can trace their route off of the island, find them that way.'

'Same call I'd have made,' Vega said. 'Difference is, your call comes with the weight of the US government behind it. Got to make this quicker, right?'

'You would sure hope so, wouldn't you?'

O'Rourke kept her voice upbeat as she spoke. She wanted Vega motivated. And that meant not revealing that, whatever government weight it had, her team had found no trace of the van after Front Street, not until it had hit the Overseas Highway a full thirty minutes later.

That gap was a problem, but it was not one she wanted to share. At least not yet.

O'Rourke moved their conversation along.

'While that's being done, how about we focus our minds on those containers. Sergio, anything jumping out at you?'

Vega did not answer immediately, his eyes fixed to the screen. O'Rourke could almost see his mind running through the available information, and so she was ready when he finally wanted more.

'Twenty-one containers,' Vega said, more to himself than to anyone else. When he spoke again, it was very much directed at O'Rourke. 'And you think there's caesium in each of them?'

'I do.'

'Twenty-one boxes of the stuff. How much would that even be?'

'Based on an estimate of a little over one hundred and twenty pounds per box? That gets us to the ballpark of a ton.'

'Is that how much you were expecting?'

'Shit no, son. Not even close. That's more caesium in one place than I've ever even heard of.'

'Then why the weight assumption on the boxes? Where's that from?'

O'Rourke aimed the remote and skipped the footage back to where the first figure arrived at the van. She pointed at the screen.

'Not one of those boys is finding those boxes an easy carry. None of them are buckling, sure. But from the body language you can tell they're blowing. Now Liberation, the one thing it's sure has hell got these days is manpower. They don't need to send any string beans down here. These fellas, they were picked because they were up to the job. And *still* it's a shift. That says to me that there's a good load in each box. When you throw the number we see here into the mix, the most obvious target weight for the full load's got to be a ton.'

Vega nodded his head. He seemed impressed by O'Rourke's working.

And so he should be, O'Rourke told herself. *That guesstimate makes a whole lot of sense.*

'OK,' Vega continued. 'Let's say that's right. Then what are we looking at?'

O'Rourke did not answer. She was checking her maths again. To make sure she was right before she shared the horror with anyone else.

'O'Rourke?'

She looked up this time. The recount was in and the news was not good.

'I think we're looking at dirty bombs,' she finally said. 'And judging by the amount of caesium we're seeing here, I think we're looking at a whole lot of them.'

TWENTY

2.20 p.m. EDT

The sky outside of Dempsey's window was a shade of the most brilliant blue, free of the slightest hint of cloud. At a cruising altitude of forty-five thousand feet, the Learjet 75 in which he and Eden Grace were travelling would have been little more than a dot from the fields and towns below.

From up here, it felt like the whole world.

Grace was sitting on the wide leather seat directly ahead of him, her back to the cockpit. The holdall she had brought with her from the ISB was on the adjacent chair, an arm's length away across the narrow aisle. It had contained four intelligence files, as well as other items Dempsey had asked her to bring.

One of those files was now in her hands; thinner than the other three, it related purely to what had happened in Key West. Dempsey held the thickest of the four, but he already knew the content. For now, his attention was on Grace.

'So the first APB, it relates to Cam Arnold only?'

'That's right,' Grace replied. 'It has a warning that he is deemed armed and dangerous.'

'But no detail of what he's supposed to have done?'

'It says murder and the APB is focused on the Keys, but it

doesn't state a location or the identity of the victim. We made enquiries and found out some more. Not much, but enough to know that it was one victim, a kind of local area security guard, killed at a Key West marina in the early hours.'

Dempsey took on the information, for what little it told them.

'OK. So we know next to nothing from that alone, then. What about the next APB?'

Grace set the thin file aside and picked up her tablet. She had received an email shortly before boarding the plane. Its content had added a new dimension to the case.

Dempsey's interest in Liberation was not limited to Cam Arnold. And if the second APB was correct, neither was last night's murder.

Grace was still looking at her screen as Dempsey continued.

'So the new one tells us what? That Cam Arnold is travelling north in a grey long-wheelbase Dodge Sprinter van?'

'Licence plate JGF 5101. Out of Ohio,' Grace added.

'And on this one, he's not alone?'

'No. He's still listed as suspected armed and dangerous, but he's thought to be travelling in company with four other men. They're down as "do not approach".'

Dempsey took a moment to think.

'That's a jump. Suggests to me that they now think this a unit.'

His mind moved quickly. On to the next conclusion.

'So what do we think they collected from the marina?'

'What? There's nothing in the APB about . . .' Grace paused. A moment later and she understood. 'A dead guard at the marina, a full crew of men and an extra-capacity haulage vehicle.'

'Safe assumption?'

'Safe assumption.'

Neither spoke for a minute or so, and Dempsey looked out of the window during the silence. He was clearing his mind of the many possibilities that now filled it. For now, they were all speculation, and so none of them were worth the time it would take to think them through. Instead he focused on the sky. On the blue.

'You think this Scott Turner guy is one of the four in the van?'

Dempsey turned to face Grace as he considered her question. He had told her as much about Scott Turner as he wanted for now, but Grace was a professional. She would not ask for more if she did not feel she needed to know. And Dempsey was grateful for her instincts.

'Maybe he is,' Dempsey replied. 'Maybe not.'

'You think he would involve himself in a murder?'

'I can't be sure,' Dempsey confessed. 'I knew him when he was a kid. Back then, no. He was gentle. Bookish. But that was a long time ago, Eden. And he's been with Arnold – with Liberation – for close to two years. He can't be the same boy after that.'

Grace waited a beat. Then another. She seemed hesitant to make the next point. Dempsey appreciated her caution, but he did not need it.

'You want to know what I'll do if he *was* a part of it,' he said. He could see from the look in Grace's eyes that he was right. 'If he willingly played a role in killing an innocent man, Eden, then he'll be treated just like anyone else. He's an adult. He makes his own choices.'

'And yet you were flying down here before you even knew that Arnold had help. Just on an association.'

'I got on this plane in the hope I could stop something. That whatever Arnold was doing, I could deal with it before Scott got himself dragged in. I owe the kid that much.'

'But if it's too late and he's one of the five? If he's already involved?'

'If it's too late then it's too late.' Dempsey had discussed Scott Turner enough for one day. He wanted to move on. 'Truth be told, there's a good chance this is out of our hands already.'

'What? Why?'

'Think about it. That APB, it didn't take us long to reach a conclusion, did it? That Liberation were unloading something from that dock and transporting it away in the van. We're not the only ones who can put two and two together. And with their history, we're not the only ones likely to be taking an interest in Cam Arnold.'

Grace thought for a moment.

'You mean Homeland Security?'

'I'd be surprised if they weren't already all over this, yeah,' Dempsey confirmed. 'And if they are, we might not have enough authority to pull Scott Turner out of whatever trouble he's gotten himself into. Not even if we wanted to.'

TWENTY-ONE

3 p.m. EDT

S cott Turner looked straight ahead as he exited the Burger King and headed back to the Jeep. In one hand he carried a four-cup drinks holder, in the other an oversized paper bag that carried enough food for six men.

Most of it was for just one.

The restaurant was in north Jacksonville, a short drive off of the I-95 and far closer to the Georgia state line than it was to Key West, where their journey had started. They had been on the road now for just over nine hours, with the drive split evenly between Brooks and Turner.

Four and a half hours each, with this food and fuel stop marking the end of Brooks' shift at the wheel.

Brooks and Clemons were waiting in the parking lot at the side of the restaurant, leaned with their backsides against the hood of the Jeep. Both men had long hair — mullets were surprisingly common amongst the anti-government contingent, Turner had noticed — and in that moment they reminded him of every cover from every bad 1980s rock album he had ever seen.

Just missing the guitars, Turner laughed to himself. *And the class.*

He chose not to share the thought. Clemons was as young as he was, but his life had been narrow in comparison. He was unlikely to get the reference. And Brooks? Brooks would no doubt take it as an insult.

Which, Turner had to admit, it really was.

He moved the large food bag into the same hand as the drinks holder, reached inside and pulled out a smaller bag. Testing it for weight, he threw it to Clemons.

'Whopper, extra-large fries and a sundae pie.' Clemons snatched the bag from the air. 'Sauces in the bag.'

Three steps more and Turner was with them. He reached between the two waiting men, placed the drinks holder onto the hood and pulled out a large cup. He took a half step back and handed it to Clemons.

'And before you ask, Sprite with minimal ice.'

Turner turned to face Brooks as he removed a second cup, which he kept for himself. He nodded his head to indicate the final two cups, still on the hood.

'Coke no ice in one and a hand-spun shake in the other. Both yours.' He raised the large bag that was still in his hand. 'Plus about ninety per cent of what's in here.'

Brooks reached out and grabbed at the bag, seizing it just as Turner pulled out his own burger and fries.

'You get everything I asked for?'

'You mean did I manage to get a fast-food order right? Yeah. Somehow I was up to that job.' Turner cast a sideways glance at Clemons as he spoke, but his focus remained on Brooks. 'You always eat that much, Kenny?'

'What if I do?'

'Nothing. Nothing at all. Just . . . well, it's a lot of food, man.'

'I work hard. I need the calories.'

'Sure. Sure, I get that.'

'What's that supposed to mean?'

'Jesus, Kenny. Nothing. It's supposed to mean nothing. I guess after all that driving you've done today, I'm sure you *need* two double whoppers and a chicken burger.'

'Why don't you mind your own fucking business, huh?' It did not take much to push Brooks' buttons. 'Fucking scrawny, bad-teeth fucking third-world Brit telling an American how to eat. Go fuck yourself.'

Brooks shoved a fistful of fries in his mouth as he pushed his backside off the Jeep and stalked away. A broad smile spread across Turner's face as he went. Brooks' reaction amused him; just about the only part of the man he did not despise was the comical volatility. It was just ridiculous enough to be funny. He glanced towards Clemons to share the joke, but he noticed that their third man had looked away.

Clemons did not want to be seen laughing, Turner guessed. And when he took just a moment to think about it, he could understand why. Brooks was unpredictable, sure, but he would still hesitate to lose it with Cam Arnold's right-hand man. Clemons had no such protection.

Being the easiest outlet for Brooks' anger was concerning Clemons, Turner could see. And so he pulled back on the antagonism.

'You ready for your leg of the drive, Cliff?'

The change of subject was intentionally transparent.

'Uh-huh,' Clemons grunted in reply. He took a moment to swallow a mouthful of burger before saying more. 'Ready when you are.'

'Get going as soon as you're done, eh?' Turner lowered his voice. 'Let Bruce Banner over there eat in the back.'

Clemons took a sip of Sprite to wash down his food. He seemed to be thinking.

'We still aiming for Summerville by night?'

'We are,' Turner replied. 'That keeps us on schedule. And should mean you get the shortest shift of the day.'

'And what about Cam? Is he gonna meet us there?'

It was the first time Clemons had questioned him about their plans. Brooks had raised the same subject earlier and Turner had happily responded with a lie. He wished he did not have to do the same to Clemons – the more time he spent with him, the more he liked the guy – but he did not have much choice.

Arnold had shared the details of his plan with Turner alone. There were very specific things Arnold still had to do, and very specific reasons that he had to do them. All of it was necessary to achieve their ultimate goal, but none of it was easily explained. It had been Arnold's decision to keep the rest of the team in the dark about what would follow. As much as Turner had grown to like Clemons, now was no time to disobey orders.

'He's heading north by a different route,' Turner explained. It was an answer with a kernel of truth; Arnold *was* heading north. At least from Key West. Turner just omitted to say how far.

'But where—'

'And just what the fuck are you looking at, huh?'

Brooks' raised voice cut Clemons off. It caused both men to look across the parking lot, towards the sound. A new car had joined them in the parking lot; it had attracted both Brooks' interest and his anger.

Turner looked around Brooks, towards the car. It was an ageing 3-Series BMW, sun-damaged and unremarkable. There was nothing he could see that could have caught Brooks' eye.

Nothing but its occupants.

'I asked you a fucking question.'

Brooks' voice was louder this time. More angry. With a final look towards Clemons, Turner moved away from the Jeep and began to jog the short distance that separated them.

'Whoa. Whoa. Whoa.' Turner called out as he moved, careful not to use Brooks' name as he tried to get his attention. It worked. Brooks turned, the look on his face one of pure hatred.

'What the fuck is it now?'

'What is it now?' Turner glanced past Brooks as he spoke. He managed a better view of the car's driver and passenger. Two girls. Twenties to thirties. And both black. 'Man, you're screaming and shouting at two girls in a damn car park. You think that's a good idea right now?'

'They were looking straight at us,' Brooks replied. Neither his anger nor his volume had lessened. 'Why they doing that? What the fuck do they want?'

'Who gives a shit?' Turner hissed his response.

'I fucking do.' Brooks was now almost shouting, his finger now poking at Turner. 'And so should you. What's got their interest, huh? Why are they paying so much fucking attention to us? That don't worry you, no? Who they might be, that don't worry you?'

'What worries me is that two women who had no need to be suspicious of us have now been given *every* bloody need. By *you*. Now stop being paranoid, calm the fuck down and get back in the car before they call the police.'

Brooks looked back towards the BMW as Turner spoke. It did nothing to calm him. But then it wouldn't, Turner realised. Because it was the mere appearance of those inside it that had caused his anger. Two black women who, Turner assumed, had dared to meet Brooks' eye and to no doubt hold his gaze? To a man like him – to a man with rampant levels of prejudice but who lacked the intellect to properly hide it – everything about that was unacceptable.

Of the many reasons Turner hated him, Brooks' racism was by far the strongest.

'I'm not going to tell you again.' The younger man kept his voice low as he stepped close to Brooks, injecting all of the authority he could find. 'Either walk away and get back in the Jeep, or we drive away without you and we tell Cam why. It's your choice.'

Brooks turned to face him. His expression was intense, his eyes unblinking. For just a moment, Turner thought that Brooks would attack him. It caused a rush of adrenaline to flow, preparing his body to fight.

A fight Turner was unlikely to win. At six foot three he had a good four inches on Brooks. But the shorter man was also the heavier man, and by some distance. At least thirty-five pounds of hard, practical muscle separated them. As did the very different lives they had lived prior to their involvement with Liberation. Brooks had spent fifteen years as a bouncer and hired thug, while Turner had been just a year away from his PhD in Nuclear Engineering when recruited by Cam Arnold. And so Turner was right to be relieved when Brooks stepped back, moved around him and headed to the Jeep.

Turner took a deep calming breath. He could feel his heart beating hard in his chest. But one glance towards the BMW told him it had been worth the risk.

The relief on the faces of the two young women made him feel good about himself.

For Scott Turner, that feeling of self-worth – of pride in his own actions – was rare these days. And so it was with a warm glow that he turned and followed Brooks.

TWENTY-TWO

2.20 p.m. CDT

Colonel Miles Walker closed his eyes and rubbed a large, callused hand across his sweating forehead. It had been a few hours since the commanding officer of the Facility had been informed of the death of three inmates during an attack.

An attack in which the dead men were the instigators and the killer was a single prisoner.

In that time, the necessary clean-up had been completed. Three bodies were now in the morgue, two hundred and eight inmates were back in their cells, and the man they all called Joshua was in a holding room.

With everything back under control, it was time for the colonel to be briefed on just what the hell had gone wrong.

'Who were they?'

It was the obvious first question, directed at Captain Wesley Bickle.

The metaphorical eyes and ears of the Facility, Bickle's role placed him outside of Colonel Walker's staff. His official position was simply termed 'army intelligence', a status that made his relatively low rank irrelevant. Bickle had been in place at the Facility years before Walker's appointment and there was no doubt he would be there long after the colonel was gone.

'The dead men are Adeel Ibrahim, Gustav Roach and Steven Kunis.'

Bickle listed their names with all the dispassion Walker would expect. As if they were items of inventory, for all the importance his tone attached to them. On any other day Walker might have called him on it.

Not today. Today he kept his eyes shut as he carried out a mental rollcall.

Adeel Ibrahim.

That one was easy enough. Like many of the Facility's inmates, Ibrahim was an Islamic extremist. He had been seized for planning terrorist attacks of a scale that would terrify the general public, assuming the public ever got to hear of them. But what the people did not know could not scare them, the government seemed to think. And so Ibrahim – like one hundred and thirty-six other men of his ethnicity, beliefs and intentions – had been locked away without publicity and without trial.

A shadow prisoner, left to rot his life away in the Facility.

Or at least he had been, Walker thought. *Up until this morning . . .*

Gustav Roach.

Steven Kunis.

These two took the colonel a little longer, but a moment more and he had them. A pair of military-trained conspiracy theorists and patriot movement extremists, they had been apprehended after an attempted anthrax attack on the Pentagon. Taken alone, it was not an offence that would have placed them in the Facility. But the investigation that followed their arrest had uncovered their other activities.

Walker didn't care about the details of those activities. The fate of the two men – incarceration in a top-secret facility where civilians were imprisoned without trial or hope of release – said all he needed to know.

With the victims now identified in his mind, he opened his eyes and shifted his focus back to the two men now seated in his small office.

Bickle was in a chair to his left, its back against the office side wall and with an open window just over his right shoulder. It could have been closed for all the impact it had on the stifling heat within. The Texas climate in July was hot, dry and still; the lack of any noticeable movement of air made the interior almost as unbearable as the near-desert outside.

Directly ahead of Walker – and seated despite his low rank of corporal – was Deontay Bush. He was close enough that the colonel could see the sweat as it dripped from his shaved head down to his neck, staining the neck of his army greens.

For now, though, Walker's focus remained on Bickle and on the information he thought the Facility's intelligence officer was more likely to provide.

'What's the connection between the three?'

'Apart from the obvious, sir?'

'What's the obvious?'

'The fact they were all working together today.'

The captain's answer sounded dangerously close to condescending; it might have been, but Walker had chosen to regard Bickle's tone as just a natural quirk. It was the only way the two men could coexist. He forced the irritation from his own voice when he replied.

'Then yes, apart from that.'

'Apart from that, Roach and Kunis, sir; they go back a way.'

'I'm aware they do. They're here . . . they *were* here . . . for the same crime. But what connects them to Ibrahim?'

'Absolutely nothing I'm aware of. Muslim extremist alongside two racist rednecks. It's not the most obvious team-up.'

Walker did not reply. The statement was hardly a revelation. Instead he turned to Bush.

'And you, Bush? You're sure they were all working together on this? You're sure this didn't just start with Ibrahim, and Roach and Kunis jumped in as opportunists?'

'If I went on just what I saw, Colonel, then no. This was coordinated. But it's more than that. We searched the scene and we searched the bodies. And Roach and Kunis, sir, they were armed with the same Ka-Bars as Ibrahim.'

'Are you serious?'

Walker already knew the answer; of course Bush was serious. But still he had to ask. Because if correct, the presence of the Ka-Bar military combat knives was extremely problematic.

'Sir, yes. For all the good it did, they *all* had them.'

'Three Ka-Bars?'

'Yes, sir.'

'And two out of the three dead men had military training?'

'Marine Corps, sir. Both of them.'

'And still Joshua killed them all in seconds? While unarmed?'

'He wasn't totally unarmed,' Bickle interrupted. His tone was flippant, suggesting he found this funny. 'He had his plastic spoon.'

Walker glanced at the captain for just a moment. He considered if he should say something. If he should caution Bickle for an inappropriate attitude. The thought passed an instant later. He had enough problems to deal with already; he did not need Army Intelligence causing him more.

He looked back towards Bush.

'You know what this means?'

'Yes, sir. It means that someone has smuggled those weapons into the Facility.'

'And?'

'And that someone has to be one of the team, sir.'

'Exactly.'

Walker did not like the answer, but Bush's assessment was correct. Barring a few very rare exceptions – federal officers, mainly – the Facility's inmates had no contact with the outside world. No visitors. No correspondence. No packages. Nothing.

They did not exist to anyone outside of the compound's walls.

So anything coming in from outside, it's been carried in. And the only people who can do that are my *people.*

It was an unwelcome thought, but it was not a surprise. Walker had long been aware of the problems within the Facility. When the state puts its ultimate undesirables all in one place and leaves them with no future – with nothing to live for – then it creates an inevitable problem. There was not an inmate in here who did not have enemies on the outside. Some of them powerful. Some of them entire governments.

And sometimes, to those enemies, life imprisonment was not enough.

Add an inmate population filled with proven killers who had nothing to lose, suddenly those same enemies had the means on hand to get the job done. All they would have to do was to make someone like Roach or Kunis or Ibrahim an offer – money to family would be the main one, Walker guessed – and they would have their hired gun.

Or their hired Ka-Bar wielder.

But to actually communicate that offer? And then to arm the men who had accepted it? *That* required inside help. *That* required corrupted guards.

If he were to be truthful, that thought bothered Walker far more than the three deaths. To him, corruption within his ranks was hard to comprehend. Walker was a ranger. A unit where the command structure was everything. Where the weak links that now surrounded him would have been identified and dealt with during selection.

That was his reality. *That* was his experience. Not *this*.

Unfortunately for Walker, the higher he climbed, the further he was taken from the 75th Ranger Regiment and from the life of a soldier. He had become a politician not by choice but by promotion. And that had forced him to become a thing he had never been: a man of compromise. A man who had to think carefully before acting on the tone of lesser men like Bickle. Men who, in his past life, he would have dismissed via the knuckles on the back of his hand.

It was not the life he had chosen. Nor was it the life he wanted.

A ranger colonel? Like hell am I.

The thought depressed him daily, but there was no time for that now. He had to focus on the case at hand. And so he turned to Bickle.

'Why Joshua?'

Bickle seemed surprised by the question.

'How would I know that?'

'You're intelligence, aren't you? Try and show some. That

man is the most dangerous human being within these walls. Shit, I'm not even sure "human being" is an accurate description after what he pulled today. So why him? Why does anyone take on a fight they can't win?'

'I doubt they thought they couldn't—'

'Shit, stop being such a goddamned smart-arse, Wesley, and try helping the process. How about that, huh?'

For once, Bickle seemed to have no answer.

'So I'll ask again. Why Joshua? Why pick *that* fight? Who benefits?'

Bickle hesitated. When he finally spoke, his tone was different. Both the condescension and the amusement were gone.

'Joshua's got more enemies outside than anyone else in here. The people he killed in the years before they caught him? It's like a who's who of the rich and dangerous. With him as the target, it could be almost anyone.'

'Anyone who knows he's in here, anyway,' Walker corrected. 'That can't be too many, surely?'

'It's enough, Colonel. The Facility, it's not the steel-trap secret we all like to think it is. When Joshua was taken out of the game, plenty would have done the math about his fate.'

'So you're saying what? That asking who's behind this is an impossible question?'

'Not an impossible one, no. But it is a damned difficult one.'

'Then I guess you'll need to get started right away, won't you? Because I want to know who the hell is targeting an inmate in my prison. Then I want to know which of the greedy bastards on staff helped them recruit and arm the suicidal sonsofbitches who went up against him today. You got that?'

Bickle did not respond. His eyes were fixed on the floor.

'I asked you a question, Captain.'

Bickle looked up and opened his mouth to speak, only to be interrupted by the sound of Deontay Bush clearing his throat. It was a reminder to both officers that the corporal was present, and a clear indication that he had something to offer.

Both men turned towards him.

'Something you have to say, son?' asked Walker.

'Just a thought, Colonel.'

'What is it?'

'It's about Joshua, sir. Another reason he could have been targeted.'

Walker was confused.

'Another reason? You mean other than all the shit he pulled before they stuck him in here?'

'Yes, sir. Possibly, anyway. I'm not saying it's any more likely. Or that it's even *as* likely. But I thought, you know, it's best to look at everything, right?'

'Right. So what is it?'

'It's just that Joshua, in case you didn't know, sir, in the last year or so, he seems to have given himself a job.'

'A job?'

'A role, sir. Whatever we want to call it. You're aware of a prisoner called Peyton Travis?'

'Travis is an inmate in my prison, Corporal. You can safely assume I'm aware of the man.'

'Then you'll know, sir, that Travis has disavowed the cause that put him here.'

'I know what bullshit the shrinks tell me, yeah. They've said that what Travis did was the result of a breakdown. And that he's better now.'

'You don't believe that, sir?'

'No, I don't believe that. A man has a breakdown, he drinks whiskey and he cries on the sofa. Worst ways, he jumps off the roof or he sticks a pistol in his mouth. Travis formed a damned anti-government militia and plotted to kill thousands. That ain't the same thing, son.'

'Well, sir, it seems he's distanced himself from that movement now. And in the last twelve months he's made no secret of it. Whatever the reason for him doing that, he's made himself hellish unpopular with the anarchists and the patriots and the anti-federalists in here with him. Men like Roach and Kunis. In other words, sir, Joshua's got a lot of enemies on the outside. But Travis, he's got a lot of them *in here*.'

'Sorry, son, you've lost me. The attack was on Joshua. So just what the hell does it matter how many enemies Peyton Travis has got?'

'It matters because of Joshua's role, sir. And because Travis was sitting right next to him when he was attacked.'

Walker sat more upright in his seat. His eyes fell on Bickle.

'And you didn't think to mention this detail?'

'It didn't seem relevant,' Bickle explained. 'Every account we have, they went for Joshua. Not Travis.'

'And those accounts could well be right, sir,' Bush interjected. He seemed determined to keep his contribution on track. 'But that doesn't mean that Travis wasn't the ultimate target. Joshua, he seems to have appointed himself as Travis's personal bodyguard. It's been that way ever since Travis came out as being all reformed and anti-white supremacy and such. Since then, Joshua's had his back. And everyone knows it.'

Walker took a moment to consider Bush's theory.

'You think Travis is on the level, Bush?'

'I don't think I'm qualified—'

'Neither am I but I told you what my gut said. So what does yours tell you?'

Bush took a deep breath and in that moment Walker knew what answer would follow. The young soldier would not need to steel himself if he was going to agree with his commanding officer.

'I think the man is what he says he is,' Bush finally replied. 'I think he's telling the truth.'

'Tell me why.'

'Because look at the risk he's taking, Colonel. With the white supremacy and the patriot bullshit, he was already hated by half the inmates in here. But at least he had protection. At least he had others with the same ideology. By condemning what he was, he's lost that. Worse than that, he's got another whole category of lunatic, all ready to kill him too. Why the hell would he bring that on himself?'

'And yet it's been, what? Over a year since he went public. And he's still alive.'

'All due respect, colonel, but there's one reason and one reason only that he is.'

'Because if someone wants Travis, they have to go through Joshua.'

'Yes, sir.'

'And plenty of people in here want Travis.'

'Yes, sir. The only reason Travis is still breathing is because of the man he's got beside him.'

Walker nodded his head. As cynical as he was about the kind of road to Damascus moment Travis was meant to have experienced, he could not just dismiss what his men were telling him. And if what Bush thought was true, then it created a whole new line of inquiry.

He turned to Bickle.

'And all of this, none of it seemed relevant to you?'

'It does now, Colonel. I didn't see the connection that Corporal Bush made.'

'Damn right, you didn't. Time to make up for that. Add Travis to your enquiry. I want to know if he was to be the real target once Joshua was out of the way. Or whether this was just an attack on Joshua himself.'

'Sir.'

'And while you're on that, I want to know what's connected Travis and Joshua. I want to know why they've bonded.'

Walker turned back to Bush before Bickle could respond.

'Where is Joshua now?'

'He's in a holding room, sir. He's waiting to be interviewed for the investigation.'

'And Travis?'

'Back in his cell, sir. The cell he usually shares with Joshua.'

Walker thought for just a moment. He had been unaware that the two men were cellmates, but it explained the connection. Partially, at least. But there had to be more to it because, from what Walker knew of Joshua, he was not one for emotions and friendships. The fact of their twenty-four-seven co-habitation? That alone was not enough. But right now it *was* convenient.

He stood up, his eyes fixed on Bush.

'OK, here's what we're going to do. I want Joshua out of that holding room and back in the cell now.'

'Sir? His interrogation isn't—'

'Those killings, son, they were as clear a case of self-defence as any one of us has ever seen. A few more questions won't change that. But if you're right and this whole thing was designed to get Joshua out of the way so someone could get to

143

Travis, us sticking him in solitary does that just as well as him being dead, doesn't it?'

Bush nodded in understanding.

'So let's not risk a fourth death today. If Joshua being in the room with him is keeping Travis alive, let's get Joshua back *in* that room.'

'Sir.' Bush rose to his feet. 'I'll see that's done now.'

'Good work.' Walker turned to Bickle. 'Now let's see *you* being that efficient, shall we? Get to work.'

TWENTY-THREE

2.35 p.m. CDT

Peyton Travis was sitting upright on his bunk, a book resting on his knee. He could not have missed the sound of the heavy iron door being unlocked, which was no doubt why the book was down and his eyes were on the entrance as Joshua stepped into the cell.

Joshua took a stride forward as the door slammed behind him, then another as the sound of the locking mechanism clicked in. He took a look at Travis, held his eye for a moment and then headed for his own bunk.

The cells in the Facility were not typical of an American prison. Each housed two inmates, but beyond that there was no similarity to the jails depicted on TV. There were no bars, instead just a sealed room with a single doorway. Their size, too, was very different. The average cell in a normal prison was six feet by eight feet, with one bunk stacked on top of the other. In the Facility they were twenty by twenty, with the two regular bunks placed across the room from one another.

The idea, Joshua figured, was to make life less unbearable. The discomfort in most jails was designed as a deterrent. To make it a place to which no inmate would want to return.

Whether or not that worked didn't matter here; every single inmate in the Facility was in for life, and so deterrence was meaningless. Instead the logic was switched on its head: behave and enjoy the relative comfort of the cell.

But step out of line? Do that and there was The Tank.

Joshua had spent more time in The Tank than he cared to remember. An unfurnished, unlit six-by-six space where a man of Joshua's six-foot-three frame could not fully stretch out. It was the Facility's idea of punishment. And it was where Joshua had expected to spend the next month, after the violence of the afternoon.

It was a surprise, then, to find himself back facing his own bunk. But that was not the reason that he now stood motionless, his eyes fixed upon it.

'Three, four, five, six annnnd seven.'

The words came from across the cell, spoken in Peyton Travis's smooth Ivy League accent. And yet they mirrored exactly the words that were in Joshua's mind as he counted off the seconds before he could allow himself to take a seat on his bunk.

'Bed's still there, then,' Travis said, his tone mocking. 'Didn't disappear while you waited.'

Joshua ignored the comment. With his mattress now beneath him, he had taken off his shoes, placed them tightly together facing out and he was now counting again.

Always the number seven. Seven touches. Seven seconds. Seven . . . whatever. Joshua knew how strange the compulsion must seem to those without it. And if he ever admitted it to himself, he knew how detrimental it was to his life.

He no longer required the perfection to which his obsessions had led. He did not need to be the perfect shot with a pistol or with a rifle or any of those other things that used to keep him alive. His OCD had led him to practise those skills endlessly and so back then they had been productive.

Now? They were a hindrance. Tics that Peyton Travis found endlessly amusing.

'I suppose those shoes will run off if you don't wait, will they?'

Joshua ignored him again as his count hit seven. Only then did he swing his legs onto the bunk and push his back against the cell wall. Once settled he tapped the mattress on either side of his thighs, seven times each hand, before reaching into his pocket for the pack of Marlboro cigarettes he had been denied back in the holding room.

'You have to do that in here?'

For the first time, Joshua glanced back at Travis. He lit a cigarette as he did so and made a point of blowing a plume of smoke in the direction of the other bunk.

'I put up with enough of your toxic shit. You put up with mine.'

'You know what that does to your health?'

'Less damage than a Ka-Bar, that's for sure.'

Travis put down his book. Joshua did not need to glance at its title: *Philosophical Explanations* by Robert Nozick. Travis was a voracious reader but he clung to that particular copy of that particular book as a lifeline, checking it out of the Facility's library weekly.

He met Joshua's eye, his expression withering.

'Those three amateurs stood no chance and you know it.'

'You know who sent them?'

'Why do you assume they were there for me? Why not you?'

'Anyone coming after me, they won't send the Three Stooges. They were for you.'

'You're probably right.' Travis smiled as he spoke. A smug, self-satisfied grin. 'Lucky I have you then, isn't it?'

'For now,' Joshua replied. 'Not forever.'

'Who needs forever?'

Travis's smile remained in place as he reached for his book, opened it at a page halfway through and began to read.

For a moment, Joshua just watched, the urge to snap Travis's neck as powerful as it had ever been. He would not act on it – he *could* not – but the temptation was strong. And so he did all that was open to him. He took a final drag on his Marlboro, stubbed it out in the ashtray next to his bunk and blew the smoke towards Travis's side of the cell.

As ever, it was not nearly enough.

TWENTY-FOUR

3.50 p.m. EDT

Cam Arnold looked up and to his right as he approached the automatic doors of the Fort Drum Service Plaza. A large, dark bulb looked back at him.

Security camera, Arnold knew. *Disguised so the sheep won't know they're being watched.*

He suppressed a smile, looked ahead and strode through the open doors, into the identikit mini-mall of gift shops and takeout stands that formed the heart of the plaza.

'We gonna eat?' Paul Holly asked, following just a step or two behind. Holly was now wearing a baseball cap, which Arnold assumed was an attempt to blend in, based on its Florida Gators emblem. Holly was from Arkansas and so wearing anything other than a Razorbacks cap could only be a disguise.

Arnold was amused by the effort.

With what's coming, it'll take more than a hat to avoid attention.

'Yeah, we're getting food. But we're bringing it with us,' Arnold explained. 'We need to keep on schedule.'

The doors slid closed behind them as they made their way forward. It sealed them in, keeping the essential air conditioning inside while keeping out the sound of heavy dance music that was now being played at full volume in the parking lot.

Ahead of them was an impressive but unhealthy set of options for eating on the move. Dunkin' Donuts. KFC. Nathan's Famous. Even an Arthur Treacher's Fish and Chips, presumably for the tens of thousands of Brits who drove the Turnpike between Orlando and Miami each year.

Arnold turned to Holly.

'It's on me. What you having?'

Holly thought for a moment.

'If we get a family bucket of chicken, that's gonna last, right?'

'You're making the most of that offer, huh? I didn't say I was feeding you all the way north.'

'No, but, you know . . .'

'Yeah, I know. Whatever. Chicken it is.'

'Thanks, Cam.'

Arnold had already stopped listening. His use of the words 'all the way north' had been deliberate; chosen to maintain Holly's belief that they were taking a long, slow journey back to Pennsylvania in their disguised Dodge Sprinter. A journey delayed by frequent stops that were designed to interfere with any algorithm that might be used to trace their progress through highway cameras.

Some of that story was true. Certainly the reason for the stops and for the fresh livery and the fresh plates now on the van. But the destination? As Arnold figured it, Holly did not need to know that he would never see Carbon County again.

The thought led Arnold naturally to the next part of the plan. He turned to look back outside. His view from here was poor, thanks to the sheer size of the plaza and its distance from the parking area. But still, he could see that the music was beginning to attract attention.

It didn't give them too long.

He turned back to Paul Holly.

'You need anything else while we're here?'

Holly paused. Thinking again. The man made no decision quickly, Arnold had noticed.

'Couldn't hurt to hit the head,' he finally offered.

'OK. Go. I'll order while you're gone.'

'Thanks.'

As Holly walked away in direction of the restrooms, Arnold stepped forward and approached the KFC counter. He was just about to order when interrupted by the sound of Holly's raised voice.

'Don't forget the gravy and biscuits, Cam.'

It had been eight minutes since Arnold and Holly had crossed the threshold into the plaza. Long enough for them to order a meal, for that meal to be served and for both men to use the facilities.

And long enough to guarantee that the dance music blaring from the open windows of the grey Dodge Sprinter had attracted exactly the attention on which Arnold had counted.

Arnold glanced upwards and to his left as they walked outside. Another look at the camera. From this angle he could better trace its view. He could see what it could see. He turned his head again and faced front. Towards the van. From here – from where the camera was placed – the Sprinter was distant but visible. Enough for at least some details to be clear.

It told Arnold what he needed to know. What was about to

happen would be recorded. By this camera at least. Perhaps by others.

More don't matter. One's enough.

The sound of the music – played at full volume on the expensive, base-heavy system Arnold had installed into the Sprinter long before he had travelled to the Keys – was hard to bear, even from the distance of the plaza's doors. It only got worse as they drew closer.

Others seemed to agree. The parking area was not heavily populated; the Florida afternoon heat made the cool plaza far more attractive than the burning asphalt outside. But of those few who were there, every head was turned towards the van.

Arnold passed the bucket of chicken and sides to Paul Holly as they crossed the main access road between the plaza and the parking lot. With his right hand now free, he moved it down and back, to feel for the pistol he had tucked into his waist.

A SIG Sauer P226. Arnold's pistol of choice, all the way back to his time in the US Marine Corps. If he could help it, there was no other handgun he would use. It was not superstition. The P226 really was just better than anything else on the market.

From one hundred yards, the music was near deafening, even for Arnold. And yet it made him smile. He had been careful to choose the type of sound that would have the effect he was looking for. That would guarantee both attention and irritation amongst anyone nearby. He had settled on something called 'aggrotech'.

It had been a good choice.

Two plaza guards began to walk towards them as they approached the Sprinter. The men had been examining the van, no doubt called over by customers in complaint at the noise.

Arnold had noticed them fifty yards back. And he had noticed *them* notice *him*.

It had taken that distance for the guards to be sure where he and Holly were headed. Now, though, as Arnold closed in on the Dodge, there could be no doubt.

'What the hell's the idea, fellas?'

The first guard shouted above the music. He was the older of the two by maybe twenty years and was by far the less imposing. His body language suggested a lack of confidence not matched by his words. Arnold had not expected him to take the lead.

'He asked you a question, guys.'

The second guard spoke when Arnold and Holly were five steps closer. Neither had acknowledged what his colleague had said, which – from the second guard's tone and his body language – Arnold thought had angered him.

Arnold said nothing. Just kept on walking. Holly did the same.

'What the fuck is your problem, man?' The second guard again. His attention was now fully on Arnold. It suggested that he, too, was attuned to body language; he knew who was in charge. 'Listen, you need to—'

Whatever the second man had intended to say, Arnold did not give him the chance. From just feet away, he pulled the SIG from his waist and fired two shots into the man's brain. A heartbeat later and he had turned the gun onto the dead man's colleague.

Two more shots and he, too, was put down.

A single second. No more. And all without Arnold breaking his stride.

He looked around as he climbed into the driver's seat of the

Sprinter, threw the pistol into the door's open compartment and switched off the speakers. What bystanders there had been were nowhere to be seen.

Hiding out of sight, no doubt.

It left nothing to see but parked cars and two dead bodies.

Arnold turned the key and the ignition came to life. It sounded near silent to his ears; unsurprisingly when, just moments ago, they had been assaulted by full-volume aggrotech and gunfire.

He looked to his right, towards Holly, who had climbed into the van's cab beside him. Holly seemed shocked. Which he had every right to be, Arnold figured, since he'd had no warning of what had just occurred. But he said nothing.

Arnold put the van in to drive, hit the gas and – as he felt the Sprinter pull away – he indicated to the bucket that was now on Holly's lap.

'What are you waiting for? Pass me a wing.'

TWENTY-FIVE

4.45 p.m. EDT

The streets of Key West were an early evening mix of heat, alcohol and the kind of crowds that Eden Grace had not seen in more than a year. The combination left her sure of why it had taken thirty-two years and a potential national emergency to bring her here.

To some, the place was a paradise. But to Grace . . .

The island was not what she had expected. Or at least that was true of what she had seen so far; the back seat of a US government sedan was perhaps not ideal for a definitive assessment, she realised, but it at least gave her a flavour.

The furthest south Grace had been before today was Miami. Her Venezuelan-born father had been raised there and it was where his family – what was left of it – still lived. Grace had liked Miami, but she had not been back since her father's death. The city, with its heavily Latino culture and cuisine – and with endless memories of his smiling face – reminded her too much of what she had lost.

Grace realised now that she had expected much the same of the Keys. Not the memories, but the culture. If anything, their location further south suggested that an even heavier Central American influence was likely.

Already she knew that she had been wrong.

Unlike the art deco and stylised design she remembered from Miami, the architecture here was almost colonial. The buildings were mostly wooden-fronted and old-world, painted white and standing a maximum of two or three storeys. And as for the people? As close as Key West was to Cuba, Grace could spot just a handful of Latino faces. All lost in a tide of reddened white skin.

It's like Orlando skipped right past Miami and headed straight here.

'Problem?'

The question came from her right.

Dempsey was seated next to Grace, in the back of the sedan that had been waiting for them at the airfield on Boca Chica Key. They had been on the ground for under ten minutes. Since then, the car had been making slow progress over a short distance.

The pace of life in the Keys did not lend itself well to urgency.

'Just checking the place out,' Grace replied. 'You been down here before?'

'Not here. Closest I ever got was Cuba.'

'I guess you didn't get your passport stamped for that one, huh?'

'No passport. It wasn't a holiday.'

'Ah. Right.'

Grace stopped herself from asking the obvious follow-up question, something she had learned to do in the past year. Instead she turned away, back towards the window.

Dempsey's past was as intriguing as anyone Grace had ever

met, but it was also, for the most part, confidential. As an agent of the British Military and then British Intelligence, Dempsey had seen and done things about which he could not talk. He regretted much of that life, Grace knew. He had told her that himself. And it was, she was sure, more than he had told almost anyone else. So she knew that his guilt for unforgivable acts was fierce.

And yet, even as the Bureau's resident Joe Dempsey expert, Grace was aware of how little she really knew about him. Cuba, for example. Why would a British government assassin have been in a hostile nation just ninety miles from the United States? There could only be one explanation and it was not one Dempsey would want to discuss.

Nor was Dempsey unique in Grace's new world. Shui Dai, her usual case partner, had been recruited from the Chinese Secret Service. Considering the rivalry between the two countries, there was no chance that Dai had not worked against America's interests at some point. And the others? Sure, Dylan Wrixon and Kate Silver were Americans, but Sal and Adama? Who the hell knew what they were up to before Dempsey had recruited them?

It was perhaps the most important thing Grace had come to understand about the ISB generally, and about Alpha Team in particular.

Whatever we've done in our previous lives, the team is our family now.

It had been a difficult transition for her. As it had been for others, she was sure. But in the past year, as she had come to see the world more and more through international eyes, Grace had realised how damaging blind patriotism can be.

She still loved her country. That would never change. But the kind of cooperation that came with the ISB, enabling them to protect the world from the many who would harm it, had convinced her of the importance of a global view.

And yet for all that, the team's focus did tend to remain on the United States. When a single country dominates the world, it is that country that draws the world's attention, both good and bad. The US, she had discovered, faced more threats than any other First World nation. Threats that were best neutralised early.

Exactly why we're here.

She turned back to face Dempsey. He was sat at the other end of the car's back seat, Dylan Wrixon's tight polo top already ripping around his thick biceps.

'So what do you think we're up against? You think Liberation intend to do something here? Looking at this place, it doesn't seem like a target for their kind of group.'

'What makes you say that?' Dempsey asked. 'You think half the people here probably agree with their cause?'

It was a fair question. The support for movements like Liberation was more common in the south than the north and it did not get any more south than Key West. She also doubted that a Caucasian-heavy holiday destination was the natural target for a group of white supremacists.

But no, it was not that.

'More to do with what they could achieve here,' Grace explained. 'The buildings are small and they're easily replaced. And the island itself, it's too far from the mainland to have the kind of impact on everyday infrastructure that a terrorist attack aims for. Or even to cause the same fear. The further an attack is from a major city – from what people see as their real life – the less it impacts their day-to-day existence. So no. I don't think this place is a target at all.'

'Then what were they doing here?'

'Like you said, the murder took place at a dock. Then a little later an APB on a truck? Got to be disembarkation and then movement of illicit goods north.'

'What illicit goods? Drugs? Weapons?'

'Too many other options to say that. To simply pick one without evidence or analysis. That *would* be an assumption.'

Dempsey smiled. Grace knew that he was testing her. Everything was a lesson, and she was learning from a master.

'And what about the theory that they're taking whatever they collected north? How is that not an assumption?'

'Second APB. The first just named Cam Arnold and it seemed to be focused on Key West. The later one threw in the Dodge Sprinter and his four companions, and it spread the net up to the mainland. There has to be a reason for the increased geographic focus. If Homeland Security have taken point on this, they must know something that makes them believe the van is heading north.'

'Sound reasoning,' Dempsey observed. 'And I suspect we'll be getting those blanks filled in for us pretty soon.'

He indicated ahead as she spoke. Grace redirected her gaze through the sedan's windscreen and saw what Dempsey already had: yellow plastic tape, now visible in the near-distance. It looked like a police cordon, except for the two black-suited men who appeared to be controlling access.

Their appearance suggested something more.

'Homeland?'

'Homeland,' Dempsey confirmed.

TWENTY-SIX

4.55 p.m. EDT

Dempsey's first thought as he stepped inside North Bay Marina's clubhouse was one of relief. It was not what he would have expected of himself and it said all it had to about the unusual intensity of the heat outside.

The naturally cold concrete from which the building was constructed was well hidden by the exterior's wooden facade and by the carefully plastered white interior. Regardless, its cooled temperature filled the room with the effectiveness of a refrigeration unit. Combined with well-hidden, near-industrial-strength air conditioning, it made the space an oasis from the tropical sun.

The sedan had been unable to pass Homeland Security's on-site operational centre at the entrance to the marina. This had forced Dempsey and Grace to walk the final short leg of their journey. Less than one hundred yards, it was still far enough for them to get some idea of the extreme climate. Even dressed in casual clothes far more suited to the environment than Grace's black suit, Dempsey had been grateful to step into the cold.

Both agents had their ISB credentials in hand as they walked through the entrance doors. They had already been examined by the Homeland agent posted just outside the building, but both knew they would need them again.

The hit of the A/C focused Dempsey, as if he had taken a lungful of pure oxygen. It seemed to do the same to Grace, who must have felt the heat outside even more keenly than him. She seemed instantly more alert as she scanned the building's interior.

The marina reception had been decorated with an eye to wealth. Dempsey could have guessed that from outside; the yachts alone confirmed North Bay as a preserve for the rich. What he saw now only strengthened that conclusion. Even when crowded with Homeland Security and police personnel, there was enough marble and original art visible to identify the place for what it was.

Not that the rich would be welcome today. Today, the North Bay Marina clubhouse was a government outpost. A temporary headquarters for the United States premier department of intelligence.

Immediately ahead of them, surrounding what would usually be the front desk, was a huddle of agents. At least that was Dempsey's guess. The clothes were usually a giveaway – the standard federal kit, identical to what Grace was wearing right beside him – but two of the group were dressed differently. In clothes much more suited to the weather.

One of those two seemed to be leading the discussion. Or at least she had been, until she noticed the arrival Dempsey and Grace. Their presence in the reception area brought the conversation to an end.

Dempsey noticed that the initially curious expression on the lead agent's face had quickly turned to irritation. She considered this an interruption. And she was not happy.

'Something I can do for you people?'

The question, asked with an accent that Dempsey could only place as 'Mississippi Delta', confirmed that he had been right about the hierarchy. She was the shortest of the group by some distance, and the oldest. Somewhere in her early fifties, he guessed.

He moved forward, remaining a step ahead of Grace.

'I'm Agent Joe Dempsey, from the ISB.' Dempsey held up his credentials as he spoke. Grace did the same. 'This is Agent Eden Grace. You were told to expect us?'

'The where?'

Dempsey's eyes flitted from the lead agent to the man who had spoken and noticed he was the only other member of the huddle who was 'out of uniform'. He watched as the man turned to the woman. 'O'Rourke, what is that?'

The question confirmed to Dempsey that the man was no fed; if he were, he'd have heard of the ISB.

'It's the International Security Bureau,' Dempsey explained. 'From the United Nations. We're on the same team.'

O'Rourke – as Dempsey now gathered the lead agent was called – took a step forward. This resulted in her four subordinates and their still-unnamed interloper facing Dempsey and Grace in a line, with their boss now ahead of them like some wildly undersized quarterback.

She held out her hand as she spoke and Dempsey took it in his own.

'I'm Special Agent O'Rourke. And for my sins, I'm in operational command of this shitshow. So yes, sir, I was told to expect you. But I wasn't told why. You mind putting that right for me, son?'

Dempsey smiled. Despite the slightly confrontational

question, he could tell from her easy manner that she was curious rather than genuinely irritated by their intrusion into her case. That would make things easier.

'Nice to meet you, Special Agent O'Rourke.' Dempsey could not match O'Rourke for charm but he could sure as hell be polite. 'And I'm sorry if it seems like we're muscling in here. We're really not. We just received notice this morning that Campbell Arnold has been implicated in a murder in Key West. Our system has Arnold flagged as connected to the terrorist group Liberation. And Liberation are of particular interest to our team at the ISB.'

'Why?'

'They're terrorists, Special Agent O'Rourke. Why would they not be of interest?'

'Liberation are *domestic* terrorists, son. By their very nature. They're anti-federalist, anti-government, anti-union. And anti-people who look like me. What's that got to do with the *International* Security Bureau?'

O'Rourke put particular emphasis on the first word of the agency's title, to make her point clear. It made Dempsey smile again. Even when being blunt, she somehow did it with warmth.

'Misleading title, that,' Dempsey replied. 'It just means we have jurisdiction to act anywhere in the world, in any United Nations member state territory. We're like an extra intelligence service, Agent O'Rourke. Just not one that's confined to a single country.'

The amused expression on O'Rourke's face made Dempsey's smile grow wider.

'But then I think you already knew that, didn't you?'

'This ain't my first rodeo, Agent Dempsey.'

'I wouldn't dare suggest otherwise.'

'I bet you wouldn't. But would you dare answer my question? What is it that's got the ISB all keen on Cam Arnold and Liberation?'

'They're just one of a hundred groups we're monitoring.'

Dempsey glanced at Grace as he spoke. What he had just said was a lie but he had no intention of mentioning Scott Turner. Not until he had to. His glance was an instruction for Grace to follow the same line.

He turned back to O'Rourke.

'What with the resurgence in the patriot movement, we figured you guys needed as much help as you could get. So, like I said, Cam Arnold's name was flagged and we were sent down to assist.'

'To assist? You're not here to run your own agency investigation?'

'What good would that do? You're Homeland Security. You've got resources we can only dream of. No, Agent O'Rourke, we're here to assist you in any way we can.' Dempsey indicated behind her. 'Like I said to your man, we're on the same team.'

O'Rourke smiled. A smile which, for the first time, Dempsey was sure was real.

'OK. Well, I guess I'd be a fool to say no to an offer like that, wouldn't I? But if you're gonna help, first you'll need to know what we know. Because this ain't as simple as a murder on the docks no more.'

TWENTY-SEVEN

5.20 p.m. EDT

Cam Arnold pulled the spice-coated skin from a still-warm chicken leg and threw it through the van's open window, aimed towards the bush beyond. It was a decision he instantly regretted, even as he watched the salty mix of deep-fried flour and carcass fly through the air.

Shit.

They were parked deep in wetland country, on one of the few accessible roads that came off the Blue Cypress Conservation Area, and Paul Holly was working at the back of the open Dodge Sprinter. A position which left the poor guy open to his surroundings, Arnold had realised. And so not the smartest of circumstances to be throwing out 'treats' that could attract predators.

The thought made Arnold shudder. Not for Holly's sake but for his own. He pressed the electric window control and watched the glass roll up, shielding him from the dangers of the Florida wildlife outside. It was exactly eleven hours since they had left Key West and, though sundown was still three hours away, the light was dimming.

Screw being out there when it gets dark.

Arnold's reptile phobia was always going to be a problem at this stage of the scheme. Along with the need for two pairs of hands to apply the large replacement decals to the side of the van, it was why he had needed to include Holly at all. For this stage of the plan to work, the journey from Key West had to be staggered by a succession of irregular breaks and by repeated changes to the disguise they had applied to the Grey Sprinter. The only place those breaks could take place without detection was as close to off-road as the Dodge could handle.

In Florida, that meant swampland.

He could feel the movement in the back of the van. Just as he had for the past twenty minutes or so. Holly was working hard. The removal of over a ton of cargo – even in individual one-hundred-and-twenty-pound containers – was no easy task in a climate like this. It would have been tiring for two men. But with Arnold sidelined it must have been exhausting.

Still beats the shit out of the alternative, though, Arnold thought.

He felt no guilt at sitting this part out. The idea of moving into the bush and encountering some Floridian reptile – a gator or, even worse, one of the damned Burmese pythons that now terrorised the Everglades – was just too much for him to handle.

And besides, I've done enough so far.

The thought was interrupted by the sound of the van's back door slamming shut. Arnold glanced at the driver's wing mirror. The closure of the door suggested that the first phase of the work – the part that could take them away from the van and into the bush – was done. That impression was confirmed by the sound of the second door.

It left just one thing to do. And phobia or no phobia, this was not something Arnold could sit out.

He opened the door and stepped out with care, his eyes drawn to the spot where he knew the chicken skin had landed. He could see nothing there, but that gave him little comfort; Arnold knew from his own personal experience that nature's camouflage was a hell of a lot better than the military's. Still, he had no choice. This next part was a two-man job.

Arnold walked to the end of the van and found Holly exactly where he had expected him to be. Standing just ahead of the rear doors, Holly was holding a container of soapy water that had been carried in the back of the van and applying it to the delivery firm signage they had applied to the Sprinter that morning. The idea was for the chemicals in the water to loosen the decal adhesive, allowing them to peel it away.

Holly was dripping with sweat. He had finished his lone task fast and was wasting no time with the next one.

To get it over with and get out of here, most likely.

Arnold stepped forward and used his thumbnail to try to loosen the delivery sign. He looked across at Holly as he worked, noting that Holly did not look back.

'You good?' He kept his tone light. It gave Holly every chance to ignore the question and just get on with work.

It did not work.

'I thought you were a marine?'

Holly did not glance towards Arnold as he spoke. Both that and the tone of the question itself were signs of a disrespect he had never before shown. After all, it was because of Holly's usual blind obedience that Arnold had chosen him for this journey.

The change in attitude put Arnold on edge. Unexpected was the last thing he needed right now. He did his best to ignore it.

'I was a marine,' he finally replied. 'Five years active. Why?'

Holly did not answer. He just carried on with his work, but Arnold could see that something was coming. That something was bothering the man.

'Come on. Tell me why you asked.'

This time Holly bit.

'Just ain't never heard of no marine who's shit-scared of snakes is all. Ain't never seen a Green Beret who can't handle the jungle.'

Arnold smiled. As strange as it seemed for Holly to show him such an attitude, if this was all the problem was, well, he could handle that.

'It was in the damn jungle where it started,' Arnold replied. 'I was fine with the things until then. No problem at all. Then afterwards? No way.'

For the first time since Arnold had stepped out of the Dodge, Holly looked at him as he spoke. His expression, though, was blank; Arnold could not tell if he was curious or irritated. Or just plain harassed by the work effort he had put in.

'So you want to know what happened to me?' Arnold asked. 'What caused the phobia?'

'No. No, I just want to get this done.'

That answers it, then. Irritated it is.

Arnold made no more effort to speak. Instead he turned his attention to the job, wetting and pulling at the van sign until it peeled away from the rear doors. It was a quick enough task with two. In less than ten minutes they had cleared the back, the front and the left-hand side of the Sprinter.

It was only once they moved to the right-hand side that

Holly spoke again. When he did, Arnold realised what was really bothering the usually compliant soldier.

'You know there's no way the cameras at the pit stop missed the signs on this van, right?' Holly had placed the water container at his feet. 'You know they'll have recorded it all?'

'I know that. That's why the signs are coming off. And the plates. It's why we've got more of both.'

'Yeah, I get that. In fact we got four more sets of each. All different. I didn't think much of it before, when we put the first set up. But after the pit stop? I gotta ask: you planning to kill a lot more people on the journey north, Cam?'

At first Arnold said nothing. He just met Holly's stare and returned it. He knew his actions would have caught Holly off guard, but he still hadn't really expected him to question them. Certainly not with this amount of confidence. Arnold considered how he should respond, and immediately realised he had few options.

If Holly had confronted him *after* putting on the new decals? If he had done that, then Arnold could have answered as he pleased. Sure, it would speed up what was to come. But not by much.

But as it was, he had to be careful.

'And if I am?'

'If you are, I think I should have been told that part of the plan, don't you?'

'Since when were you in command here, Paul?'

'I'm not trying to be in command of anything. But I do think I should know if I'm being asked to put myself in the firing line. I didn't sign up to be treated like a fool, Cam. You killed that patrolman at the docks without telling any of us it was gonna happen. Then you killed those two guards at the pit stop. Now maybe the patrolman needed to go, I don't know about that. But I do know those guards were a set-up. The music. The whole thing. You lined them up to kill them. Why?'

Arnold's mind was working quick. Holly had questions, but so did he.

'You've been quiet about this almost an hour. You said nothing when it happened. So why now?'

Holly hesitated before he answered. When he spoke again, he sounded just a little less confident.

'Time to think. I ain't like you, Cam. I ain't all quick-witted, 'specially when that sort of shit comes out of nowhere. But I been pondering, and I don't like where this is going. There ain't no way we ain't getting nabbed for this.'

Arnold paused to think. He did not like the direction the exchange was taking.

'You can't be so sure of that, Paul,' he finally said. 'There's a lot more to what we're doing than you realise. Remember, if you get caught then I get caught, too. You really think I'd take the risk that I'm not around to finish this?'

'Then why are you?'

'Why am I what?'

'Taking the risk. Because you sure as hell are, Cam. And if you can't see that, man, I've got to question what the hell I've been following.'

'Now hold on a god—'

'Jesus, man, I cut myself off from my damned family for you. To follow *you*. I trusted you, man. And now you're telling me you can't see the shit you're driving us into. You can't see the target you're putting on our backs? What the hell, Cam? What kind of goddamned vision is that, huh?'

Arnold exhaled long and hard. Holly would never understand what was going to happen. Arnold knew that. But right now he needed the man, and Holly was not taking no for an answer.

'Look, I just need you to trust me. I swear, Paul, I'll—'

'I ain't trusting anything I don't know for sure. Not now. Not after this. You want me to trust you, Cam, you swear to me that this ain't gonna happen again.'

'Paul, you don't understand.'

'What I understand is that any more killing gets us caught and then that's game over. So it's your choice. You want me to stay on board with this? You find another way. Clear?'

Arnold stared hard at Holly as he spoke. The ultimatum was pushing him to his limits. So was the disrespect. But still, Holly had left Arnold no choice.

'OK. We'll find another way.'

Arnold bent down as he spoke and picked up the container of water at Holly's feet. He then threw what remained of its content over the final panel sign and began to peel away at the adhesive. Holly just watched, his expression now even angrier than it had been before.

Arnold knew why. Holly didn't yet have what he wanted.

'Your word, Cam,' he repeated. 'I ain't doing nothing more without your word.'

Arnold stopped what he was doing and turned to face Holly one more time.

'You've got it. You have my word.'

Ten minutes later and the Sprinter was near transformed. All traces of the parcel delivery service and the Florida plates were gone. Replaced by a Georgia index and the distinct signage for a motor parts company Arnold had registered in Savannah two months ago.

Holly, too, seemed to have changed. Or at least his mood had improved. The conversation had continued as they'd worked and Arnold had detailed the changes he would need to make to the plan, to still achieve what they had set out to do. Holly, he was sure, had failed to follow most of the detail; he just seemed pleased to be trusted again.

I guess it's true what they say about the simple things, Arnold thought to himself.

The light had dimmed further. Arnold looked around nervously. The conversation and the work had distracted him, but his fears returned fast. The sun was no doubt still strong nearer to the main road, he knew. Once they were out from under the coverage of the Everglades. But in here, it was getting dark fast.

He turned to face Holly.

'So we're good now, right?'

'We're good.' Holly smiled as he spoke. A happy soldier once again.

'OK. Then let's get back in the van. We've got to wait another hour off the highway to stay on schedule. I sure as hell ain't doing that out here.'

'Damn right.'

Arnold opened the driver's door, climbed in and used the open compartment on the inside of the door to slam it shut. As he did so, he reached inside the compartment and felt the grip of the same SIG Sauer P226 he had used at the Fort Drum Plaza. Bringing himself upright, he moved the pistol into his right hand, raised it towards the passenger door and, as the door opened, he fired two shots.

The impact sent Holly careering backwards, away from the door and into the bush behind. Arnold moved almost as fast in the same direction, to close the open door. As he did, he did not even glance down. Holly no longer deserved a second's thought.

He refused to follow the plan. And so he had to die.

It would affect what was to come – *it speeds up the schedule, anyway*, Arnold thought – but still, Holly's death was necessary. He had brought it on himself.

And now the dumb bastard's gonna be someone's dinner.

TWENTY-EIGHT

5.50 p.m. EDT

O'Rourke stretched back into the cold leather of the North Bay Marina manager's chair. She took a sip of piping hot coffee and – for the first time that day – she allowed herself to close her eyes.

It had been a long twelve hours and the clock was still ticking.

O'Rourke had awoken in Key Largo at 5 a.m. At almost exactly the moment Cam Arnold had slit the throat of Ricardo Garcia. From that moment to this, the work had not stopped.

First she had made the early-morning journey to Key West. Then, upon her arrival, she had overseen the investigation of Garcia's death. First as an observer hoping to be wrong. And then as the agent in charge, once Cam Arnold's involvement had been confirmed. She had followed that by leading her team's examination of the marina and as good as confirming the DOJ intelligence that Liberation – led by Arnold – had collected caesium-137 from a waterborne source.

A sheer ton of the stuff. Enough to make at least ten dirty bombs. And all of this on US soil.

Those developments alone would have been an exhausting

day for anyone in O'Rourke's position. But there was more. So much more. The departure of the caesium-loaded Dodge Sprinter van from Front Street was where the questions really began.

It made sense to O'Rourke that the cargo would be taken to the mainland. It was a theory agreed upon by her team. No one saw Key West as a likely target for a dirty bomb. And certainly not from Liberation. Attacks had very specific aims. They could be symbolic. They could be designed to damage infrastructure, disrupting day-to-day life on a massive level. Or they could be no more than terror itself; kill enough people in one blast so that those left are too scared to go about their normal lives.

None of these aims worked if the target was Key West. There was nothing here of national symbolism, except maybe the Southernmost Point Buoy. And that wasn't exactly difficult to replace. As for infrastructure? There was none. It was a tourist destination. A few streets of bars and restaurants, all bordered by beaches and marinas.

An attack here wouldn't slow the US a jot.

As for terror in itself being the aim, on this O'Rourke agreed with Dempsey and Grace. An attack off the mainland, this far from what most American's saw as 'real life'? It was just too remote – too detached – to be effective.

No. Key West was not the target. The caesium was heading to the mainland in the back of Cam Arnold's Dodge Sprinter, guarded by three no doubt heavily armed men with little care for their own safety.

It was a sound theory. The problem was, at the moment, that theory was all O'Rourke had.

She opened her eyes at the thought. Her rest, if she could call it that, was over. There was work to be done.

Reaching out for the mouse, O'Rourke clicked the DNDO computer terminal that had been fitted in the office just five minutes ago and brought the screen to life. A moment later and she had accessed the traffic camera compilation put together by her team. The display filled with familiar images; footage she had already seen five, maybe six times today.

It had been the logical next step. The Dodge Sprinter had driven away from the marina just after 5.45 a.m. and though Key West was not well covered in terms of traffic and private security cameras, there were still enough to trace the broad movements of a vehicle. O'Rourke had expected, then, to see the Sprinter join the Overseas Highway portion of US Route One at the junction with Flagler Avenue no later than 5.50 a.m.

She had been right about the destination. She had been wrong about the time.

On the footage she now watched, the Dodge passed the Flagler Avenue camera at 6.20 a.m. A full thirty minutes later than O'Rourke had anticipated, and far longer than the vehicle's journey from point A to point B could possibly take.

The discrepancy was a serious problem. Key West was not the target. O'Rourke could not be more sure of that. But a staging point? Perhaps the place where the bombs would be put together? Or even just a storage point for the caesium, to avoid the risk of moving it in the window between Garcia's death and the identification of Cam Arnold as his killer?

Neither made any logical sense, and yet the extra thirty minutes were hard to explain in any other way. There were no cameras between Front Street and Flagler Avenue, but that was also true in several other directions from Front Street. And thirty minutes was just about how long it would take for the cargo to be driven to another location – to a warehouse, perhaps

– and unloaded. Whether for storage or even for preparation into bomb form.

O'Rourke could think of no other reasons for the thirty minutes. But still she did not like either as a theory.

As a staging point, the flaws were massive. Building the bombs here would then require their movement over hundreds of miles to the nearest viable target: Miami. And thousands of miles more if the target was somewhere else.

Which is a hell of a risk to take with ten live bombs, unless one hundred per cent necessary.

Which it's not.

The warehouse possibility was more likely, but even that had its flaws. Primarily because they could not have known that Arnold would need to kill Ricardo Garcia, could they? Which meant they would have needed a warehouse available 'just in case'. Garcia's death was all that made the drive back to the mainland risky. If he had lived, the journey would have been danger-free.

But even if they *had* been cautious enough to make such contingency plans, how hard would it be to find the warehouse? Key West was not over-burdened with storage spaces. Finding one recently rented would be no difficult task. And even if that was extended to short rentals on residential properties, again, it was a small place. Armed with radiation detection equipment, O'Rourke's team would find the caesium in short order if it was still on the island.

Which was why she had already put them to work.

As much as she believed that the caesium was heading north, O'Rourke had hedged her bets. A full contingent of KWPD and Monroe County Sheriff's deputies had been brought in to bulk out her own small team, and for the past two hours they had been sweeping every conceivable storage facility on the Key.

So far they had found nothing. Just as O'Rourke had expected.

No. It's gone. There's some other reason for that van's delay. I just need to work out what it is.

She clicked on through the footage, chapter by chapter. Her analysts had done their job well. Each new display showed another sighting of the Dodge, each on a camera sequentially north of the last. Wherever the Sprinter had been for its extra half hour on Key West – whatever Cam Arnold had been doing – the ultimate aim was to head back to the mainland. That much was clear.

How far they intended to go into the mainland, however, was not.

Almost as soon as the van passed the US Route One milepost, the trail went cold. Every camera from that point to Florida City and then further on to Miami had been viewed. And viewed again. The Dodge Sprinter appeared on none of them.

The van had hit the mainland. And then it had disappeared.

It was a terrifying mystery. A vehicle containing enough caesium-137 to radioactively devastate ten heavily populated targets was now in the hands of a known terrorist organisation and unaccounted for on the US mainland. And if it was not located soon, it could be taken literally anywhere throughout the continental United States.

O'Rourke just stared at the screen. At the increasing stream of traffic heading north on Route One. Images she had seen again and again already today, none of them showing the vehicle she was looking for.

She pushed her chair backwards, away from the desk, and lifted a hand to her brow. She was tired, and it was not just the hours. It was not just the stress and what now looked like the hopelessness. They all played their part, but O'Rourke had to accept that it was more than that. As much as she hated to acknowledge a weakness – to admit something about which she could do nothing – she could no longer avoid reality.

It was her age and it was her health. After everything she had done – everything she had achieved – O'Rourke knew she was no longer young enough nor well enough to be living this life.

The latter was noticeable at a glance. No one could fail to notice the extra weight she carried. One hundred and seventy pounds was too much for a woman who only stood five foot one. That extra baggage would be hard work even if it were the result of overconsumption, but it was not. O'Rourke had been slim her entire adult life. Hell, she had been called a 'skinny bitch' more times than she cared to remember. The weight gain had been sudden. And it had been relatively recent.

Those who did not know O'Rourke personally no doubt thought it was her lifestyle just catching up with her. Junk food and sugary drinks usually go hand in hand with the long, erratic hours she worked. But O'Rourke's few friends knew better. She had always eaten well and hadn't touched a soda in thirty years.

No. The extra weight was just the most visible symptom of a massively underactive thyroid. As she had discovered only recently – when she had finally forced herself to confront the unknown and find out what was behind her deteriorating health – her metabolic gland had effectively shut up shop five years ago. Since the diagnosis, she had been experimenting with various treatments, trying to find what would work for her. So far without success; the chronic pain, severe fatigue and weight gain showed no sign of abating.

The final symptom was impossible to hide, but up to now O'Rourke had concealed the others well. She'd had no other choice. Not if she wanted to keep doing what she was doing, for as long as she could do it.

Her career predated the creation of both Homeland Security in 2002 and of the Domestic Nuclear Detection Office in 2005. Back when she had started, the responsibilities she held today would have been vested in the State Department. And the very idea of a black woman heading one of State's most vital teams? Unheard of.

The world of 2021 was different, sure, but it was a world that O'Rourke and women like her had built through pain and through sacrifice. She wasn't about to walk away from that, from the life she had strived to create. Not until she had to.

O'Rourke was older than most people assumed; she had turned sixty-one just two weeks ago, which made her about a decade older than she was usually pegged. But it still felt like yesterday when – aged nearly thirty – she had made the switch from law to intelligence. In the three decades that had followed, she'd done everything possible to achieve the position she now held. And she had done it for herself. Sure, she was happy to be a pioneer. She was glad that other women were now on the ladder behind her.

But she had never pretended that the advancement of womankind was her driving motivation. O'Rourke's jet fuel was ambition. A need to be the best at what she did. And, she was sure, most would agree that she was.

She wasn't about to let her health change that.

No one's gonna see me struggle, she thought to herself. *No matter how hard this one gets.*

The alert tone on her console sounded like a boxing bell, telling her that a new email had arrived. It broke through her thoughts, bringing her back to the moment.

O'Rourke leaned forward so she could reach her mouse. With it, she opened the email and read its contents. Then she re-read it. And then, for the second time, she pushed her seat back from the desk.

She finally understood.

TWENTY-NINE

5.55 p.m. EDT

'How many of the possible locations have been searched?'
Dempsey was sitting in the reception area of the North Bay Marina clubhouse, on a chair just a few feet from Sergio Vega. He and Grace had been brought up to speed on everything Homeland Security had learned since the death of Ricardo Garcia, and O'Rourke had outlined the continuing efforts to locate the Dodge Sprinter and the caesium.

It told them a lot, confirming most of their own conclusions. But there was more Dempsey wanted to know. For him, the picture still did not make sense and so, with O'Rourke now in her temporary office, he took the chance to speak to a non-Homeland member of her team.

'At last call, I think we'd got through approximately sixty-five per cent.' Sergio Vega checked his tablet screen as he spoke, to ensure his figures were correct. 'Yeah, that's it. Sixty-five per cent.'

'That's quick work.' Dempsey was genuinely impressed.

'It's a big team O'Rourke pulled together. There are two hundred police officers and deputies on this right now. And twenty specialists from the DNDO, one for every team.'

'Big operation. How'd you drum up so many bodies?'

'Every leave cancelled, everyone off shift called on, skeleton staff working as law enforcement on the island. And even then we didn't hit two hundred. We had to call in help from outside. Other Keys.'

'Good time to be a criminal in Key West.'

Vega was looking outside as Dempsey spoke, through one of the large floor-to-ceiling windows that flanked the main doors to the clubhouse. He seemed distracted. His own words had been trailing off and it seemed that Dempsey's reply hadn't yet registered.

When it finally did, Vega turned back to face the ISB agent. 'What?'

'With all the cops on search duty. It's a good time to be a criminal in Key West.'

'Yeah. Yeah, I guess it is.' Vega smiled as he spoke. 'Lucky those criminals don't all know that, huh?'

Dempsey took a moment to glance outside, for some indication of what had caught Vega's attention. All he could see was Grace speaking to Agent May.

May had stepped outside for a cigarette and Dempsey had indicated for Grace to join her. His rationale was the same as his own conversation with Vega; with their new 'alliance' with Homeland Security less than an hour old and so far from settled, they were likely to get more information from the non-Homeland members of the team than from O'Rourke's regulars.

This meant taking their chances where they found them.

'Missing the sunshine out there?' Dempsey asked. He nodded towards the window as he spoke, aware that Vega's attention was not on the weather.

Vega must have caught the subtext because he now seemed embarrassed, but he did not acknowledge the underlying question with an answer. An unspoken denial that did not convince Dempsey for a second. Dempsey could see exactly what it was – *who* it was – that had Vega's attention. And as much as he thought that kind of distraction to be a bad idea, this was not his team.

Which makes it none of my business.

'You will let me know if the search of the island pulls anything up, Sergeant Vega?'

'Yeah. Yeah, of course, no prob . . .'

Vega stopped speaking before he was finished, his attention once again caught by movement outside. Dempsey followed his eyeline, turning just in time to see the main doors to the clubhouse open and May stride in. Grace was alongside her and they both headed directly to Dempsey.

'O'Rourke has news,' May announced. Her tone was serious, her focus was now fully on Dempsey. 'She wants to see the two of us in her office.'

'Fort Drum Service?'

'Yes.' O'Rourke had checked and rechecked every aspect of the email and its various attachments before calling Dempsey and May to her office. 'One hundred per cent.'

'And where is that, exactly?'

'It's on the Florida Turnpike,' O'Rourke replied.

'Yeah, but how far along it? How far north have they managed to get, Agent O'Rourke?'

O'Rourke took a deep breath before she answered. From that alone, Dempsey knew it would not be good news.

'It's almost one hundred and ninety miles on from where they were last spotted.'

Dempsey shook his head. That distance? It changed everything.

'And this was two hours ago, was it?'

'Give or take,' O'Rourke replied. 'And I know what y'all gonna say next. Those two hours, they could put them another hundred miles further north by now. I realise this ain't ideal.'

Dempsey could see that O'Rourke had taken a hit. The pressure she was under seemed almost physical, as if its weight were threatening to overcome her. To add to it would solve nothing. Only information would do that.

'Any idea what led to the shooting?'

'You'll see for yourself on the footage,' O'Rourke replied. 'Looks to me like they tried to speak to him and the sonofabitch just gunned them down.'

'There's got to be more to it than that,' Dempsey said. 'With what he's hauling in that van, he would be desperate to avoid attention.'

Dempsey paused. His own words had sparked a question.

'The van. You've had an APB out on that van now for half the day and, from what you told me earlier, you've got half of southern Florida under siege, searching for them. You've even got access to a whole web of traffic cameras. With all that, how did you miss the van as it headed north?'

O'Rourke simply shook her head, the same look of defeat in her eyes. She reached out to her console screen and turned it around so that it faced Dempsey and May. Then she clicked her mouse.

'Watch the clip.'

An instant later and Dempsey was watching footage of two men as they walked through a set of automatic doors. One of them – the bigger one – Dempsey recognised as Cam Arnold. He couldn't see the other man clearly, but from what little visibility there was, he was much too short to be Scott Turner.

Dempsey kept his eyes on Arnold. And what he saw surprised him.

'He looked right at the camera. He knew it was there and yet he looked right at it.'

'That was my first instinct,' O'Rourke replied. 'Not much attempt at a disguise, either.'

'None.'

O'Rourke skipped the footage back so they could watch it again. And then again.

'Any other thoughts?'

'Just that first one,' Dempsey replied. 'Arnold as good as bowed to his audience. Why?'

'Good question, keep it in mind. What about you, Nicki? Anything to add?'

'Nothing.'

'What about the other guy? Any idea who he is?'

'None at all,' May replied. 'He keeps himself well covered.'

'I thought you'd say that. OK, I'm gonna run forward eight minutes. That's when they leave. But when I'm skipping through, y'all look right ahead at the van in the distance in the parking lot. That's the Sprinter.'

'What happens with it? The other three get out?'

'No sign of them, but maybe they couldn't. Probably not safe to leave the caesium.'

'What, then?'

'Just watch.'

O'Rourke skipped the footage forward. Even at eight times run speed Dempsey could see that the van was attracting attention. Other customers from the parking lot were approaching, as if there was some disturbance coming from within. He looked at O'Rourke.

'There was music left on while they were in the stop,' she explained.

'Loud enough to bring people over like that?'

'Seems that way.'

Why would he do that? Why bring attention to the van?

Dempsey looked back at the screen as the runtime hit eight minutes. O'Rourke clicked her mouse and reduced the play to normal speed. Ten seconds later and they were back to Cam Arnold and his companion. They were walking out of the plaza, their backs to the entrance camera.

At least at first.

'He looked up again,' Dempsey said. 'He looked straight up at the camera. Arnold wants us to be sure that it's him.'

'I thought the same,' O'Rourke replied. 'Then I thought that maybe he just wasn't sure it was a camera. Maybe he was taking a closer look, wondering what it was.'

'Maybe.' Dempsey was not convinced. 'But that shit-eating look on his face? I don't know.'

'It probably don't matter. Just keep watching.'

As much as he disagreed – something was telling Dempsey that it really *did* matter – he did not need the instruction; his eyes had not left the screen. He watched as Arnold and the second man walked towards the van. And he noticed for the first time that the crowd outside it included two guards.

It left him in no doubt of what was to come. The next few seconds came with the full knowledge of how it would play out and so Dempsey was unsurprised as Arnold pulled his pistol and shot both guards dead.

Unsurprised, but confused.

'Why did he do it? Why did he kill those men? Over a noise complaint? He could have just said sorry and walked away. They were no threat to him. He didn't . . . he didn't *need* to do that.'

'Maybe there was more to it than we know right now,' O'Rourke replied. 'Or maybe he's just got a hair trigger.'

'No, that doesn't make sense. If he's shipping what we think he's shipping in that van, why the hell take that risk? Why even have music playing loud enough to draw attention? Why look up at the camera? Twice? None of this makes sense.'

'Hold that thought, son, and we'll circle right back. For now, you need to see what comes next.'

Dempsey did as O'Rourke had suggested. The footage had continued at normal speed and so it had taken until now for Arnold to fire the engine and begin to drive the van. Naturally he headed for the exit, a route which brought him closer to the camera.

And one that gave Dempsey his first clear view of the vehicle.

'Crafty bastard.' Dempsey shook his head. 'How did none of us think of this?'

May stepped closer to the now-frozen image as Dempsey and O'Rourke exchanged understanding.

'Is that what I think it is?' she asked.

'It's the Dodge,' O'Rourke confirmed. 'We've been looking for a plain grey Sprinter with Ohio plates. That thing he's driving, it's covered in the coloured decals for a delivery company. And they've switched the damned plates. It's like a completely different vehicle.'

'Jesus Christ. We've been looking for the wrong van.'

'No. We've been looking for the *right* van. How were we supposed to know the bastards would transform the damned thing?'

'Oh, come on!' May seemed barely able to hold her temper. 'You think that's going to fly in Washington? We've got ninety per cent of Florida's law enforcement searching the southern tip of the entire damned state. We've got every available Homeland unit working with them. All because we were convinced they had to be somewhere south of Florida City. And now we find out that these sonsofbitches have been driving hundreds of miles north without a care in the goddamned world?'

'That's how fieldwork goes, Nicki. It ain't all plain sailing. Shit happens, girl. And when it does, we deal with it.'

'That's not good enough, Bambi. If this goes wrong, it reflects on Justice as much as it reflects on you.'

'Are you kidding me?' O'Rourke rose from her seat, her eyes fixed on May. 'Are you really gonna stand there and lecture me all uppity-like on Justice?'

'I mean it reflects on the DOJ—'

'I was born at night, Nicki. But I wasn't born *last* night. I know you mean the DOJ. Now maybe you need to remember who greased those wheels that got you there in the first place.'

'And how long do I owe you for that?'

May's voice was low and deliberate. She was holding herself back. Dempsey suspected that she had more to say. A glance in his direction seemed to remind her that they were not alone.

She looked back at O'Rourke.

'I've got to report in to Assistant AG Milner at the DOJ within the next thirty minutes. When I do, I want to be able to tell him that we're ahead of this, understood?'

'And how do you suggest we achieve that?'

'Have we got any more traffic footage of the van?'

'It's been fifteen minutes, Nicki. You tell me.'

'An APB at least?'

'You trying to insult me now?'

'No, Bambi. Like I said, I want us ahead of this. And maybe the best way to do that is actually *getting* ahead of it. They're headed north. If Fort Drum is two hundred miles up the mainland, that puts them level with Orlando right about now, assuming a two-hour drive since that footage. So let's get ourselves *further* north. Let's get a jet to Jacksonville and let's get set to meet the bastard en route.'

'You telling me what to do now? You ain't got a day's worth of experience in the field and you're taking control of where we go next?'

'Jesus, Bambi, it's just common sense. It's—'

'I run my operation, Nicki. Me. You got that?'

'I—'

'Me. Now get the hell out of this office. Now!'

Dempsey remained motionless. For just a moment May did the same, standing her ground. There was much more going on here than he could know, Dempsey realised. A long history of . . . something. It had worsened what should have been a minor disagreement. Now it threatened to do more.

Threatened, but did not. Without another word, May turned and marched out of the room. She slammed the office door behind her. A moment later and O'Rourke retook her seat and reached for the desk phone.

Dempsey watched as she put the handset to her ear and was put through to a subordinate.

'Get us a jet,' he heard her say. 'I want to be in the air to Jacksonville within the hour.'

NO WAY TO DIE

O'Rourke put down the receiver and looked up at Dempsey with a smile.

'Can't stand for that kind of insubordination from anyone, son. Not in company. But a good idea's a good idea. Ain't no education in the second kick of a mule.'

THIRTY

6.45 p.m. EDT

Scott Turner took the lead as he and his two companions were taken to their booth.

The restaurant was quiet. Turner spotted just three occupied tables. Even now, months after the success of the Covid vaccine and with lockdown eased, eating out remained much less common than it had been.

Even with the strides that had been made in beating the virus and the overall success of the vaccination programme, Turner would have been lying to himself if he denied a preference for the restaurant's drive-through service. However low the risk of infection might now be, staying outside cut it even further. But with the company he was in, there was just no way he could have made that suggestion. For the fanatics of Liberation, care for their health came a very distant second to asserting their freedoms.

Except for the freedom to not die from stupidity.

'OK, gentlemen. This'll be your booth for this evening. I'm gonna leave you with some menus and your waitress, Diane, will be over to take your drinks order. OK?'

The hostess guided each man into the booth as she spoke. She placed Turner and Clemons on one side and Brooks on the other, careful as she did so to avoid any kind of physical contact. Turner and Clemons smiled in reply. Brooks, though, seemed irritated by the whole process.

'Is she gonna be dressed like bomb disposal, too?'

Brooks' question seemed to take the hostess by surprise. For a moment she just looked at him. Debating whether she should ask his meaning, Turner guessed. If that guess was correct, she seemed to decide against it.

'OK. You all have a nice meal now, fellas.'

'Goddamn ridiculous state of affairs.'

Turner looked across at Brooks. Unlike the hostess, he had no need to question what had upset his colleague. It would be the same thing it was yesterday evening, when they had eaten in Key Largo. And yesterday afternoon when they had stopped just outside Miami.

The same old scratched record. Masks. Handwash. Keeping a distance. Pretty much any sensible precaution, really.

Turner resisted the urge to shake his head. Brooks would notice, he was sure of it. Just as he was sure that it would lead to another disagreement. The man was a fanatic who could argue all day long against government control and the state's intervention in the lives of citizens and all the other craziness that obsessed him. There was nothing Turner could say that would dissuade him from his views.

Because dissent, he had discovered, only angered Brooks further.

Brooks and the rest of them.

Turner glanced off to his right. Towards the only two people he could see standing in the large, near deserted room. One of them was the hostess. She was speaking to the other – a younger woman, barely more than a girl – near to the kitchen doors. With no sign of any other serving staff, Turner guessed that the girl was their waitress.

Diane.

He was proved right just seconds later as he saw the hostess point towards their table, her expression unfriendly.

That'll be the usual Brooks warning, he thought. *Spit in the shrimp sauce for us, then.*

'These people. Every one of 'em. No fucking idea of how the world really works.'

Turner looked back to face Brooks. The man had been muttering under his breath since his comments to the hostess, words which Turner had happily missed. Now that they were louder he found it impossible to ignore them.

With an exaggerated sweep of his arm, Turner gestured to the room around them.

'What people, Kenny? There's no one here.'

'Exactly. Look how easily they've been controlled. By some bullshit, made-up virus. Look around everywhere we've been. Florida. Georgia. Now South Carolina. All of 'em. Empty stores. Empty diners. And a bunch of fucking sheep in masks. For what, huh? For control, that's what.'

Turner wanted to answer. He wanted to point out that Florida had been thriving precisely *because* it had closed down last year. In a stroke of luck, the state had elected its first Democrat governor of the twenty-first century in 2019. And so, at the outbreak of Covid-19, the state had shut down promptly and effectively, preventing the spread of the virus and allowing the economy to open up and recover quickly once the vaccination program was in full swing.

He also wanted to say that Summerville, South Carolina – where they were right now – had done the opposite to Florida.

This state's governor had ignored the directives from the White House. He had authorised the reopening of schools and colleges, of bars and restaurants, of everything President Knowles' team had recommended should stay shut to stop the spread.

He had done that before the pandemic was under control. And the result?

Just look around yourself.

Turner wanted to say these things, but he could not allow himself the pleasure. Brooks was an idiot – a nasty, ignorant fool – but then so was almost everyone who had joined Liberation in the last year. Conspiracy theorists and gun nuts. Low-hanging fruit, all of them. Plucked by Cam Arnold as soldiers for the small army he had put together.

Willing bodies for the cause.

Turner understood that Arnold needed men like Brooks. And men like Cliff Clemons, he had to remind himself. Clemons was far less vocal and a whole lot less vicious, but his beliefs were much closer to Brooks' than they were to Turner's.

Arnold needed these people, all of them, and Turner needed Arnold. It left him with no choice, then, but to tolerate the paranoid rants that somehow circled from coronavirus vaccinations to Chinese insurrection to the world-ending dangers of 5G technology and then back around again. With no option but to stay silent in the face of bizarre theories, from conspiracy within the White House itself to fantasies of the federal government brought crashing down by a coalition of the righteous.

To challenge these beliefs, as absurd as they were, could undermine everything Arnold had built. Turner could not risk that. Not now. Not when they were so close.

Everything comes with a price, he told himself often. *Why should manpower be different?*

'So, you boys ready with a drinks order?'

Turner looked up, happy for the interruption. He noticed that Clemons seemed just as relieved. For Brooks, it would be little more than a pause.

'Diane, is it?'

'It is.' Diane indicated the name tag on her shirt. 'Thanks for noticing. I like your accent. Australian?'

'It is,' Turner lied with a smile. He was used to his English accent being mistaken for something it was not. A combination of the American inflections it had picked up during his years in the US and of a general inability to place a dialect. And useful when travelling under the radar. 'I think we're ready to order drinks *and* food.'

'Well, that's great. The kitchen'll be pleased to be plating up for a change, instead of putting everything in plastic.'

'I noticed the queue of cars,' Turner replied. He was grateful for a moment of non-conspiracy-based conversation. Plus it would be a bonus to get Diane onside, if only to offset the spit potential caused by his association to Brooks. 'Has it been like that for a while?'

'Since about a month after the lockdown ended. We were busy as all hell to start. Then the infections went back up. Frightened people off. Now we never get fuller than this. Just a whole lotta takeout.'

'Ah, stop with the infection bullshit, would you?'

Turner, Diane and Clemons all turned towards Brooks.

'Just what the hell is wrong with you people? Can't you see when you're being played? You know this is all about the vaccine and what it can do to your DNA, don't you? Fucking sheep, every one of you.'

Diane's expression changed. As young as she was, she

seemed unwilling to tolerate the rudeness. Turner could see the anger in her face as she opened her mouth to answer. He acted first, before she could speak. The last thing he needed was a scene.

'So, Diane, we're gonna take two Sam Adams and a Coke, please.'

He spoke firmly, bringing attention back to him. Satisfied that he had interrupted in time, he made a show of looking at the menu, but with one eye on Diane as she composed herself from Brooks' rude interruption.

'Do you recommend the coconut shrimp, Diane?'

Another attempt to engage. To put Brooks' rudeness behind them. Turner waited for the waitress's focus to return to him. She took out her notebook and turned to him, although he noticed her eyes still furtively glancing over to Brooks.

But as irritated as she still was, her attention was back on the job.

'What do you think? Is it a good choice?'

'It's . . . yeah, yeah, it's our most popular appetiser.'

'That settles it, then. We'll start with two coconut shrimp and, I think, a langostino lobster dip with chips. Then for mains, we're gonna go with two blackened catfish and a New York strip. Plus French fries all round.'

Diane nodded. Her previous good humour was now gone. Not that Turner was surprised; Brooks could do that to anyone. Still, he regretted the change in atmosphere. He had been enjoying the conversation.

'That everything?'

'It is, yeah. Thanks, Diane.'

'OK.' She forced a smile. There would be no more friendly chat. 'The kitchen'll be right on it.'

'Who the hell do you think you are, ordering for me?' Brooks spoke as soon the waitress had stepped away. As ever, he made no attempt to keep his voice low. 'I'm a grown-ass man. I'll order my own goddamn meal.'

'Yeah, you really looked like you were focused on the menu.' Turner was reaching the limit of his patience. His voice became a hiss as he spoke again. 'If I'd let you go on, you'd have insulted half the restaurant and we'd have been asked to leave. Which, knowing you, would have involved the cops being called. You think that's a good idea, do you?'

'I wouldn't have—'

'You wouldn't have what? You can't help it, Kenny. You could start an argument in a fucking phone box. We can't have that. We need to stay on Cam's schedule and that means reaching Summit Hill in two days. Sooner if we can. You think we're gonna manage that with you kicking off every time we stop for a bite?'

Brooks stared back at Turner from across the table. He wanted to say something but he was stopping himself. Turner knew why. He had used Cam Arnold's name for a reason; a reminder of his own connection to the man Brooks seemed to idolise.

An awkward, angry silence fell between them. Turner was happy with that. Comfortable or not, it beat listening to more of Brooks' bullshit.

Clemons, though, seemed to think otherwise.

'So . . .' he began. He seemed unsure of what to say to break the silence, and when he spoke again, his faltering voice betrayed his nerves. 'You, er, you said "mains" back then when you meant entrées. Seemed like your English was showing a little there, weren't it?'

Turner looked towards Clemons. For a moment he was confused; it seemed a strange comment to make. Then it struck him.

He's changing the subject. Trying to distract Brooks from the argument.

The irony of Clemons' tendency to play peacemaker was not lost on Turner. For a member of a semi-militarised anti-government militia, his aversion to aggression was unusual. Did it show he wasn't really one of them, Turner had wondered in the past? That he was essentially human driftwood, somehow caught up in the rapids of Liberation?

Or maybe he's just shit-scared of Kenny Brooks?

Either way, Turner appreciated the effort to move things along.

'I thought my English was always showing,' he replied. 'Not that she placed it.'

'You really think I need reminding that I'm taking orders from a Limey?' Brooks' interruption was directed at Clemons. 'You might be fine with that, you little Yankee pussy. But it don't sit well with me.'

'Jesus, Kenny. Why does everything have to be a conflict, man?'

Clemons' tone was almost pleading but still Brooks seemed to take his words as a challenge. His hands came crashing down on to the table and he began to push himself up.

Bastard's just spoiling for a fight, Turner realised.

He reached out and gripped Brooks around his thick wrists.

'Either stay in your seat or leave, Kenny. But do what you're about to do and this mission's dead.' Turner could feel his heart pumping fast. He was trying hard to disguise his own fear. 'Your choice, pal. But if we're not where we need to be when the time comes? Well, I would not want to be you if that happens.'

Brooks eyed Clemons as Turner's words sunk in. Turner followed his gaze and saw that Clemons had backed into his seat, his face turned towards the floor.

'We're supposed to be a unit,' Turner continued. 'We're in this together, so this sort of shit, it's not helping. It's not helping at all. Now if you're as pissed off as you seem to be, how about you call it a night?'

Brooks slowly turned towards the younger man, his expression still angry.

'So I got to miss my meal because of this chicken shit?'

'No, you have to miss your meal because you can't be let loose in polite company. And that's on you, Kenny. Not me. And not Cliff. Besides, there's a vending machine at the motel. If you're hungry, use that.'

Turner watched his words hit home. He could see their effect. Brooks wanted to tear him apart with his bare hands. But he would not do it. Turner had the protection of being Cam Arnold's man and so Brooks' hands were tied.

Both men knew it and so for all Brooks' piercing stares and spoken threats, this was only going to end one way.

'Cam won't always need you, your lordship. You know that, right?'

'Then make sure you come see me when he doesn't.' Turner smiled as he spoke. A broad, confident grin. 'And I'll be waiting. Until then, you follow orders. Now go.'

The threat had done the opposite of what Brooks had intended. It had been meant to intimidate, yet all it had achieved was to confirm that – for now – Turner was safe.

He released Brooks' wrists and watched him leave. Then he

stood up, moved around the table to face Clemons and caught the eye of the waitress. He signalled for her to come over and then took his seat.

'Thanks for that.' Clemons spoke before Turner was even settled. 'That guy, he's just . . . he's just . . .'

'He's a dick,' Turner finished for him. 'But right now he's a useful dick. So we've got to tolerate him.'

'And what about when this is done? You're not afraid he'll come looking for you?'

'Let him.' Turner smiled again at the thought. At the images that crossed his mind. 'When this is done, Cliff, if he comes looking, he won't find me alone. And what he *does* find, it'll be a whole lot more trouble than he's ever known.'

Clemons nodded his head as if he understood. Which, Turner knew, he did not.

'Anyway, thanks again for stepping in. I owe you.'

'Don't mention it.'

'Can I help you, sir?'

Both men looked up; the waitress was back.

'Yeah, Diane, thanks. I just wanted to apologise for the manners of the guy we had with us. He's gone now. He won't be eating with us after all.'

'Well, that's a shame.'

'I think we all know that it's not.'

'Well, OK, then. If we're all on the same page.' Diane laughed as she spoke. 'Will you need his food coming off the order?'

'I don't think so,' Turner replied. 'It's been a long day. I think we can manage a little extra between us. Keep it all coming, Diane.'

'Consider it done.'

'You're not gonna get it boxed up for him?' Clemons asked.

'Not a chance. Like I said, there's a vending machine at the motel.'

'You're asking for trouble, Scott. That guy, he's not right.'

Turner took a moment to look at Clemons. To consider his comment. It felt like a strange one, coming from another extremist. But then Turner had always had his doubts that this description truly fit Cliff Clemons.

'You say that like you're surprised, Cliff. What did you expect to find when you joined up?'

'With Liberation, you mean? I . . . I don't really get what you're asking?'

'You know what the movement believes, Cliff. What Cam believes. And what he's willing to do too.'

'You mean that guard this morning? I never knew that was gonna happen, Scott. I never knew anyone was gonna get hurt. Did you?'

'No. No, I didn't.'

'Then you must have been as surprised as me.'

Turner was intrigued. He had assumed he was the only one shocked by Cam Arnold's actions that morning.

'Cliff, you must know what we're all here to do. What this mission is. You must have expected violence?'

'Not like *that* I didn't. I knew some people might get slapped round a little. But nothing serious. Not . . . not that.'

'But you're still here.'

'Where else am I gonna be? I'm in this now. What good will it do me to walk away? Besides, you're still here, ain't you?'

Turner smiled. He could not argue with the statement. Nor did he intend to. He had no urge to explain himself to Clemons. It was enough that he knew his companion a little better.

'Yeah. Yeah, I suppose I am. Proper pair of contradictions, aren't we?'

'Cam can pick 'em, huh? What a team. A super-smart English guy who uses words like "contradictions", a goddamn psychopath who wants to kill half the people he meets. And then me. Some guy who's not even sure why he's here any more.'

'You don't have to stay, Cliff. You don't have to take this risk. Not if you've changed your mind about all this. You could just disappear. I won't try to stop you.'

This time it was Clemons who smiled.

'Kind of you but I'll be honest, I ain't got nowhere else to be. Besides, we're in this together. We might as well see where it ends.'

THIRTY-ONE

6.50 p.m. EDT

O'Rourke stepped out of the sedan and onto the tarmac at Boca Chica Key. The car had brought her within twenty yards of a Gulfstream G500. Belonging to one of Key West's richest men, right now the plane was in the service of Homeland Security. A contribution from a local concerned citizen. Or at least it would be presented that way.

In reality, its billionaire owner had been given no choice. Homeland needed a plane, and this was the nearest one that matched O'Rourke's requirements.

Most of O'Rourke's team was already on board, along with Dempsey and Grace from the ISB. The engine was already running and so O'Rourke was surprised to see Sergio Vega and Nicki May still on the tarmac, just a few feet from the open door.

'What's happened?' O'Rourke shouted the question, an effort to be heard over the roar of the jet engines. 'The van been spotted?'

'No,' Vega shouted back. 'Still no sign.'

'Problem, then?'

'Not a problem,' Vega replied. 'Just something we've been discussing.'

'What is it?'

'It's the timing,' Vega explained. 'Nicki and I, we've been looking at it. And it doesn't make sense.'

'Whatever it is y'all are thinking, does it change the need to go north?'

Vega looked at May. She nodded her head to him. Permission to speak for them both.

'No. But it might affect where we go from there.'

'In that case, it can wait till we're in the air,' O'Rourke replied. 'We got to get this ship moving. And besides, I can't hear a damn word you're saying over the sound of those engines.'

'You mean you want me to come with you?' Vega seemed surprised.

'You're part of the team, ain't you? Now get your butt on board.'

Vega smiled and began to turn towards May. Whatever it was he had intended to say to her, O'Rourke cut him off.

'What's the matter, Sergio, engines made you deaf? Get on the damn plane. Nicki and I need to talk.'

Vega hesitated, his gaze shifted from O'Rourke to May and then back again. For a moment he seemed unsure, then he made up his mind. With a nod but without a word, he turned and boarded the jet.

O'Rourke did not watch him go. Her eyes were fixed on May.

'I'm sorry, Bambi,' May shouted before O'Rourke had a chance to speak. 'I went too far.'

'You're damned right you went too far, Missy.'

'I was just stressed about the way things were going. I lashed out.'

'I was there, honey. I know what you did.'

'I know. I just . . .'

'What's done is done, Nicki. Am I happy about it? No, no I ain't. And I'm a little sore you did it while the English guy was watching. But we ain't got time for this now. We've known each other too long and too well to let a little thing derail what we're here to do. So that's it done, understood? It's over.'

May smiled nervously.

'This is the part where I'd usually say "no hard feelings", right?'

'Don't go pushing it now.' O'Rourke wanted the distraction over. 'And what about your new friend? Sergio? His thing about the timings? Is it worth hearing?'

'Very much so.'

'Really? In that case, how much of it really is his thing?'

'Let's just call it a joint effort.'

'Yeah. That's what I thought. OK. Get yourself up those steps. You can bring me up to speed once we're in the air.'

THIRTY-TWO

6.53 p.m. EDT

'That'll be sixty-seven dollars and eighty-four cents for the gas, the water and the chips.'

The attendant spoke from behind a clear Perspex screen, with only a small opening at the bottom with room for both a card machine and cash.

Cam Arnold could not estimate the age of the barrier. It was worn and more than a little battered, with scratches and chips that suggested hard contact. The damage told Arnold that the screen was there to protect the attendant from robbery rather than what he still called 'the China Virus'.

A conclusion that had allowed him to stay civil.

He took a wad of cash from his pocket, counted off seventy dollars and told the attendant to keep the change. The rest went back into the clip and then back into his pants. He did not wait for a receipt.

There were two people in the queue behind him. The first was six feet from where Arnold stood, the second six feet more. Both were wearing masks.

Goddamn sheep.

Arnold turned and headed towards the exit, and as he moved

he walked within a few inches of both waiting customers. It was a deliberate act, designed to antagonise. Florida had no law requiring that a person had to be masked when inside a store, which meant these guys were wearing theirs by choice.

By choice.

The thought pissed Arnold off. It was not the kind of caution he had expected to find. Certainly not in Florida. And so he took pleasure in their discomfort as he breached social distance, coming uncomfortably close without a face cover of any kind.

Neither man said a thing as Arnold passed them. Both looked down, unwilling to meet his eye; Arnold was a muscular, imposing man, so their reticence did not surprise him. He was used to it. But it did give him the chance to study them. Just a moment each, but that was long enough for him to peg them both as part of the problem.

Each man was holding a credit card, ready to pay for their overpriced fuel directly from their instantly traceable bank accounts. That made them willing adherents to an interconnected system of control overseen by the governments and the corporations that together ran the world.

To Arnold, that made them every bit as unacceptable as the bastards who 'owned' them.

Bees in a hive. Waiting to be fucked and conditioned to say thank you when it happens.

He walked through the door, stepped outside and passed another waiting customer. The first of three, all of them forced to stand in a line outside due to the gas station's 'three customers at a time' rule. Yet another concession to the ridiculous constraints the US government had imposed in response to a staged pandemic. And yet another example of companies keeping those restrictions up when even the government had lifted them.

Corporate control. Even worse than Washington's bullshit.

Two of the three people in the line were maskless. The third – the only woman, standing in second position – was not.

Arnold shook his head as he walked back to his van. Even the six-feet distance the three were keeping irritated him. The fact they were obeying that instruction when it was no longer even a law. It had been bad enough during the lockdown, when people had stuck to the rules to avoid a fine. But this lot? Here and now?

Now they're doing it because it's suggested.

By their betters. By their rulers.

They're the problem. As much as the government. As much as big business. These fucking automatons, doing exactly as they're directed.

The Dodge Sprinter was parked at pump six, illuminated by both the dimming sun and the sodium lights of the gas station forecourt. The livery Arnold had applied with Paul Holly back at the Blue Cypress Conservation Area looked less fresh already. The Florida climate has that effect, Arnold knew. New becomes old real fast in the heat and the humidity of a swamp. And so the Savannah Parts Company signage looked as authentic as any other working vehicle.

It was exactly as it needed to be, under the old plan. Just another indistinct van, making its way along the Turnpike. Ready to attract a little attention when the time was right, before transforming into something new and blending back into the crowd. Or guerrilla tactics, as Arnold had explained it to Turner.

Make some noise now and again, he had said. *Keep their focus where we want it. Then, when we're ready, we spring the trap.*

The only problem, thanks to Paul Holly's death, was that the 'when we're ready' element had changed.

Arnold had moved on as soon as Holly's body had hit the bush, but he had not moved far. Once he was just a short distance out of Blue Cypress, he had stopped the van and waited. Irregular movement was built into the schedule, but this time Arnold needed it for another reason.

He needed time to think. To assess the impact of Holly's death and to determine the best way to proceed. Without Holly it was impossible to disguise the van again; applying the livery was a two-man job. It left Arnold with just one more 'attention-grabber'. One more time when he could draw focus before he stripped the van, changed the plates and moved to the final phase.

It was two transformations less than he had planned, which in turn meant a big leap forward in the schedule. Arnold had no doubt that he had done the right thing by shooting Holly – a weak link is a cancer and needs to be dealt with as soon as it's spotted – but still, he had to be sure that his people could deal with the change of pace.

Timing was everything. It was essential that Scott Turner reached Carbon County as the next player came onto the board – his expertise was key – and so that had to guide how and when Arnold next acted. And if Turner, Brooks and Clemons were on schedule, they would be more than a third of the way to Pennsylvania already, on track to hit Summit Hill by noon on the day after tomorrow.

The question, then, was would Turner react the right way when he saw the news? Would he know to hit the gas? Arnold had no way to warn the kid that the plan had moved up – with phones so easy to trace, any contact Arnold made with him would risk Turner's location being revealed – and so everything depended on Turner doing the right thing when the starter's pistol was fired early.

Arnold had been asking himself that for hours and the truth was, he just did not know. He was still struggling with the question when he heard the tone of a WhatsApp notification. He reached out for his phone, read the message and a grim smile spread across his face.

Well, that was well timed.

The decision was made.

Arnold reached out and tapped the screen on the Sprinter's satnav, to bring it alive. He reviewed his current location on the map – Whittier, Florida – before typing in his destination.

Fifty-six miles. An hour, give or take, if I head straight there.

A few more moments' thought. It was close to perfect. The timing. The distance.

Once the plates were changed and the signage was stripped off – once Arnold was back to a plain grey dodge – he could make his way slowly to where he needed to be. Hell, he could even park up somewhere dark, to give them the time they would need.

But first he had to give them one more signpost.

The thought made him laugh as he realised what he had yet to do. What he had failed to check.

A signpost ain't worth much if they can't see it.

He opened the door, stepped out of the van and walked towards the road, looking all around him as he moved. What he saw – or, more accurately, what he did *not* see – was a disappointment. Either there were no security cameras covering the forecourt, or they were well hidden enough that even he could not spot them.

Meaning there might only be the camera over the store entrance. And that ain't getting a clear shot of the van.

For a moment he reconsidered what he was about to do. Maybe it would be better somewhere else. Somewhere with more camera coverage.

Maybe . . .

Arnold found himself staring into the forecourt as he ran through the possibilities. His eyes drifted back to the line of customers. The first guy and the masked woman had now gone inside. It left the third guy, who remained mask-free, and two more customers who had joined him in the line.

Both in masks. Both keeping their six-feet distance.

Both of them part of the problem.

His eyes returned to the first man. The guy without a mask. And in that moment he made his decision. With his smile growing wider, he strode back to the Sprinter, opened the driver's door and took out his pistol.

THIRTY-THREE

6.08 p.m. CDT

Joshua kept the form of each press-up, squat thrust and tuck-jump combination perfect, even as his count approached thirty. He hated the name of the exercise – a burpee – but there was no better way to stay fit in the confines of his cell.

Twenty-five.

Twenty-six.

He was breathing hard but then he always did. Four sets of thirty at full intensity would have been an effort for an Olympian. So for a forty-six-year-old with no access to a gym? They were near torture.

Twenty-seven.

Twenty-eight.

Joshua had been in the Facility for almost four years. Or forty-three months, to be exact, and precision was important to a man like him. Forty-three long months with no word of or access to his family or to the world he knew. And then ahead of him, who knew how many more.

The intention for Joshua – as for every inmate – was that, sooner or later, he would die here.

In the years before his imprisonment, in the decade during

which he had made himself the most feared assassin on the planet, Joshua had heard talk of this place. Never more than rumours, they were tales of a prison for the very worst of the worst. A place which, by its very nature, had no former residents to confirm its reality.

Looking back, he had never dismissed the idea. It had made logical sense that such a place should exist. But he had given it little thought beyond that. He had certainly never expected to find himself here.

The day that Joshua had assisted in the shooting of a former American president had changed that. From that moment on, with his family under threat from his employer and with DDS agent Joe Dempsey hunting him from London to Belfast and finally to the Republic of Ireland, the Facility had been one of only two likely fates.

The Facility. Or death.

Death he had considered more likely. He knew that entanglements with Dempsey rarely ended any other way. And while he was very nearly proved correct, a combination of fine Irish medics and his own sheer will to live had seen him survive.

Looking back, he was not convinced that was quite the victory it had seemed at the time.

Twenty-nine.

Thirty.

Joshua's feet landed for the last time and he immediately doubled over and grasped his ankles, stretching his hamstrings tightly.

Maintaining his physical fitness had been essential from day one. The legend of Joshua carried many advantages, none more prevalent than a fearsome reputation for violence. That legend made his day-to-day life easier than it was for most, but it was inevitable that it would occasionally be tested.

Knowing what would lie ahead, since his arrival he had done all he could to reach and maintain his physical peak. It was no easy task. His age and the injuries he had sustained from his showdown with Dempsey were high hurdles. But he had overcome them both and, in a short time, he had established his position at the top of the Facility's hierarchy of violence.

With hindsight, he wished he had allowed himself to be just another inmate. Because by being the alpha, he had attracted the attention of Peyton Travis.

And Peyton Travis came with complications.

Pulling himself upright, Joshua took a few moments to stretch off his chest and his triceps before heading for the large basin in the corner of the room. Like the toilet, it was behind an opaque partition and so he had a little privacy as he soaked a large flannel, lathered it with soap and used it to wash down his bare torso.

It was a welcome moment of isolation that was not to last.

'Turn the tap off, would you? I'm trying to watch Fox News.'

Joshua looked at his own reflection and noticed his brow had furrowed. A sign of his confusion. He walked to the end of the partition and looked around. The TV had been on as he'd exercised, but he had paid no attention to what was showing.

And nor, he had assumed, had Travis.

'Since when did you start watching TV?' Joshua asked. 'And when the hell did you start to listen to the news? I thought it was all bullshit.'

'It is,' Travis replied, distracted by what was on-screen. 'But sometimes even an idiot box can be useful. I want to hear this.'

Joshua did as he was told. Not from any sense of obedience – ordinarily a 'domestic' instruction from Travis would elicit the opposite response – but because he was intrigued. Travis hated television.

Joshua, then, wanted to know why this bulletin was an exception.

The report was half done as Joshua began to listen, but he quickly caught up with the main details. A shooting at a service station in Florida, two guards killed, unprovoked gunfire, suspect armed and dangerous. Nothing too unusual, as far as he could tell.

He looked back towards Travis as the story came to an end.

'You know something about that?'

Travis said nothing. He hit mute on the remote and picked up his book.

'That a yes, is it?'

No answer.

'This mean I can expect more trouble, then?'

Travis did not even look up.

'Wonderful,' Joshua said, this time to himself. 'Just wonderful. Thanks for the heads-up.'

He moved back to the basin, re-soaked the flannel and started where he had left off.

THIRTY-FOUR

7.32 p.m. EDT

Eden Grace closed the final page of the manila file and looked straight ahead, towards Dempsey. He was already looking back, as if waiting for Grace to finish. A near-identical yellow file sat on the empty seat to his right.

'What do you make of it?'

'There's no more in there than we already have,' Dempsey replied. 'Yours?'

'Less. Same material on Cam Arnold and on the history of Liberation as was in ours. Not as much on current members. There's no mention of Scott Turner in here at all. They don't seem to know he exists.'

'And who exactly is Scott Turner?'

The question caught both Dempsey and Grace unawares. Neither had noticed O'Rourke approach. It was hardly a surprise; unlike the Homeland team, they were seated towards the rear of the Gulfstream G500 fuselage and so were closest to its engines. It was a luxurious way to fly, sure. But it was far from silent. The sound of the PW814 engine now powering the plane to five hundred and sixty miles per hour had easily drowned out the agent's footsteps, but not their voices.

Dempsey glanced back to Grace and raised an eyebrow. An instruction to follow his lead.

'He's just a name in our files,' Dempsey lied. 'Believed to be a member of Liberation.'

'You think he's one of our guys? One of the four with Arnold?'

'Statistically unlikely,' Grace offered. 'By your own count there are at least two hundred members of Liberation now following Arnold. Chances of any particular one of them being in the four, they're not high.'

'But he could be.'

'He could be, yeah,' Dempsey replied.

'Then tell me about him.' O'Rourke took a seat across from the two agents. 'If he means enough that you're discussing him, then I need to have heard of him too, right?'

Dempsey gave Grace an almost imperceptible nod. She knew its meaning. They had done all they could. With O'Rourke now looking for details, they could no longer hold back without being overtly dishonest.

The time had come to throw Scott Turner to the wolves.

'We think it's unlikely that Turner would be with them,' Grace explained, 'because he's no field guy. He's a brain. When he was recruited, he was a student at MIT. Not top of his class or anything like that, but still bright as hell. And he's certainly as capable as Liberation could want.'

'Capable at what?'

'At nothing that bodes well. Turner was a nuclear physics specialist. Theoretical and practical. If he's a man with bad intentions then he's the last person we want laying his hands on any quantity of caesium-137. And we sure as hell don't want him having a ton of the stuff.'

O'Rourke nodded her head as she cast her eyes upwards, to the plane's ceiling. She seemed to be considering what she had just been told. A few seconds more and she was ready to continue.

'And your theory on why he's not with them now?'

'Because assuming he *is* their weapons guy,' Dempsey offered, 'then it's likely they're taking the caesium to him. There's no way he could have weaponised it in those missing thirty minutes in Key West. No one could have. If they'd just holed up once they reached the mainland then yeah, he could be with them and he could be at work. But they haven't been holed up, have they? They're still moving. Have been all along. And that must mean the un-weaponised material is being taken north. Why would Arnold risk doing that if the guy who can do the job is sitting on the seat right next to him?'

O'Rourke took a few moments to consider Dempsey's conclusion.

'What about if he's had more than the missing thirty?' she finally asked. 'Not holed up the whole time, maybe. But still, a few hours here and there?'

'I don't follow?'

'Something Nicki and Sergio were just saying. About the distance travelled.'

'What about it?'

'We have them hitting the mainland just before eight forty a.m. Then we have them at Fort Drum at ten to four this afternoon. That's seven hours to drive two hundred miles in a straight line. Absolute worst ways, distance like that, it's a four-hour journey. You and me, we'd been thinking the delay was them stopping to keep things irregular, make it harder for us to spot the van once it was disguised. But what if we were wrong? What if they needed those hours for something else?'

'You mean something like bomb-making?'

'That was their theory.' O'Rourke indicated to May and Vega, at the far end of the fuselage with the Homeland team. 'I didn't think it made much sense, since it would need someone who was capable of weaponising the stuff. But if this Scott Turner fella is with them . . .'

Grace felt her blood run cold.

'Then they could have used that time to build the bomb,' she said, concluding the thought O'Rourke had left hanging.

'That doesn't make sense.'

Grace turned to Dempsey. She was hopeful of what he might say. That he would prove O'Rourke wrong. It was not personal. She just did not want a one-ton dirty bomb travelling unseen on the American mainland.

None of them did.

'Why not?' O'Rourke asked.

'It's a waste of the caesium. The van, there's only so much it can carry. And a ton of caesium is only as damaging as its blast radius. A Dodge Sprinter, on top of that one ton, it's not carrying enough explosives to do justice to that much radioactive material. With that limit on payload, a tenth of that much caesium would do as much damage as the whole lot.'

Grace looked from Dempsey to O'Rourke, waiting for her reaction. Grace's education in radiated conventional weapons was barely a few hours old, but still, what Dempsey had said made sense to her. She just hoped that O'Rourke would agree.

'We're assuming common sense and logic on this lot, are we, son?'

'From what I've seen so far, yeah,' Dempsey replied. 'And from what I know of Scott Turner.'

'OK. In that case, yeah. That makes sense. Which means

either they're not going to waste that much caesium on one bomb. Or . . .'

'Or they've unloaded the rest of it already,' Dempsey concluded. 'Which would mean they've shifted ninety per cent of it to another vehicle or to storage or whatever. And they're driving a single mobile WMD.'

Grace felt her pulse quicken. She had been hoping that Dempsey's analysis would make things better, not worse. That optimism had gone as he continued to speak.

'Which could explain why we only saw two men at Fort Drum.'

'It could.'

None of the three spoke for a moment. For Grace, the enormity of what they could be facing was just sinking in. She assumed the same was true of Dempsey and O'Rourke. That they, like her, were now grasping for some easier conclusion. When neither one spoke, she filled the silence.

'All of this . . . it's all just conjecture right now, surely?'

'It is, yeah,' Dempsey agreed. 'But it's also as likely as any other possibility. And it's more likely than most. Which means we have to proceed as if it's a fact.'

'Agreed.' O'Rourke's voice was quiet. 'Now what do we—'

'O'Rourke, you need to hear this.'

The interruption came from May, still at the front end of the fuselage. O'Rourke got to her feet and turned towards her. Dempsey and Grace did the same.

'What is it?'

'It sounds like it's Cam Arnold. If it is, he's done it again.'

'Done what, exactly?'

'He's shot up a gas station. In Whittier, outside of Orlando. Five people dead, one survivor.'

'You've got to be kidding me?'

'I'm really not.'

O'Rourke was silent for a moment and so Dempsey stepped in.

'You said outside of Orlando. North or south?'

'South.'

'How far?'

'Fifty miles, give or take.'

'That's hundreds of miles south of where he should be by now, if he's making his way out of state.'

'My thoughts exactly,' May replied. 'Added to what we were just discussing, I'm not convinced he is planning to leave Florida at all.'

'How sure are we that it was him?' O'Rourke asked.

'There's security footage being uploaded right now.' This time it was Vega who replied. 'But from the description? It sounds like him. Right down to the grey Dodge Sprinter with decals and out-of-state plates.'

Dempsey and May locked eyes. Almost as one, they turned back to O'Rourke.

'We need to turn this plane around,' May said.

'Why?'

'Bambi, he's driving a van-sized radioactive bomb. He's had all the time in the world to arm the thing and now he's fifty miles outside of the biggest tourist trap on the planet. That can't be a coincidence.'

O'Rourke said nothing, her eyes widening as she considered what May had suggested. It was clear that she had not considered the possibility of Florida's theme parks as targets. A moment later and she had made her decision.

She walked to the plane's intercom and connected to the cockpit.

'Turn this plane around now. We're going to Orlando.'

THIRTY-FIVE

7.40 p.m. EDT

Dempsey noticed himself squinting as he looked at his tablet screen. A pointless effort to see more than the gas station camera had recorded. After four views, he had witnessed all that it had to show him.

Which is not very much. And sure as hell not enough.

Grace was once again on the seat across from him, with O'Rourke and her entourage now back at the other end of the plane. The two ISB agents had divided the work between them, with Grace reading the report on the shooting while Dempsey studied the footage.

Both had finished more quickly than anticipated.

'The camera, it's all interior,' Dempsey said. 'I can see it's Arnold and I can see he just walks in and starts shooting. But I can't see how or where it begins, or any of what happens outside.'

'According to the witness report, that's where the shooting started,' Grace replied. 'Outside. Do the customers in the store not react to the sound of gunfire?'

'No way to tell. The camera's literally positioned to cover the door. Anyone inside, they're not on-screen.'

'Well, that's a hell of a system they've got set up.'

'Not exactly state of the art, no. So what else does the report say?'

'Nothing you don't already know. The murdering bastard walked right up the line of customers outside and just started firing. Five dead. Two outside, three inside. Only one person left alive.'

'Any indication how they survived?'

'What do you mean?'

'I mean were they shot and injured? Or were they untouched?'

Grace checked her file.

'Untouched.'

'Customer or staff?'

'Customer. The only attendant on duty is one of the dead.'

'Man or woman?'

'The attendant or the survivor?'

'The survivor, Eden.'

'Man.'

'And that man, was he inside or outside when the shooting happened?'

'He was outside. Is that important?'

'Could be. Was he in the line or was he filling up with petrol?'

'He was in the line. Everyone there, other than Arnold and the attendant, was a customer waiting to pay. Why does that matter?'

'I'm just making sense of the facts. Cam Arnold's no fool, especially with a gun in his hand. Five years in the Marine Corps. And he left behind an impressive military jacket, right?'

'He saw a lot of action, yeah.'

'And by all accounts he was good.'

'Yeah. Seems to have been.'

'OK. Then apply what we know to that person. He takes down five people – all in a gun-heavy state like Florida, so he can't be assuming no one's going to fire back – but then he leaves one unharmed?'

'Maybe . . .'

Dempsey waited for Grace to finish, but she did not. He knew her well enough to know why. Whatever theory she had been about to raise, she had already analysed and rejected it. It was a reminder of how fast her mind could work and how suited she was to the ISB.

When Grace stayed silent, Dempsey continued.

'And remember, if the shooting started outside then Arnold had to pass the survivor on the way in and again on the way out? All while he was firing his weapon. And yet he let the guy live. He let him off without a scratch, even. And he did that both times. Does that sound like any spree killing you've ever heard of?'

'No,' Grace replied. 'No, it doesn't.'

'Exactly right. We need to look again at the survivor. Odds are, Arnold left him unharmed for a reason.'

Grace did not respond immediately.

Another trait that makes her so suited to the work, Dempsey thought. *She thinks things through before she speaks and before she acts. All too rare.*

The thought process did not take her long. A moment later and she understood.

'You're not thinking the survivor was a friend or a . . .'

'Could be anything,' Dempsey replied. 'We rule nothing out. But it's unlikely, no. That petrol station, it seems like a pretty random selection. So while we have to look for a connection, it strikes me as more likely he left that person alive for another reason.'

'You got a theory, Boss?'

'I've got the beginnings of one.'

'Care to share?'

'It's just . . . you notice how much Cam Arnold seems to like a camera?'

Grace thought for a moment.

'You mean at Fort Drum?'

'I mean everywhere. Ricardo Garcia, killed in view of the only camera covering the marina. Then the services. And now he leaves a near perfect eyewitness alive for no apparent reason, on the one occasion when there're no cameras to do the job for him.'

'You think he *wants* to be seen?'

'I do,' Dempsey replied. 'Now we just have to work out why.'

THIRTY-SIX

8.16 p.m. EDT

Cam Arnold reached for the air conditioning temperature control, pressed down and continued the pressure until the gauge changed from a number to a single misspelled word.

'Lo'.

The cold air hit hard. Every vent that could be manipulated to face the driver's seat had been. It was overkill even for the wet Florida heat – the van told him that it was still eighty-one degrees on the other side of his windows, a ridiculous temperature for the hour – but it wasn't the weather that was causing Arnold to sweat.

Arnold had spent the last twenty minutes at the rear of the parking lot at Orange County Convention Centre. A short wait, but a necessary one; the journey from Whittier had been quicker than expected. Less than an hour, including the time it had taken for him to strip the van bare of its signage and switch the plates one final time.

It had placed him well ahead of his hastily re-worked schedule.

The next step of the plan was its most dangerous, because

from the moment he left the parking lot, Arnold had little control. For that reason, the timing had to be perfect.

He did not have far to travel – three miles at most – but by now he could expect every pair of law enforcement eyes to be searching for him. Arnold had done enough, he was sure, to signpost his destination. The shootings alone should have done that, but if they had not then his contingency would have kicked in.

They would know by now where he was heading. They would know where the threat was directed. It was essential to the proper working of the plan that they did, but it also made every moment he was back on the road a risk.

Arnold would do everything he could to come through this next stage alive. Not because he feared death – he had no wish to die, but he did not fear it – but because if *he* failed then the whole scheme failed with him. Everything he believed in depended on the next thirty minutes and on the web he had woven to achieve his goal.

It was enough pressure to cripple a normal man. And enough to make Cam Arnold sweat.

He used a handful of paper towels – left over from Paul Holly's KFC bucket – to wipe the dripping perspiration from the back of his head, before opening his door and dropping them onto the concrete floor of the parking lot. The heat that rushed in, even from just that moment, cancelled out the effects of the A/C.

It quickly recovered once the door was closed again.

Arnold leaned back into his seat and took a deep breath. It helped to clear his head and to lower his heart rate. Another breath and it was lower again. A third and he felt almost like himself. Almost calm.

It did not last. The sound of a WhatsApp tone made him reach out for his phone, his heartbeat rising again. The message was short and displayed on the locked home screen.

'Team in air, heading to target. Ten mins.'

Arnold stared at it for a few seconds. Long enough for his nerves to resurface.

Another deep breath and he pushed them back down.

Time to do this.

Putting the van into reverse, he manoeuvred out of the space, shifted to drive and began to move slowly towards the exit that would place him on Orlando's International Drive.

THIRTY-SEVEN

8.25 p.m. EDT

O'Rourke pressed the headphones tight against her ears as the Bell 407 helicopter banked sharply. She listened hard for a connection, doing her best to ignore the churning feeling in her gut and lower throat.

The journey from Orlando International Airport to International Drive was barely ten miles direct, but by road it was closer to thirteen. And since the only thing O'Rourke was sure of right now was that Cam Arnold was not flying, they had to follow the traffic below to have any chance of spotting him.

The long, sweeping highways that separated Florida's tourist attractions from one another did not make for an easy journey. The repeated sharp banks and lurches were not kind, not to O'Rourke's stomach or to anyone else's.

So far the discomfort had been without reward. Just a minute or two from their destination, they had seen nothing.

'How far out are you?'

O'Rourke was forced to shout her question into her mic over the roar of the rotor blades. It was directed at Joe Dempsey, currently in a second chopper with Eden Grace and two agents from O'Rourke's team, and heading towards Buena Vista Drive.

The two agents, though miles apart, were connected via their mobiles, with the signal patched through to their respective headphones.

'Seven miles to go for us. Following the I-4 like you said.'

'And no sign?'

'You'd already know if there had been. Anything from the local police?'

'Same answer as yours.'

O'Rourke looked around as she spoke. Her companions – two male agents plus Nicki May and Sergio Vega – would want to know what Dempsey was saying, but none of their headsets were tuned in to the same signal; theirs were on a passenger signal that ran through the chopper's central console. It was a lack of news that was easily relayed, though, and so O'Rourke did not need to explain over the deafening sound of the helicopter. Instead she just shook her head. Then she pointed down, indicating for her team to keep their focus on the street below.

They had a van to find.

She took a deep breath and returned to the call.

'I hope your gut's as reliable as you were convincing, Mr ISB.'

'It's the only run that makes sense,' Dempsey replied. Like O'Rourke, his reply was almost a shout. 'They're the only two targets right now. It's got to be one or the other.'

'I'm counting on your instincts, son.'

'It's the right call. Your own team think so too.'

O'Rourke nodded her head in agreement and instinctively glanced towards May. As O'Rourke's protégée and one of the few people she trusted completely, May had backed Dempsey's call.

Hell, she came up with the broadest part of it.

Both May and Dempsey *were* right. O'Rourke was sure of that.

The movement of the Dodge Sprinter was only logical if it was bringing Cam Arnold to Orlando. Why else take the route he seemed to have followed? And why else take whatever time-consuming detour he had, other than to offload the excess caesium and weaponise the van-sized explosive device he was now driving?

And just where the hell else could he be heading?

It was not the only possibility. O'Rourke knew that. But it was the worst one. And it was the most immediate. And so, as Dempsey had said, they had to proceed as if it were a certainty.

With that settled, the targets as good as chose themselves.

Ask any person in the Western world to name a tourist destination in Florida, odds are the answer will be Disney. It was logical, then, for Arnold to be aiming for one of the big parks. A little research and that was narrowed down further. Magic Kingdom, though the most well known, could be ruled out. It was remote. Hard to reach from the massive parking area and so protected by distance from a normal blast radius. Epcot was unlikely too, for much the same reason.

But Hollywood Studios and Animal Kingdom? Their parking lots were right outside their entrances. A dirty bomb in the back of a van there would cause untold damage and a catastrophic loss of life. The perfect choice.

Except for one thing: right now, neither one was open. It was close to 8.30 p.m., thirty minutes after the gates closed and a solid two hours since the bulk of the guests would have started to leave. And while there was no guarantee that Arnold was going to act tonight – O'Rourke had already argued that, in all likelihood, he would already be holed up somewhere, ready to act tomorrow – they had to assume the worst.

They had to assume that whatever he was going to do was imminent. And that narrowed down the possibilities.

It was Dempsey who had done the maths, building on May and Vega's reasoning to focus on the most likely targets. For a night-time attack, he had argued, there were only two real possibilities: Disney Springs and Universal Resort's CityWalk. Two huge social and retail magnets, filled to the brim with shops, restaurants, bars, clubs and who knows what else.

Both overflowing with tourists and guests on a hot July night.

And both easily accessible by road.

He's right, O'Rourke reassured herself. *If it's tonight, it's one or it's the other.*

The Bell 407 banked again. Left this time. It caused O'Rourke to look outside. To their right was a large man-made volcano which, even in the dark, looked to have an enormous water park surrounding it.

And straight ahead?

Rollercoasters. Lots of rollercoasters.

'We're just reaching Universal now,' O'Rourke said, into her mic. 'I'll contact you with an update as soon as we have anything.'

'Still six more minutes for us,' Dempsey replied, 'but I'll do the same.'

O'Rourke felt herself nod again. A pointless gesture in a conversation where she could not be seen.

'I'll be waiting to hear. Good luck.'

'The same to you.'

She clicked off the phone connection, rejoined the closed

audio group within the chopper and, as she spoke, she looked from agent to agent.

'This could be it, so be ready for anything. We take this sonofabitch alive if we can. But if we can't, I don't want anyone losing sleep over a kill. You got that?'

All four members of O'Rourke's team spoke as one, confirming their understanding of their orders.

'Ma'am.'

'Good. Now let's get this done.'

THIRTY-EIGHT

8.28 p.m. EDT

Tony Sheehan walked out of the 7-Eleven, holding up two Ben & Jerry's cookie dough sandwich bars and two bottles of Coke as he headed back to the patrol car. A display for his partner. The sound of a chopper overhead made him look up. It was unusual to get them so close to the parks.

The distraction, though, lasted just a moment.

'You trying to kill me or something, Sheehan?' Sergeant Billy Valentine of the Orlando Police Department was only half-joking. 'I'm supposed to be watching my figure. What happened to the ice pop?'

'Ah, come on, Sarge. You can't say no to cookie dough.'

'I know I can't. That's the damn problem.'

Valentine took the ice cream sandwich and the sodas as Sheehan climbed back behind the wheel and started the engine.

'You want me to open this for you?'

'Please, Sarge.'

Sheehan manoeuvred the patrol car backwards, shifted gears and began to make his way out of the lot. International Drive was immediately ahead, with Universal Boulevard crossing it around two hundred yards further along to the left.

Sheehan was signalling right, and so his attention was on the traffic from that direction as Valentine passed him the already melting ice cream. He took it absent-mindedly, his focus already on something else.

'Sarge, what was that BOLO again?'

Sheehan did not take his eyes from the oncoming traffic as he spoke.

'Grey Dodge Sprinter, 2018 model. Last seen all signed up as a Savannah Parts Company, but might have stripped them or replaced them. Two men in the front cab, three in the rear. Driver is either a big guy with a military cut and a black T-shirt, or a smaller guy wearing a white polo shirt and a Gators baseball cap.'

Valentine reeled off the details from memory. As of the last half hour, every patrol car in Orlando had been instructed to be on the lookout for the vehicle and the men he had just described. The same BOLO had been repeated five times since then and so the meaning was clear.

This one was serious.

Valentine followed Sheehan's eyeline as he spoke and would have seen why the patrolman had asked the question. Heading towards them – just yards away, about to pass in the direction of Universal Boulevard – was a grey Dodge Sprinter.

'Only one guy up front,' Sheehan observed as the van crossed their path. 'Buzz cut, black top.' He turned to Valentine. 'Wrong numbers, right description. Your call, Sarge.'

'Follow him.'

Sheehan threw his untouched ice cream sandwich from his open window and did as his sergeant instructed.

Cam Arnold signalled to turn right. The junction with

Universal Boulevard was just ahead. That placed him maybe two minutes from the start of Universal Resort. Three and he'd be directly outside CityWalk.

Whole lot further than I thought I'd get.

The traffic signals ahead were red as he waited to turn. He glanced in his side-mirror as he waited, just in time to see the Orlando Police patrol car he had passed moments earlier pull left onto International Drive.

The same patrol car that had been signalling right, Arnold observed. He felt his stomach tighten. There had to be a reason they had changed their mind.

And that reason had to be him.

'You see the patterns in the dirt?'

Sheehan was driving at ten miles per hour. A reasonable speed to approach a red traffic light, it gave Valentine some breathing space. Thinking time before he had to make a decision.

'No,' Sheehan replied. 'What you seeing?'

'Look closer. The streaks running down through the dirt. You follow them back up, you see a big square patch on either rear door where the paint's cleaner than it is either above or below.'

Sheehan brought the patrol car to a halt, just a few yards behind the Sprinter.

'You think something was covering the doors?' he asked.

'Could be. A temporary decal would account for that, wouldn't it? Something about a Savannah auto-parts shop, maybe?'

'I guess it would.' Sheehan looked down. 'What were the plates we're looking for?'

'Georgia plates. Savannah again. PQQ1 151.'

'These ones are local. Orlando CYD 193.'

'You don't think they'd change the plates when they stripped off the signs?'

'Yeah. Yeah, I guess so. So what do you think?'

'I think we don't have much choice, Tony. Hit the lights.'

Sheehan did as he was instructed. The single wail of the patrol car's siren coincided with the illumination of its dark red lamp.

Valentine stepped out of the car and stood to his full, imposing height. A hard stretch, alleviating the lower back compression that came from a shift spent in a seat. A moment later and he was down again, as he lowered his head back through.

'Call the stop in, run the plates and coordinate with the BOLO. If this is our guy, they're gonna want to know.'

Arnold felt a rush of adrenaline at the sound of the siren and the sight of the red light.

It was a welcome release.

He had been on edge since the death of Paul Holly. The loss of his second man – necessary as it had been – had impacted his schedule. And in doing that it had created uncertainty. Doubt as to when the inevitable confrontation would occur.

Now he knew, and the injection of his fight or flight hormone had transformed his nervous anticipation into something far more pleasurable.

It's about goddamned time.

Using his right-hand mirror, he watched as the patrol car's passenger stepped out. A big man in a sergeant's uniform. Six-five or thereabouts, weighing around two fifty. Maybe more.

Arnold's SIG had not left his side since the gas station back in Whittier. He had switched out the used magazine and replaced it with a full seventeen-round clip since the shooting, but otherwise it had remained untouched. Just waiting for the moment he would need it again.

That moment had arrived.

A glance to his left-hand mirror confirmed that the driver of the vehicle had remained in place.

He's calling in the stop.

That process would include running the plates, which would – Arnold knew – come back as belonging to a black 2010 Chevrolet Camaro. It was an intentional attribution rather than a mistake. One designed to ensure that *this* would be the stop that triggered the end.

Not that it's gonna take the plates. Not after this . . .

'CYD 193. Yeah, local plates. Fast, would ya?'

Sheehan watched as Valentine approached the Dodge. The sergeant was moving slowly and with caution, his right hand carefully placed on the butt of his pistol. He moved from the passenger's side to the driver's side and began the short walk from the vehicle's rear to its front.

The patrol car's dashcam was recording exactly what Sheehan could see, but it was providing no sound. Luckily for him, it was not needed. If there was one thing Valentine could do, it was shout.

'STAY IN THE VEHICLE AND KEEP YOUR HANDS ON THE WHEEL.'

The police sergeant was moving steadily as he shouted his instructions to the unseen driver. He was now just yards from the cab, following the procedure for a traffic stop exactly, just with added aggression and a whole lot more caution.

Sheehan could only hope that would be enough.

'HANDS WHERE I CAN SEE THEM.'

Valentine had not hesitated as he strode forward, which suggested to Sheehan that the driver was obeying the shouted instructions. All patrolmen were trained to use a vehicle's side-mirrors to their advantage; they provided a clear view of the person inside. Large van mirrors worked best and it seemed from the sergeant's body language that whoever was inside was doing as instructed.

'Bravo Two Two Delta, this is dispatch.'

Sheehan's eyes flicked down to the radio. He put the mic back to his mouth.

'This is Bravo Two Two Delta. Go.'

'Results on Orlando Index Plate CYD 193. That's a negative on the description you gave. CYD 193 is registered to a black Camaro, Bravo Two Two Delta. Repeat, black Camaro.'

Sheehan was moving by the time he heard the word 'negative'.

He was out of the car before the repetition of 'Camaro'.

And he was moving towards Valentine – his voice raised to its maximum – before he could hear the second transmission, designed to stop him.

'Bravo Two Two Delta, this is dispatch. We have your location. Backup is imminent. Until it arrives do NOT engage. I repeat. Do NOT engage.'

From where he sat, Arnold could watch the large police sergeant without taking his eyes from his waiting pistol. The shape of the Sprinter's display console allowed for that; it rose to a peak just ahead of the steering wheel, which had allowed him to place his SIG on the plastic slope that headed back down towards the bottom of the vehicle's windscreen.

It was a poor design, given the standard stop protocol of most police departments. It allowed someone like Arnold to place their hands on the wheel while keeping their weapon just inches from their fingertips. That in turn made someone like the approaching sergeant far more vulnerable than they deserved to be.

For Arnold, it was a design flaw that made the Dodge pretty much perfect.

He kept his hands still, resting lightly on the wheel but careful not to grip it; a grip could cost him moments and, with what was about to happen, moments mattered.

The patrolman was just yards away, as visible to Arnold in the side-mirror as Arnold was to him. From here it was clear that his hand was not just resting on his pistol; it was wrapped around the butt with a forefinger on the trigger, ready to be drawn and used in an instant. Arnold felt the threat of a smile, brought on by a mental image of a quick-draw shoot-out between himself and the inevitably slower man.

And then, in an instant, the thought was gone.

Arnold saw the activity before the cop heard it. And so his hands were off the wheel as the first shout made the patrolman turn.

'SARGE! DRAW DOWN! NOW!!'

It was a natural human reaction for the big man to do what he did next. It was also the very worst choice he could have made.

The patrolman was already looking away as Arnold gripped

his SIG. He had stopped in his tracks, less than two yards from the driver's door, and he had turned to face the shouter.

The big patrolman's movement gave Arnold no more than an extra second. But with the difference between life and death just a fraction of that time, it made the outcome inevitable. The driver's door was open and Arnold was halfway out before the first cop could turn back to face him.

The patrolman went down with the first three shots, delivered from feet away and clustered in his chest. A quarter of a second at most. As he fell, it took just a slight readjustment of Arnold's arm to move his bead from one cop to the other.

The extra distance meant nothing to his aim. Three more shots, this time from five yards instead of one. Just as quick and all equally grouped around the second man's heart. The younger cop was dead before he could lift the pistol that now dropped clear of his right hand.

Arnold lowered his weapon and looked around. There was no traffic behind him, but what had happened could not have been missed by the cars moving along Universal Boulevard, or by those that were now held at a signal as they waited to turn left towards the resort.

Arnold did not give them a second thought. His focus was already elsewhere: on the fact that the second cop had called in the stop.

Which means more of them are on their way.

THIRTY-NINE

8.29 p.m. EDT

'I don't give a shit what permissions you do or don't have. I want this chopper put down in that road. And I want it done now.'

O'Rourke turned from the pilot to May.

'Make sure he gets us down there. No excuses.'

O'Rourke did not wait for a response. She was used to being obeyed and had no fear that May would disappoint. Instead, she turned her attention to her headphones. She switched frequency from the helicopter's closed audio group and connected instead to her mobile.

The call was answered on the first ring.

'You have him?' Joe Dempsey did not waste time on niceties.

'We will shortly,' O'Rourke replied. 'Turn that boat round and get yourself to Universal Boulevard. You were right, he's coming for CityWalk.'

'You're sure?'

'Cops stopped a grey 2018 Dodge Sprinter with indications its signage had been stripped, a driver matching Arnold's description and plates associated to a 2010 Camaro. Good enough for you?'

'And then some. We're on our way.'

O'Rourke cut the line without another word. A moment later and she felt the front end of the Bell 407 lurch downwards. They were descending. And they were doing it fast.

She gripped the handle above the door for stability and switched back to the closed audio group, just as the pilot began to speak.

'Special Agent O'Rourke, I've heard from dispatch at the Orlando PD. Something's wrong. They've lost contact with the unit that called in the Dodge. What should I do?'

'Put us down.'

O'Rourke had already considered all possibilities. She looked around at her team.

'Either Arnold's guys have taken down the unit or the unit have taken them. My money's on option one. If that's correct it means they're turning right and coming up here any minute now. When they do that, they find us. You all ready for this?'

'Ma'am.'

The team spoke as one. Even Vega. It was exactly as O'Rourke would expect. They were primed and ready to act.

There was nothing more she could ask from them or say to them. All four were now armed with automatic Colt M4 Carbine assault rifles with two backup pistols each. The same fire power as the team with Dempsey, all supplied by the Orlando PD's SWAT unit before they had boarded the two police choppers. Vega had assured O'Rourke that he was familiar with the weaponry. She knew for herself that the other three had had all the training they needed.

This was happening. And they could not have been better prepared.

Shame that don't guarantee a win.

The police report had noted only one man in the cab of the Dodge. A man matching Arnold's description, but still a man alone. It was, though, no assurance on the numbers faced. O'Rourke had seen the tapes. Five men had left Front Street in that vehicle. And while it was likely that most had split off with the rest of the caesium, she had to be prepared for the worst.

She had to prepare for all five to come out shooting.

At least five, she corrected herself. *How the hell do we know they didn't pick up more on the way? Ain't no rule that says they can only drop off.*

It was the first time the thought had occurred to her. She was just about to share it, but before she could she was interrupted by the reassuring feeling of contact. The chopper was down. A few more seconds of manoeuvre and it was settled.

O'Rourke looked out. She could see that the pilot had positioned the vehicle lengthways across the northbound carriageway. At forty-one feet in length, it was enough of an obstruction that the Dodge – once it arrived – would struggle to pass.

Good man.

'Everybody out,' she ordered. Leaning forward, she tapped the pilot on the shoulder. 'You too.'

By the time O'Rourke had climbed down, all five of the helicopter's other occupants were in the street. All between the jackknifed vehicle and the slight hill where the road crossed International Drive.

The two agents and May fanned out exactly as O'Rourke would have ordered, had any order been necessary. Vega did the same, taking up position at the end of the line, level with May. All four were evenly distanced across the carriageway, each with an M4 raised and pressed against their shoulder.

Enough firepower to stop even a speeding van, O'Rourke hoped.

Because if it's not . . .

She turned to the pilot. He seemed unsure of what to do.

'I suggest you run,' O'Rourke shouted, over the sound of the still-slowing rotor blades.

'What?'

O'Rourke pointed towards the road behind the chopper.

'Run, and don't stop running. This thing that's coming, if we can't stop it, it's going to do some real damage. You don't want to be anywhere near it when it goes off, son, believe me. So you need to run.'

The pilot hesitated for a moment.

'RUN.'

This time he did as ordered.

O'Rourke did not watch him leave. She turned to face the same direction as her agents, walked the short distance that brought her level with them and drew her pistol.

FORTY

8.34 p.m. EDT

Cam Arnold allowed himself a grim smile as he observed both the traffic ahead of him and the carnage he could see to the left of the Sprinter.

Minutes had passed. Minutes in which he had sat and watched as the world around him froze.

He had ignored three different green lights that would have allowed him to turn right onto Universal Boulevard. To leave the scene of his latest fatal crime. He had his own reasons for waiting, but as he did so he found himself fascinated by the actions of others.

Arnold could understand why no one had yet come to the aid of the two fallen cops. Anyone who had seen him shoot them could have no doubt that they were dead. And anyone else?

Who the hell's gonna approach a stationary van with a mad gunman at the wheel?

No, all of that he understood. That was just plain common sense.

It was the opposing vehicles that intrigued him. The line of cars on the opposite side of International Drive, all lined up to turn left. To head where he was heading. Because if Arnold had ignored three sets of signals, then so had they. Three green lights, all of which would have allowed them to head away from the scene.

And yet not one of them had dared move.

What's stopping them? he wondered, his fascination a welcome distraction from his own wait. *Do they think the bad man in the van's gonna ram them if they cross his path? Or maybe they're waiting to see what happens next, once the cops arrived?*

He had no way to know the answer. All he knew was that these people had done nothing. They had not intervened. They had not turned around. They had not continued on their way. They had just stayed rooted to the spot, safe inside their metal cages, waiting for . . . something.

More goddamned sheep, he thought. *Just dying for their instructions.*

The distant sound of sirens broke through Arnold's distraction. He opened his window and closed his eyes, to focus on the noise. It only took a few seconds to be sure. To know that they were getting closer, and to know that they represented more than one police vehicle.

His smile widened as the sound became clearer.

Holy shit. By the noise of it, it might just be all of 'em.

It was exactly the response he needed. Shifting the van into drive, he ignored the red signal and finally took the right-hand turn onto Universal Boulevard.

FORTY-ONE

8.35 p.m. EDT

'What the hell's happening down there?'
O'Rourke was struggling to control herself. To deal with the fear of what could come over that hill at any moment. It was far from a new feeling but, as the seconds changed to minutes, she was finding it near impossible to hide her nerves.

'Is there no update from police dispatch?'

The enquiry came from Nicki May and it was pointless in the circumstances; if there had been an update then O'Rourke would not have asked her own question. Her natural reaction, then, was to snap back exactly that, but she resisted.

'NO UPDATE.' She shouted the reply, ensuring that the answer reached all four of her team and not just May. That effort to be heard somehow hid the fear in her voice. It was a welcome side effect. 'WE'RE STILL IN THE DARK HERE. STAY SHARP.'

The instruction was to herself as much as it was to her team. And she knew that it was necessary.

They must be feeling this too.

With the time that had passed, she was now convinced

that the police intervention on International Drive had been unsuccessful. Arnold and whoever was with him must have been prepared for a stop – *with their actions so far they've fairly been inviting one*, she thought – and so the odds were on the side of the Liberation gunmen if that stop turned violent.

Especially against a single patrol car.

O'Rourke shook her head at the thought. One patrol car, underprepared and underarmed, taking on a van filled with five gun-toting extremists. Maybe more. That was just no match and so it was ending only one way.

Cam Arnold was coming. He was taking his time about it, but he *was* coming.

And he's bringing a whole lot of trouble with him.

There were many different ways O'Rourke could see this playing out. Only one of them ended well. And unfortunately for her and for her team, *that* scenario – the one where Arnold was alone and gave himself up without a fight – was the least likely of them all. If Dempsey and May were correct, then Cam Arnold was on a suicide mission.

And men who come to die, they go down swinging.

It was that thought that made O'Rourke so fearful of what was coming. Homeland Security had trained her to handle a firefight. Just as it had trained the two agents alongside her, and just as she had trained Nicki May. But this was no simple shoot-out.

The biggest threat here was not the guns being carried. It was the weapon that Arnold was driving.

The likelihood was the Sprinter contained a dirty bomb, almost certainly armed with at least some of the caesium landed this morning. That was the consensus conclusion of the Homeland Security team, of May and of Vega, and of Dempsey and Grace. And O'Rourke was confident that they were all correct.

With that knowledge, the calculation of damage had been a simple enough task. Simple but devastating. The thought of it made O'Rourke turn and survey the area around her, to see for herself the reality of what those figures truly meant.

It was a safe assumption that the conventional core of the bomb would be ammonium nitrate-based. And it was only logical that the van would be filled close to capacity. If both of these conclusions were correct, this left them facing a device that incorporated eight five-hundred-pound barrels of the stuff. A payload that was two-thirds the size of the bomb that had torn through Oklahoma City in 1995. Enough to wipe out an area the size of at least ten city blocks, and to badly damage maybe half that distance again.

Instant death to everyone within half a mile. And that's before we throw in the radiation.

She looked towards CityWalk. At this time of night, one of the two busiest sites in central Florida. And now, she was sure, Arnold's target.

The chopper had landed as far from the perimeter as it could while still maintaining a 'must pass' point. It was the best they could do, but it was not enough. If O'Rourke's team stopped Arnold here but did not stop the bomb, CityWalk would still be hit. Maybe not as severely. Maybe with fewer lives lost. But the destruction would still be unthinkable.

O'Rourke could not let that happen. They had one chance to stop this. One chance to save at least five thousand lives. And one chance to survive it themselves.

If they were going to achieve any of that, they would achieve it here.

'AGENT O'ROURKE.' The shout came from May, just as the lead Homeland agent was turning back to face her team. 'HE'S COMING.'

O'Rourke felt her heart rate spike as the Sprinter came into view. It was at the apex of the long, humped bridge across Interstate-4. Perhaps six hundred yards in a dead-straight line from the four M4s and the single Glock 19 that were now all raised and aimed, ready to bring Cam Arnold down.

'ORDERS, AGENT O'ROURKE?'

The second shout came from beyond May. From Vega.

O'Rourke hesitated as she tried to focus on the Dodge. It was moving slowly, well below the speed limit, but it was still moving. And with every yard it covered, it increased its destructive range over the resort behind her.

'AGENT O'ROURKE?'

Vega again. He needed an answer. They all did.

The van was four hundred yards away now. And it was getting closer. O'Rourke raised her pistol, her hand shaking. She knew that she had no real choice here; that she had to open fire before the van was in range to wreak havoc on CityWalk behind her.

But what if a stray bullet from her team ended up setting the bomb off? Or one of Arnold's unit ignited the weapon from within the back of the vehicle while she and her team were focused on the van's driver?

And what if we're wrong entirely? What if the bomb ain't even in the van no more, and then we've taken out the only man who can tell us where it was?

She would be responsible for the consequences in those scenarios. Every last one of them. But then if she waited too long . . .

This flurry of thoughts and the stress of the moment had distracted O'Rourke from the sound of the engine and of the rotor blades approaching overhead. She was shocked, then, when the second Bell 407 helicopter swooped down from above, behind the oncoming van.

For just an instant her eyes left the Sprinter and flitted up to the new chopper. A figure was perched on its right-hand side, practically hanging out of the open door with an M4 aimed downwards at the rear of the Dodge. A glimpse of denim and a near-uncovered muscled arm was enough to tell O'Rourke who it was.

Dempsey.

She brought her focus back to the Sprinter, reached for her earpiece and switched its frequency to match up with her phone. The connection was instant. And so was the message.

'There's no heat signature coming out of the back of that van.'

It was the voice of Eden Grace, coming through loud and clear. Someone else was shouting in the background – Dempsey, O'Rourke assumed – but she could not make out the words. They were drowned out as Grace spoke again.

'I repeat: there is no heat signature coming out of the back. The driver is alone.'

O'Rourke was confused.

Arnold's alone?

The fact did nothing to alter the threat of the bomb itself: Arnold could set it off easily enough, or there could be a timer or even a remote. But with no one hidden in the rear of the vehicle, it at least narrowed the risks and reduced O'Rourke's targets down to one.

She opened her mouth to give the order to shoot but, before

she could say a word, the Sprinter came to a halt. It was an unexpected development and it made O'Rourke hesitate. Just for an instant, but long enough.

'ARNOLD HAS HIS HANDS RAISED,' May was shouting as loud as O'Rourke had ever heard her. 'INSIDE THE VEHICLE. HIS HANDS ARE EMPTY AND THEY'RE RAISED. HE'S . . . HE'S SURRENDERING.'

O'Rourke looked across at May. If she was right, if Arnold was giving up, then they had to take him alive. It was their best chance of finding the bulk of the caesium and the rest of his team. Maybe their only chance.

But if May was wrong . . .

O'Rourke paused over the dilemma.

Dempsey, clearly unaware of this development, did not.

The second chopper was descending fast, now just feet from the ground, but the ISB agent seemed in no mood to wait. Dempsey jumped before touchdown and took off towards the Sprinter's left side the moment his feet hit the floor.

Once on the ground, Dempsey moved fast.

Grace had taken over comms with O'Rourke from inside the helicopter, which meant using Dempsey's phone to connect to the Homeland agent's, with the line patched through to their chopper headphones.

This left Dempsey without an earpiece and so he was no longer connected to either woman. Combined with the sheer noise of the rotor blades drowning out all other sound, he had no means to communicate his new theory with either team. A fact that made time even more of an imperative: there was none left to waste.

As Dempsey raced ahead he realised that he was entering a six-hundred-yard potential kill zone, where an order to fire could come at any moment. And where, if his theory was wrong, Arnold could detonate a bomb without warning.

The second threat did not concern him; Dempsey was convinced of his own conclusions. But that same threat *did* impact on the first because if others still believed a bomb to be an immediate threat, a hair trigger became all the more likely.

It left him with no other option. He had to put himself into the kill zone, in the hope that his presence would be enough to stop O'Rourke's team from taking action of their own.

Dempsey did not slow as he reached the back of the vehicle. The clock was against him. From the body language surrounding the shouted exchanges amongst the Homeland group ahead of him, he knew he had just moments.

'BOSS. YOU NEED TO CALL THIS.'

The shout came from the agent to O'Rourke's right. Former special forces, O'Rourke remembered. He was no doubt itching to act instead of watching a second team take the lead. O'Rourke ignored his plea, her focus never leaving Dempsey as he moved closer to the van.

'EYES, NICKI?'

'ARNOLD HASN'T MOVED A MUSCLE. HIS HANDS ARE UP AND THEY'RE EMPTY.'

O'Rourke hesitated. For all the enthusiasm of her men, her instinct told her that May was correct. If she was not, why had Arnold failed to detonate the bomb? Sure, he wasn't as close to the target as would be ideal, but he had to know he wasn't getting past this point. And even from here the damage would still be horrific.

Plus this ain't the only bomb. We kill Arnold when we don't need to, what chance have we got to find any others?

She looked towards May, who seemed to sense both O'Rourke's gaze and her uncertainty.

'He's surrendering, Bambi.' This time May did not shout. 'He's surrendering. We're federal agents. We're not executioners.'

May's words spurred O'Rourke into making her decision. Arnold *had* to be taken alive.

But Dempsey can't know that, can he? He can't know Arnold's surrendering.

O'Rourke already knew the answer to her own question and it seemed to be confirmed as the ISB agent reached the front of the van, his intentions all too clear.

As May cried out in horror and began to sprint away towards him, O'Rourke could only watch as Dempsey raised his weapon.

Dempsey ignored the movement in his peripheral vision as he closed in on the driver's door. At least one of O'Rourke's team had started to move. To run towards him. Whatever their reason, it was too late to stop and check.

Arnold was just feet away. Half a second at Dempsey's pace. A moment that could be the difference between life and far too many deaths to contemplate.

He did not hesitate as Arnold finally came into sight and, with the assault rifle's stock still jammed hard into his right shoulder, Dempsey pulled the trigger.

*

'NICKI, GET BACK HERE!'

Even before she had finished it, O'Rourke knew that her shouted order was a waste of breath. Nicki May had moved an instant before Dempsey had reached Cam Arnold's door, breaking into a sprint as she tried to close the distance between them.

May's efforts, though, were as fruitless as O'Rourke's. With so much distance to cover, she had barely managed five yards before the sound of three shots brought her to a horrified halt.

FORTY-TWO

8.39 p.m. EDT

The eruption of gunfire made O'Rourke wince. Not from the noise itself; that she was well used to. Instead, it was the fear of what could follow.

Fear of a failsafe, there to detonate the bomb in the event of Arnold's death. A risk she had been well aware of when the decision was hers, it was somehow harder to handle when it had become someone else's.

A second passed. Then another. Neither one brought an explosion. But they did bring confusion. As O'Rourke opened her eyes and refocused on Dempsey, she saw him drag a very much alive Cam Arnold from the Sprinter's cab and throw him face first to the hot asphalt of Universal Boulevard.

What the hell?

Arnold hit the floor hard, his head impacting directly with the ground. If O'Rourke had been thinking clearly, she would have understood the intentional physicality of Dempsey's approach. It was maximum non-lethal force, designed to incapacitate and prevent any effort at remote detonation.

O'Rourke, though, was *not* thinking clearly. She was preoccupied with just two facts:

Arnold's alive.

And so are we.

O'Rourke was rooted to the spot as those thoughts ran through her mind. Most of her team seemed to have suffered the same reaction. Three of them were standing still, their weapons lowered, unsure in that moment of what to do next.

The fourth – Nicki May – was the exception.

May was already moving fast again. The shots had delayed her but not for long. She was already halfway to Dempsey and Arnold.

It was the mental kick O'Rourke needed. Her protégée had shrugged off the shock. She was doing her duty. O'Rourke had to do the same. And so did the rest of her team.

'MOVE!' O'Rourke was already running as she shouted the instructions. 'KEEP THAT BASTARD PINNED TO THE GROUND!'

Vega had not needed the order. He had set off after May a moment before O'Rourke herself. The other two agents had stayed in position until instructed to do otherwise. Less than a second later and they were already ahead of their team leader.

Three hundred yards was no great distance but still it took O'Rourke almost a minute to cover the ground. Her team were faster, leaving her an out-of-breath spectator as each of them reached Arnold and the Sprinter ahead of her. By the time O'Rourke joined them, Dempsey had stepped back and her two agents had their muzzles low, pressed into the neck and the back of an unmoving Liberation terrorist.

O'Rourke pulled in a painful intake of air as she slowed her pace. She gave Arnold the briefest of inspections, enough to see blood dripping from where his forehead had struck the floor, an impact that seemed to have left him insensible, before she stood up and addressed Dempsey.

'You didn't shoot him?'

'No.'

'But the gunfire?'

'That was to disorientate him. Rifle discharge right by his ear, next best thing to a flash-bang.'

'But what about the bomb?'

'He was never going to set off a bomb, Agent O'Rourke. That's not what this was about.'

'And just what the hell am I supposed to make of that?'

'He's been leading us to this point all day,' Dempsey explained. 'The killings. The cameras. The timing of the whole thing. All of it was a trail. All of it was designed to bring us *here*. To keep our focus on *him*, all while the caesium disappeared into the night. He planned for us to take him down, exactly like we have.'

O'Rourke was shaking her head even as Dempsey spoke.

'Son, I ain't saying you've only got one oar in the water, but that kind of thinking, that's just not what we need here. We need my team to—'

Dempsey turned away before O'Rourke had finished speaking. For a moment she was speechless. She was not used to her words being dismissed. But then, with the hulking agent no longer blocking her view, she noticed the position of the team from the second chopper.

They were just feet from the Sprinter's rear doors and Dempsey was heading towards them.

'EDEN. OPEN IT.'

Grace, who must have been standing out of sight at the back of the vehicle, obeyed Dempsey's shouted instruction before O'Rourke could countermand it. She stepped into view just a moment later.

'It's empty, Boss. Nothing in there at all.'

O'Rourke could do nothing to disguise her surprise.

'Nothing?'

'Not a thing, Agent O'Rourke,' Grace replied. 'It's like Dempsey figured. We've been played.'

O'Rourke looked around, at the scene that surrounded her.

Two choppers. Federal and state agents. A terrorist taken alive. And all of it was for . . . nothing?

No. Hell no. That ain't right. It can't be.

She pushed past Grace, moved around the van and looked through the open doors, needing to see it for herself. It was exactly as the ISB agent had said. Apart from a few rolls of plastic – more decals, she realised – the rear of the van was empty.

The boxes she had watched being loaded in Key West? The caesium? It was all gone.

Both the sight and the implications that came with it seemed to make the world spin. Reaching out, O'Rourke gripped the van's rear door as she steadied herself. For a moment she thought she might pass out. The deep lungfuls of hot air that she forced herself to pull in did little to dispel that feeling.

Where is it?

The question only made her worse.

Where in the hell is it?

'The bomb was never here, Agent O'Rourke.'

She tilted her head, to look towards Dempsey.

'The whole thing was a ruse. Wherever the caesium is, whether it's already a bomb or not, it was never in this van. It was never with Arnold. At least not once he'd hit the mainland, anyway. It's long gone and we have no way to know where. That's why I had to step in. I didn't have time to tell you and I couldn't risk anyone firing on him. We had to take him alive.'

O'Rourke took a few moments more. Her head was beginning to clear as she listened to Dempsey's voice. A few more deep breaths and she had found her own.

'How?' she finally asked. 'How did you know?'

'I didn't,' Dempsey replied. 'Not until you told us he was here. And then still not for sure until we got the negative heat signature on the empty rear section on the van. But something's been bothering me since the plane. It was how Arnold killed the patrolman at the marina, in full view of the only camera in the place. A camera he looked straight at, almost like he knew it was there. Same thing at the service plaza. And then the witness he left alive in Whittier. None of those killings were necessary and every one of them guaranteed our attention. Why would he take that risk? Why would he leave that trail? If he actually had a bomb and if he intended to reach this target?'

'But if you were figuring on this already . . .'

'I wasn't keeping it from you. The idea was still forming when I left you, but then you called through and the timing clinched it. When you confirmed the traffic stop you confirmed the target, but you also confirmed that he'd reached here at just the right moment. All the way through Orlando as public enemy number one and he gets here just minutes after you? And all without police attention until he was practically on top of you? That's no accident. He waited somewhere nearby. Somewhere off-road and hidden. And he did that to give us time to get here. He wanted us here, Agent O'Rourke. In fact, he *needed* us here.'

'But why?'

'Because he wants something. And whatever that is, he knows we can't refuse him.'

O'Rourke listened. As she did, she felt a knot growing in her gut.

What Dempsey was saying, it made sense. Dreadful, unarguable sense. Arnold had focused Homeland's attention – *her* attention – on himself. It was a classic, basic diversion. And somehow O'Rourke had bought it. She had aimed her full attention and with it the attention of Homeland Security and half the law enforcement of Southern Florida, all on Cam Arnold.

All while a literal shit-ton of radioactive material made its merry damn way up to and across the state line, most like. Toted on the lord knows what kinda wheels.

O'Rourke took a step back while the full enormity of the situation sank in. As she moved, she looked around.

At Dempsey and at Grace, now standing together just feet away.

At May and at Vega, both within earshot and both ashen-faced.

And at the two Homeland agents who were covering Arnold. They seemed oblivious to what had been discovered in the rear of the Dodge. Their focus, unlike that of everyone else, remained on him.

On him.

On Cam goddamn Arnold.

The name alone brought clarity to O'Rourke's mind. Clarity and anger.

That piece of fucking redneck shit . . .

O'Rourke's pistol had not left her hand during all that had happened, but this was the first time she truly felt it. Her grip tightened around its butt as she moved, striding between May and Vega and towards the man she could now see moving on the floor ahead.

'GET THAT SONOFABITCH TO HIS FEET.'

The order was unnecessary. The two agents had been joined by a third from Dempsey's chopper and he was already covering Arnold while his colleagues dragged the Liberation man up. Arnold was unsteady. His eyes were wild and his face was a mask of the blood that poured from the wound to his brow.

None of which slowed O'Rourke for even a heartbeat.

'WHERE ARE THEY? WHERE ARE THE BOMBS?'

Arnold seemed to be regaining his equilibrium.

'ANSWER THE QUESTION, DAMMIT. WHERE THE HELL HAVE THEY TAKEN THEM?'

Arnold was improving with every second. His eyes were more focused. His back straighter. O'Rourke watched as he pulled himself to his full height. She waited for his answer. What she got instead was a smirk.

It was more than she could handle. Perhaps the day had taken a bigger toll than O'Rourke could admit even to herself. Perhaps her age and her condition really were too much for her now. Or perhaps it was the effect of the latest set of meds she was trying out. Whatever it was, Arnold's reaction seemed to flip a switch in O'Rourke's mind and she did something she had never done before.

Stepping forward without a word, she thrust her hand upwards, grabbed Arnold by his throat and pulled his head lower. As she did, she lifted her Glock and pressed its muzzle into his wound.

'TELL ME WHERE THEY ARE!'

'BAMBI! NO!'

O'Rourke heard May's shout. She chose to ignore it.

'TELL ME!'

'STOP IT!'

May again, only this time the DOJ agent was unwilling to be dismissed. With her shouted protest ignored again, she took her objection to the next level. Stepping forward, she forcefully pushed O'Rourke's pistol from Arnold's head and pulled her away.

'GET THE HELL OFF OF ME!'

O'Rourke shrugged May off, her temper giving her unexpected strength. May had clearly not expected the force and so the lighter woman was sent stumbling backwards by a wild sweep of O'Rourke's arm. She had at least achieved her objective; the Homeland agent immediately freed Arnold and instead turned her full, angry attention on her DOJ subordinate.

O'Rourke's first instinctive thought was for her weapon, but she managed to overcome it; she kept her pistol down. Her anger, though, was free-flowing. She had no intention of holding *that* back.

May must have seen it in her eyes. She stepped back with her hands raised and her palms facing out, putting as much distance between herself and O'Rourke as she could. Distance that O'Rourke fully intended to close until an interruption from her right cut through her fury.

'*You're* what they sent?'

O'Rourke stopped moving.

Cam Arnold's voice was softer than she had expected, his accent not dissimilar from but less pronounced than her own. It stopped her from taking another step. After the briefest of distractions, all eyes were now back on him.

'They trusted *this* to one of you?'

O'Rourke resisted the bait. She knew what Arnold was saying. What his words meant. It was no more and no less than she would expect. And right now it was irrelevant.

She turned back to face him, her neck craned to meet eyes that were set over a foot above her own. When she spoke, all the anger had left her voice. It left just cold authority.

'You're going to tell us where the bombs are. And you're going to tell us now.'

Arnold smirked again.

'Sounds to me like that suit and badge you're wearing, they've gone and made you kinda uppity. Like you're the one giving the orders here.'

'I *am* the one giving the orders here, son.'

'No, ma'am.' Arnold said the last word in a tone as mocking as O'Rourke had ever heard. 'No, you ain't. You see, you need me. Because without me, you ain't never finding what was in the back of that van. And we both know what happens if you don't.'

O'Rourke bit her tongue. There was so much she wanted to say. So much she wanted to do. But she could not. Arnold was right. Even beaten and bleeding in the street and with two assault rifles aimed at his head, he had the upper hand.

She took a deep breath and a single step back.

'What do you want?'

The smirk grew into a broad, arrogant grin.

'I want the release of Peyton Travis. And I want it done now.'

13 JULY
2021

FORTY-THREE

12.10 a.m. EDT

Dempsey set a plastic tray down on the metal canteen table, grabbed one of four oblong tinfoil wraps and took his seat against the wall. He began to peel away the shiny skin. At first oblivious to the three pairs of eyes watching him, his distraction did not last long.

He gestured towards the remaining burritos.

'What? You've all got one.'

Grace and Vega both moved forward as Dempsey spoke, as if his words had been a starter's pistol. May stayed still, her eyes sweeping from the tray to the man who had just delivered it.

'How do you eat that garbage,' she asked, 'and still look like . . . well, like *you*?'

Dempsey did not address the question himself. Instead he looked to Grace.

'Eden, tell Agent May the first rule.'

'You eat what you can, when you can.' She took a slug of ice-cold water and then pushed the tray towards May. 'Same principle as sleep. You never know when you'll get the next chance.'

'It's disgusting. I'd rather go hungry.'

'Suit yourself, Agent May. I'll go get you an apple.'

'No, please, I'm fine.' May stood up before Dempsey could get to his feet. 'I work better on an empty stomach. I'm going to head outside for a cigarette.'

Vega shifted in his seat.

'You want some company?' he asked.

'No thanks, Sergio,' May replied. She smiled warmly at the detective as she spoke. 'I need to be alone, to think a little. What happened back there with Bambi? On the bridge? I need to work out how to deal with it.'

'You did the right thing,' Vega replied. 'She'd lost control, you had to intervene.'

'It's not as simple as right and wrong. Not between me and her, anyway. We go back a long way. I need to deal with it. Honestly, eat your . . . your food.'

May gave Vega another smile as she reached out and touched his shoulder. He grinned back, his eyes flitting from her face to her hand. If Dempsey had harboured any doubts that the man was smitten, they would have been dispelled in that moment.

Not that he'd had any such doubts. And not that he intended to mention it, either. It had been none of his business when he had first noticed it back in Key West and it remained none of his business now.

'You're a fast mover, Sergio Vega.'

Dempsey glanced at Grace in surprise as she spoke. He had not expected her to comment either. And if the deep reddening of his cheeks was any indication, neither had Vega.

'I . . . I . . . erm . . .'

Vega seemed lost for words.

Or mortified, more likely.

Dempsey suppressed a smile as Grace's own colour began to match Vega's. A misstep like this was rare for Grace; she of all people made a point of respecting the division between work and private life. And so it was not often that Dempsey got to watch her squirm.

'It's not . . . it wasn't a criticism, Sergio,' Grace stammered. 'Sorry, I didn't mean to pry.'

The silence that followed made the situation even more excruciating. Grace glanced towards Dempsey for help. He shook his head with a smile; he was enjoying this far too much to help. She frowned in return, sensing the fun he was having at her expense. Vega still seemed unsure what to say in reply, while Grace would no doubt be happy if neither ever spoke again.

Dempsey looked from one to the other as they both avoided eye contact, his smile widening as the awkwardness of the moment grew.

The silence continued as they ate what was left of their food. For Dempsey, once the humour had passed, that quiet was welcome. It offered a pause in what had so far been an unpredictable twelve hours and gave him time to think.

He glanced at his watch.

12.15 a.m.

5.15 a.m. in London.

Even with his delayed flight he should have touched down four hours ago. With the inevitable ISB upgrade to first class, he would have been well rested, and so he would have been awake and just hours from seeing the closest thing he had to a family.

To seeing Michael and Sarah. And meeting the boys.

My godsons.

As much as that thought unsettled him – as much as he questioned his suitability for such an important role – right now there was nowhere that Dempsey would rather be. It had been far too long since he had been home. Since he had last seen the people he loved.

And yet somehow he had ended up here. Four thousand miles from where he should be. And for what? Why *was* he here, now that Cam Arnold was in custody? Certainly not to take the lead in the man's interrogation, that was for sure. O'Rourke and her Homeland team were off doing . . . whatever they were doing, while Dempsey and the other outsiders suddenly seemed much less welcome.

Out of the loop and killing time.

The thought left him frustrated, only made worse by the knowledge that he could be elsewhere.

They had arrived at Homeland Security's Central Florida Office shortly before 11 p.m. It had taken them forty minutes to secure the scene on Universal Boulevard following Arnold's capture. Once done, responsibility of everything other than Cam Arnold himself had been passed to the Orlando Police Department.

Only then had they been free to make the flight from Orange County to where they now sat: Fort Pierce, Florida.

The Sunset City.

Had this been Dempsey's operation, that flight would have been followed by Arnold's immediate interrogation. That man had information they required. He knew the whereabouts of both the caesium that had been landed that morning and of Scott Turner, the man likely tasked with weaponising the radioactive material into a series of mini-WMDs.

For Dempsey, the extraction of that information would have been his absolute priority. But, as he had been made very aware, this was *not* his operation.

It was Agent O'Rourke's operation. Or, more accurately, it was Homeland Security's.

And Homeland did things their own way.

O'Rourke had checked in with her superiors from the scene of Arnold's arrest, giving them an overview of the position. That summary had included the fact that Arnold was holding Homeland to ransom – information on the caesium in exchange for the release of Peyton Travis – and it had been this complication that had set the political wheels in motion, leading to a strict instruction from O'Rourke's superiors: no further interaction with Cam Arnold until the United States secretary for Homeland Security reached Fort Pierce.

The instruction had taken Dempsey by surprise. It would not have been his approach. Not by a long shot. But then Dempsey was not a part of Homeland Security and so he lacked the luxury – or was it the burden? – of the full picture. O'Rourke, on the other hand, knew everything she needed to know and she had seemed to take the development in her stride.

And even if she had not – even if she had been as dissatisfied as Dempsey – she had done as she was ordered.

O'Rourke's obedience to her superiors meant that Arnold had been sat alone in an otherwise empty interrogation room for the past ninety minutes. Untouched, unquestioned and unchallenged, all while a ton of radioactive material was moving ever further into the continental United States. And all while Dempsey – a trained interrogator – was sitting barely three hundred yards from the man who could guide them straight to it.

None of which makes any bloody sense at all.

The sound of chair legs scraping on floor tiles cut through Dempsey's thoughts, making him look up. Vega had pushed his seat back and climbed to his feet. The only trace left of his burrito was its foil wrapping, now crushed into a ball on the table ahead of him. Vega reached down and picked it up, before doing the same to Dempsey's.

'You done with that, Agent Grace?'

He indicated what remained of Grace's meal.

'Yeah, I'm good. Can't eat as much as you guys.'

The detective looked towards Dempsey.

'You want to finish Nicki's?'

'No thanks, Sergio. I've had enough.'

Vega scooped up the remaining food and foil before turning and heading for a bin that sat open next to the cafeteria register. He returned with a handful of paper towels and used them to clean the table of the few crumbs and grains of rice dropped from the tortilla wraps.

'You this tidy at home?' Grace asked.

'Made that way by my mother,' Vega replied. Dempsey could detect a hint of pride in his voice as he retook his chair. 'She always said that we didn't have as much as the family next door, but what we did have was cleaner than theirs. I guess it stuck.'

'My father did the same with us,' Grace replied. Her effort, Dempsey could tell, to move beyond the earlier awkward moment. Sharing rare details of her own personal life. 'Must be a Latin thing. My mother sure as hell didn't buy into it.'

'Your dad, where's he from?'

'He was Venezuelan. Born there, raised in Miami. He's not with us any more.'

'I'm sorry to hear that. It's hard when you lose your people.'

'It is. But we keep the lessons and we pass them on, huh?'

'Yeah. Yeah, we do. I sure won't be forgetting those lessons, anyway.'

'Your mother, is she still around?'

'She is. My dad, too. I'm lucky.' Vega turned to look towards Dempsey. 'And you, Agent Dempsey? Do you see much of your family?'

Dempsey had expected the question; it was almost inevitable, given the conversation so far. But inevitability did not make it a subject he wished to discuss.

'Never really had any.'

'You never—'

'You can't miss what you never had, Sergio.' Dempsey rose to his feet. As clear a message as he could give that the subject was closed. 'I'm going to find O'Rourke. The longer we wait to speak to Arnold, the less chance we have of finding Scott Turner or the caesium.'

He began to turn towards the doorway that led out. As he moved, he could see that Vega was about to speak. An apology, most likely, but before he could form the words he was stopped by a touch of Grace's hand and an almost imperceptible shake of her head.

The unspoken exchange made Dempsey smile as he strode from the table. As she always did, Grace had his back.

'What are you going to suggest to O'Rourke?' Grace called after him.

'That we should get first shot,' Dempsey replied, stopping and turning back to face them. 'At least we should if the secretary is going to be much longer. Waiting was O'Rourke's order, not ours.'

'You really think she'll go for that?'

'I think she's as keen to get this done as we are. And besides, if you don't ask you don't get.'

The final word had barely left Dempsey's lips as the door to the cafeteria opened behind him. Dempsey turned at the sound, just in time to see Nicki May re-enter the room.

'I thought you were going to speak to O'Rourke?' he asked.

'That has to wait,' May replied. 'Secretary McMillan just landed. He's getting a full debrief in ten minutes and we're all expected to be there.'

FORTY-FOUR

11.12 p.m. CDT

Colonel Miles Walker slowed as he approached the front gate and lowered the driver's window on his white Tesla Model X. His military ID was hanging from the rear-view mirror but he knew it would be unnecessary; as unusual as it was for him to drive himself – or to be returning to the Facility four hours after heading home for the night – entry would require no more than a glimpse of his face.

'Colonel. Welcome back, sir.'

The guard ripped off a crisp salute as he pressed the entry button that opened the first barrier. The man gave no suggestion of surprise at Walker's irregular reappearance; the Facility's team had been told to expect him.

He drove passed the gatehouse and the open access point with a salute and a nod, but without a word. The business on which he had been called back was serious and it was secretive, which meant that even now Walker had very little knowledge of why he had been dragged out of bed. It had left him in no mood for small talk.

The next point of entry was one hundred yards beyond the first. Like the previous gate, it was the only route through an electrified wire fence that stood thirty feet high, the last five feet of which were laced with shredding razor-wire. Between them the two boundaries created a featureless open space that no escaping inmate could hope to survive; the gun turrets that were dotted every one hundred and fifty feet along the inside perimeter guaranteed that.

For Walker, that same one-hundred-yard no man's land was as risk-free as any freeway or residential road, easily passed as the front gate closed and the second opened. For a prisoner, it was the final insurmountable barrier to a free world they would never see again.

The rest of the journey inside took just a few more minutes. First through another gate in another fence, both identical to the first two. Then through the walls of the Facility themselves, via their single point of physical entry: double-height iron doors that could only open with the simultaneous turn of three individual keys, each one held by a different member of the institution's staff. And then finally through another internal security gate, behind which was a small parking lot reserved for Walker and just four other members of the Facility's military personnel.

It was one of those four who was there now, awaiting the commanding officer's arrival: Captain Wes Bickle.

The fact that Walker had expected to see him made Bickle's appearance no more welcome. Walker's natural dislike for the intelligence officer did not help his mood, any more than the late-night twenty-mile journey or the unusually intense exterior heat that now hit him as he climbed out of the driver's seat.

'What the hell is this all about, Bickle?'

'It's about Peyton Travis, Colonel.'

'I know *that*, captain. It's everything *else* I don't know. How about you change that?'

'I don't know a whole lot more myself, sir. Just that we've had a message from the Department of Justice telling us to prepare Peyton to be moved.'

'Moved? Moved to where?'

'We don't know. In fact, we don't yet know if the move will even go ahead. We just need to be ready in case it does.'

'What the hell does that mean? Why have I been called in for something that might not even happen?'

Walker was growing less patient by the second. And he had good reason. All this uncertainty and the lack of explanation, it was . . . disrespectful. To him, to his rank and to the institution that was under his command.

The situation irritated him enough that he did not wait for Bickle to answer before opening the secure door that led into the building and on to a short corridor. Nor did he speak again as he made his way to his office, which sat at the hallway's end. Only once he was behind his desk did Walker return his attention to the intelligence officer who had followed.

'Well? What's with the uncertainty?'

'I don't know the answer to that, Colonel. All I know is the order that came down. We're to immediately prepare Travis for transport and then await further instructions.'

'And we're supposed to deal with the transport how, exactly? I can't spare the bodies for a safe transfer. Not without calling in a team off-shift, but they want me to do that near midnight? It's too short notice. It just doesn't work.'

'They've thought of that. According to the message, if he *is* going to be moved, they'll be sending a team from Homeland Security. We just need to hand him over. Which is an irregular process and so we can't formally do it without your say-so. That's why I had to call you in, sir.'

Walker sat back and considered what Bickle had just told him. In his three years at the Facility he had overseen the transport of maybe ten prisoners. On each of those times their movement had been arranged weeks in advance and always for the same purpose: to be interrogated for information they might hold, then returned to his custody until they were needed again.

If they ever were.

It was not unique, then, for an inmate to be transported out of the Facility. But at this sort of speed? With no warning and no preparation time?

And no certainty that it'll even happen?

It raised far too many questions in Walker's mind. They were questions he knew even Bickle could not answer, a fact which made him even more uncomfortable. For a moment his mind wandered; it caused him to stare past the captain – now seated in the chair that faced the desk – as he thought through the situation.

An instant later and his focus was back.

'What do you make of this, Wes?'

It was an honest question. For once Walker had the feeling that he and Bickle were on the same team. The US military against the DOJ. It allowed the protective shield he usually deployed with the intelligence officer to slip.

'I don't know what to say, Colonel,' Bickle replied. 'I've told you what I know.'

Walker shook his head as he opened his desk drawer. He took out two weathered glass tumblers and a bottle of Hillrock Bourbon, splashed two fingers' worth into each glass and pushed one across the table. He took a mouthful from his own before speaking again.

'I'm not asking for what you *know*. I'm asking for what you *think*. This is weird, right?'

'Yes, sir. Yes, it is.'

'You ever encountered a situation like this before? Before I was here?'

'Never once. Every time one of the prisoners has been needed, we know well in advance. Sometimes an investigator might turn up without much notice, but even then it's a minimum half a day. And they *never* don't show. But for a transport out? That's written in stone, Colonel. That's done with the same precision as transporting the president himself.'

Walker nodded his head. Bickle was telling him nothing he did not already know, but still the confirmation was welcome.

'And we've never had a team in from outside to facilitate?'

'No. The handover never happens here. That'd be too many new faces in the place if we did it that way. Normal protocol is for our own team to take the prisoner where he needs to be and to return him when done. It means they remain in our custody for the longest possible period.'

'So why the change? Why deviate so far from settled practice?'

'Some sort of emergency would be my guess, Colonel.'

'Mine as well,' Walker agreed. 'Whatever it is, it must be a fluid situation. And whatever Travis might be needed for, it's got to be so last-minute that they aren't even sure about it themselves. Makes you wonder what shit's going down out there, doesn't it?'

'Makes *me* wonder what the hell Travis could have to do with it,' Bickle replied. 'The man's been in here near on a decade. What part can he have to play in any kind of national emergency?'

'Good point.' Walker paused a moment. He was considering a new question. 'You think this could have anything to do with today?'

'You mean with Joshua and the mess hall?'

'Yeah. Like Bush said, what happened today could have been an attack on Travis as easy as on Joshua himself. You think it could be connected to whatever this is all about?'

'Can't rule it out. And it would be a coincidence, timing-wise. But I think it's unlikely.'

'Why?'

'Because Travis has a lot of enemies in here. All the noise he's made rejecting his old cause, he's pissed off a lot of people who used to look up to him. Throw in the reason he's here. The white supremacy stuff. That has the other side of the aisle gunning for him, too. Odds are that if the attack *was* aimed at him, it's related to his past.'

'And what if this is about that too? His old life?'

This time it was Bickle who took some time to think.

'I guess we just don't know.' he said. 'And maybe we never will. Maybe they won't even come for him.'

'Maybe not. But we have our orders, so for now we have to presume they will.'

Walker swallowed the last drops of his bourbon and indicated for Bickle to do the same.

'And that means you need to get him ready.'

FORTY-FIVE

12.35 a.m. EDT

'How sure are you about the caesium?'

The question came from Ray McMillan, the US Secretary of Homeland Security.

Seated at the head of the long conference table that dominated Fort Pierce's main meeting room, McMillan naturally commanded the full attention of the room's occupants. His position gave him a level of importance matched by few others.

Young for the role – a few years older than Dempsey at most, putting him in his early forties – he carried the kind of authority that could only come from absolute competence. He was typical of the appointments made by President Knowles in the past eighteen months. Men and women who, above all else, understood their roles and their duties and who knew best how to discharge them.

The table was divided between Homeland and the outsiders. Nicki May sat to McMillan's left, with Dempsey next to her, then Grace and Vega. Directly opposite them sat the five Homeland operatives, with O'Rourke to the secretary's immediate right. So far she had taken the lead in the meeting, outlining the facts of the operation and what the team had surmised to now.

McMillan had absorbed it all without making a single written note. With the summary now over, he had questions.

'If we haven't examined the material, how can we be sure it's actually caesium?'

'We can never be one hundred per cent certain without a seizure, Mr Secretary,' O'Rourke began, 'but we're as sure as we can be in the circumstances. There was no visual identification but there *was* a clear residual signature that indicated radioactive material. We followed it all the way from the end of the jetty to the marina's entrance, where Arnold's van was parked. A strong, direct route, sir. Most important, that signature was nowhere else thereabouts. Just a straight line from Point A to Point B. The same straight line walked by Arnold and his men. It suggests with little room for doubt that it came from the containers they were carrying.'

'And the quantities you're suggesting? Do we have any direct evidence to say you're right on that? A ton of caesium-137, Special Agent O'Rourke. That's . . . that's . . .'

'That's a whole shitload of trouble, sir.'

O'Rourke's suggestion caused Dempsey to suppress a smile. He found her matter-of-fact style refreshing, particularly now it was coming naturally and not being played so heavily for effect. But he suspected Ray McMillan did not share his enthusiasm for her informality. He glanced to Grace beside him, looking for her lead. Her time in the White House had taught her when to remain expressionless around a politician and when to react.

Right now, she was a blank slate. Dempsey mirrored her frozen pose, with only his eyes moving from O'Rourke to McMillan as he awaited the secretary's reaction. When it came, it was surprising.

'I'm sure we can find a better description if we have to,

Agent O'Rourke, but yeah, that really *is* a shitload of trouble. So how sure are we?'

There was no humour in McMillan's voice as he spoke. Nor was there any sign of it in his eyes. Still, his adoption of O'Rourke's inappropriate turn of phrase told Dempsey a lot. This was a serious man with a serious role and, right now, a serious problem on his hands. There were many politicians who, less suited to their position, would have buckled under that stress. The type who would have taken this as an opportunity to lash out. To reprimand a subordinate for a breach of protocol.

McMillan had done no such thing.

He knows there's a job to be done. And he knows that nothing else matters.

Compared to many politicians Dempsey had encountered, it was a breath of fresh air.

'We can't be certain on the quantity,' O'Rourke continued. 'But we've made logical deductions. With the size and the number of containers we saw being carried to the Sprinter – and with the fact that none of them looked to be an easy carry – it makes sense for the total load to be a ton. Maybe a little more or a little less either way, but it's the safest working assumption.'

'Can I ask something?'

Dempsey raised his hand politely as he spoke. An acknowledgement that he was a stranger here, both in terms of agency and nationality. A Brit from the United Nations, speaking up in a meeting of US federal agents.

'Please do, Agent Dempsey.'

'Thank you, Mr Secretary. I'm just wondering, sir: why does the quantity matter? Even a small amount, with the right payload of explosives, is enough to kill thousands.'

McMillan waited a moment before he answered, his eyes moving across the line-up of outsiders. He was either considering whether he should respond at all, or he was assessing his audience for how he delivered what was to come. Finally he spoke.

'I want to put my cards on the table here, Agent Dempsey. As if this room were Homeland and Homeland only. Can I assume everyone here understands what that means?'

This time he glanced at Vega; the only man in the room who came from outside the intelligence community.

'All *four* of us follow your meaning, Mr Secretary.' Dempsey's reply was intended to take the attention away from an individual who lacked credentials and back to a group that did. 'Whatever you have to say, it's within these walls only.'

'Well, your word is evidently good enough for the president, Agent Dempsey. Which I guess makes it good enough for me. So here's the long and the short of it: we know that something's coming. We have done for a while now. The resurgence in the threat of domestic terrorism in the last year is like nothing we've ever seen. Our intelligence services are at war with a whole section of our own population and it's only a matter of time until they hit us hard.

'And the fact of the matter is – and I realise what I'm about to say is unpalatable – whatever that attack might be, it's kind of *necessary*. We're talking about thousands of US citizens here, many of them trained by our own armed forces. As long as they're just making noise, there's only so much we can do about them. Their whole "big bad government" bullshit, if we go in too hard then we just make that true and we bolster their cause. But if they were to act? If they were to follow through on some of their threats . . .'

'Then the government could be justified to go back at them,' Dempsey offered. 'You're saying you need a Pearl Harbour.'

'Pearl Harbour. Nine-Eleven. Call it what you like, the answer's yes. These sonsofbitches are growing and it's happening all over the country. Even in states that have no history of a patriot movement or white supremacy or any of that shit. They're infiltrating our schools, our police, our military. Their ideas are taking hold, Agent Dempsey. And the Covid lockdown – something we had to do to beat that damn virus, for the sake of the population that *includes* these assholes – it was like throwing gasoline on a smouldering fire. And yet right now, for all our knowledge of what we face and how bad it could become, there's almost nothing we can do about it.'

'Until there's a serious attack.' This time it was Grace who spoke.

'Exactly. And that leads me back to your question. The quantity matters, Agent Dempsey, because it tells me what we can expect. And if I know that, I know what I can allow. A single bomb, conventional in size? We can live with that.'

For a moment there was silence. Not even the sound of breathing.

The reality of what McMillan had just said about the rise of domestic terror groups was undeniable. Dempsey had witnessed the massive growth in anti-government and white supremacist movements in the last year and he was aware of how powerless federal agencies were to combat them for as long as they remained loud but non-violent.

But viewing a dirty bomb as convenient? Thousands of deaths as a reasonable price?

'You can't seriously mean what you just said?'

The words came an instant before Dempsey could say them himself. He turned to the far end of the table. Towards Vega.

'You heard what Agent Dempsey said, right?' Vega continued. 'Thousands of people dead. Even with a tenth of a ton.'

'Detective . . . Vega, is it?'

'That's right.'

'Detective Vega, please don't look at this as if we *want* an attack of that magnitude. Deaths in that number, it could be the worst terror attack ever carried out on American soil. No president wants that on his watch, believe me. The question we have to ask ourselves, however, is how does it balance against what could become a full-blown civil war? Because in the grander scheme of things . . .'

'Screw the grander scheme of things.'

Vega's voice was raised. Of everyone around the table, the Key West lawman had the least experience of politics. It gave him an honesty that Dempsey now envied.

'We're talking about the deaths of a thousand innocent people. More than that, most likely. You want to go to war with the gun nuts and the rednecks and all that bullshit, you don't let people die just to justify it. You get your ass on camera and you make a goddamn case.'

'Detective, this—'

'This is all moot, that's what this is.' May slapped her hand onto the table ahead of her as she interrupted, her tone angry. 'You're debating the efficacy of allowing a single attack to happen. But this *isn't* a single attack, is it? One ton of caesium . . . there's no way any terrorist group wastes that on one bomb. Not when a tenth of that amount will do exactly the same damage.'

'What does that mean?'

May looked past Dempsey and Grace towards Vega. She took a moment to compose herself and to suppress her temper loss before answering his question. She seemed keen that her irritation was not directed to him.

'It means ten bombs, Sergio. Minimum. And *that* means a terror campaign, which Homeland can't allow.' She turned back to face McMillan. 'Because a single attack is a rallying call, isn't it, Mr Secretary? It'll win you the support you need to take these groups on. But a campaign? A campaign is a problem. A campaign will make the White House look weak. And a second, third, fourth attack? That'll quickly sap the will to fight. So if we're sure about the ton – and we *are*, Mr Secretary, we *are* sure – then we're back to where we started. We're back to finding the caesium, we're back to finding Scott Turner and we're back to stopping Liberation before they can act. At all costs.'

McMillan did not hurry to answer. He leaned back into his chair, his eyes now fixed on May. The natural time to respond came and went, but still he stayed silent, his gaze not shifting. Finally he sat forward and brought his two palms down gently onto the table. When he spoke, his tone was almost gentle.

'You're right, Agent May. If it's a ton – and I'm taking it from you all that it is – then all bets are off. We have to find it. And if we're going to do that, we have to do something we can never admit.'

'Which is what, sir?' O'Rourke asked.

McMillan turned to face her.

'We have to go negotiate with a terrorist.'

FORTY-SIX

1.05 a.m. EDT

O'Rourke lowered herself into her seat and took her time to get comfortable. She said nothing as she moved herself back and forth and side to side, settling in for what could be a long shift. It was part necessity and part act; a show, intended to demonstrate to Cam Arnold that he was not the most important person in the room.

In the chair next to her was May. That decision had been made by McMillan and was very much against O'Rourke's wishes. Even without their earlier confrontation as a factor, she would have preferred to have Dempsey alongside her.

But orders were orders and so here they were.

Arnold was positioned across the table from them both. Well within what would otherwise be touching distance, his wrists were cuffed to a thick metal loop in the table's centre. It provided just enough give for his comfort, while protecting the two women from the physical threat he would otherwise pose.

O'Rourke watched Arnold as she opened the thick manila file that she had carried into the room. Inside was everything Homeland Security knew about the man. His whole life in one

long, meticulous record. She had moved his one-sheet profile –
complete with photograph – so that it was now the front page,
positioned where it could not be missed. To someone with
Arnold's ideology, a privacy-destroying page of information all
about him would be a red rag to a bull.

Or at least that was O'Rourke's intention.

Arnold, though, did not give the file so much as a glance.
And May seemed to warrant just as little attention. Instead his
eyes remained fixed on O'Rourke, unblinking as the silence of
the room grew ever more oppressive.

Finally Arnold cracked a smile.

'They teach you this in Gestapo school, do they?'

There was genuine amusement in his voice. It told
O'Rourke two things.

This sonofabitch thinks he's funny.

And he thinks he's in control.

'Ironic it's you who brings up Nazis.'

The comment came from May. It caused Arnold to finally
turn his head and acknowledge her presence.

'Go educate yourself on irony, sweetheart,' Arnold replied,
his tone utterly dismissive. 'Then come back to me when you're
able to keep up. Until then, leave this to the grown-ups.'

His gaze shifted back to O'Rourke.

'Now how about you and me stop playing games and you
tell me how you're doing on my demands. You got Peyton
Travis heading this way yet?'

'Peyton Travis died ten years ago,' O'Rourke replied. 'But
you already know that. You also know that the US government
don't negotiate with terrorists. So even if he were alive, we
wouldn't be running to get him on your say-so.'

Arnold's smile widened as O'Rourke spoke. He ignored her

pointed use of the word 'terrorist' – thrown in in the hope of a reaction – and instead he focused on the first part of her answer.

'Peyton Travis was taken into custody ten years ago as a political prisoner. *That's* what I already know. And it's what you know too.'

'Whoever you're getting your information from, I suggest you go ask for a refund. Peyton Travis—'

'Is currently incarcerated in a top-secret, military-run prison you people call the Facility,' Arnold interrupted. 'He's being held without trial and has been for the last decade. You want to continue to deny that, Agent O'Rourke? Or are you and I gonna stop playing games here and start talking straight?'

O'Rourke hesitated for just a moment. She forced herself to face forward, trying hard to give no indication of what she now knew: that Arnold's intelligence was one hundred per cent correct.

Her silence, as short as it was, seemed to be enough.

'Maybe you're not the adult in the room after all.' Arnold's eyes moved from O'Rourke and towards the large mirror that was built into the wall behind them. 'Maybe I need to speak to your boss on the other side of that two-way. Is that it? You need his permission to tell the truth here, do ya? I guess that figures.'

'Figures how?'

Arnold ignored the question and raised his voice. He was now speaking directly to the occupants of the hidden observation room.

'Gotta tell you, fellas. Knowing you're there, it's a hell of a relief. For a while I really thought you'd trusted this whole thing to one of them. Good to know it's all just for show.'

'There's no one behind that mirror that I answer to,' O'Rourke lied through gritted teeth. As much as it bothered her to admit it, Arnold was getting to her. 'This is *my* operation. Does that bother you? That you've been brought in by a black woman?'

Arnold's eyes refocused on O'Rourke.

'Maybe it would, if me being here had a goddamn thing to do with you. But you got to know it didn't, right? You got to know that I'm just where I want to be?'

'Come on. Are we really gonna sit here and talk this foolishness?'

'Ain't nothing foolish about it. They know what I'm saying.' Arnold gestured to the mirror as he spoke. And then May. 'And I reckon she does too. But since they're making me deal with the slow kids, let's use language you understand. I *planned* for you to catch me. I gave you every damn clue and crumb I could. Because I *wanted* to be in this room. I *wanted* to be having this here conversation.'

'You expect us to believe—'

'I don't give a damn what *you* believe. All that matters to me is what the white man hiding behind that mirror believes. What *he* knows. And right now, what he knows is this: my people are out there with enough caesium to bring this government to its knees. They got it and they know how to use it. And so now your boss can do exactly what I want, or he can watch your United States of America burn.'

Arnold's fixed gaze returned to the mirror, his voice once again raised.

'And frankly, fellas, right now I'm not too fussed which choice you make.'

Ray McMillan showed no emotion as Arnold spoke. He remained stock-still, not moving an inch back from the two-way mirror even as the Liberation man addressed him directly. It was a near perfect poker face, betrayed only by the slightest bead of sweat that had trickled from the top of his hairless head and now moved past his ear.

In the small, air-conditioned room they were in, that bead of sweat could only be the result of anxiety.

Dempsey was standing at the other end of the mirror. The space between them allowed him to observe McMillan while O'Rourke engaged Arnold. To study his reaction, however well hidden. And that observation confirmed to Dempsey that Arnold's claims were true.

'Where's the Facility?'

McMillan half-turned at the question.

'Are you suggesting that he's right about that?'

'I'm not suggesting anything. He *is* right about it.'

'You've decided that just from what that lunatic said?'

'No. I decided it from how you rolled with what he said. If Peyton Travis is dead like he's supposed to be, you wouldn't have steeled yourself to show no reaction to Arnold's statement. So, the Facility. Where is it?'

'Texas.' McMillan's reply was instant. It confirmed the impression Dempsey had already drawn: the secretary for Homeland Security was utterly practical. He wasted no time pushing a lie that he knew Dempsey would reject. 'Eighty miles outside of San Antonio.'

'And how many untried men are you holding there?'

'Two hundred and eight as of midday yesterday.'

'Very precise. Suggests a recent briefing. Which I guess means arrangements are in place?'

'To move Peyton Travis, you mean? Of course they are. We're against the clock here, Agent Dempsey. And if the decision *is* made to bring him here, I need that done without delay.'

'So we're suddenly in a hurry, are we? It didn't seem so urgent while we waited around for you to fly in.'

'That's because we didn't know what our decision would be then, did we? We didn't know that we'd be looking to stop these lunatics.' McMillan finally turned to face Dempsey. 'But now we do and so now we're in a hurry. It really is that simple and yet it feels to me like you and I are on the edge of having a problem here. Are we, Agent Dempsey?'

'About what part, sir? About the fact you were willing to turn a blind eye to a one-off bomb? Or about the secret prison you're running where you're letting un-convicted men rot?'

Dempsey could not keep the disgust from his voice as he spoke. McMillan seemed unfazed.

'Pick one,' he replied, his tone lacking any hint of concern. 'Either will do. Because if we *do* have a problem, well, as much as the president might have your back, this is *my* operation. And *I* don't need complications. Do we have an understanding?'

'We do,' Dempsey replied. 'For now, anyway. Until this is over.'

McMillan turned away before he replied, his focus already back on the interrogation room.

'Good enough for me.'

'OK. Let's assume for a moment that you're right about the Facility. And about Peyton Travis.' May spoke with confidence, filling the silence that had been left by O'Rourke. '*If* it exists – and *if* he's alive – what do you gain by his release?'

'Gain?' Arnold replied. 'What's *my* gain got to do with anything?'

'You've gone to a lot of trouble, Cam. You've put it all on the line. There's got to be an upside in this for you.'

'That's the problem with you people. You're a bunch of weak-willed liberal fucking sheep. To you, everything is about what you can get. What you can take. What you can steal. It's about what you're entitled to be given. You tell the world that you're this shining city on the hill. Humanity at its best. But, at the end of the day, you're just a big old melting pot of shit, all thrown in together with no cause or vision or . . . or . . . anything.

'But that ain't *my* people, sweetheart. We know what patriotism is. We know what brotherhood is. And Peyton Travis, he's one of us. And if you think we're gonna forget about him. If you think we're gonna walk away and leave a soldier behind. Well, lady, you got a whole lot to learn about Liberation.'

'It's been ten years.' This time it was O'Rourke who responded. 'A decade. You and that brotherhood of yours? You already left him behind. Hell, you don't even know that he's the same man as he was back then.'

'Ten years don't mean shit.' For the first time there was venom in Arnold's voice. Hatred. And it was directed entirely at O'Rourke. 'We've been in this fight since 1861. Before that, even. This is a long game we're playing here. Has to be, when so many of our own are betraying their race and taking sides with the likes of *you*. No, ten years don't matter. He knows we'll come for him in the end. He knows it's just a matter of time.'

O'Rourke looked at Grace in disbelief, their earlier issues now forgotten in the face of Arnold's fanaticism. Grace simply shook her head. Like O'Rourke, she seemed to have no reply to what the man was saying.

It confirmed what O'Rourke already knew: there was no victory to be had by engaging a ranting madman.

Instead, she changed the subject.

'Maybe you're right. I guess we'll see. Right now, though, there's something else I wanna know. Where's Scott Turner?'

O'Rourke watched as Arnold's angry smirk faded. Just for a moment, he looked unsure of himself. It was gone in an instant, replaced by the same belligerent facade. But it had lasted long enough for O'Rourke to see that he had been rattled.

He didn't expect that name.

'Who wants to know?' Arnold looked again towards the mirror as he asked the question.

'That'll be Homeland Security that wants to know, Mr Arnold.' O'Rourke knew an attempt at diversion when she saw one. 'Now quit prevaricating and answer the damn question. Where is he?'

'Why?'

'Why do you think?'

'You first.'

O'Rourke resisted an urge to frown. Arnold's change in attitude was confusing; it seemed to be more than a reaction to a name he did not expect them to know. Whatever it was, O'Rourke had no idea. But she could not let Arnold know that. Not while he was on the ropes.

She leaned forward and placed her elbows on the table. Her face was now tantalisingly close to Arnold's restrained hands. O'Rourke made a point of looking down at them before she spoke again. Studying the scars and the damage around the knuckles.

'You gettin' frustrated now, Cam?'

'Don't remember giving you permission to use my first name.'

'I don't remember needing it.' O'Rourke indicated to his clenched fists. 'I bet you'd like to have those hands wrapped around my throat right about now, right?'

'Ain't like I'm trying to hide that fact, is it?'

'True enough. But now. Right now. Now that you know we're on to your little friend. I bet you'd like to choke the life right out of me.'

'Trust me, lady. I don't need no excuse to want that. I just got to look at you, sitting there in your suit and speaking like you're civilised folk.'

O'Rourke smiled. His racism was no longer having the desired effect. When Arnold had been calm and in control, it had been pointed. Directed with precision. But now?

Now it was just desperate.

'You telling me this sudden discomfort of yours, that it's not related to the fact we know who Scott Turner is?'

'Why'd you keep bringing that boy up?' Arnold's eyes flitted from O'Rourke to May. 'Why are you so interested in him?'

'Why does the name seem to hit you so hard, Cam?' O'Rourke asked. 'There some . . . special bond between you two? You get a little close for comfort back at redneck terror school?'

'Fuck you. I ain't a faggot.'

Arnold smirked at his own reply. An attempt to seem unaffected, O'Rourke could tell. It did not work.

'Why are you so concerned about him, then? About the fact we know his name?'

'I ain't concerned about nothing. I just don't see why we're changing the subject, that's all. When we're here to talk about Peyton Travis.'

'Was it you that recruited Turner? What was it? You needed his big old science brain to get to work on the caesium? Is that where it's heading now? To Scott Turner?'

Arnold did not respond. Instead he sat back into his chair – as far as his cuffs would allow – and he smiled. First at O'Rourke. Then at May. In that moment the Homeland agent knew that she had broken the golden rule.

She had asked one question too many, revealing that she did not know as much as he might have thought. When Arnold spoke again, it was clear that he had regained his composure. And with it, he had reclaimed the room.

'Now how about we get away from the kid, get back to where we started and you tell me when the fuck I'm gonna see Peyton Travis.'

'What do you make of that?'

McMillan turned to face Dempsey as he spoke.

'She had him,' Dempsey replied. 'And now she doesn't.'

'But why?'

'She gave too much away. Nailed her colours to the mast by asking about the caesium. If us knowing that Turner's the bomb-maker was what concerned Arnold then that would have been the right move. But from his reaction, it seems that wasn't the problem. He thought we knew something else about Turner. Something we don't. Whatever that was, it had him worried.'

'What could it be?'

'Who knows? It could be anything.'

'Maybe what O'Rourke said earlier was right – that maybe they've been involved?'

'Can't rule it out,' Dempsey replied, 'but I think it's

unlikely. If Arnold's gay he'd have to keep that well hidden. It's not the sort of thing that goes down too well with bigots. So hooking up with another member of Liberation, that seems much too risky for a man who's been so careful for so long. He's spent ten years keeping that movement alive and building it back into a force. He wouldn't risk that for sex. Not when he could just go get that away from prying eyes. Besides, to my knowledge, Scott Turner's straight.'

McMillan nodded his head, his eyes narrowing. He had more questions. Dempsey could tell. And the ISB agent could anticipate what they might be.

'To your knowledge,' McMillan parroted. 'And just what is "your knowledge", Agent Dempsey? We never got to that in the briefing, did we? So how about you tell me now: just why is Scott Turner of interest to the ISB?'

'He's not,' Dempsey answered. 'He's of interest to me. This one is . . . it's personal.'

'Not any more it's not. Not if you intend to continue being a part of this operation. So what is it? You've got a history with this guy?'

'No, not with him.' Dempsey looked back into the interrogation room as he spoke. His eyes once again fixed on Arnold and the smug, self-satisfied grin that had returned. 'With his father.'

'His father? You've got to be kidding me.'

'Do I look like I'm kidding?'

'No. No, I guess you don't. Come on, then. What was your relationship with Turner's father?'

Dempsey took a deep breath and looked McMillan directly in the eye.

'I'm the man who killed him.'

FORTY-SEVEN

1.48 a.m. EDT

Scott Turner jerked awake in confusion, staring into his dark, unfamiliar surroundings. In that moment he wondered where he was. An instant more and he knew both the answer and why he was suddenly conscious.

A series of loud, heavy bangs shocked every last residue of sleep from his system and sent him crashing towards the night table at the side of his motel bed. As unsuited as Turner was to the life he had embraced, Cam Arnold's training had been thorough. Such aggressive knocking in the middle of the night had to be viewed as a threat.

Turner grabbed his Smith & Wesson 640 revolver and cautiously moved towards the door. The banging had stopped. All he could hear now was the heavy thump of an insistent beat. Someone close by was having a party.

He looked through the peephole, expecting to see either a drunken partygoer or an angry resident choosing the wrong room for his complaint. He was surprised, then, to see no one there. The fact made little sense until, seconds later, the banging started again.

It was the same sound as before, and it left Turner in no doubt that he had been correct: someone *was* beating on a door.

Just not my door.

He climbed to his feet and walked to the front of the small room, towards the large, curtained window that made up at least half of its front wall. Careful not to make any noticeable movement, he slowly widened the natural gap where the curtains met and peered outside.

Turner's room was on the second floor of the motel and so his first view was of both the parking lot below and of the road beyond it, lit up in the darkness by the tall neon signs advertising the businesses that flanked the highway.

He ignored those details. From here, with the dampening effects of the walls and the curtains reduced, he could see and hear much more. And so he now knew exactly why he was awake.

Kenny fucking Brooks.

Just the name tightened Turner's grip on his pistol. Just the thought of the man. He had been nothing but a thorn in Turner's side since they had left Key West. And now there he was, Turner could see. Shirtless, angry and smashing a thick, battered fist against the door of the motel room that was two down from Turner's own.

'Jesus Christ.'

Turner said the words aloud as he stepped away from the window. He opened the door and stepped out, onto a long balcony that took a ninety-degree turn at the end of his room, creating the motel's elongated 'L' shape. Brooks was near a closed doorway a few yards beyond it. He was animated, pacing like a caged animal.

'KENNY.'

It was nearly 2 a.m. but Turner had no reason to keep his voice down. Anyone he could wake would already be up, if not from Brooks' assault on the door then most certainly from the deafening music that was coming from beyond it. The sounds of a party in full swing were much clearer now that Turner was wide awake and outside.

'KENNY,' he shouted again. 'WHAT THE FUCK ARE YOU DOING? GET BACK IN YOUR ROOM.'

'FUCK YOU, LIMEY.'

Brooks did not even look around as he shouted back. Turner's English accent had been enough for Brooks to recognise the voice and – as always – he seemed to have no intention of following the younger man's orders. In fact, he did the opposite, raising his fist and once again beating on the closed door.

'TURN THAT SHIT OFF,' he shouted. 'PEOPLE ARE TRYING TO DAMN WELL SLEEP.'

Turner shook his head. Brooks was not entirely wrong. The music and the sound of the partying from inside the room *was* loud. But still . . . the irony of that statement, screamed into the night air at 2 a.m.

As laughable as it was, Turner had no time to find it funny. Brooks was already banging the door again, this time even harder. Turner watched as it shook under the weight of the older man's hard, weathered knuckles.

From the sounds that were coming from inside, the room was crowded. And if Turner was any judge of human nature, the patience of that crowd had to be wearing thin. He realised that he had to get Brooks inside. Somehow he had to avoid what was beginning to look inevitable.

A second later and his time had run out.

The door was swung open before Brooks had finished

banging, knocking him off balance and causing his arm to flail comically as the wooden resistance disappeared. Not that Turner had time to find any humour in the sight; before he could even register what he had seen, he watched Brooks take two strides back to the balcony railing before a near giant stepped out of the room.

The looming figure had to duck as he walked through the door and out into the open. He dwarfed Brooks in both height and width. His size alone could have been enough to identify him as a football player, but any doubt was dispelled by the way he was dressed: the Charleston Southern Buccaneers jersey he wore fitted him perfectly, while the number sixty-three on its chest even suggested his position.

'And just what the fuck do you want, asshole?'

Turner knew what he had to do. What he *should* do. He *should* defuse the situation. Brooks would never back down, not even from what appeared to be one of the local college's offensive linemen; a bigger, stronger, much younger man. And so Turner knew that he should step in before this thing escalated.

And yet the thought that Brooks might get his comeuppance at last? It made Turner hesitate.

It's not like he hasn't asked for it.

The thought was gone as quickly as it had arrived, dispelled by a response faster and more violent than even Turner had anticipated. He had at least expected to see an exchange of words. Perhaps some posturing. But Brooks evidently knew better. This fight was a mismatch, and so the only chance he stood was to hit first and hit hard.

Brooks did exactly that. He hit first. And, for good measure, he also hit dirty.

The insult had barely passed the linesman's lips as Brooks drove his fist upwards. A less experienced street fighter would have aimed for the jaw, an instinct as natural as it would be foolish; no one reached the level of competitive college football without the ability to ride out a head-strike. Brooks made no such mistake. Instead, he used the height difference to his advantage and stuck upwards with a rising right cross, connecting flush in the centre of the bigger man's throat.

The linesman staggered backwards towards the doorway, his huge hands clutching helplessly at the skin and cartilage that had failed to protect his collapsing windpipe. The desperate reflex left him defenceless to what Brooks did next, as the Liberation man lifted his right leg and stamped forward with all of his weight on his opponent's exposed knee. The impact was as devastating as it was unnecessary, ending a fight that was already over by sending the footballer's leg joint in a direction it was never made to go.

Brooks stepped back and watched the man fall before turning his attention back to the open doorway. Turner looked on in horror, frozen to the spot, as Brooks raised his arms and shouted into the still packed room.

'WHO'S FUCKING NEXT, HUH? WHO'S FUCKING NEXT?'

'We gotta stop this.'

Turner spun around at the words. He had not realised that Cliff Clemons had joined him on the balcony. Like Turner, Clemons was dressed in just his boxer shorts.

'We gotta stop this now,' he repeated.

Turner nodded his head in agreement and began to move. He gripped his gun tight as he closed the short distance between them. Unlike Brooks, he had no view through the door to the room. And so he did not know what might be coming. But he could tell from Brooks' body language that what he had witnessed was only a pause in the violence that lay ahead.

A pause which, from the way he now saw Brooks visibly tense, was about to come to an end.

Turner accelerated for the final few feet and raised his revolver, just as the first body came rushing through the open door.

'DON'T FUCKING MOVE.'

Turner's shout was loud enough and close enough to make the newcomer turn his head as he came at Brooks. Combined with the sight of Turner's gun, it might even have been enough to stop the heavily built man in his tracks. But Turner would never know, because Brooks did not give him the opportunity.

With momentum behind him but his focus distracted, the newcomer had made it easy for Brooks to step aside and use the man's barrelling forward motion against him. A heavy collision with the balcony railings was inevitable, made all the worse as Brooks grabbed at his passing clothing and used it to ensure that collision was head first.

Turner did not need to watch the second man fall. Nor did he need to check that Brooks had done what was necessary to keep him down; if there was one thing he could assume from Brooks, it was maximum violence at all times. Instead, he focused on the doorway and on the room beyond, fully aware that there were only so many young men they could successfully take on.

And only so much commotion they could cause.

A third man – wider than the first, taller than the second – was just feet from the door as Turner aimed the revolver inside. The man did not come any closer. As Turner knew it would, the gun trumped both numbers and physicality. A fortunate reality as he counted off six more obvious football players and at least as many teenage girls inside.

'Every one of you, step back.' Turner had lowered his voice but kept the intensity. 'Get against the back wall.'

The group did as they were told, revealing as they moved a room that was a mess of empty beer cans and the smears left by lines of cocaine. It really *had* been a party.

The sound of a man loudly struggling for breath threatened to distract Turner but he resisted the urge to turn back. Some of those against the wall seemed unable to do the same. They looked past both him and the gun, towards the door.

Towards Brooks.

'Don't look at him,' Turner ordered, gesturing with his weapon. 'Look at me. Look. At. Me.'

Every wandering eye did as instructed.

'Now all of you, any phones. Take them out and throw them at my feet.'

He waited while they all did as instructed. As they fumbled through their pockets, there was a strangled moan of pain from behind.

'WILL YOU STOP THAT SHIT?' Turner shouted over his shoulder. He did not need to see what Brooks was doing to know that it would be sadistic. And utterly unnecessary. 'ENOUGH.'

His eyes had stayed on the line-up, their mobile phones now in a clumsy pile just ahead of him. Satisfied, he pointed at the landline phone that was sat on the nightstand by the bed and gestured to the player nearest to it. Like every other man in the room, the guy outweighed Turner by at least fifty pounds.

'You. Rip that phone out of the wall and then rip the wire out of the receiver.'

The man did as he was told.

'Now join the rest of them back there.'

Once the man had returned to the wall, Turner took two strides back. It brought him almost level with the doorway. Close enough that he knew he could be heard by Brooks and Clemons. Before he spoke he looked down at the linebacker, now prone on the floor and still struggling for breath. It seemed to Turner that the man's injury was restricting his oxygen intake rather than cutting it off completely.

But what the hell do I know about it? The poor bastard could be dying right there.

Whatever the reality, Turner was in no position to help. Careful to keep the group in his peripheral vision, he shifted his gaze from the injured man to Brooks. When he spoke, he kept his voice as low as he could. To avoid being heard inside.

'We've got to get out of here. Now.'

'What's the matter?' Brooks smirked. 'Bit of action and you wanna cut and run?'

'Actually, yeah. That's exactly what I want to do. Because there's no way the police haven't already been called for your "bit of action", you fucking lunatic. And we can't afford to be arrested for it. Not now. So go get dressed, get your stuff and get to the car.'

Turner did not wait for a reply. He turned to Clemons.

'You do the same,' Turner instructed. 'Then go grab my things too. Meet me back here. You've both got two minutes, then we're getting the hell out of this shithole. Now go.'

FORTY-EIGHT

2.25 a.m. EDT

'So, it appears we're at an impasse,' McMillan concluded. After an hour spent interrogating Cam Arnold with no results, O'Rourke and May – along with McMillan and Dempsey – had rejoined the rest of the team to bring them up to date on developments.

Or, more accurately, on the fact that the interview had achieved nothing.

'I would say we are, yeah,' O'Rourke replied. 'That man ain't telling us nothing. Not until he knows that Peyton Travis has been released. Probably not after that, either. Even if we did let it happen.'

'And what makes you think we *won't* let it happen?' McMillan asked.

The question took O'Rourke by surprise. Of all the possibilities she had considered since taking Arnold into custody, giving in to his demand had not been one of them.

'We . . . we don't negotiate with terrorists, sir. That's our line in the sand, surely? We're the United States government. We can't—'

'That's the thing about lines in the sand, Special Agent

O'Rourke. If the tide's strong enough, those lines move. And sometimes they disappear altogether.'

O'Rourke said nothing. The expression on McMillan's face told her that she would be wasting her time. He looked around the room before speaking again, his words no longer directed at anyone in particular.

'Look, I came here tonight with an open mind. Probably way more open than any of yours. But you convinced me what Liberation are planning. What they're capable of pulling off. We can't let it happen. Not at any price. We have no idea where Scott Turner is, or any of the other men from the marina that night. We don't know where any of the caesium is. We have no other leads. Right now the only route we have out of this is to do as Arnold asks. Unless anyone here has a better plan?'

O'Rourke felt a fast beat flow through the vein in her temple as she listened. A sure sign that her blood pressure was rising. The sensation came as no surprise. What was being suggested went against everything she stood for. She had to find another way.

'Maybe if you gave us the time to come up with a better plan, at least?' she pleaded. 'Instead of just accepting the easy route?'

'You think this is an easy route? You think this is an easy decision? *I'm* where the buck stops on this one, O'Rourke. *I'm* the one who's considering bringing a dead man back to life. This isn't the goddamned easy route. But unless you're about to tell me otherwise, it might just be the *only* route.'

'There has to be another way,' O'Rourke implored. 'He's a terrorist, Mr Secretary. He's—'

'There's much more at stake than that. One man's terrorist is another man's hero, O'Rourke. How many statues do we have in this country of men once regarded as terrorists? The implications of what Arnold is asking for go far beyond the principle of with whom we do and do not negotiate. If I authorise the release of Travis, I am acknowledging the existence of the Facility. And when that happens, what do you think the world's reaction will be?'

'You're suggesting the world doesn't know about it already?'

The question came from Dempsey and it caused McMillan to look away from O'Rourke.

'Of course I'm not suggesting that it's entirely unknown. At the highest level, anyway. But since when was that the same thing as being known outright? And since when did public reaction have anything to do with genuine outrage? If I have to acknowledge that we're holding hundreds of civilians without trial and without hope of release? We'll be crucified internationally.'

McMillan turned back to face O'Rourke.

'And yet that's what I'm going to be forced to do. Unless we can come up with an alternative, that's all I *can* do. Because even international outrage beats the hell that Liberation are now capable of inflicting upon us. And so if Arnold can stop that—'

'But if we just had time—'

'What if we *don't* have time? What if we see the first bomb today? This morning, even? They have the material, O'Rourke. We know that. And they've got the know-how, thanks to Turner. If he's with the caesium already – and you know he most likely is – then we could be hours away from the first attack. Shit, we could be too late already. We have to act now.'

O'Rourke said nothing. She knew how she wanted to respond. She wanted to remind McMillan of the immutable rules of this world. Of the consequences of bending in the face of a threat. But she knew it would do no good. And she knew that she had no other argument.

She could only hope that Dempsey or May could do better.

'Anyone else got anything to say on this?' McMillan asked. 'Before I make the final call?'

'I think it's a mistake,' Dempsey said. 'Everything we've seen today, no doubt going back to the first tip-off about Key Largo, all of it has led us here. All of it put *Arnold* here. And I believe him when he says that it's precisely where he wants to be.'

McMillan paused for just a moment before replying. And in that breath, O'Rourke found some hope.

'OK. And why does that matter?'

O'Rourke watched the ISB agent carefully as he thought through his response. Like her, he clearly saw this as their last chance to do the right thing. To deal with Liberation without bowing to their demands.

Dempsey's hand reached up and touched the ragged six-inch scar that ran the length of his left cheek. An unconscious tic, O'Rourke guessed.

He's feeling the pressure, too. He knows we're a whisker from the wrong ending here.

'Because that's meticulous planning,' Dempsey replied. 'And the release of Travis is part of that plan. We can't play right into his hands like that. Not when we don't know what his endgame is. Travis is a dangerous man to bring into this and even once he's out there's no guarantee Arnold would tell us anything. I know we need to do something to prevent a potential disaster. And we need to do it quickly. But we've been one step behind Arnold all along. More than one, if we're honest. If we do as he asked now, we'll just make the situation worse for ourselves.'

'I'm hearing a lot of opinions, Agent Dempsey.' McMillan's tone was a little uncertain as he snapped out the words. 'What I'm not hearing are any solutions. If we go along with what he's demanding – if we release Travis – then we're at least buying ourselves some time as we arrange it. Time to locate these other crazy sonsofbitches.'

'And you think what, that an extra few hours will be enough?' Dempsey asked. 'It's not worth the risk. Travis is a maniac with a brain the size of a planet. Once he's outside those walls, he's a bigger threat than Arnold could ever be.'

'Actually that's not entirely true.'

May's voice broke through the exchange. O'Rourke glanced sharply towards her, while all other eyes in the room turned in her direction as one.

With everyone's attention caught, she continued:

'You don't know what's happened with Peyton Travis during his time at the Facility. More importantly, Arnold doesn't know either. In my opinion, Travis could be our most valuable asset here and I think we should bring him in.'

'What the hell are you talking about, Nicki?' O'Rourke felt a chill of cold anger as she registered May's words. Dempsey had been standing her ground and that had given her some hope. Now she sensed their opportunity to stop Liberation's one demand begin to slip away.

'I'm talking about the rehabilitation of Peyton Travis. I've read the psychiatric reports myself, built up over a decade of treatment. He's changed. He's disavowed everything about Liberation. Everything about who he was.'

'That doesn't sound right. The man was a fanatic,'

Dempsey said. 'Men like that, they don't just wake up with a change of heart.'

'Unless what he did was connected to some emotional or mental health issue,' May replied. 'Unless those beliefs were never really his. Not the real him. Which is what his medical doctors have concluded.'

'Doctors can be fooled. Especially by a man as brilliant as Travis. He could be lying to try to get released.'

'That would be entirely pointless,' May replied, 'and a man as brilliant as you say Travis is would know that. Rehabilitation would never achieve his release. No amount of change in an inmate's character or beliefs makes a difference with the Facility. You go in there, you go in for life. Travis knows that. And once inside, there's absolutely no contact with the outside world, which means Arnold doesn't know about any of this.'

'Well he sure as hell knew of Travis's continued existence. *I* believed he was dead. If the place is so watertight, how does Arnold even know he's there?'

'There's no possibility of contact with an inmate once that inmate's inside. But that doesn't rule out a leak about the fact they're in there. That sort of information, it's not behind the same walls as the prisoners themselves. And like the secretary said, the Facility might not be public knowledge but it's not the Kennedy assassination, either. We've got better kept secrets.'

'At this point it doesn't matter *how* Arnold knows about the Facility or that Travis is in there. What matters is that he *does* know.' McMillan turned back to May. 'So what's your suggestion, Agent May?'

'We brief Travis. We tell him he can help us. Offer up some sort of amenity, something he wants, and bring him in. Arnold clearly still worships the man. If he didn't there's no way he'd have gone to these lengths for his release. He's expecting Travis to be on side. And that makes it likely that he'll tell Travis the plan and location of the caesium if we bring the two of them together. Then Travis tells us.'

O'Rourke stared at her former protégée. In theory it made sense. But after the time she'd spent with Arnold – and, over the years, with others like him – she didn't buy it. She shook her head.

'No, I'm sorry, It's still too risky. He may claim to be converted in there, and let's say for a moment I believe that, because how the hell do I know? What's to stop him having another "change of heart" once he's out and he's face to face with his old life?'

'I agree,' Dempsey said. 'I know his kind. They don't give up their views that easy. There's just not enough proof that his rehabilitation is real.'

'How about six attempts on his life in a single year? Is that convincing enough?' May placed her finger on a page of the file that sat ahead of her. 'Two by black inmates, motivated by his time with Liberation. And four by men who used to worship the ground he walks on, up until he came out and denounced the movement. That's two attempts for what he used to be, Dempsey. And four more because of what he has become. Because he has chosen to repudiate the Liberation movement and everything they stand for. Everything he used to stand for. Is that good enough for you?'

'Seven attempts and he's still alive? You sure they've been trying hard enough?'

O'Rourke heard the undisguised scepticism in Dempsey's tone. She opened her mouth to add her own, but the secretary for Homeland Security beat her to the punch.

'Enough.' McMillan slapped his right hand on the table, calling the exchanges to a halt. 'Agent May is right. If Peyton Travis has disavowed Liberation then there's no way Arnold could be aware of that fact. And that changes everything. Travis is just about our best possible bet to come through this thing in one piece. This debate is over. I want him here as soon as possible.'

He turned to O'Rourke.

'The DOJ have already made the arrangements to collect him from the Facility, in case this was the route we took. It won't take much to turn that into an escort from there to here. No offence, O'Rourke, but on this leg I want Agent May taking point.'

He turned to May.

'An armed DOJ team will be waiting for you at Vandeveer Airbase, ten miles out from the Facility. O'Rourke and her team will accompany you to back them up, just in case. Anything goes wrong here, no one's going to say Homeland didn't carry its weight.'

O'Rourke looked on with dismay. For the third time in twenty-four hours, May – the woman O'Rourke had mentored and guided, who she genuinely saw as her baby sister – had undermined her. This was a mistake. She felt it in her gut.

Sadly for O'Rourke, her gut would not be enough to dissuade McMillan.

The secretary climbed to his feet and turned his focus to Dempsey.

'And you, Agent Dempsey? I can't order you to join O'Rourke but, from what the president tells me, we'd be crazy to leave you out.'

'We'll go,' Dempsey confirmed. He indicated to Grace and Vega. 'All three of us. We've come this far.'

McMillan hesitated. It was clear to everyone that the offer had not included Vega. And perhaps not even Grace. O'Rourke was sure that Dempsey knew that, too, but if McMillan thought the same he did not show it; with just a nod of the head to confirm the personnel, he was heading for the door.

His departure left just the Key West original team in the room. O'Rourke's own Homeland squad. The stragglers she had picked up along the way. And the 'friend' who had just usurped the leadership of her team.

However O'Rourke had expected the operation to play out, it sure as hell was not like this.

FORTY-NINE

2.40 a.m. EDT

Scott Turner rubbed his palm against his right eye socket, careful to keep what that left of his vision on the sodium-lit road. The dark, featureless horizon of the I-95 was rolled out ahead of him. Seven hundred miles long, give or take, from this point to Carbon County, Pennsylvania.

It was a drive Turner had been dreading for the long, stark miles that lay ahead, but right now the spread of empty lanes ahead was a relief. Keeping to the US-17 speed limit and taking every precaution to avoid attention, it had taken nearly forty minutes for the Jeep to travel from their Summerville motel parking lot to the interstate. A near forty-mile journey, with Turner primed over every inch for the appearance of a red light and the sound of a siren.

Fear had kept him awake and nerves had kept him focused. With the roads near deserted, he had been convinced that some police attention was inevitable. Attention that would no doubt end badly once Kenny Brooks got involved. Somehow it had not happened. Despite what Brooks had done at the motel – hell, despite what Turner had had to do himself – they had made it out of Summerville, they had passed their journey's halfway mark of Walterboro and they were now exactly where they should be: heading north on the road that would take them 'home'.

That they were on that road at all was a triumph after everything they had been through. And yet it was not entirely ideal. Because while they were nearly four hours ahead of schedule, Turner was operating on barely two hours' sleep. Not a problem when wired by the anticipation of arrest. But very much a problem now that this fear was behind him.

He reached out for the bottle of now warm water that sat in the front console. Cliff Clemons was asleep in the front passenger seat next to him and so Turner was careful not to touch him as he placed the bottle between his own knees, reached into the storage shelf on the inside of the driver's door and felt around for the touch of thin, cold metal.

The single foil layer of caffeine tablets was the only item in there and so he found it quickly. Taking out three white tabs, he popped the cap on the water bottle and sucked in the few mouthfuls that were left in there, washing the caffeine down in the process.

Turner dropped what was left of the tablets back into the door's open compartment before turning his attention to the now empty bottle. For just a moment he thought about throwing it into the back seat, towards Kenny Brooks' head. The mental image made him smile. Waking the bastard with a start would give him at least a moment of pleasure.

Except once that moment's over, the arsehole will be awake.

Turner dismissed the idea, placed the bottle back into the console's empty cup holder and kept his eyes on the road. A focus that made him miss the signs of Clemons stirring in the seat beside him.

'How you feeling?'

The sound of Clemons' near-whispered voice came as a welcome shock.

'Been better,' Turner replied. 'We didn't need that shit back there.'

'You mean back at the motel,' Clemons asked, 'or the shit in the back seat?'

Turner did not need to look to know that Clemons was smiling at his own crack.

'Both,' Turner said, a grin now spreading across his face. 'What about you? Wish you'd taken my offer back at the diner?'

'I can't say I ain't feeling a mite regretful. But then what would you be doing without me, just you and crazy eyes back there? I reckon you need me here more than I need to be elsewhere.'

'You might be right, Cliff. You might be right.'

'You want me to take a shift at the wheel?'

'In a few hours. In the meantime, try and get some sleep. We've got a long journey ahead.'

FIFTY

4 a.m. CDT

Joshua opened his eyes at the sound of the cell door's locking mechanism.

Before the first bolt had even moved into place, he had glanced towards the cheap plastic timepiece on his wrist.

Before the second he was on his feet.

And before the third he was just three steps from the cell door, primed and ready for whatever might be coming. At 4 a.m. and after what had happened yesterday, it was unlikely to be anything good.

He felt himself relax as the cell door opened slowly. The lack of urgency suggested that he was wrong. Anyone coming for him or for Travis in the night was unlikely to give up the advantage of surprise by moving with such leisure. That conclusion was strengthened when the cell's lights were switched on.

Murder tends to happen in the dark.

Joshua took a step back, his defences down, as Captain Bickle stepped through the door. The sight of the short, whippet-thin intelligence officer caused him to exhale hard. An unwelcome presence at the best of times, Bickle was the last person Joshua wanted to see before dawn. In that moment, he almost wished it *had* been someone looking to finish the job.

He kept the thought to himself, but he made no effort to hide the disdain that lay behind it.

'What do you want, Bickle? How many times do I have to tell you? I've got nothing to say to you or to anyone else.'

'Who says I'm here for you?'

Bickle hardly even glanced at Joshua as he spoke. His eyes were on the far corner of the room. Where Peyton Travis was now pushing himself upright.

'What the hell's going on?'

Travis directed the question to Joshua and seemed to only then notice their guest. Unsurprisingly, the sight of a senior Facility officer did nothing to change his irritated attitude. And like Joshua, he did nothing to hide it. If there was one thing that Travis had not lost after a decade locked up, it was a sense of his own importance.

'What the hell are *you* doing here, Bickle? Have you got any idea what goddamn time it is?'

Joshua could feel a bristle of . . . of . . . something as the words hit the captain. He could not place exactly what that something was. Irritation? Impatience? Maybe even a feeling of chastisement? Joshua did not know which, but it was not the first time he had seen Travis stop a man in his tracks like that.

It was a reaction with which Joshua was familiar from his own life, but in his case it was natural. He was tall, fit and strong, and perfectly capable of killing ninety-nine per cent of human beings with his bare hands.

But Peyton Travis? The only thing that was *not* physically average about the man was his hair, still unusually thick for a man in his mid-fifties, even if it was now greying fast. The effect

Travis had, then, had nothing to do with physicality or violence. It could only be described as a presence. And while that was lost on a man like Joshua, it had a visible effect on most others.

Bickle certainly felt it now. Joshua watched as the intelligence officer pushed through it.

'This place works by my watch, Travis. By my time. Not yours. Now get up. You're going on a little trip.'

The hard words would have meant more if they had not followed such an obvious nervous pause. Joshua would have been amused by the exchange, were it not for the announcement that Travis was to be moved. That was unexpected and it put Joshua on edge.

'What trip?' he asked.

The fact that the question came from Joshua caused Bickle to turn.

'And what the hell has that got to do with you?'

Joshua felt his jaw clench. It was an unconscious movement, brought about by uncertainty. For the first time in a very long time, he was unsure of what was now expected of him.

Bickle took two steps forward, shortening the distance between them to less than a foot. The intentional invasion of Joshua's personal space derailed his train of thought.

'Well, inmate?' Bickle demanded. 'Do you want to tell me how Travis's movements are any business of yours?'

Joshua looked down at Bickle as the man spoke and he was aware of exactly what this was: an attempt by the intelligence officer to regain the front foot after Travis had thrown him off balance. Bickle was compensating with a display of strutting arrogance, towards a man who he knew could kill him in a heartbeat. It was a fearlessness born not from courage but from the fact that he had the power of the US Army behind him.

Just another bully, Joshua thought to himself. *And I hate bullies.*

'What about if I make it my business?' Joshua allowed a sinister grin to spread across his face as he fixed his eyes on Bickle's.

Bickle smiled at the question. A smug, over-confident expression. Then he nodded his head towards the doorway. The response was immediate. Two guards entered behind them, one after the other. Each one was large enough that Joshua could literally sense their looming presence.

Joshua glanced in their direction before matching the captain's smirk with one of his own.

'You really think they're going to be enough?'

Bickle's expression stayed fixed but his eyes widened. It betrayed his uncertainty, and so it should; Joshua had done more than enough in his life – hell, even just during his time in the Facility – to justify that question. Bickle's overconfidence visibly seeped away and he all but recoiled as Joshua leaned downwards, reducing their seven-inch height disparity to barely two.

When he spoke, he made sure that Bickle could feel the heat of his breath upon his face.

'Believe me, little man. You don't want to come second in this one.'

Somehow Bickle stood his ground. As intimidated as he clearly was, he could not allow himself to back down. It led to a bizarre David and Goliath stand-off, only there was no way that David was going to win this one.

Luckily for Bickle, he did not need to.

'That's enough, fellas. Stand down. Both of you.'

Travis spoke with the voice of a man who was used to

being obeyed; a natural, superior authority that he had not lost during his decade in the Facility. This time Bickle did not react. Whatever Travis's X factor might be, it was no match for the fear that Joshua could impose. For at least that moment, the captain's focus remained on him.

For Joshua, though, it was a direct command. Whatever his personal relationship with Travis, whatever animosity he had for the man, when it came to a situation like this, he accepted that Travis was in charge.

And like any good soldier, Joshua respected that chain.

He stepped sideways without hesitation, moving himself away from both Bickle and his two subordinates at the cell doorway. Aware of how unexpected his movement could be, Joshua was careful to keep it unthreatening, so as to avoid any knee-jerk reaction from the captain's gorillas. The sudden change left Bickle visibly confused and Joshua could understand why. The situation had escalated quickly before resolving itself in an instant.

It made him smile.

The highs and lows of working in a madhouse.

'So are you going to tell me where I'm supposed to be going?'

Bickle turned at the sound of Travis's voice. But only for a moment. Then he turned back to Joshua. He had the look of a man who suspects a trick is being played but cannot work out what that trick might be.

'I'm talking to you, Bickle.' Travis pulled on a T-shirt as the intelligence officer turned to him once again. He tugged the bottom of the top down, to cover his protruding gut. 'Where am I going?'

'What does it matter?'

Bickle seemed irritated by the events of the last few minutes. All his usual self-satisfaction was gone, but so was his earlier natural deference to Travis. All that was left was impatience.

'It might not matter to you but I don't get out of here too often. Be nice to know where I'm heading. And even nicer to know why.'

'Where you're going? No. You don't get that. As for why, you'll see soon enough.'

'Which means you don't know yourself.' Travis smiled as he spoke, his tone utterly certain. 'Don't worry, Captain. We won't think less of you for that.'

Joshua watched as Travis leaned down, pulled on his white sneakers and began to tie their laces. It was an obvious strain. An inevitable side effect of the extra weight the man was carrying around his waist. Once done he stood upright and pulled in a long breath.

Standing tall, he stepped closer to Bickle and took full advantage of his few extra inches in height.

'But doesn't it bother you that they won't tell you where I'm being taken? An intelligence officer with no access to intelligence? Must be more than a little deflating for the ego. I mean, what are you even for if they don't share intelligence with the man whose job it is to know it?'

Bickle smiled in return. Joshua could tell why. As much as he did not like the man, he knew that Bickle was no fool. And certainly not dumb enough to fall for the crude trick Travis was trying to pull.

'You really think that shit's going to make me tell you what you want to know?' Bickle asked. 'Credit me with a little more brain than that, Travis. And save the manipulation for the idiots locked in here with you.'

Travis smiled in turn. It was an obvious ploy, he must have realised. One never likely to succeed. And so he seemed unfazed by its failure. He turned without another word and walked back to his bed. Leaning down with another groan, he picked up the single book that was sat on his bedside table.

Nozick again, Joshua knew. Even without seeing the cover.

'You can't bring that.' Bickle's tone betrayed his intention. There was no rule that prevented Travis from taking his book. It was just an attempt to score a hit. 'Put it back.'

'You can't be serious,' Travis said. 'It's just a book.'

'Put it back.'

Travis hesitated for a moment. As if weighing his options. Finally he did as he was asked, replacing the item on the small nightstand next to his cot. He then turned back to face Bickle, who showed him his back in reply and strode towards the door, past the two silent guardsmen. It was a petulant reaction and it made Travis smirk as he began to follow.

He was three steps closer to the door when he felt Joshua's outstretched hand on his chest. Travis turned to face him.

'You don't forget our deal,' Joshua said. 'When you're out there. First thing you do, understood?'

Travis did not answer. Instead he held Joshua's stare, giving no indication of agreement or dissent.

'The first thing you do,' Joshua replied.

'Take your hand off the prisoner.'

The instruction came from the larger of the two guardsmen. His voice made Joshua look up and in that moment Travis took his opportunity. He pushed Joshua's arm aside and started walking fast, reaching the door in two strides. Once there, with a two-man human wall between them, he looked back into the cell.

And then he smiled.

FIFTY-ONE

6.15 a.m. EDT

The Dough Boys diner was sat on the edge of Interstate Drive, a near-dirt road that had been laid down back when the I-95 first made its way through the outskirts of Dunn, North Carolina. Like the other small businesses dotted along its length, the diner had first opened to service the workmen in town to construct the highway.

And like those other businesses, it had stayed long after those workmen were gone.

Scott Turner looked around the diner's square interior. His booth aside, there seemed to be two other customers and three staff. Quiet for a place like this, even just after 6 a.m.

'What ya having, hun?'

The voice of the diner's only waitress made him start. A sure sign that his nerves were shot. Which was probably to be expected after everything they had been through in the last few hours.

'You need more time or what?' she asked, seemingly irritated by the lack of response.

'Why? You got more people waiting to be served?' Brooks asked.

Turner blanched at the idea of another confrontation. He'd assumed Brooks would have felt right at home here: everyone was white, no one wore a mask and there was a large Confederate battle flag proudly displayed on the diner's back wall. But no. There was, Turner now realised, no way to satisfy Kenny Brooks.

The guy would start a fight with Robert E. Lee himself.

'Sorry, long drive,' Turner interjected before the waitress could respond to Brooks' challenge. 'We're all a bit zonked. Could you give us a few minutes and just bring us three coffees?'

Turner almost sighed with relief as she walked away. He could not have handled defusing another situation right now. Not when all he wanted to do was to eat.

Not when there's country-fried steak for breakfast.

The thought made him smile. For all the time he had lived in the US, he had retained many of his British quirks. Enough for the likes of Brooks to think of him as a Limey sonofabitch, at least. But even Turner had to agree that many things were better here than back home, and one of those things was the way the Americans ate breakfast.

He came from the land of the 'Full English'. But deep-fried breaded steak with mushroom gravy? At 6 a.m.?

The sign of a place that has its priorities straight.

'Something amusing you?'

Brooks' voice carried its usual threat of unrestrained aggression. The question told Turner that his momentary happiness had been evident on his face. And it meant that the moment was now over. Turner returned his attention to the man who sat across from him.

'If something was amusing me, you can be sure it wasn't you.'

'Keep it up, boy—' Brooks tapped his temple with his finger as he spoke '— it's all getting noted. And when you ain't useful any more . . .'

'So you've said.' Turner leaned forward. 'And like *I've* said, when that time comes, I'll be more than happy to accommodate you. But until then, how about you wind your neck in and stop doing everything you can to get us pinched? Eh? How about that?'

Brooks did not move back even an inch. He held Turner's gaze as a cruel, crooked smile grew on his face. The younger man understood its cause. They both knew how any future fight between them would end. And if there had been any doubt about that at all, it had been dispelled by Brooks' display of violence back in the motel.

No. A one-on-one confrontation with Kenny Brooks would not go well for Scott Turner. And Brooks knew it. But what he did not know was that Scott had no intention of being the only Turner in that fight . . .

He pushed the thought from his mind. As pleasing as the mental images were, Turner had no time for them now. They were still five hundred miles south of Carbon County. Ten more hours at least, all in the same car. And with three, maybe four more stops. To fully embrace his hatred of the man would make those hours unbearable. And it was not like Turner would ever see him again once they reached Summit Hill.

'Holy shit!'

Cliff Clemons' horrified tone made Turner's head spin in his direction. When he did, he saw that Clemons was pointing upwards and away from their booth. Towards the thick wide-screened TV that was mounted behind the diner's counter.

'That's Cam, ain't it?' Clemons was trying to keep his voice down, Turner realised. And he was failing. 'And that . . . that's the van.'

Turner followed Clemons' pointed finger. It took no more than an instant to know that he was correct. That the man being manhandled on the screen – being dragged violently from the floor to a waiting helicopter – *was* Cam Arnold.

'It's Cam, Scott. Right?'

Turner said nothing. Every detail of what was being played out on-screen, under the hyperbolic headline 'Terror in Orlando', was exactly what Cam Arnold had told him to expect.

All except for one thing.

Turner looked at his watch.

'We have to move. We have to move now.'

'What the hell is that?' Even Brooks seemed shocked. 'If Cam's been caught . . .'

'I'll explain everything as we go.'

Turner was thinking fast. What they had just seen, it was at least ten hours ahead of schedule. And he had no idea when this had even gone down; it could have been hours ago. That timing changed things.

'And where's Paul?'

'What?'

'Paul,' Clemons said again. 'It's only Cam on there. You think Paul got away?'

'He's probably already in the chopper.' Turner got to his feet as he spoke. 'We've got to go. That arrest, it's too early. It puts us off the pace.'

'What do you mean, too early?' Brooks' eyes narrowed as Turner stepped out from the booth. 'What's too early? What the hell do you know?'

'I know that Cam had to be caught.' Turner nodded as he

spoke. There was nothing to be gained from keeping them in the dark. Not now it was done. 'That was always the end point of his plan. The only way it could work. I also know it wasn't supposed to happen until later today. Which means we're against the clock. We need to get moving. Now.'

Brooks looked from Turner to the screen and back again. The Englishman could see his mind working. And it did not take Brooks long for him to reach the inevitable conclusion.

'How come you knew this and we didn't?'

'Because Cam didn't think you'd ever agree to him sacrificing himself for the bigger picture. That's why we didn't tell you. Anything else you need to know, I'll tell you in the Jeep. We've got to get our arses to Summit Hill and we've got to do it fast.'

Clemons was now out of his seat and out of the booth. Brooks paid him no attention as he slowly rose from his own. His eyes did not leave Turner.

'You think we're just going to obey you now, do you?'

'You do whatever the hell you want to do,' Turner replied. There was no time left for patience. 'Either come with me or don't come with me. It's one hundred per cent your decision and frankly I couldn't give a shit. But whatever you're going to decide, do it quick.'

Brooks moved out of the booth, his eyes still fixed on Turner.

'It's a five-hundred-mile drive,' he said. He stepped closer as he spoke, into Turner's comfort zone. 'Whatever the hell's going on, you think this sudden rush of yours is gonna make a difference?'

'It will,' Turner replied. 'Because we're not driving. Not now.'

'What?'

'We don't have time. Not if we're going to keep Cam's plan on track. The only way to get ahead of this is to fly.'

For just a moment Brooks looked puzzled. Turner could tell that he had not expected the decision. It gave the younger man a temporary advantage and he took it before Brooks had time to think.

'Both of you get back to the Jeep,' he said, his eyes drifting towards the near-empty counter, 'while I settle up the bill. And once you're there, get on Google and find the way to the nearest airport.'

FIFTY-TWO

5.30 a.m. CDT

Dempsey opened his eyes as the wheels of the Boeing C-17 Globemaster III touched down on the tarmac at US Air Force Base Vandeveer. A glance at his watch told him that the flight had taken three hours. What it could not tell him was that he had slept every minute of that time.

He had needed the rest. The 5 a.m. start and the stress of the day had left him flagging. But with just a few hours' sleep and a long-overdue change of clothes – from the ill-fitting outfit Grace had brought him at LaGuardia to the all-black special ops kit he had sourced at Fort Pierce – Dempsey felt like a new man.

He looked across at Eden Grace and Sergio Vega. They were seated next to one another on the transport plane's side-wall seat, directly across from him. Grace was still unconscious, her legs stretched outwards into the body of the spacious but bare fuselage and her head rested awkwardly against Vega's shoulder. Like Dempsey, she had changed her clothes, from a black suit to the matching style of combat fatigues he now wore.

Vega, too, had made the swap but he could not pull off the look as well as Grace. The disparity in their appearance was not helped by the fact the detective had clearly enjoyed no sleep at all, leaving him with deep dark rings around his eyes. The sight amused Dempsey; by the standards of his own experience, it had not even been that bumpy a ride.

I guess flying blind in a transport kite isn't for everyone.

'Everybody up.'

The sound of Nicki May's voice echoed out over the roar of the engines.

May was standing in the centre of the plane, turning a full three-sixty as she addressed her team. Her circle stopped for a moment as her eyes fell on Vega, who became all too aware right then of the attractive woman now resting her head against his shoulder. He moved to his right without warning, away from Grace. The sudden lack of support jerked her awake.

The detective's concern seemed misplaced. May's gaze had moved on before he had shifted even an inch. Now in command of the operation, she had more important things to consider than whatever attraction had developed between them.

'My DOJ unit is waiting for us on the tarmac,' she announced. 'We're ten miles from the Facility. Which means I want to be heading back here inside twenty minutes max. Everyone got that?'

Not one of O'Rourke's Homeland team replied. Instead, every one of them looked to her, presumably to speak for them. The chain of command they were used to.

Despite that, O'Rourke said nothing. It left a silence that was unacceptable at this stage of an operation and so Dempsey stepped in. As much as he had come to respect O'Rourke, and while he hesitated to usurp her position as May had done, the mission was more important than anyone's ego.

'Got it.' Dempsey spoke the words loud and firm, making sure that everyone could hear. He looked around the fuselage before he spoke again. 'We all have.'

With that Dempsey climbed to his feet, collected the FN P90 submachine and the two Glock 19 pistols he had stowed on the fuselage weapons rack and headed towards the rear of the plane. As he knew they would, Grace, Vega and then the Homeland team all did the same.

O'Rourke joined him at the back of the plane. She was quiet, making her impossible to read.

'This is just for now, you know?' Dempsey kept his voice low, not that it was necessary. The sound of the C-17's rear cargo door made him impossible to overhear. 'We'll be heading back to Fort Pierce within the hour and then it's back to being your operation. Let her enjoy her moment.'

'I ain't fussed whose operation it is,' O'Rourke replied, 'and I'm way too old to think this job is about friendship. Any problem I have with Nicki, we'll sort that between ourselves when this is all done. The only thing that concerns me is *what* we're doing. This ain't the right move. I know it. You know it too.'

Dempsey shook his head.

'Not our decision to make.'

'Spoken like a true soldier. Doesn't make it the right call, though, does it?'

'No, Bambi. No, it does not.'

Dempsey looked down and to his left as he spoke, in time to see the slightest smile crack on O'Rourke's face. It was the reaction he had hoped for; a clear signal that he had her trust.

Knowing *that* was worth the risk of an angry response.

'You gonna make a habit of calling me that?'

'Only if you want me to. You like it better with an English accent?'

'Sounds as out of place in English as it does Mississippi, and every other damn accent in between. So what, I should start calling you Joe?'

'Dempsey will do.'

'Exactly. Glad we agree.'

Dempsey did not answer. Nor was one expected. Instead he stepped forward as the rear cargo door settled onto the tarmac and revealed a waiting convoy of five identical Chevy Suburbans. Like the C-17 in which they had been flown here, the line of dark SUVs was far more than they needed to transport just nine operatives.

But it was exactly right to move nineteen.

Dempsey did not need to count the number of black suits who were now standing by the waiting vehicles. He knew this drill as well as anyone. Ten would make it four per truck once the nine bodies from the plane and Peyton Travis himself were added to the mix. Any more than that would only obstruct immediate egress from the cars in the event of a firefight.

Any less and, well, why have less when you've got the whole DOJ at your disposal?

It was, as Dempsey had often observed, just the way the Americans did things.

When you've got unlimited resources, why wouldn't you use them?

It was a view May seemed to have fully embraced. She strode past Dempsey and O'Rourke without a glance, putting enough distance between them that she was able to turn and face them as she reached the first vehicle.

'O'Rourke, you're with me in the lead car. Dempsey and Grace, car two. Two Homeland pairs in three and four. Sergio, you're in the rear.'

She waited just a moment, looking from face to face as if

expecting some dissent, or at the very least some comment. When none came she grabbed the front passenger door of the first Suburban, swung it open and then turned back to what was now her team.

'Let's do this.'

FIFTY-THREE

5.35 a.m. CDT

Colonel Miles Walker studied Peyton Travis from across his seat, staying silent as he surveyed the man from head to toe.

He was not impressed.

In the three years since taking command of the Facility, Walker was sure he had met or at least seen every one of its two hundred or so prisoners. And yet he had no memory whatsoever of the man who now stood just feet from him. That fact left Walker perplexed. If Travis had made so little impression on him, just how the hell had he amassed a cult of fanatical followers?

The prisoner was dressed in a blood-red jumpsuit, with his wrists and ankles shackled to the same four-piece chain. It was hardly necessary. At six feet tall and fitter at age fifty than most were at twenty-five, a skilled army ranger like Walker had nothing to fear from the shorter, older, out-of-shape man. But rules were rules and if Travis was leaving the Facility, he was doing so in restraints.

Whatever the psych reports say.

'So I hear you're a part of the master race, right?'

The thought amused Walker as he looked from Travis to the statuesque Corporal Deontay Bush, flanking the prisoner from a few steps behind. The physical contrast between the two could not be more stark, and nature's favour had not followed the white supremacist philosophies that had put Travis behind these walls.

'How do you want me to respond to that, Colonel?' Travis seemed unfazed by the question. 'What do you want me to say? That I don't believe those things any more? Would there be any point in me doing that?'

'Not really,' Walker replied. 'Leopards don't change their spots, do they? Maybe just rearrange them a little when they need a new kind of camouflage.'

'I understand your scepticism. But I would have thought, what with all the attempts on my life since you've been here, I might at least deserve the benefit of the doubt.'

'Nothing doing, I'm afraid. Far as I'm concerned, the only time I can trust that an attempt on your life was genuine is when I see your corpse. And right now you're a whole lot too alive for my taste.'

'Then I guess I'm fortunate that not everyone's as closed-minded, aren't I?'

Walker said nothing in response. Instead he just continued to survey the man.

'Anyway, Colonel, now we both know where we stand with one another, how about you give me some idea of where I'm going this morning? Who's coming for me?'

'I wouldn't tell you if I knew. Which would be more enjoyable than admitting I don't, now I think of it.'

'Well, at least you're honest,' Travis replied.

'Makes one of us, at least.' Walker stood up from his seat and moved around the table, bringing him face to face with

Travis. 'Now tell the truth. What's with the change of heart? What are you hoping to gain?'

'Absolutely nothing, Colonel.' There was no effort in Travis's voice. As if it meant nothing whether Walker believed him or not. 'I'm here for life. Whatever happens. I know that. And I know that my treatment here by you and by whoever follows you, it won't change whether I'm a good man or the man I used to be. The only thing that's changed is my safety. By speaking out against the things I did, I put myself at risk from the people in here who still think that way. And by bringing attention to those terrible things that I did in my past, I put myself at risk from every black man, every Asian man, every Muslim man in this place.

'Now tell me, Colonel. As an intelligent, educated person, why on Earth would I fake something that only has a downside?'

Walker took a half step back and lowered himself to sit on the edge of his desk. It brought his head down to Travis's chest height and so he looked up.

'Not such a risk when you've got Joshua on your payroll, though, is it? A trained killer protecting you twenty-four-seven? Where's the threat?'

'I don't have anyone on a payroll any more, Colonel. And certainly not Joshua. Can't a friend stand up for another friend in need these days?'

'That man hasn't got a friend on this planet, Mr Travis. That's what's got me stumped. Why he'd look out for you. But you know what, you're right: I don't need to know the truth. Rehabilitated or not, when you're done with whatever they want you for, you're back here with me. And even if you *are* a changed man, you're still a prisoner in this facility and you'll be treated as such. You got that?'

'Fine by me, Colonel.'

Travis meant those words. Walker could tell. Neither his tone nor his expression changed at all as their exchange ended, and that confirmed to Walker that Travis had no interest in whether the Facility's commander believed him.

It was dismissive and, if Walker was honest, it irritated him.

He tried to banish the response as he stood up from the desktop and began to move back towards his chair, but before he got halfway he was stopped by a movement at the office door.

It was Bickle. The captain announced himself with two words.

'They're here.'

FIFTY-FOUR

5.42 a.m. CDT

Dempsey stepped out of the Chevy Suburban and took in a deep, hot lungful of the desert's morning air. The sheer dryness caused him to cough, as if a vacuum of atmospheric moisture was sucking the fluid from his body.

He leaned back into the heavily air-conditioned truck, picked out a bottle of cold water from the inside of the door and took a deep swallow. The relief was instant.

'Everything alright over there, Boss?'

Grace had exited the Suburban from the opposite side and had walked around the back of the vehicle to reach him.

'Dry throat,' Dempsey explained. He offered her the open bottle. 'Need some?'

'Just did.' Grace held up a half-empty bottle of her own, her eyes sweeping their surroundings as she did so. 'So this is what a secret prison looks like.'

'Were you expecting something else?'

'I don't know what I was expecting. But I don't think it was something so . . . typical.'

Dempsey nodded in agreement. Grace was right. The Facility really was the very definition of ordinary. Or at least as ordinary as a stereotypical prison building at the heart of a top-secret military research facility – one covered by a strictly enforced no-fly-zone – could be.

So not so ordinary at all, then, Dempsey conceded to himself.

But he could still see what Grace had meant. For all its unique security precautions, the Facility resembled every fictional state penitentiary in every television show Dempsey had ever seen. The wire fences. The guard towers. The thick, sheer stone walls. All it lacked were orange-suited meatheads lifting weights in the yard.

Give it time. It's not even 6 a.m.

'Is it just me, or is this place a hell of a lot hotter than the Keys?'

'It's not just you, no,' Dempsey replied.

'That's Texas for ya.' Both Dempsey and Grace turned at the sound of O'Rourke's voice. Neither had seen her approach from the other side of the lead car. 'Hotter than the hinges on the gates of hell.'

'Seems apt,' Dempsey replied. He pointed towards the prison's triple-height front doorway as he spoke. 'Since they seem to be opening them for us.'

Grace and O'Rourke turned to face the same direction without another word. All three watched as the entrance to the Facility's main building parted in the middle, so slow that it seemed almost for effect. Gradually, though, the gates opened, making way for the group of men who had been stood behind them.

At the group's centre was a middle-aged man in a red jumpsuit. Shorter than any of the guards around him by several inches and older by decades, Peyton Travis's face was still recognisable from the decade-old photo Dempsey had seen in the intelligence files.

'That the guy?'

The question came from Grace's left. Dempsey looked past her to see that Vega had now joined them.

'It is,' Dempsey replied.

'So everything that's happened? Ricardo and everyone else who's died? That was all for *him*?'

No one responded. Not that it was needed. Vega provided his own answer.

'This world makes no damn sense.'

Dempsey kept his agreement to himself. For now his focus was on Nicki May as she stepped forward, towards Travis and his security detail. She was approaching alone, taking complete control of the handover. Whether or not it should have, that bothered Dempsey.

Screw Ray McMillan, he thought to himself. *This is O'Rourke's operation.*

'Anyone else interested in hearing what they have to say?' he asked.

'Damn straight,' O'Rourke replied.

'That's what I thought.'

Dempsey strode forward, past the second Suburban and then the first, quickly gaining on May as she closed in on the Facility team ahead. He did not need to look to know that O'Rourke had kept pace, with Grace and Vega staying a few deferential steps behind.

Ahead of them were eight men in uniform, all of them US Army. That fact alone made Dempsey more comfortable. He had served in the British rather than the US armed forces, but the military was the military. It had a culture. To a soldier, meeting an ally's unit was like a Catholic stepping into a church on the other side of the globe.

Different, but the same.

Dempsey stepped closer, now just feet behind May. As he did so, he noticed that seven of the men ahead wore the tan berets that identified them as 75th Ranger Regiment. One of the world's elite units and maybe the best the US had, their deployment here said everything about the security that surrounded them.

With rangers on the guard, Dempsey realised, *this place is as close to being impregnable as any location on Earth.*

The group's commanding officer – a ranger colonel, according to his beret and the eagle insignia on his collars – stepped forward, first with a salute and then an outstretched hand. Both were directed at Dempsey, although he was still a step behind May. Dempsey was surprised by the misogyny of the assumption, but he was also conscious that he was outranked. He had little choice but to return both gestures.

'Miles Walker.' Walker's grip was as firm as Dempsey would expect. Aged maybe fifty, the colonel had kept himself in ranger shape. He seemed every bit as fit and as strong as Dempsey himself. 'Glad to have you people here.'

'Glad to be here, Colonel. I'm Agent Dempsey from the International Security Bureau.' He indicated to May, who had taken a step back to match Walker's step forward. 'And this is Agent Nicki May from the Department of Justice. Agent May is the agent in charge for this collection, sir.'

Walker frowned a little as he turned to face May. His expression suggested surprise, but nothing more than that. Dempsey detected no embarrassment from the man about his mistake.

'It's a pleasure to meet you, Agent May. And thank you for arranging the movement of the prisoner. Ordinarily we'd provide the transport detail, but given the short notice . . .'

'That was understood and appreciated, Colonel. The clock's against us on this one, so whatever we had to do to make it happen.' May moved her head slightly, to look past Walker. 'This him?'

'Yes, ma'am. This is Peyton Travis.' Walker turned as he spoke. It was a clear message that he expected the prisoner to listen up. 'And if he knows what's good for him, he's going to be a very useful resource to you folk today. Isn't that right, Mr Travis?'

'I'll help in any way I can,' Travis replied. '*If* I can.'

Dempsey did not blink as he watched the exchange. And nor, he noticed, did Travis. Whatever the truth of the man, whatever Travis knew or did not know about the activities of Cam Arnold, there was one thing Dempsey had learned from just the last few moments:

Whatever it was about him that allowed him to build Liberation – whatever unerring confidence that took – it's still there.

Knowing that was a start, at least. But it was not nearly enough information for Dempsey to make a proper assessment of what they faced. They needed more and they needed it quick.

Dempsey noticed a thick manila file, held in the hands of the only man on Walker's team who wore no beret and no insignia of rank. Dempsey did not need to wonder about the difference. Every specialist unit had an intelligence officer. Right now, he was looking at Walker's.

Dempsey pointed to the file.

'Is that his custody record?'

'It is,' Walker replied, following Dempsey's gesture. 'A full copy of it, at least. It's a heavy read, Agent Dempsey.'

'But maybe a necessary one,' Dempsey replied. 'Do you mind?'

'Knock yourself out, son.'

Dempsey stepped forward and took the file from the silent intelligence officer. Then he stepped back to his position just behind May and handed it to Grace.

'Scan through,' he said, 'and we'll discuss it on the plane.'

Grace took the file without a word, turned and headed back to the second Chevy. Dempsey did not watch her go. His attention was instead caught by the sound of Peyton Travis's slow, precise voice as it filled the still morning air.

'Is anyone going to tell me what this is all about?'

'You'll know soon enough.' May sounded impatient. As if Travis's question was an irritation. 'Once we get to Florida.'

'Really, Agent May?' There was something in the man's tone. For a person in a position of zero control, it carried an authority that made no sense. 'You don't think Florida's a long way to go just to find out I've nothing to tell you?'

Dempsey watched as May's expression turned quizzical. Travis had caught her attention. And he knew it.

'Let me explain this slowly,' he continued. 'Let's say, shall we, that you're mistaken in what you think I know. Wouldn't it be better to find that out now? Because if I don't have the information you want, Agent May, what's the point in the journey?'

May hesitated. Travis had undermined her and in that moment she seemed unsure how to respond. That uncertainty, Dempsey was sure, came from her inexperience of command. And so it did not surprise him that Walker felt the need to step in.

'Let's call it one last chance to see the world, then, shall we?'

Walker grabbed Travis by the collar as he spoke and pulled him forward. It was an unexpected display of brute physical strength, causing Travis to stumble as he was propelled from the spot.

'He's all yours, Agent May.' The colonel's eyes shifted to the prisoner. 'Until she's done with you. Then you're mine again, and you'd better hope I've been told all about your exemplary behaviour.'

Dempsey watched the display with interest. It was a show, he realised. An attempt to keep Travis in his place. He understood why it was necessary, but was unconvinced that it would have the intended effect. If Travis had not been cowed by a decade in the hellhole that stood behind him, a few threats were unlikely to make much difference.

May, though, seemed encouraged by Walker's actions; her momentary loss of confidence looked to disappear as its cause stumbled towards her. She stepped smoothly to one side to avoid Travis's uncontrolled movement and turned to the four closest DOJ agents.

'Get him in the back seat of the centre truck and secure those restraints so he can't move. And make it quick.'

The DOJ quartet did as instructed. Within moments they had taken control of the now silent Travis and were manhandling him to the waiting motorcade.

'Feels strange to see an inmate leaving without my men around him.' Walker paused for a moment, as if considering his own comment. 'Well, leaving upright, anyway.'

'He'll be back soon enough, Colonel,' May replied. 'You won't have time to miss him.'

Walker nodded his head, his expression grim.

'I hope he gives you what you need.' He looked towards Dempsey and O'Rourke. 'All of you.'

'Thank you, Colonel.'

May followed Walker's eyeline and, for the first time since they had joined her up front, she looked directly at the two agents beside her. The glance was fleeting. As if they were an irrelevance.

'If you have the transfer papers, Colonel,' she said, turning back to Walker, 'we can get them signed and then get going.'

Walker's intelligence agent stepped forward, a small file in hand. He offered it to May, who reached out and took it without a glance. She flicked through the few pages before turning her attention to O'Rourke.

'Get back to the vehicles while I deal with this,' she instructed. 'You're riding with me in the third car. I want us either side of Travis.'

'Ma'am.'

If O'Rourke had any problem with the deliberate display of authority, she did not show it. A picture of professionalism, she kept her tone deferential and did exactly as instructed. Dempsey moved with her.

'She's taken to the big chair fast enough,' Dempsey said as they moved away. May's barked order had not strictly been to him, but he had taken it as his cue to leave. Vega, too, had joined them, leaving May alone with Walker and his team. 'Good job holding your tongue.'

'Ain't gonna be for long,' O'Rourke replied. She sounded almost happy. 'We get back to Florida, I'm back on top. And when that happens, believe me, Nicki's gonna wish she was a red-headed stepchild.'

Dempsey laughed. It was the first time he had heard the expression, but it required no explanation. And for once, he could tell O'Rourke was not using it for effect. The DOJ agent was going to regret how she had conducted her temporary command.

'Rather her than me,' Dempsey chuckled.

O'Rourke looked up to reply, a smile now on her face, too. But before she could say another word, they were both interrupted.

'Boss. You need to see this.'

Dempsey looked straight ahead, towards the sound of Eden Grace's voice. Grace, in turn, was moving towards them fast. She was holding Travis's file open in her hand. From the look on her face, whatever she had found inside was not good.

'What is it?'

'You need to see for yourself.'

Dempsey took the file from Grace's hand, scanned the page and saw it in an instant. The name should have been lost in the information sheet's densely packed detail, yet to Dempsey's eye it stood out.

He looked at Grace without a word. His mind was suddenly fighting to stay focused against the torrent of conclusions and deductions that were sweeping through it.'

'That *is* him, right?' Grace asked.

Dempsey nodded his head in reply. It was all he could manage, with his mind now racing as it was. The name . . . *that* name . . . it was shocking enough on its own. It meant that he was alive. All this time, he was alive and he was *here*.

They had lied. For four years, they had let Dempsey think that he had killed the man. That realisation was like a physical blow to the gut, but right now that was not the issue. Right now, what mattered was how that lie could relate to Peyton Travis, to Scott Turner and to Liberation.

'So what does it mean?'

'I don't . . . I don't know,' Dempsey replied. 'But it's got to mean something, right?'

'Got to,' Grace agreed.

'What's going on?' O'Rourke asked. The question broke through his thought process, forcing him towards clarity. O'Rourke needed an answer, which meant Dempsey had to find her one.

'It's Travis,' he finally said. 'He wasn't as isolated in here as we thought.'

Dempsey looked over at May, who was headed towards them. Without another word of explanation, he strode off to meet her, his pace urgent.

'Nicki, we need to halt this. We need Travis back inside the Facility.'

May did not break step as she drew closer.

'Don't be ridiculous. We've got orders.'

'Then you need to override them. There's more to this than we realised.'

'What the hell are you talking about?' May's eyes fell on O'Rourke, Grace and Vega as she swept past Dempsey. She shook her head in apparent exasperation. 'Enough of this bullshit. Bambi, I told you, you're riding with me. Get in the damned vehicle.'

O'Rourke opened her mouth to respond, but May's attention was already on her companions. On Grace and on Vega.

'And if you two are moving with us then you need to find a spot now, because I'm not being thrown off schedule.'

With no sign that May intended to slow, Dempsey reached out and carefully grasped her arm.

'Nicki, you need to listen to this. This is a mistake.'

'Get your hand off of me.' May finally stopped walking. She spun to face Dempsey, pulling her arm from his deliberately light grip as she did so. 'What the hell is wrong with you? You're supposed to be some specialist field agent, right? Then why the hell are you being spooked by nothing?'

'It's not nothing,' Dempsey replied. 'There's something wrong with this. With all of it. Travis's cellmate. I know him. His name's James Turner. He's Scott Turner's father.'

For just a moment, May seemed unsure.

'Scott Turner. Are you . . . what . . . Jesus, who the hell *cares*? What the hell difference does that make?'

'I don't know yet,' Dempsey answered. 'But it means something. Travis is in here, isolated from the outside world and by all accounts a reformed man. And yet his cellmate's son just happens to be a member of Liberation? That's no coincidence. It can't be.'

'Maybe not,' May replied, 'but I'll ask you again, what difference does it make? So Turner joins Liberation because his father is in the Facility. So what?'

'Listen—'

'No, *you* listen. I'm in charge here. I'm not O'Rourke. And I'm not in the habit of letting every goddamn waif and stray tag along and have his say. Truth is, I'm not even sure why you're here, Agent Dempsey. But I do know that if you're going to stay with my team, you'll do so silently. We're on the clock here and I will not allow this bullshit to delay my mission. You got that?'

Dempsey said nothing. He stood motionless, his eyes fixed on May's own. Of the twenty answers now threatening to trip off of his tongue, he knew that he could allow none of them. His silence left only the sound of the waiting motorcade until May spoke again.

'I'll take that as a yes.'

She moved away without another word, towards the open door of the third Chevy that would place her next to Travis. She climbed inside and had her door slammed shut by a waiting agent, who then climbed into the same vehicle's driving seat.

None of this interested Dempsey; he had already turned back to Grace, Vega and O'Rourke.

'You need to join her,' he said, his focus now on O'Rourke. 'She's only thinking about her career. About her orders and about executing them to the letter. It's made her oblivious to the threat that man could be. You need to be next to her, making sure she does the right thing.'

'Agreed.'

'And Grace, you need to go too. You and Sergio. Get yourselves into the last Chevy and keep your wits about you.'

'You think something's going to happen?'

'I don't know,' Dempsey replied. 'If it does, between you guys, Homeland and the DOJ, you're all stocked up like a small army. But something's not right so you *do* need to be ready. Just in case.'

'And what about you? You're not coming with us?'

'I'll make my own way back to Fort Pierce. If we're going to find out what's really happening here, first I need to go speak to a dead man.'

FIFTY-FIVE

5.55 a.m. CDT

Dempsey felt the uncomfortable sensation of nervous energy as he waited for the corner door to be opened. It was not a new feeling. In fact, there had been a time in his life where sickening anticipation was almost his default mood. That had been in his years of active service for the British Army – first as a soldier, later as an assassin – when he dealt in life and death on a near daily basis.

He had no such reason to be fearful today. Unlike the years he had spent either preparing for an open firefight or dug into a hillside as he awaited the perfect shot, there was no risk of death here. And little chance that what was coming would descend into violence.

And yet even with that reassurance, his heart was beating fast.

It was a unique reaction to a unique set of circumstances, Dempsey knew. He did not welcome it, but he did at least understand it.

Less than fifteen minutes had passed since his discovery that James Turner – the man now better known by the alias Joshua – was alive. A fact which Dempsey had not questioned for almost four years. Not since he had left the infamous assassin for dead on a forest floor in the Republic of Ireland, fifty miles outside of Dublin.

Dempsey had been told back then that Joshua had been found barely alive, badly beaten from their fight and with three bullets having torn through his left lung. The prognosis had been bleak and so, when finally told that Joshua had lost a near month-long fight for life, Dempsey had accepted that without question.

The realisation that he had been played, then, made him feel naive. Dempsey knew how governments worked when in the shadows. Hell, those shadows had once been *his* battleground. And if they were willing to send a man like him to end a problem with a bullet, they sure as hell wouldn't baulk at taking less extreme measures when they deemed a public trial inconvenient but death unnecessary.

For the worst problems, there were men like him. It only made sense, then, that for others there were solutions like the Facility. Dempsey should have considered that fate for Joshua, he now realised. He should not have just accepted what he had been told. But the fact was, he had done exactly that. He had been so sure that James Turner had died at his hands.

Right up until he saw that file.

The revelation had hit him like a freight train. In a fairer world, that would have been enough for one day. But when was Dempsey's world ever fair? And so, along with the discovery that his old friend was an inmate of the Facility, he'd also learned that Joshua had now spent almost three years as Peyton Travis's cellmate.

Each fact alone was shocking enough. But together? Together they were dizzying. Even to a man like Dempsey.

He placed his hands flat on the heavy metal table ahead of him as he heard footsteps approach the far door. He could feel the sweat that had formed on his palms. A result of his increased heart rate and the stifling early-morning temperature. He chose to ignore it as he listened to the sound of the door being unlocked.

The door opened and for just a moment Dempsey felt the urge to stand. He had no idea why. Joshua had never outranked him. Quite the opposite, in fact. It was a strange reaction, then, but not one that Dempsey had time to analyse as a face from his past – a face he had never expected to see again – stepped into the room.

Dempsey rose to his feet, in that moment understanding his own compulsion. Whatever their former ranks and whatever their current status, Joshua deserved to be met as an equal. Whether he realised it himself or not.

Joshua's face gave away nothing as he set eyes on the man who, above all others, was the cause of his downfall. He held Dempsey's gaze for no more than a second, his expression blank, before turning to the two guards who had entered the room behind him.

'You boys should wait outside. Whatever's brought Captain Camelot here, he won't want you hearing it.' He held up his wrist restraints as he spoke. 'And you can take these off. This guy doesn't need protecting. Not even from me.'

FIFTY-SIX

5.56 a.m. CDT

The five-vehicle convoy raced along the featureless desert road at over eighty miles an hour. Nicki May had insisted on covering the distance between the Facility and US Air Force Base Vandeveer as quickly as possible. Fast enough, it turned out, that even the advanced suspension on the top-of-the-range Chevy Suburbans struggled to mask the potholes in the road's surface.

Grace had nabbed the front passenger seat of the rearmost Chevy, with Vega sitting directly behind her. From here she had a clear view of both the vehicles and the route that lay ahead. Not that either offered her much distraction. It was still not quite 6 a.m., a time at which – if such a thing is possible – the desert is even *more* deserted.

'So what did Dempsey mean when he said he had to speak to a dead man?'

Grace turned in her chair, so that she could see Vega.

'Travis's cellmate,' she replied. 'The one he mentioned to Nicki. Dempsey used to know him. Until today, he thought he was dead.'

'What do you make of all that?'

'Who the hell knows? It could be nothing. It could just be a coincidence. But I think Dempsey's right. We shouldn't have left without knowing more. Screw the schedule, Nicki should have waited.'

'Damn right she should have,' Vega agreed. 'I don't get why she's acting like this.'

'You don't know her, Sergio. Not really. Maybe this *is* her. Or maybe she's not handling the pressure of command well. I've seen that before. Lots of times. Decent agents turned into assholes by the need to get things right.'

'We'll see, I guess. Once we get back to Fort Pierce. We'll see if the old Nicki's back. Once she's just one of us again.'

Grace nodded, choosing to not pursue it further. Vega was a grown man and he would make his own choices. For his sake she hoped he would not be disappointed. But she had her doubts.

'How far out are we from the air base?'

Vega's question broke the short silence. Grace glanced towards the speedometer.

'Can't be more than seven minutes at this rate. Assuming no one blows a tyre on these damn roads.'

'Good. The sooner we're in the air the better. That whole exchange back there has left me on edge.'

'Best place to be,' Grace replied. 'It keeps you vigilant. And if Dempsey's right, that's exactly what we need to be.'

'Do you think he is?'

'For all the good it does us, Sergio, in my experience Dempsey is *always* right. It's best to assume that's not changing today, so I recommend you do what the man said. Just keep your wits about you. Stay alert and stay alive.'

FIFTY-SEVEN

5.58 a.m. CDT

Joshua sat back as far as his screwed-down metal chair would allow and slowly scanned the seated Dempsey from head to toe, and then back again. His expression, as it had been since they had first known each other, was impossible to read. But his thoughts, Dempsey knew, could not be friendly. Not after everything they had been through.

Whatever those thoughts were, they would have to wait. Joshua did not know it yet, but they had no time to dwell on ancient history.

'Listen, Jim—'

'It took you long enough to show your face,' Joshua interrupted. 'I thought you'd have had the balls to come sooner.'

'I didn't know you were here,' Dempsey replied. 'I didn't even know you were alive.'

'Bollocks. You're the DDS golden boy. There's no way they'd keep this secret from you.'

'There's no such thing as the DDS any more. There hasn't been since we last saw each other.'

'You mean since you shot me?' Joshua's tone was flippant.

As if what had happened between them was just an everyday occurrence. 'What happened then? Why'd they shut it down?'

'Look, Jim, we don't have time—'

'I've got nothing *but* time thanks to you. So if you ever want to get to what you're really here for, you're going to have to indulge me first. I don't get many visitors, Captain.'

'It's Joe. You know it's just Joe.'

'It was *never* just Joe. Not even back in the day. Not even with all that "no rank amongst brothers" bullshit. I didn't buy it then, I'm not buying it now. You got that, *Captain*?'

'Think what you like, Jim. I'm not here to fight.'

'That makes a change.'

'I'm here about Scott, OK? He's in trouble and I'm trying to help him. So how about we stop this shit and we focus on what matters, eh?'

For the first time, Joshua's facade slipped. There was genuine concern in his eyes. When he spoke again, he did so slowly.

'What about Scott?' he asked. 'What do you know?'

'I know you've been protecting Peyton Travis. You've been keeping him alive in a prison full of people who want him dead.'

'Says who?'

'Says your file. And so does every officer I've spoken to in the past fifteen minutes.'

'So?'

'So I know you've been doing it for Scott. Travis's organisation has been going from strength to strength in the last year. Recruiting left and right. Young men, mainly. Some of them bright, Jim. Some of them very, very bright.'

Joshua sat back in his chair. He took time to study Dempsey. When he finally spoke, all the confrontation had left his voice.

'What you're getting at, I can't say it. It can't come from me.'

'What do you mean?'

'I mean I don't know who's listening. I don't know where he has ears. And I'm not risking what's mine. So if you have something to say – if there's something you know – then just fucking say it.'

This time it was Dempsey's turn to stay silent. He studied Joshua, looking for some hint that his apparent helplessness was an act. Finding none, he made the only decision he could.

'Scott's working with Liberation. You know that and that's why you were protecting Travis. Am I right?'

'Are you for real? You think my boy's *working* with those sick fucks? Jesus. I remember you used to be good at your job. He's not working with them.'

'Trust me. He is.'

'And just how the fuck would you know that, eh?'

Dempsey's eyes narrowed. He was shocked that Joshua needed to ask.

'How do you think I know? Do you think I'd just leave them after you were gone? I told you, I thought you were dead. I thought *I'd* killed you. But whatever the hell *you* became, *they* were still family to me. He was still the boy I watched grow up. So I did the right thing. I found them – Lisa and Scott – when I came to America. And I looked out for them. I made sure they were OK.'

'You went near my family?' Joshua's voice began to rise. He was angry now and he made no attempt to hide it. 'After what you did to me? After you put me in here? You had the audacity to speak to *my* wife? To *my* son?'

'I didn't go near them.' Dempsey raised his hands as he

spoke. An indication for Joshua to stay calm. 'I said that I looked out for them. I made sure they were safe. Tried to make any problems they had go away. And I made sure they had access to your money. That's all.'

Joshua nodded his head. The anger was still there, just beneath the surface. But at least he no longer seemed ready to erupt.

'Didn't do a very good job with Scott then, did you?'

'What does that mean?'

'What does that fucking mean? You've just told me my son's part of a terrorist organisation. Bit of a disaster on your watch that, isn't it?'

'I'm not a miracle worker. I couldn't force the kid to stay in school. Any more than I could force him not to get wrapped up in all that Liberation bullshit. He's an adult. He makes his own choices.'

'Choices.' Joshua's voice was quiet. 'And how sure are you that it *was* a choice?'

Dempsey hesitated again. He was beginning to suspect . . .

'One hundred per cent. But surely you'd already know that? If you were protecting Travis for Scott?'

'How long have you known me, Joe? And you think I'd have protected Travis just because my son had joined the movement he'd started? My boy joins some sort of bollocksing redneck cult and suddenly I'm just onside? A compliant little bodyguard? Fuck off.'

The combination of Joshua's answer and his tone left Dempsey unsure of himself.

'It seemed too much of a coincidence,' he said.

'Do you not remember me at all? I mean, does that *really* sound like the way I'd deal with this?'

Dempsey said nothing. He had enjoyed minimal time to think through the various possibilities before reaching the most likely conclusion. Now he was beginning to doubt his reasoning. Doubts that only increased as Joshua continued.

'If my son had been seduced by those hillbilly arseholes, I wouldn't have been *protecting* Travis. I'd have been *torturing* the slag. Forcing him to dump Scott out of the thing. It's simple as that. You think I'd be looking after him out of some sort of solidarity? Because *Scott's* in then *I'm* in? Is that it?'

'Then why?'

'Because Travis told me that Scott was a hostage, that's why. That my boy was a prisoner. The fat little shit even showed me pictures to prove it. This wasn't a collaboration, Joe. This wasn't me getting on board to support my suddenly racist fuck of a son. This was *blackmail*. It was Travis's safety for Scott's safety. Simple as that.'

'Jesus.' Dempsey considered the implications of what he had just been told. 'So . . . so they didn't recruit Scott for his expertise? They didn't groom him for his ability to make a bomb? They did it so they could get to *you*. So they could get Travis protected.'

'What do you mean, make a bomb?'

'It's why we thought Scott was with them. Because of his background. Nuclear physics.'

'Travis doesn't need someone to make a bomb. He's one of the top weapons designers on the planet. You think he'd need to go out and headhunt some geeky kid from college?'

'Well, he's been in here ten years, his expertise can hardly be much use to them.'

'Only if you assume he didn't make what he needed before he was caught. Trust me, whatever he needs to create chaos, it's likely been safe and hidden for the past decade. All it needs is *him*.'

The words made Dempsey's blood run cold.

All it needs is him.

'So this whole thing with Scott. It was just a way to control you?'

'It was. And they were smart enough to sell it in the only way that would stop me killing Travis myself. If they had Scott – if he was a prisoner – then what could I do but obey?'

'But the file. It says that Travis was being targeted by his own people.'

'You've no idea how accurate that is,' Joshua replied. 'He *was* targeted by his own people. But they weren't *former* people. The attacks on Travis, they were paid for *by* Travis. Not that they knew that. They were amateurs who stood no chance, to make sure he was never really in any danger even if I was having a bad day. How do you think they got weapons in here? You think someone without Travis's resources could do that?'

Dempsey sat back into his chair. What Joshua was telling him, it made perfect sense. After all, the attacks on Travis had been the proof they needed of his rehabilitation. But if they hadn't been real . . .

His eyes fixed on Joshua.

'So you've no doubt, then? That it's all an act? That Travis is still part of Liberation?'

'He's not a *part* of it,' Joshua replied. 'He never stopped *running* it.'

'But how?'

'The man's a fucking billionaire. You think that kind of money can't walk through walls? Even *these* walls? God knows how many channels of communication he has in and out of here. But for specifics – for orders and instructions – there's a book back in our cell. He uses it to communicate, via the prison librarian. He checks it in when he has a message to go out. Checks it back out again when messages come in. It's that simple when you can afford to buy people.'

Dempsey took a moment to think. The implications were many, but the conclusion was inevitable.

'And so he knew this was coming? He knew we were taking him out of here?'

'He didn't just know, Joe. He planned the whole thing.'

'Which means . . .'

'Which means that everyone who follows him knows, too,' Joshua confirmed. 'Which I guess now includes my son.'

Dempsey began to rise from his seat. His thoughts were arriving thick and fast, and they were coming out as words that were no longer meant for Joshua or for anyone but himself.

'All of this. The caesium. The shootings. Even taking Cam Arnold into custody. It was all a misdirect. It was all designed so we'd take Travis outside of these walls.'

He locked eyes with Joshua one last time.

'Jesus Christ. This whole thing's a jailbreak.'

FIFTY-EIGHT

6.01 a.m. CDT

Eden Grace looked at her watch and then across to the speedometer on her left. A swift mental calculation told her the rough distance the convoy had left to travel before it reached the air base.

Two miles, give or take.

The thought gave her little comfort. Sure, the distance remaining was better than the eight miles they had just covered. And the closer they came to a military facility – even one as minor as Vandeveer – the less likely it was that the five speeding Suburbans would be seen as anyone's viable target.

But two miles is still two miles. And if this thing has Dempsey worried . . .

The heat was already causing optical illusions in the distance; what looked like sheets of water in the heart of the desert, caused by the refraction of light through the parched, burning air. The effect combined with the sand and dust kicked up by multiple sets of speeding wheels on the road ahead, making it near impossible for Grace to risk assess what was left of their route.

'Can't be far now.'

Grace could not tell if Vega was asking a question or making a statement. Either way, she did not reply. Right now her attention was on an object in the far distance. Something she could not quite identify.

'Do you see that?' Her question was to the vehicle's driver. One of Nicki May's DOJ team. 'Beyond the dust cloud. Is that something in the air?'

'I . . . I think . . .' The driver squinted as he tried to adjust his vision. 'I'm not sure, ma'am. I think maybe there's something. Or maybe not.'

'No. No, there's something. I'm sure of it.'

'What is it, Eden?'

Grace ignored Vega's question as she reached out for the Suburban's two-way radio handset and pressed down on the transmit button.

'This is Agent Eden Grace in Suburban Five. Seeking an ID on the airborne object ahead. Over.'

Grace instinctively held the handset away from her ear as she awaited a response. The AN/PRC-119F was an effective frontline communication device that was trusted worldwide, and for good reason. But what it was not was subtle. Grace had experienced the radio's temperamental volume control before. Her hearing would not forgive her if she made that mistake again.

A second passed. Then another.

'This is Agent Grace in Suburban Five. Do we have eyes on the sky? Over.'

Grace's heart was beating hard as she waited for a response, her eyes still fixed on the growing dark object she could see ahead.

Two more seconds of silence passed.

'Is anyone receiving? Over.'

Nothing. Not even static.

'Something's not right.'

'It's just a gremlin.' The observation came from the driver. His tone was almost nonchalant. 'It's not like they've gone anywhere. We can see them all right ahead of us.'

Grace looked to her left, to face the speaker, though she had not listened to a word he had said. Her thoughts had been elsewhere as she assessed their situation.

An assessment now done.

'Get off the road. Now.'

The driver did not seem to realise that this was not a request. When he replied, his earlier nonchalance was replaced by irritation.

'What? Why the hell—'

'We're driving full speed towards an unidentified aircraft, at the same moment as someone's jamming a radio system that supposedly can't be jammed. All while we're in a convoy that carries a prisoner who made a billion dollars building impossible shit for the military. You think any of that's a coincidence?'

'I . . . I . . .'

'JUST GET OFF THE DAMNED ROAD! NOW!!'

From where O'Rourke was seated – next to the rear passenger-side door of the third Suburban, with Travis to her left, May beyond him and a DOJ agent occupying the spot ahead of her – her view of the road ahead was limited.

And uniquely for her, it was not something the senior Homeland agent had even noticed.

O'Rourke was renowned for both her attention to detail

and her operational awareness. It was part of the reason that a middle-aged black woman from the poorest part of the Mississippi Delta had risen to a professional status where 'white', 'male' and 'privileged' were the first three unwritten tick boxes on the application form. And yet right now, that focus was somewhere else entirely.

She kept her eyes fixed straight ahead as she ran back over the events of the past few days.

The call had come when? O'Rourke looked at her watch. *Seventy-three hours. Shit. Was it really just three days ago?*

It seemed so much longer, with everything that had happened in that time. But O'Rourke could not allow such questions to distract her. Her focus had to be absolute. She needed to understand this.

How did we get here? And what does the journey tell us?

The call that had set this whole thing off – the tip that a consignment of caesium was heading to Key Largo – had come from May. O'Rourke had never questioned that. It was intelligence picked up by the Department of Justice but better placed with Homeland Security, so it made perfect sense that May would bring it to her. Their friendship went back years; who better for May to trust than her mentor who just happened to work at Homeland's Domestic Nuclear Protection Office?

Even now, even after May had pulled a career move that O'Rourke could never have expected, that fact was the one thing that tempered the feeling of betrayal. The reality that, ultimately, this *was* May's case. It had begun with her. So why should she not . . .

A mental alarm slammed O'Rourke's analysis off course.

Nicki's case.

Nicki's tip.

She silently turned her head and looked past Travis, to the woman on the seat beside him.

It was Nicki who brought us to Key Largo.

It was Nicki who brought me to Key West.

As if she could feel O'Rourke's gaze upon her, May turned and looked back.

She implicated Liberation and Cam Arnold.

She supported Dempsey about Orlando.

May shook her head as O'Rourke's own eyes began to widen in horrified realisation.

She fought to bring Travis out of the Facility.

'Bambi, I'm sorry.'

Jesus, she even stopped me calling the shot on Arnold at Universal.

'I really am.'

O'Rourke went for her weapon. May did the same, a heartbeat sooner and with her pistol in easier reach. If they'd had the chance to complete the draw, there could be only one winner.

But that chance did not come.

'Is that what I think it—'

The question came from the driver's seat, just ahead of May, but before he could finish his sentence – and before O'Rourke and May could reach their weapons – the air outside of their Suburban seemed to ignite.

FIFTY-NINE

6.03 a.m. CDT

Deontay Bush felt the full weight of the heavy metal door slam outwards the moment he turned the key. The sudden force made him step back. A stumble, almost. He regained his footing in an instant, just in time to dodge the impact of ISB Agent Joe Dempsey as he sprinted through the doorway and into the corridor.

Bush reacted in a heartbeat.

'GET THIS DOOR CLOSED AND LOCKED.'

He was already moving as he shouted the order to the private who had manned the room beside him. Bush knew he could trust his colleague to do as instructed, and to do so fast. That trust was vital, because Bush also knew that no one outside of Colonel Miles Walker's command had any right to roam free inside the Facility.

Whoever the hell they might be.

'AGENT DEMPSEY.' Bush was gaining on the agent as he called out his name. Even from a standing start, he was the faster man. 'STOP, SIR.'

But Joe Dempsey did not do as instructed. Instead he took the left turn that lay just ahead of him. The same turn they had taken in reverse just ten minutes earlier, as they had made their way to the interview room. That choice told Bush two things.

He's retracing our steps.

And he's about to hit another locked door.

Seconds later and Bush was proved correct on both counts. Dempsey had reached the barred gate that divided this secure section of the Facility from the administrative area beyond; the location, the agent would know from earlier, of the various rooms assigned to the prison's officers.

Bush had no doubt that this was where Dempsey was heading – directly to Colonel Walker, most likely – and there had to be a good reason for him to be in such a hurry.

But this was still the Facility.

And the Facility had rules.

'Agent Dempsey, you need to—'

'I need to get through this gate,' Dempsey interrupted. 'I need to see the CO. I need to see him now.'

'Agent Dempsey, sir, can you—'

'Just open the gate, Corporal.'

'What the hell's going on here?'

The question came from the other side of the bars, causing Bush to look past Dempsey and into the corridor beyond. Colonel Walker, no doubt attracted by the commotion, had left his office and was already striding towards them.

Bush opened his mouth to reply, but Dempsey beat him to it. When he spoke his voice was calm and authoritative. It was a tone that left no room for doubt.

'Colonel, you've got to radio Nicki May. She's driving into an ambush. They all are.'

SIXTY

'GET CLEAR OF THE CAR!'

Grace grabbed Vega by the collar as she shouted the order. At first she had to physically drag him away from the Suburban, but only for a moment. Vega lacked Grace's training but he was smart and his natural response was still good; a second later and he was matching her pace.

They moved fast, away from the prone vehicle and into the sweeping cloud of dust that had been thrown up when its wheels had shifted off-road. Grace cast just a single glance back as they went. It was long enough to see two things: that the driver had also cleared the car and that he was now heading the wrong way.

He was running *towards* the now slowing convoy.

Grace did not let the man's mistake slow her own progress; there was nothing she could do from here to make him turn around and, if she was right, it would not matter anyway. As he closed in on the fourth Suburban, the unwitting DOJ agent was as good as dead.

It had not occurred to Grace for even a moment that her instinct might be wrong. That the aircraft she had seen bearing

374

down upon them might actually be from Homeland or from the DOJ. Or even from the US Air Force, scrambled out of Vandeveer.

No. Grace had called this one right. She knew that already, and so the shock of the first explosion was purely physical.

She had barely an instant to register the sound of the impact before its shockwave hit. The force smashed into her from the side as she sprinted towards the road, sending her crashing face first into the desert sand.

She pushed herself back up to her feet. The skin on her palms and fingertips had been both cut and burned by the rough, hot ground, but Grace had no time to notice. Her eyes were on the carnage now ahead of her; on the flaming wreckage of what had been the first Suburban.

But it was not the explosion that concerned her. That damage was done and there was nothing that could change it. Instead, it was a sound she could barely make out that sent her pulse racing.

Small arms fire.

The noise seemed distant, a result of the damage the explosion had done to her hearing. But those gunshots, the unmistakable sound of an ongoing attack, warned Grace of the devastation that was still to come. Her eyes followed it to its source: assault rifles being discharged from the open doors of the aircraft Grace had spotted from the Suburban. It was close enough now for Grace to recognise it as a heavily armed, military grade Huey helicopter.

And for her to realise that the chopper was positioning itself to fire again.

'SERGIO, MOVE!'

She grasped Vega again as she screamed, forcing him to act

just as she had done moments before. Vega had somehow stayed on his feet through the impact of the shockwave, but the death and destruction he now saw had left him rooted to the spot.

It was shock, Grace realised. A natural human reaction that had been drilled out of her by intensive Secret Service training, with any residual traces eradicated by her time with Dempsey. Vega had enjoyed neither of those advantages and so his response was to be expected. But understandable was not the same as acceptable. Not in a combat situation.

If he wants to live, he needs to move.

'NOW, SERGIO!'

Grace pulled at Vega's collar, hard enough to break through his stupor and get his frozen feet moving. Together they stumbled clumsily into the road and then across it, towards a shallow ditch that Grace had spotted running along its far side. They moved as fast as their bodies would allow, with every step wracked by pain and injury, the toll of the hit they had taken from the shockwave.

A few seconds and they were down, behind the cover of a natural parapet; compressed dirt, randomly formed alongside the highway to create a short, eighteen-inch-high wall that was topped by the road itself.

It was as meagre an obstruction as Grace could imagine, but it was enough. And it was just in time as the shallow bank guarded against a second, much closer explosion. The fourth Suburban, the one ahead of their own, Grace guessed. The ground around them shook at the impact and the already burning air felt hot enough to roast them where they lay, but both were unharmed.

At least by that one.

Grace moved upwards for just a moment, rising for a view of

the road. She was down again just as quickly, her assessment of the likely target confirmed. The fourth car, like the first, had taken a direct hit from whatever ordinance it was that the chopper was firing.

No way anyone's surviving that, Grace told herself. *Not in the car. Not outside it, either.*

'WHAT THE . . . EDEN . . . WHAT THE FUCK?'

Vega's voice was loud, Grace could tell. It had to be for her to hear him over the roaring sounds around them and her own temporarily impaired hearing. Still, she ignored both his shout and the sound of a third explosion – this one further away. Car two, she assumed – as she methodically checked herself for injury. With what she suspected was coming, she needed to be certain of her own capabilities.

The wave had hit them both hard, leaving her with an unwelcome combination of a groggy mind, a sick stomach and muscles that felt like they'd been through a car crash. For now, though, that seemed to be the extent of the damage.

With no obvious major injury, Grace knew that she could still do her job. When the time was right, she could still fight back. With that clear in her mind, she reached for her shoulder holster, gripped her pistol and drew it. Only then, once she was fully prepared, did she turn to face Vega.

'Are you hurt?'

A fourth explosion – the closest so far – drowned out Grace's question. Its shockwave was impossible to ignore, even with the protection of the bank; it seemed to suck the very oxygen from the air, even while they were shielded from physical harm.

'ARE YOU HURT?' Grace asked again, raising her voice above the sound of devastation that now surrounded them.

'AM I HURT? JESUS, EDEN. WHAT THE FUCK IS HAPPENING?'

'JAILBREAK,' Grace shouted back. 'THEY'VE COME FOR TRAVIS.'

'WHO HAVE? WHO ARE "THEY"?'

'LIBERATION WOULD BE MY GUESS. BUT DOES IT MATTER? ARE YOU HURT?'

Vega did not reply. He seemed to need time to register what was happening. To think through what they had just escaped.

And to realise who was still out there.

'WHAT ABOUT NICKI?' His voice was even louder now. Driven up in horror. 'NICKI AND O'ROURKE. THEIR CAR . . .'

'THEY'RE IN THE SAME TRUCK AS TRAVIS,' Grace shouted back. 'AND THERE WERE FOUR EXPLOSIONS, NOT FIVE. WHOEVER'S IN THAT CHOPPER, THEY WON'T FIRE ON THE GUY THEY CAME HERE TO RESCUE.'

Vega hesitated. When he finally spoke again his voice was lower. Still loud, but no longer the shout it had been.

'But how would they know which car?'

'An insider. Has to be. None of this works without one.'

Grace was not looking as she answered. Her attention was focused on the movement of the dust and sand and smoke that surrounded them. Each seemed to be forming a vortex, all spinning in directions of their own. Grace did not need to risk a glimpse of the road to know what this meant.

The chopper's landing.

'Who?'

Grace turned to face Vega. With her mind elsewhere, his question made no sense.

'Who what?'

'The insider,' Vega explained. 'Who is it?'

'It's not you, it's not me and it's not Dempsey.' Grace indicated through the bank of earth, in the direction of what she presumed was their now devastated Suburban. 'And it's sure as hell not the poor sonofabitch who was driving us. Beyond that, it could be anyone.'

Vega looked nervously towards the dirt wall, all that lay between them and what was left of the convoy. He wanted to raise himself above it, Grace realised. Just enough so he could see beyond. She was relieved that he resisted. With almost all other targets now gone, that was the only sensible choice. And right now, that was exactly what she needed Vega to be.

Sensible instead of rash.

It was the only chance they now had to stay alive.

O'Rourke looked around. Her surroundings seemed . . . unfamiliar. And unnatural. For a moment she could not work out why – hell, she couldn't even work out *where* – but that changed as the pain in her right temple burst through her bewilderment.

Everything came back at once. A rush of consciousness and agony that she could have done without.

She did not need to check if the two men in the front seats were dead. Both were slumped forward lifelessly into their seatbelts, towards the Suburban's shattered windshield. It was from there, O'Rourke slowly realised, that the confusion of her surroundings had come. The intense sun was still beating through the rear window to her right and through the open passenger door to her left, but the front of the vehicle was somehow shrouded in darkness.

She peered closer and realised why. From the damage to its front, the vehicle must had been driven onto the desert dirt at speed, directly into one of the thick, rock-hewn bushes that flanked the road. It must have been moving fast enough for the combination of stone and shrub to devastate the front of the vehicle, bringing it to a dead stop in a matter of inches.

It was the only conclusion. And it left nothing but questions.

How had they . . . why had they . . .

O'Rourke's mind focused, an observation from an instant earlier now returning to its centre.

The open passenger door.

Her disorientation was gone. Replaced by absolute certainty and cold fury.

Nicki.

The image of May's face – the mouthed words of meaningless apology – were fixed in O'Rourke's mind as she unclipped her seatbelt, pulled out her pistol and climbed across the back seat of the Suburban. She moved in a semi-crawl towards the open door, taking far more time than she should. She was slowed by a combination of her head injury and overall poor health. But she would let neither hindrance hold her back.

O'Rourke had one thought in her mind. One burning objective: to make Nicki pay for what she had done. She knew she might never achieve it – she did not know how long she had been out and so May could be long gone by now – but she had to try.

And if I ain't too late . . . if she's still here . . .

A moment more and O'Rourke was out of the car, but not in the way she had intended. She had reached out for one final moment of support – one last place of purchase as she pulled her body through the vehicle – but, her head still groggy, she had miscalculated. Her outstretched hand found only air, causing her full weight to fall forward and down.

O'Rourke tumbled through the open door and hit the ground hard. She took the impact on her outstretched hands, dropping her weapon as she went. Somehow she avoided any contact with her already injured head. Not that any further blow was needed; as she lay on her front and tried to regain her lost breath, O'Rourke realised just how off-kilter the world seemed.

She took a few moments more. It was not nearly enough time to recover. It was barely enough to bring her breathing under control. But it was all the time she had. If Nicki May *was* still here, that could change at any moment.

O'Rourke pushed her body up from the floor and looked all around her. At first she could not see clearly, which was as much an effect of the bright sunlight as it was her head injury. Slowly, though, her focus returned. When it did she could see for herself the blood that was now on May's hands.

Jesus, girl. You go wrong, you don't do it by halves.

The carnage was all around her, with burning trucks in every direction. All of the other four vehicles for the convoy, each one devastated by what could only be missile fire. Which meant they had each been a target except for the Suburban that had been carrying Travis.

If O'Rourke had harboured any doubts at all, they would have been wiped away now.

Her eyes locked on to the nearest smouldering wreck. It was the second SUV, she surmised, based on its position. O'Rourke took a moment to study what she could make out of its remains. To be sure that her instinct was correct. It took no longer than that. Even with her mind working at less than full speed and viewing from a distance, O'Rourke knew her subject: the damage done by a missile was visibly distinct from a bomb or a landmine, with even the trajectory making a difference to how the debris would spread.

It was a missile, she told herself. *And it came from the sky. But where?*

The answer revealed itself almost as soon as she began to look for it. Even with her heart now pumping hard and the pain in her head worsening with the pressure, O'Rourke was almost certain of what she would find. And yet somehow, when she did, it still seemed unexpected.

Holy shit.

For a sound that she had not even registered until that moment, the roar of the helicopter's engine was deafening. It had, she now realised, been *all* she could hear from the moment she had regained consciousness; a sound so all-pervasive that it had become the soundtrack of her groggy tragedy.

The chopper must have touched down to the ground just as O'Rourke first saw it; close enough, at least, that six of its passengers were out with their assault rifles raised before she had even properly registered the sight. All six were moving forward as one, fanned out in exact increments and closing in on a point two hundred yards from O'Rourke's position, all seemingly heading to the same spot.

Military-trained, O'Rourke told herself. *And they ain't ours.*

She leaned forward and picked up her fallen pistol – a standard-issue SIG Sauer P229 – and checked to make sure it had not been damaged by its fall. Seconds later and it was ready, a single 9mm round in the chamber, fifteen more in the magazine and another fifteen in the reloader she now slipped into her waistband.

Satisfied that she was armed and ready, O'Rourke took a deep breath and pushed herself upright.

Thirty-one rounds against six automatic rifles. Another deep breath. Then a thought that almost made her laugh. *For a moment there, I thought we were in trouble.*

The line stayed with O'Rourke as she began to move, the image of a favourite movie providing a necessary distraction from reality as she raised her weapon and strode forward. Only one fate awaited her, she knew that. But the lives of these men and women, of fourteen federal agents and of Eden Grace and Sergio Vega . . . they were on her.

It was O'Rourke who had been played. It was O'Rourke who had believed every word May had told her.

She redoubled her grip on her pistol as she closed the gap between her and the six men from the helicopter, aware that they seemed to be heading sideways to her advance. Towards a spot she could not see.

Hundred and fifty yards.

O'Rourke estimated the distance. Her pistol was neither lethal nor accurate from here and so any shot would be a waste of ammunition. She had to get closer. She could only hope that the gunmen's attention stayed fixed ahead of them as she did so.

Hundred and forty yards.

Forty more until a shot would be lethal, ninety more until it would be accurate. And that was on O'Rourke's best day.

Hundred and thirty yards.

She was breathing hard now, her pistol beginning to wave visibly with each step. She pushed on, never allowing her pace to drop.

Hundred and twenty yards.

O'Rourke stumbled. Just for a moment, but long enough

that she needed to catch and reset herself before she could move again. As she did so, she scanned to the right, in the direction the group of six were headed towards. It was a movement of just a few inches as they were now yards from their target, but it was enough to banish every ounce of fatigue from O'Rourke's body.

Nicki.

May and Travis had been obscured by the swirling sand and dust thrown up by the helicopter rotors, but they were finally visible as they rushed forward to meet the six gunmen. There was no hesitation at all in their movement, which told O'Rourke what she already knew: these men – these mercenaries or these self-proclaimed Liberation freedom fighters, whatever they wanted to call themselves – were here to spirit Travis away to safety.

A prison break, O'Rourke now realised. *This whole thing was a goddamned long con. Every last bit of it.*

She gripped the pistol harder, steadying her hand. And then, for the second time in twenty-four hours, she began to run. Still a hundred yards back, her 9mm rounds could now be fatal in the unlikely event that they hit something that mattered. For O'Rourke, that was just about as good as her odds were going to get.

And so she opened fire.

Travis, May and their rescuers were fifty yards from the helicopter and double that from O'Rourke. There was no chance she was going to reach them in time and almost as little that her bullets would do any damage at all. And yet still the sound of her gunfire caused Travis to act.

For just a moment, what was now a protective huddle of eight moving bodies came to a halt. A second later and it was moving again, but this time as a group of seven. Nicki May had split off and was now facing the approaching O'Rourke. She had an assault rifle raised to her shoulder and she stood stock-still as O'Rourke's wild shots flew past her, all missing by a margin that made them no threat.

Thirteen.

Fourteen.

O'Rourke's eyes were beginning to lose their focus as she counted her own bullets. The world around her started to spin and she could feel her knees weakening as she slowed.

Fifteen.

By now she had no real expectation that any shot would hit its target. She was still fifty yards away. The very outside of the range of accuracy with a SIG pistol and way beyond what O'Rourke could manage in her present state. It was with no confidence, then, that she applied the kiss of pressure that fired the weapon's final round.

Sixteen.

O'Rourke stopped moving and, with her eyes never leaving May, she ejected the empty magazine and reached into her waistband for its replacement. Clicking it into place and chambering a round, she began to lift the pistol to fire again.

It was a shot she would never make.

Grace watched in horror as May stepped from the huddle of bodies, a rifle raised to her shoulder and pointed towards O'Rourke. She had spotted May perhaps thirty seconds earlier, standing with Travis at a short distance from where the chopper set down. At first Grace had denied her own suspicions. She had wanted May to be onside. Wanted this to be a last-ditch attempt on her part to keep custody of Travis.

That hope had been all but extinguished when the two – Travis *and* May – were enveloped by the six arriving 'rescuers'. But even then Grace had clung to the most unlikely of explanations: that May had simply surrendered herself to the inevitable and that what she had witnessed was the DOJ being taken as a compliant hostage.

Grace was unsure why she wanted to deny the most obvious explanation. Maybe it was simple ego; after treating May as one of their own, both she and Dempsey would have to accept the extraordinary extent to which they had been played.

Or perhaps it was for Vega. Perhaps Grace did not want him to have fallen for a bitch who'd betrayed them all.

Whatever the reason, there was no denying it now. Not when May was armed with an assault rifle and aiming it at O'Rourke, all while Travis was being spirited to the waiting chopper.

'I can't . . . I can't believe . . .'

'Believe it,' Grace interrupted. She turned to face Vega as she spoke. 'Believe it and use it. Because we're not letting that bitch kill O'Rourke. Understood?'

'Understood,' Vega replied, his voice far more firm than Grace had expected. There was no uncertainty in his eyes as he spoke. Whatever he had felt for May, her betrayal had destroyed it. 'Flank her?'

'It's the only way. You move from here, I'll go fifty yards up and do the same from there. We move together, weapons up, on my signal. Got it?'

'Got it.'

Grace moved without another word, her eyes flitting between her own path, the chopper and the stand-off between O'Rourke and May. She covered the ground quickly and so was much closer when she saw O'Rourke stop and slowly reload.

The distance between the two women had closed to a point where, with a steady hand, O'Rourke might actually hit her target. It was a fact that would not have been lost on May and so Grace knew in her gut what was coming next.

She hoped that she was wrong. That May would not . . .

The crack of the assault rifle was unmistakable. Three shots, fired in a single short burst.

Grace watched in horror as O'Rourke fell.

O'Rourke looked up, her eyes blinking wildly in the blinding light of the sun. The short burst of gunfire had taken her off her feet and hurtled her into the dust. An equilibrium-busting body-slam that had shattered what had been left of her senses. It was an almost welcome delirium; while it lasted, O'Rourke could not consider its cause.

It was a mercy she would not enjoy for long, ended by a deep, painful cough that left her lips wet with blood. The agony that came with it brought O'Rourke around from her stupor. A few seconds more and she was thinking clearly again. Clearly enough to know exactly where she was.

On her back and helpless as her life bled away into the Texan sand.

'Well . . . holy . . . shit.'

O'Rourke said the three words aloud, each one of them exhausting. The sound of her own voice told her that she was still alive. But only just. She coughed again. More blood – this time expelled as far as her navel – and more pain.

Allowing her head to fall back into the dust, she took a deep, pained breath, closed her eyes and resigned herself to her fate.

'Why didn't you stay in the car?'

O'Rourke opened her eyes.

'You were supposed to stay in the car.'

She forced her head upwards, pain ripping through her body from the movement. O'Rourke had no doubt that she was worsening the damage already done by attempting to lift herself upright, but she would be damned if she was staying on her back.

Not now. Not when that bitch is right there.

'You were supposed to live, Bambi. That's why I put you in *my* car. You could have walked away from this.'

O'Rourke could say nothing in reply. It was all she could do to stay conscious through the agony as she dragged her body sideways. To a position where she could at least lock a bloody left eye on the woman who had betrayed her.

May raised the rifle barrel.

'Why?'

It was all O'Rourke could manage to say as her consciousness began to slip away. All of her remaining energy, expended in a single word.

But a single word was all it took. May lowered the barrel again. Just by inches and not enough that anyone back at the chopper could notice.

'Why? Do you really want to know?'

O'Rourke did not reply, but her open left eye remained fixed on May.

'It was because of you,' May continued. 'I've seen what you've become. Old and beaten down and sick and exhausted. And for what? A country that's going to drop you the moment you're no more use.'

With the world seeming to close in around her, O'Rourke

could hear the words but – now barely conscious – she could no longer appreciate their meaning.

'I'm not letting that happen to me, Bambi. I'm not making the same mistake. I was offered a way out.' May raised the barrel one last time. 'And I'm going to give you yours.'

O'Rourke was out before May could pull the trigger. And so she never heard the gunshot that saved her life.

Grace ran as fast as she could – faster than she ever had before – but she still knew it would not be enough. Although close enough to see movement that proved O'Rourke was alive, there was no way she could cover the ground between them in time to stop May from taking a final, fatal shot.

But there was still hope.

Sergio can still get there.

Vega's starting point had been closer and, as Grace had now learned, the detective was fast. He was very, very fast.

Vega had covered the rough desert ground at a pace Grace could never have matched, closing the distance like a sprinter. Just thirty yards and counting from May and O'Rourke, his approach had been unseen. May's attention was still fixed on her wounded 'friend' and so in just a few more steps Vega would be close enough to take her down.

You're going to make it, Sergio. Grace willed Vega on in her mind. *Just slow down and take the shot. You can't miss.*

The thought had barely formed as May's rifle began to rise. Their time was up. For O'Rourke to live, Vega had to act. But first, Grace knew, he had to slow. There was simply no way he could fire accurately at that pace.

He needed that second more. He needed a distraction.

Grace provided it.

Aware that she could not risk hitting Vega or O'Rourke by firing from this distance, Grace lifted her arm and – without breaking step – began to fire towards the awaiting chopper. With at least two hundred yards between them, any single round lucky enough to strike it would be harmlessly deflected. But damage to the vehicle was not the point.

Grace's eyes never left May and so she saw the DOJ agent register the six shots. May's eyes flitted upwards from O'Rourke and homed in on the source of the sound. Her rifle moved with them and this time May did not hesitate. She opened fire – three bursts of three shots each – causing Grace to dive to her right in order to the avoid the volley of bullets.

Grace rolled as she hit the ground, lessening the impact and bringing her back up into a firing position; with no cover anywhere close by, a volley of her own was going to be her only protection. But before she could pull the trigger she heard another series of shots and, as she saw May react to the new shooter, Grace burst into a final sprint.

The gunshots had come from Vega, fired at full speed. Despite the time Grace had given him, he had not slowed his pace. And that, Grace knew, made his shots a lottery. That kind of gunplay was a mistake for anyone but the most skilled expert. So against a well-trained federal agent armed with an automatic assault rifle?

The question answered itself.

Grace pushed herself hard. She was determined to be wrong. Determined to reach her own firing range before May could act. Determined to save Vega's life. But sometimes determination is just not enough.

The three-round burst hit Vega full-on from less than

ten yards, with the slight upwards movement of May's barrel sending two into his chest and the third directly into his horrified face. He went down hard just as Grace came to a halt and raised her own weapon. May, though, did not stop to watch him fall. With the burst fired, she was already spinning back to face Grace.

And that gave Grace the perfect target.

Three shots fired. Three targets hit. Two to the chest and one to the head. The same grouping as Vega. Had Grace known that then she would have thought it poetic justice. As it was, she did not give it a second's thought. May was dead. As was Vega and most likely O'Rourke, and so Grace's focus had shifted to her own survival.

Even with her attention fixed on May, Grace had not forgotten the presence of the chopper. How could she, with the swirly fog of sand and dust still being whipped up by its rotors? And so it was towards the Huey that she turned as the third bullet left her Glock 19.

Grace spun quickly, fully expecting the worst. With at least six armed gunmen inside and carrying sufficient firepower of its own to have taken out four Suburbans of five, she stood no chance in any kind of confrontation. Even so, Grace was not going down without a fight.

Or at all.

She lowered her pistol as she watched the chopper lifting off, its tail turning towards her as it rose into the air. As uncertain as she had been of what she was about to face — whether that was a hard-fought execution at the hands of Travis's gunmen, or just certain death from the Huey's heavy ordinance — it had not been this.

It had not been . . . disinterest.

She stood open-mouthed as the helicopter moved away, quickly picking up speed as it put both Grace and the carnage all about her behind it. Her heart pumped hard, flooding her system with now unnecessary adrenaline as she tried to rationalise what had just happened.

He didn't wait for her, Grace realised. *After everything she did for him, he abandoned her. He didn't even wait to see the outcome.*

Not that Grace had any sympathy for her. May had chosen Liberation over her country. And she had chosen them over her friend.

O'Rourke.

With her pulse lowering and the grip of her fight or flight instinct beginning to lessen, Grace realised that she had not checked on the Homeland agent. And that, unlike Vega or May, there was still a chance that she had survived.

She was beside O'Rourke in seconds. Grace dropped to her knees and checked the agent's bloodied neck for a pulse. To her surprise and relief, she found one straight away.

She's alive.

O'Rourke's heartbeat was slow, but it was regular and it seemed at least strong enough to give Grace hope. Moving fast, she inspected O'Rourke for injuries and found three: a minor impact wound to her right temple, cuts to her hands and a single bullet hole. It seemed that two of May's three-round burst had missed their target. The third, though, had hit O'Rourke in the chest at an angle suggesting damage to her right lung. It was a wound that would be fatal without urgent medical attention. Far more than Grace was qualified to provide.

O'Rourke was alive. If she was going to stay that way, they needed help.

And they needed it now.

SIXTY-ONE

6.12 a.m. CDT

'How far out?'

Dempsey held his helmet mic close to his mouth as he spoke. The question was to the pilot of the UH-60M Black Hawk helicopter, one of two that were now hurtling through the air at two hundred and twenty miles an hour towards US Air Force Base Vandeveer.

'Two minutes to the base, sir,' the pilot replied. 'But it don't look like we're going that far.'

'What does that mean?'

Dempsey was in the rear of the chopper, sat in a fast deployment position along with ten armed US army rangers from the Facility. It was the ideal placement for immediate deployment into a combat situation but it was not designed to provide him with the best view of the route ahead. Which meant that Dempsey could not see the pillars of smoke from roughly five miles away that were now drifting up and away into the desert sky.

'It looks like we're too late.' This time it was a voice that he recognised. It was Colonel Walker, who had taken the co-pilot's seat in the cockpit. 'The convoy's been hit.'

Dempsey felt his stomach turn at the news.

'What can you see? Is it ongoing?'

'Not judging by the spread of the smoke. Those fires have been burning for a while. Five minutes at least.'

'Any sign of who hit them?'

Walker paused before responding. Dempsey understood why. At this speed the scene ahead would be growing clearer to the colonel by the second. A few more could make the difference between a guess and an informed answer.

'Doesn't look like it,' Walker finally replied. 'All I can see is four burning vehicles.'

'Four?'

'Yeah. Looks like ... wait ... no, five. The fifth isn't burning. It's off-road, but there's no smoke.'

'Any movement around it?'

'Not that I can see but we're still too far out for precise detail.'

Dempsey closed his eyes and pushed the back of his head into the wall. He could feel the gaze of the rangers upon him. Sympathetic glances from hard men who understood loss and who had heard the exchange with Walker. As far as they were aware, Dempsey had just lost his team.

He had not, of course. Of the nineteen bodies in the cars, he had only ever exchanged words with four. But one of those four . . .

'Jesus, Eden.'

Dempsey said the words aloud, his eyes opening as her name left his lips. The image of his friend's face stayed in his mind even as he looked around the combat-ready soldiers who now surrounded him. The ranger directly across gave him a wordless nod that spoke volumes:

Sorry for your loss, brother, it said. *Now let's make them pay.*

With those unuttered words in his head, Dempsey pushed the mic back to his mouth.

'Colonel, call through to Vandeveer. If these bastards were on land then we'll find them easy enough. But if they were moving by air, we'll need radar.'

'Grayson's ahead of you, son,' Walker replied, with a nod towards the pilot. 'He's already got them working on the sky search and they've scrambled two jets to intercept as soon as they have the coordinates.'

'Only two?'

'Lucky it's that many, Agent Dempsey. It's a minor base. Not much more than a runway.'

Dempsey said nothing more. They could only work with the resources they had. And chances were, they would probably be enough. Whatever aircraft had come for Peyton Travis, it would be no match for a US Air Force fighter jet.

The sensation of the Black Hawk decelerating distracted Dempsey from the point. He gripped the MK-17 assault rifle he had been provided at the Facility and dug his feet down into the floor of the cabin, to stabilise himself from any sudden movements right or left as the chopper descended. Looking out of the side door to his right, he saw the second Black Hawk mimicking the movements of the first. It could mean only one thing.

We're here.

It took less than ten seconds from the first decrease in speed to the feel of the ground beneath the aircraft. It was the kind of hard and fast landing almost unheard of in civilian aviation but which was typical of a military pilot deploying into a dangerous situation.

A second more and Dempsey was out. The rangers were deploying all around him but he did not wait for them to group. With his rifle raised and his legs pumping hard, he sprinted away from the chopper and towards the closest burning vehicle. Within ten strides he was clear enough of the swirling dust and sand to recognise the charred remains of a Suburban. A few more and he knew what had caused the damage.

He inspected the wreckage in moments. Four sets of remains. Charred and with the upper bodies all but obliterated, there was still enough left of the lower regions to count the victims. Dempsey was moving as soon as that count went beyond three, because three told him the only thing he wanted to know.

It's not Eden's truck.

He headed to the next burning wreck, his rifle now raised in one hand as he lifted his com with the other.

'Colonel, at least one of these trucks was hit by an air-to-surface missile.' Dempsey spoke as he moved, never slowing his pace. 'All four would be my bet. This was an air attack.'

'Affirmative,' Walker replied. 'That's our take, too.'

'Then we need the radar results from the base. They need to get after these bastards.'

He reached the next burning vehicle. Another body check. Four more. So still not Grace.

'Not gonna be that simple, son.'

'What?' Dempsey spotted and then headed to the next Suburban. 'Why not?'

'There was more than one aircraft picked up on the system. Way more than—'

'DEMPSEY!'

Even with Walker's voice coming through an earpiece, the

piercing shout drowned out the colonel's reply. Dempsey zoned in on its source in an instant and, through the obstructions thrown up by the still swirling rotors of the Black Hawks, he saw the one sight for which he had not dared to hope.

Eden.

Grace was a hundred yards away. A hundred and twenty at most. Whatever the distance, Dempsey covered it faster than he had in his life.

His eyes swept from right to left as he ran, taking in the details and assessing their surroundings for threats and for danger. And so he could not fail to notice as Grace turned away, back to an object that he could now see in the dust behind her.

An object which, as he grew closer, he began to recognise.

He lifted his mic to his mouth.

'Colonel, we need a medic here now. We have survivors. I repeat. We have survivors.'

SIXTY-TWO

7.34 a.m. EDT

Ray McMillan was angry. More than he had been at any time in his eighteen months as US Secretary for Homeland Security. Maybe more than he had ever been. Not that he was in any condition to sit and compare his current moods to those of the past.

He needed an outlet. And he knew exactly where to find it.

'Mr Secretary, sir, I really think you should let me deal with this.'

The advice came from Assistant Director Lee Hodges, head of the Homeland Security Central Florida Office in Fort Pierce. He offered it from a few hurried steps behind McMillan, chasing after the secretary as he stormed along the corridor towards the interrogation room.

And McMillan chose to ignore it.

'Sir, this is . . . not how this works. You can't interrogate a suspect. You're—'

'I'm the Head of Homeland Security,' McMillan snapped back. He did not look back as he spoke. Nor did he lessen his pace. 'I decide how things work. And right now, they work like this.'

McMillan reached the door of the interrogation room at the

398

same moment as he stopped speaking. Gripping the handle, he opened the door with far more force and speed than was needed and stepped inside. Then he strode towards the table that sat against the far wall, his eyes never leaving its occupant.

'Where the fuck is Travis?'

McMillan asked the question before he had reached his waiting chair. It was directed at Cam Arnold, who was seated in the same position he had taken during his earlier interrogation by O'Rourke.

Arnold responded with a broad, smug smile.

'It's done then, is it?'

'Where is he?'

'Guess I'll take that as a yes.'

Arnold sat as far back into his chair as his cuffs would allow. With their chain wrapped around the iron ring that was built into the centre of the table, his movement was limited. But had he been able, McMillan could tell, he would have had his hands behind his head and his feet up, revelling in his own success.

There was little that McMillan had not seen in twenty years in intelligence. Even less that could faze him. He was a cold, practical man and he had relied upon exactly those attributes to climb the ladder and grasp the position he now held. A position he had earned from long years of hard work. A position he deserved.

And a position that was now at risk. Trusting May. Overruling O'Rourke and Dempsey. The decision to release Travis. This whole disaster. All of it was on McMillan. There would be consequences, he knew. It left McMillan uncertain of his future, unsure of everything for which he had worked, and yet all he could see was the arrogant self-satisfaction on the face of Cam Arnold.

It was more than he could take. McMillan reached forward, grabbed Arnold's chains and pulled them hard. It caused Arnold to be dragged forward, his face colliding with the table. The secretary then held up the chains to pin the prisoner in place before lowering his own head to the same level. Now just inches from Arnold's ear, McMillan brought his voice to a near whisper.

'I've just lost a whole unit of good men. The Department of Justice even more. You think you can declare war on the federal government, then just sit back untouched by the consequences? I can make your life a living hell. And I can decide when and how that hell ends. Whether you realise it or not, you're mine. So either you tell me where Travis has gone and you tell me who else helped organise this . . . this . . . fucking massacre, or, believe me, I will have you flayed alive and cooked while you're fed to my fucking dogs.'

The words felt like an exorcism. A release of the hate that had built up in the last thirty minutes, as McMillan had seen his operation crashing down around him. With his anger vented, he felt some of his usual calm return. Stepping back, he released the chains and allowed Arnold to lift his head from the table.

The Liberation man took a few moments to compose himself before looking McMillan in the eye and allowing his grin to return.

'So you're one of the folks from behind that mirror, are ya?'

McMillan was unsure how to answer. He had not expected his threats and the violence to immediately break the man, but he had not anticipated that they would be ignored entirely.

'Come on now, there's no need for secrets here.' Arnold spoke before McMillan had a chance to break his own silence. 'Not any more.'

'You arrogant—'

'Mr McMillan, I'd hope you'd have realised by now that name calling ain't gonna help.' Arnold seemed to notice the secretary's surprise at the use of his name. It made him smile even wider and caused him to shake his head. 'You think I didn't know who you were? After everything that's happened, did you really think I didn't do my homework on who I'd be dealing with? This, sir, is why you people will lose. You underestimate us at every turn.'

McMillan stepped back, his eyes remaining fixed on Arnold. The grin was still in place. The same smug expression. Nothing the secretary had done so far had even rattled the man. For McMillan, it offered a challenge. He had to work out how to approach an educated fanatic. How to get something – anything – from Cam Arnold. He had no idea right now how he would manage it but he did at least knew what would *not* work.

He had to play this smarter.

McMillan reached out for the chair on the opposite side of the table, pulled it out and took his seat. He leaned back into it, mimicking the pose he knew Arnold wanted to adopt, except McMillan kept his arms down and his hands flat on the cold metal. An old trick he had to remember; flat, open hands would help him stay composed in the face of what might come.

'OK. You want to do this civilised, let's do this civilised. When did you turn May?'

Arnold just smirked.

'It can't have been that recent,' McMillan continued, ignoring the reaction. 'None of this plan works without her. She's a long-term mole. So how long ago did she join your little movement?'

'She alive?'

'You really give a shit?'

'No. Not one little bit. But I am curious. I just wonder if things played out like they did in my head. That's all.'

'In that case you don't need to know.'

'That's not your call, Mr Secretary. You want my information, you give me yours. Did she make it?'

McMillan hesitated. He was uncertain how he wanted to play this. It wasn't ideal to cave on the first demand, but then it hardly mattered one way or the other. As he weighed the pros and cons, he glanced at his watch. It was an unconscious reminder of how little time they really had. And it made his decision for him.

'No,' McMillan finally answered. 'She's dead. As she should be.'

'Good. That bitch had no loyalty. No principles. The ground's the best place for her.'

The secretary could not suppress a frown. He felt it furrow his brow and, as he saw Arnold notice it in turn, he immediately regretted the action.

'You thought she was one of mine out of ideology, I see.' Arnold's smile had lessened. Now it was back. He leaned forward. 'Not for a minute. She betrayed you people for money. It was a whole lot of money, sure. But still. She gave you up for a price. All of you.'

'When?'

'Year ago, more or less.'

'That's how long you've been planning this?'

'That's how long May was involved. I've been on it a whole lot longer than that. And that, sir, begs the question, don't it: if I've been working on this for as long as I have, why in the hell am I gonna give up the boss right after we got him out?'

'Because you've thought this through,' McMillan replied. He finally felt like he was finding his feet. 'Yeah, Travis is out. And yeah, we don't know where he is yet. But—'

'You like the extra blips trick?' Arnold interrupted. 'That

one was my idea. Stole it from the end of that movie. What was it? The one where James Bond plays the rich guy?'

McMillan did not respond. He would not give Arnold the satisfaction of knowing just how effective his 'blips trick' had been, but he had to agree: it *had* made pursuit of Travis almost impossible. Instead of a single aircraft appearing on the Vandeveer radar at the time of the attack, there had been sixteen. Sixteen helicopters taking off from the same location. All setting down in different spots within a square mile of one another at the time of the attack. And all leaving again at the same moment, taking sixteen different flight paths away from the area. With just two jets available to bring the choppers down and check their human cargo, it reduced the odds on finding Travis and his rescuers to one in eight.

The tactic had worked perfectly, but McMillan had no intention of telling Arnold that. Instead he continued, as if the prisoner had said nothing.

'But you're not thinking of yourself. Travis might be out, but *you're* in here. And now he's gone there's a shiny new empty cell waiting to be filled at the Facility. That one's got your name written all over it. Prison for life, Cam. No contact with anyone in the outside world. Just four walls and time to rot. But you can avoid that. There's still a way out.'

'Still a way out? Seriously? You're suggesting that if I play ball I won't be imprisoned for the rest of my life? Do you really think that's got a hope in hell's chance of working on me?'

'Listen, it's not—'

'You can't think that I didn't know this was coming. That I didn't know the consequences of being caught before I ever let it happen. I ain't dumb, Mr Secretary. Ain't even close to that. I got my eyes open wide and I knew where I'd end up.'

'Like I said——'

'That's the difference between us though, ain't it, Mr Secretary? You, you're doing your job for the title and the prestige and the money. You're doing it to keep this whole shitshow on the road. To perpetuate the swamp for as long as you and yours can keep your noses stuck right in there. When it's all said and done, you're all about you. Me? I'm cut from a different cloth. I ain't doing this for me. I'm fighting for a cause.'

'Killing for a cause, you mean.'

'Casualties of war, Mr Secretary. A war I'll die for if I got to, if that's what it takes to win. Not that any of you dumb sonsofbitches even came close to killing me. Because that ain't how you people operate, is it? Not out in the open, anyway. So damned predictable.

'And you know what the real problem is with your side in this thing? You want all the perks of this world you've created. You want the profits from the shit you pull on the small folks. But you're not willing to do what it takes to earn them, are ya? Not yourselves, anyhow. You don't mind someone else getting their hands dirty, as long as no one knows about it. But your own hands? You just don't have the courage to take that step.

'Then there's the likes of me and mine. Every one of us, Mr Secretary. We'll kill whoever we need to kill. And we'll flay whoever we need to flay. We don't just make empty threats. We follow through. And we do it knowing there's nothing the likes of you can do to stop it.'

'That's where you're wrong.' McMillan's anger was rising. Mainly because he could see some truth in what Arnold was saying. 'We can stop you. And we will stop you. And if you won't help us to do that, well, that's your choice. Don't say I didn't warn you where that choice would get you.'

'I know exactly what it'll get me. A few uncomfortable days and nights by my reckoning.'

'What?'

'That's all it'll be. For all your threats, it won't be a week until you're escorting me out of here on a fucking red carpet.'

McMillan sat back in his chair. Until now Arnold had been impenetrable, giving away nothing of value. But that last comment meant something. Unlike everything that had come before it, it was no boast. It was not a claim of willingness for self-sacrifice.

It was, if anything, quite the opposite.

'And what exactly does that mean?' McMillan asked. 'Are you saying we'll let you out of here? You can't possibly think that's going to happen.'

'Think's got nothing to do with it. You ain't gonna have a choice.'

'What the hell are you talking about?'

'Have you forgotten how this started? Are you that easily distracted? What was I moving out of the Keys, Mr McMillan?'

'I haven't, no. But I suspect you never had any caesium in the first place. You only needed the threat of it.'

'Well, you're right on one count. We had to fake the caesium trail to get your attention down there. Scott Turner came in useful for that. But just because we didn't have any down in Florida doesn't mean it doesn't exist. It does, believe me. A whole lot more than a ton of the stuff.'

'You can forget that bullshit,' McMillan interrupted. 'That dog won't hunt twice. You didn't need the caesium. Not for this to play out as you planned. We just had to *think* you had it. Besides, crazy bastards like you, if you'd had as much of the stuff as you say for as long as you say, there's no way you wouldn't have used it. Of that I have no doubt.'

Arnold's smile grew to its very widest.

'Don't think we didn't want to. Problem is, Peyton didn't want to miss out on all the fun.'

'Like I said. Bullshit.'

'Believe whatever you please. Makes no difference to me right now. Soon enough you'll know I ain't lying. And soon enough you'll be doing whatever the hell Peyton Travis tells you to do.'

'And how's that, exactly?'

'Because you're a politician. And so's your boss. And once Liberation starts wiping out millions of eligible voters with those bombs that you think don't exist, well, you'll be playing a different tune then. Once Peyton Travis has brought this country to its knees? You'll be opening the door to my cell like your life depends on it.'

McMillan sat and watched Arnold carefully. The man believed every word he was saying, he realised. He believed every threat he was making.

Worryingly, so did McMillan.

'Enough of this.'

The secretary stood up from his chair, determined to give nothing else away. He was going to learn nothing more here and time was already against them. There was work to do.

He turned and walked towards the door and as he moved he refused to react to the words shouted towards his departing back.

'I'll see you soon, Mr Secretary. Trust me on that. I'll see you very, very soon.'

SIXTY-THREE

7 a.m. CDT

Dempsey and Grace stood in silence outside the doors to the operating room of the Facility's infirmary. Inside, separated from them by hinged glass and barely ten yards of distance, the prison's four medical staff were fighting to save O'Rourke's life.

It was not the first time Dempsey had witnessed the battle that takes place once combat ends. He had done the same just eighteen months ago, back when it had been Grace on the operating table. And he had lost count of how many times before that. But no matter how often he lived through it, the experience never got easier.

Dempsey had not known the Homeland agent well but he liked her and that was not common for him. Using his own rudimentary skills, he had helped Grace to keep her alive while they waited for a medic. All without panic. All without losing his calm.

It was not just concern for O'Rourke that was now affecting him. That he could deal with. But the sight of O'Rourke on that table – the sight of anyone in that condition, in circumstances like this — reminded Dempsey of how many people *he* had put into exactly that place. Or worse.

It was not something he cared to discuss. Not even with a friend as close as Grace. Not even now. But the truth could not be denied. He had caused a level of death and suffering beyond anything he could ever repair. And there was no amount of atonement that could ever change that. No amount of good deeds to outweigh the bad.

Most of the time he could lie to himself. He could forget just how red that ledger really was. But scenes like this? They made that impossible.

Scenes like this brought home the reality.

'How's she doing?'

The question came from Colonel Walker. Dempsey had both heard him approach and seen his reflection in the glass, so his voice was expected. Grace had clearly done neither and so she spun round in surprise when she heard Walker speak.

'She's alive,' Dempsey replied. 'It looks like they're still working on the bullet in her lung.'

'It doesn't look good,' Grace added. 'They're going through a lot of blood.'

'We've got plenty of that here, don't worry.' Walker placed a hand on Grace's shoulder as he spoke. 'We're all just glad you made it through in one piece, Agent Grace. And I'm sorry about your colleague. He didn't deserve what happened.'

'He shouldn't have been there.' Dempsey's eyes remained fixed on the operating room as he spoke. 'Sergio should have stayed in Florida. His death's on me. He only came to Texas because I insisted on bringing him with us.'

'He came because he wanted to come,' Grace replied. 'He could have said no. He could have stayed behind. And if he had done, I'd be dead. So would O'Rourke. I couldn't have taken down Nicki without Sergio reaching her first.'

Dempsey opened his mouth to respond but Walker beat him to it.

'Your friend's dead because of a traitor,' Walker broke in firmly. 'Same as why Agent O'Rourke is on that table. If you two want to find any other beating of a butterfly's wings that might have led them both here, you will. It's easy enough to do. But we all know who killed him, so let's stop with the self-flagellation.'

Neither Dempsey nor Grace replied. Walker was right and they both knew it. There was work to be done and their mutual 'blame-off' for Vega's death was not going to help with that.

There would be a time to mourn the people they had lost but that time was not now.

'I've done what you asked,' Walker said, moving the conversation on to a subject more useful. 'Joshua is back in the room, waiting for you. You really think he knows more?'

'I have no idea,' Dempsey replied, 'but it's worth a try. It's not like we have any other leads right now.'

'And you think he'll help if he can?'

'I think he's as motivated as he's ever been. Hopefully that'll make him less of a stubborn, awkward bastard.'

Dempsey turned to Grace.

'You sitting in on this one?'

'Wouldn't miss it.'

SIXTY-FOUR

8.10 a.m. EDT

Fayetteville Airport had turned out to be just over thirty miles south of Dunn, North Carolina, where Scott Turner had first seen the footage of Cam Arnold's arrest. A forty-five-minute drive in morning conditions provided plenty of time to explain Arnold's plan to his two companions.

Or at least it would have, if one of those companions had *not* been Kenny Brooks.

Their Jeep had been parked in the airport's car lot by 7 a.m. but they had waited an hour before approaching the terminal itself. The change in timeframe had made the risk of a scheduled flight necessary, but it was still prudent to keep their exposure to security cameras and to other methods of tracing and identification to a minimum.

It had not been a comfortable sixty minutes, with Brooks deeply unhappy that the inevitability of Cam Arnold's arrest had been kept from him. Turner knew what the true source of that problem was. It wasn't just that Arnold was now lost to them, although Brooks surely did not like that either. But mostly Brooks just could not stand that it was 'the Limey' who had been taken into Arnold's confidence on that final point in the plan.

It was ego. Nothing more, nothing less. And that ego was threatening to bring the entire enterprise crashing down.

Turner refused to let that happen. Not now. Not when they were so close.

With Arnold in custody, the ball was rolling. The plan had not gone perfectly but Scott had played his part. His expertise in nuclear material had allowed him to fake the caesium trail in the first place. For everything to go the way Arnold planned, they had to convince Homeland Security that they were moving dangerous radioactive material. Enough of the stuff to make a string of devastating dirty bombs.

That kind of weapon, Turner and Arnold had agreed, provided the only leverage great enough to get what they wanted from the US government. And so that leverage had to be created from thin air.

It had been a simple enough task for someone with Turner's training and qualifications. Prior to the charade of carrying heavy but harmless plastic crates along the jetty, he had seen to it that the only genuine radioactive material in their possession would leak just enough that it would leave the telltale signature from the dock to the Sprinter.

A trail leading directly to the decoy crates.

It had been the perfect plan. And, Turner had believed, ultimately a harmless one. Arnold had sworn to him that there would be no victims. That promise had been the price of Turner's involvement, demanded precisely because of men like Kenny Brooks.

Brooks was, to Turner's mind, little more than a clone. One of many versions of the same man, all of them collectively forming the bulk of Liberation. Angry, violent, racist men, brought together by Cam Arnold and used to vent their inadequacies at a world they believed had wronged them. It was that kind of irrationality that had worried Turner and so he had made his condition clear:

Minimum violence. No fatalities.

Arnold had agreed and Turner had trusted him.

It was with horror, then, that he had witnessed the murder of the patrolman yesterday morning. A horror made so much worse in the last few hours following Arnold's arrest as the radio had revealed how many other victims he had left in his wake.

The thought made Turner feel sick in the pit of his stomach. He had lied to himself about the patrolman, he now realised. He had told himself that Arnold must have had good cause to do what he did, all so that he could stay on mission. He had deceived himself, all to achieve his own ultimate goal.

And now people had died.

If I had stood up then, would it have stopped him?

If I had said no, would those other people have lived?

The questions threatened to paralyse him. And yet, to Turner's shame, he found that even now he could override them. Even now, the one thing he wanted above everything else still won through.

If Arnold's plan had worked, Peyton Travis would already be out of the Facility and on his way to Summit Hill, and his cellmate would be with him.

That had been Turner's price for his involvement in the Liberation plan. The freedom of his father. And now, after all these years, Turner was just hours away from seeing him again.

It was the culmination of a driving obsession every bit as fanatical as the insane ideas which drove the true followers of Liberation. Enough that he had thrown away his normal life, thrown away his long-held hopes and dreams, and aligned himself with the one group that was motivated to help him.

After all that, there was no obstacle Turner would not overcome to see his obsession through to its end.

'Did we miss the flight?'

With his mind still elsewhere as he stepped outside of the small terminal building with their newly purchased flight tickets in his hands, Turner was surprised by Cliff Clemons' question.

'No,' Turner replied. 'We're good. We take off in forty mins.'

'How long to Allentown?'

'An hour and twenty. We'll be on the road by a quarter to eleven, Summit Hill by midday.'

Turner handed Clemons his ticket, then did the same to Brooks.

'Any weapons, anything illegal, anything that's going to cause us trouble boarding the flight, dump it in the Jeep now. This is the last step to being where we all want to be and I don't want us taking any risks with that. Agreed?'

'Agreed,' said Clemons.

Turner's focus was already on Brooks, who held his gaze for just a moment. It was his default response to any kind of order from the younger man. An instant later and he seemed to think better of it.

'Agreed.'

Turner gave an internal sigh of relief. He had come too far to allow an idiot like Brooks to derail things. He did not know how, but he would not have allowed it. Not now.

After all he had done – all the lines he had crossed – nothing was going to keep Scott Turner from his father.

SIXTY-FIVE

7.10 a.m. CDT

'Who's this?'

Joshua nodded his head towards Grace. She was sat on one of the two chairs across the table from his own. Dempsey was on the other. All three were screwed to the ground, a common prison practice. To some kinds of men, even a plastic seat was a tempting weapon.

'I'm Agent Eden Grace of the International Security Bureau.'

'The what?'

'Eden works with me,' Dempsey said. 'And she already knows who you are, so consider yourself introduced.'

'Got yourself a sidekick these days, have you?'

'We're in the same unit, same as you and I used to be. No one is anyone else's sidekick.'

'Not how I remember it.' Joshua looked back towards Grace. 'Good-looking girl. Didn't know you had it in you, Galahad. Good job.'

Dempsey resisted the bait. Nor did he explain 'Galahad', although he saw Grace lift an eyebrow when she heard it. They were here for a reason, not a pissing contest.

Joshua must have read the intent on Dempsey's face and so he kept his attention firmly on Grace. He watched her silently for a few moments, just a little longer than was comfortable, before suddenly thrusting his hand across the table. It was a test, Dempsey realised. And Grace passed it when she did not jump.

He opened his hand, offering it in greeting.

'People call me Joshua.'

'People call me Agent Grace.' She kept her hands flat on the table, making no effort to reach out and return the offer.

Turner kept his unshaken hand in position for a few seconds. When Grace made no attempt to move, he turned his attention back to Dempsey. His attitude seemed to change in an instant.

'So what happened?' he asked. His tone now seemed deadly serious. 'Did he get out?'

'He got out,' Dempsey confirmed.

'Thought so. Any idea where he's going?'

'Not a clue.' Dempsey saw nothing to gain from dishonesty. 'That's why we're here. In case you can help us.'

'And how exactly could I do that?'

'You shared a cell with him for almost three years. For one of those years you were basically working for him. Chances are he said something in front of you. Maybe let something slip. Maybe he even grew to trust you.'

'And I'd remember this over that long how?'

'Don't play games. You're you. You'd remember.'

Joshua said nothing.

'So was there something? Did he say anything in that time?'

'He said plenty in that time.'

'Anything that could help us?'

Joshua pushed himself back as far as his secured chair

would allow. He looked from Dempsey to Grace, then back again. And then he slowly nodded his head.

'Enough, yeah. I've got a good idea of where he's going. And I know what he plans to do when he gets there.'

'Where?'

'No chance. You get the what for free. The where comes with conditions.'

'Then I guess we start with the what.'

'He intends to set off a dirty bomb. A monster, in a place that could kill tens of thousands.'

This time it was Dempsey who said nothing. The answer did not surprise him. From what Joshua had said in their earlier meeting, the only thing holding Liberation back from an immediate attack was the absence of Peyton Travis. A problem they had now resolved.

Grace seemed less convinced.

'That can't be right. We believe that the caesium was a ruse. In fact we don't believe Liberation landed anything in Key West yesterday. There or anywhere else.'

'I can't help with that, love. I wasn't there. But whether they did or didn't land caesium in Florida doesn't matter, because Liberation's got a massive stockpile of the stuff. Built up gradually over the last decade and all funded by Peyton Travis.'

'That's not possible.' There was no hint of doubt in Grace's reply. 'Someone would have noticed that. You can't just—'

'You'd be amazed what you can smuggle into the country when you've got time, money and motivation, Agent Grace.'

'Really?' She was not convinced. 'You're saying they've been building up a caesium stockpile for ten years?'

'They have. Well, caesium or something else like it,

anyway. Whatever it is, it's radioactive and it's lethal. They've got enough of it to do some serious damage to this country. And that fat little fuck, Travis, he plans to get straight to work.'

Grace looked to Dempsey, her expression a mix of disbelief and concern. He could understand why. As sure as she had been, Joshua seemed more so.

'And the where?' Grace asked. 'You know that, too, do you?'

'Pretty much. Enough that I can take you straight to it.'

'No.' Dempsey's response was immediate. 'Not a chance. You don't leave this place.'

'Is that right? In that case, fine. I stay here, you have no lead and we let Travis blow the country to shit. No skin off my nose.'

'You can't be serious?'

Grace sounded outraged, her previous detached demeanour gone. The change did not surprise Dempsey. Grace had never dealt with Joshua before and so his nonchalant attitude to death must have been shocking.

'They're going to kill tens of thousands of people,' she continued. 'You can't use that threat to blackmail your way out of here. That makes you no better than Travis.'

Joshua shifted his gaze back to Grace, his stare now intense.

'I never said I was better. But this has nothing to do with me getting out of here, Agent Grace. When this is over I'll walk back in here and through those doors myself. You have my word on that. You won't even need cuffs. But this mission you're on, if you want it finished, you bring me with you.'

'But why—'

'For Scott,' Dempsey interrupted. 'He wants to be there to protect Scott.'

'Wouldn't you, Joe? If you were in my position?'

'You don't need to worry about him. I won't let anything happen to him. You know that.'

'It's not for you to protect my son. The only man I trust with that boy's life is yours truly.'

'There's no way I can get you out of here.'

'There's every way. You think I don't watch the news, Joe? You think I don't know how to read between the lines from what I see on there? To know the shit that really goes on out there? We've been living this life too long to not know how it all works. I recognise your fingerprints when I see them. You can get me out of here, released into your custody, and you can do it with a single phone call. Can't you?'

Dempsey did not react, but in his peripheral vision he saw Grace look towards him. A reaction to Joshua's words. It was, Dempsey knew, all the confirmation his former friend would need.

'That's what I thought,' Joshua said. 'So let me tell you again. My son is with this mad bunch of bastards. Somehow he's one of them. And that means that anyone who goes after *them* will be aiming at *him*, too. I can't allow that. Not unless I'm there to protect him. That's the price. Understood?'

Dempsey said nothing and so Grace opened her mouth to answer. Joshua cut across her before she could say a word.

'Don't even bother, Agent Grace. This isn't a negotiation. You take it or you leave it.'

Dempsey took a deep breath. It was the only sound that filled the silence.

'If we do this,' he finally said, 'you don't leave my side.'

'Fine by me.'

'And when we're done, you're back here. No questions asked.'

'Deal.'

'And if you try anything, anything at all, I'll finish what we started in Ireland. Got that?'

Joshua smiled. A cold, grim grin.

'I don't doubt you'll try. Wouldn't be you if you didn't.'

'Those are the rules. Yes or no?'

Joshua hesitated. He seemed to be thinking.

'You know I'm going to kill him,' he finally said. 'Whether you're right there beside me or not. Peyton Travis is a dead man.'

'That I can live with,' Dempsey replied. 'Saves me a job.'

Joshua nodded his head.

'In that case, your fight, your rules.'

'Now where are they going?' Grace asked.

'Same place we are,' Joshua replied. 'Washington DC.'

SIXTY-SIX

7.36 a.m. CDT

'It's just not happening, Agent Dempsey. Absolutely no way.'

It was the reaction Dempsey had expected and exactly why he had sent Grace to make a call before taking his seat ahead of Colonel Walker's desk. He preferred to persuade instead of pulling rank but, when it came to it, what mattered was achieving his objective.

It left him just minutes more to do it the pleasant way.

'I understand why you'd say that, Colonel. I really do. But we need Joshua. Without him, we have no chance of finding Travis before he does something terrible.'

The expression on Walker's face was unmoved.

'Put yourself in my position, son. I've just released a prisoner into the custody of another agency for the first time in the history of this institution. They made it eight miles before they were ambushed and wiped out in a coordinated hit that would make my own unit proud. That was an operation that must have been years in the planning, given all the moving parts. In those circumstances, how can I trust that the next step of that plan isn't the release of Joshua, huh? How can I be sure this isn't all a part of that same overarching objective?'

'There is no way Travis wants Joshua out of this place,' Dempsey replied. 'Not after everything he's done to the man. Travis is very far from being an idiot, Colonel. He must know that Joshua will have picked up some information after all their time together in that cell. The last thing Travis is going to want is us having access to that resource.'

'And who's told you that Joshua even knows anything? The man himself? And what, I just take that as gospel, do I?'

Dempsey could see that he was not getting through. And he could appreciate why. After everything that had happened in the past two hours, Walker would struggle to trust even his closest friend with what a stranger from the ISB was now suggesting.

And that was before they took into account who it was that Dempsey wanted to take out.

'Look, I fully appreciate your hesitance. And if there were any other way then I wouldn't even suggest this. But there *isn't* another way. What Travis has planned, we have to stop it. As it stands, we can't do that without Joshua.'

Walker hesitated.

'What about the book?' he asked. 'The one from the cell. Robert Nozick.'

'Nothing useful except confirmation of everything we already know. Including what Joshua told us. If we'd had the book earlier we could have stopped the escape. But there's nothing about where he's heading. Nothing about what he has planned.'

'How are you so sure that he even does have something planned?'

'Come on, Colonel. After all this? This wasn't some desperate run for freedom. Peyton Travis has a mission. And he has the resources – the money and the men – to pull that mission off. We have to assume that his plan is imminent. And we have to stop him. This could be our only chance.'

'And what makes you trust Joshua to stay onside?'

'I don't trust him as far as I can throw him. And in his case, I actually know how far that is. But he has other motivations. His son is with Travis. Or at least he will be. If Joshua wants his boy to come out of this in one piece, he has to stay straight.'

'And when it's done? Assuming you all come through it intact, including this son of his? You think he just comes back willingly?'

'He won't have a choice. I'll bring him back myself.'

'No offence, son, but I've seen what that man can do. You really think you're up to that task?'

'Who do you think took him down last time, Colonel?'

For the first time, Walker's mask slipped. He looked surprised. He also looked kind of impressed.

'You?'

'Me. And last time I did it alone. This time, I'll have the best team in the ISB at my back. In other words, he's going nowhere.'

Walker nodded his head, his eyes looking past Dempsey as he thought through what he had been told. It was a compelling case. Unarguable, Dempsey would have described it. But only if Joshua was to be believed.

And that, Dempsey knew, was the real issue.

'I'm sorry,' Walker finally said. 'I know what you're trying to do here and I respect it. But I just can't agree to this. I just can't—'

The sound of a knock interrupted Walker. He looked up and over Dempsey's shoulder. Dempsey had no need to follow his gaze. He already knew who was about to join them.

'Come in.'

The sound of the door opening and closing told Dempsey that Grace was now in the room. Walker indicated to the chair next to Dempsey's.

'Please join us, Agent Grace. I'm just explaining to—'

'I'm sorry to interrupt you, Colonel, but I think you need to take this call.'

Grace had not stopped moving forward as they spoke and so she was already past Dempsey as she finished her sentence. He could see her cellphone as she reached out and passed it to Walker, and he watched as the colonel put it to his ear.

'Colonel Miles Walker. Who's speaking?'

Walker made no attempt to hide his surprise at the answer. His eyes widened, darting back and forth between the two ISB agents. Dempsey understood its cause because Dempsey knew exactly who was on the end of the line. And so he did not need the confirmation that came from Walker's next words:

'Yes, Mr President.'

Grace took her seat next to Dempsey and matched his poker face. This was not how they had wanted to play it, but they had been left with no choice.

'Yes, Mr President.'

Walker's eyes were now fixed on Dempsey's. The surprise had progressed to bewilderment.

'Yes, Mr President. Thank you, sir. I'll deal with it now. Goodbye, Mr President.'

Walker pushed the red disconnect icon, stood up and handed the phone back to Grace. He then sat back down into his seat and shook his head, a puzzled expression on his face.

'You both know what that was about,' he said.

'We do.'

Another shake of the head and then a small smile broke out on Walker's face.

'In that case, there's just one more thing I want to know.'

'What's that?' Dempsey asked.

'Who in the hell *are* you people?'

SIXTY-SEVEN

8.25 a.m. CDT

The cargo compartment on the Boeing C-17 Globemaster III was 88 feet long. It had room to hold almost one hundred tons of military equipment or over one hundred fully armed, fully equipped paratroopers. It had been far more aircraft than was needed to bring Dempsey, Grace, Vega and O'Rourke's team from Fort Pierce in Florida to San Antonio in Texas.

That suitability was not about to be improved as the same plane flew back east, this time to Andrews Air Force Base in Maryland, Washington DC, with a complement of just two pilots and three passengers.

It took Dempsey a few moments for his eyes to acclimatise from the desert sun to the gloom of the cavernous interior and so at first he did not even spot Joshua. When he did, the usually imposing six-foot-three figure was almost lost in his surroundings. He was seated with his back against the wall, to the left of the plane and close to the cockpit door.

Dempsey and Grace made their way towards him as the plane's rear ramp door closed behind them, shutting out what little natural light had found its way inside. The hold was even darker with only the interior bulbs to break through the dim, but Dempsey was close enough now that he could make out the cuffs around each of Joshua's wrists. Both were attached to the bench on which he sat.

'The rangers are taking no chances then?' Dempsey indicated to Joshua's restraints as he and Grace took their seats against the right-side wall. 'Can't say I blame them.'

'And there was me thinking these were your idea,' Joshua replied. 'Just assumed you were worried about a rematch.'

'Because the last time went so well for you.'

'About as well as the first went for you. As I see it, we're one for one. Which makes us due a rubber match.'

Dempsey smiled despite himself. As much as he hated aspects of Joshua's character – as much as he despised the terrible things the man had done – he could not help but admire his character. After everything that had happened to him, Joshua was as defiant as ever.

'Maybe one day.' He forced the grin from his face. 'But not today. There's more important things going on here than us. And I'm not wasting three hours in the air on this shit.'

He felt himself jerked to the right as he spoke. Grace and Joshua lurched the same way. The C-17 was moving.

He looked at his watch, calculated the flight time and added the hour for DC.

'We'll be landing at twelve forty-five hours, Washington time. My team are meeting us on the tarmac at Andrews and we'll have backup units lined up to join us. That's going to be a lot of manpower, Jim. All in and around the capital in the middle of the day. It's not going to go unnoticed so I want you ready for that. I want you ready to take us straight to where we need to be. Is that going to be a problem?'

'I've got as much reason to get to that place as you,' Joshua replied. 'So no. There'll be no problem.'

The C-17 began to accelerate. Dempsey pressed his back into the wall, to help with the stability of his seated position.

'You remember the first time you flew in one of these, Joe?'

Dempsey did not reply. He was not here to reminisce.

'Where were we again? Pakistan?'

'Not now, Jim.'

'What's the matter, you don't want Grace to hear how green you were back then? What were you again? Twenty-three? Twenty-four?'

'Twenty-two.'

'Bloody child prodigy.'

'Child is right,' Dempsey replied. 'Now be quiet. I don't want to talk about it.'

The front of the plane began to rise as the C-17 took to the air.

'Grew comfortable giving orders, didn't you?'

'And you're as good at ignoring them as you ever were.'

Dempsey placed a hand against the wall between the hold and the cockpit, unclipped his safety harness and stood up. He looked down at Grace.

'I'm going to sit a way down there. I can't deal with another three hours of listening to him.'

'You want me to come?'

'No. I'm going to get some sleep. You should do the same. When we land I want us sharp.'

He looked back to Joshua.

'And by that I do mean *all* of us. Then we'll find out what you've still got.'

SIXTY-EIGHT

10 a.m. CDT

G race opened her eyes and checked her watch.

An hour and a half sleep. Better than nothing.

She looked across to the opposite bench. Joshua's eyes were open and he was looking straight at her. It was . . . disconcerting. She instinctively looked around for Dempsey and saw that he was in the same spot he had been in ninety minutes earlier: sat against the wall at the other end of the cargo compartment, where he was no doubt getting a better rest than Grace had managed.

That man really can sleep anywhere.

She rubbed the bridge of her nose with two fingers, stood up to stretch out and then sat back down. Joshua stayed silent throughout, his eyes assessing her every movement. It was somehow less welcome than the fact he had been watching her sleep.

'You don't buy into Dempsey's rule?' she finally asked. Conversation, Grace figured, had to be better than voyeurism.

'Sleep where you can, when you can?' Joshua asked. 'That's *his* rule now, is it?'

'Whose rule is it, then?'

'Who knows. But he learned it from me. Same as I learned it from someone else. Surprised he's claiming it as his own.'

'He's not. He just happens to live by it, that's all. Don't you?'

'When I was active in the field, yeah. But that was a while ago, love. Where I've been for the last few years, there's not much to do but sleep. So I'm all stocked up.'

Grace nodded her head. The comment made sense. She looked down towards Dempsey at the far end of the cargo hold. No sign of him stirring.

She turned back to Joshua.

'So you guys go back then, huh?'

'To the beginning,' Joshua replied. 'Well, to *his* beginning, anyway.'

'Was he always . . . always . . . like he is now?'

'Depends what he is now, I suppose. Been a long time since we knew each other. But if you don't know the answer to that for yourself, maybe it's because he doesn't want you to.'

'Why do you say that?'

'Because he was a piece of work back in the day. Same as me. I doubt he'd want you to know about *that* man. About the things he did.'

'He doesn't hide anything from me.'

'Yeah? Then why are you having to ask me?'

Grace said nothing. There was no good answer.

'Truth is, Agent Grace, no man wants a woman he's screwing to know everything about him. Especially not the bad stuff. Joe and me, we've got our issues but men don't do over other men. I wouldn't do *that* even to him.'

'We're not "screwing", thank you. We're friends.'

'No such thing, love. Not between men and women. It's not possible.'

'It is when the woman can't be interested.'

Joshua opened his mouth to reply, but as he did he seemed to realise Grace's meaning. The epiphany made him smile.

'Oh. Oh, right. No point me flirting then, eh?'

'None at all. And I didn't realise you were.'

'Shame. And there was me about to give you the sob story about four years locked up without a woman. Wouldn't have worked.'

'It wouldn't have worked anyway, Mr Turner. Straight wouldn't suddenly render me gullible.'

Joshua laughed and, as he did, everything about him seemed to lighten. It made Grace think that the prisoner was warming to her, but she remained on guard. From what Dempsey had told her, Joshua was capable of deceptions way more sophisticated than this.

'So you and Joe, then. You really are just mates?'

'As much as anyone can be with Dempsey,' Grace replied. 'He's my boss. But he's my friend, too. And I think I'm his.'

'You are. I can tell you mean something to him. That's why I thought . . . what I thought.'

'Strange your mind would go right there.'

'You're a good-looking girl. He's a bloke and he looks, well, he looks like him. Where else was it gonna go?'

Grace smiled, but this was not a direction she wanted the conversation to take. And so she changed it.

'So now you know you wouldn't be breaching the 'bro code' and blocking anything, do you want to tell me about him?'

'What's there to tell that you don't know?'

'Quite a bit, I suspect. Tell me about him when he was younger. When you first met.'

Joshua put his head back against the wall of the plane and his smile widened. As if amused by the memories he was now reliving.

'He was . . . truth is, he was something else. Closest thing I ever saw to the perfect soldier. Naive as shit, though. He believed all that Queen and Country bollocks like it was a religion. There was nothing he wouldn't do if he was told to do it. As far as he was concerned, if the British government sent him somewhere then they did that with all their homework done and every other option explored. He genuinely thought he was the last resort for the good guys. Sir Galahad, turning up when there was no other way.'

'Turning up to do what?'

Joshua opened his eyes.

'You know what. There's no way he trusts you to have his back but not to tell you what he was.'

'You mean an asset.'

'I mean an assassin.'

'For the British government. What he did, it was sanctioned.'

'And what does that make him? It was always sanctioned, love. And sanctioned don't mean shit. You think governments are the good guys?'

Joshua rolled his eyes to the ceiling of the hold as he spoke.

'Jesus Christ. I can't believe he found another one just like him.'

'I'm not like him,' Grace replied. 'At least not like *you* describe him. I don't think that way. And neither does Dempsey.'

'Well, he used to, trust me. If he got an order, the fact of where that order came from made him think it was moral and that it was just. It made him think that what he was being sent to do was necessary. The kid believed that absolutely.'

'And you?'

'Me? I just went and did my job, love. I did it because I was good at it. Better than anyone else. That was enough for me.'

'Were you as good as him?'

'Depends who you ask. I reckon I had the edge. He'd probably tell you he did. What we both know, though, is that we were out there on our own. Your mate, Agent Grace, is a born killer. Most naturally talented one I ever saw, besides myself. And that is a dangerous thing when you combine it with a belief that what you're doing is right.'

'More dangerous than combining it with a sociopathic willingness to kill for money?'

Joshua smiled again.

'Now there's no need for that, is there? Attacking me because I said stuff you don't want to hear. If you don't really want to know then you shouldn't ask.'

'Whatever you say, that's not him any more.'

'Maybe not but it doesn't change the truth. And it doesn't change my answer. You wanted to know what he was like, that's what he was like. An unquestioning soldier with a talent for death. In other words, he was one hell of a weapon.'

Grace said nothing. She wanted to defend Dempsey – to insult Joshua, to turn the tables – and yet she strongly suspected that what he was saying was true. Dempsey had told her little of his past but even that had been enough for her to realise that he was plagued by guilt.

He had not been a bad man but he had done some very bad things.

And so no matter how unwelcome Joshua's disclosure might be, it was also accurate. And like he said, Grace *had* asked.

'Tell me about your son.' It was a deliberate change of subject, to a topic that was of more immediate relevance than Dempsey's history. 'Tell me about Scott.'

'What's to tell?' Joshua replied. His tone had now changed. He sounded sad. 'He's just another kid who's been let down by a deadbeat father. No wonder he is where he is.'

'But he was doing well. He was in MIT, right? Nuclear physics? He was on track.'

'And now he's not. Travis's people, they targeted him so they could control me. And look at how easy they did it. Those redneck fucks managed to turn my boy's head in no time flat. Convinced him to buy in to their bullshit. What does that say about the job I did as a father?'

'You can't blame yourself for all of that. He's a grown man. He makes his own decisions.'

'Not if I'd been around, he wouldn't have. If I'd been there for him he'd have been too strong-minded for that bollocks. And if he wasn't, well, I'd have been there to kick his arse for being so fucking stupid. But I wasn't there, was I? I was off making a name for myself. And then I was in the Facility paying for that name. And now look where he is. No, love. That's all on me.'

Grace did not respond, mainly because Joshua was correct. If he had been a better father then Scott Turner would likely be finishing his PhD right now. His corruption probably *was* Joshua's failing and Grace was not about to lie to make him feel better.

'I'll make up for it, though.' Joshua's voice was low this time. Low and serious. 'I'll make this right.'

'I'm sure you will. And I promise, I'll do whatever I can to help you save your son.'

'Of course you will.' Joshua smiled again. His moment of sad introspection was over. He indicated to the end of the cargo compartment. 'But if you don't mind, I'll throw my cards in with him down there.'

'What do you mean?'

'I mean that no matter how much your mate's changed, him and me, we're gonna be back doing what we always did best together. And believe me, that means that Peyton Travis and every one of those hillbilly arseholes who've fucked with my boy, they're gonna die ugly.'

SIXTY-NINE

11.36 a.m. EDT

Cliff Clemons lit a cigarette and leaned back against the glass front of the Lehigh Valley Airport arrivals terminal.

The feel of the smoke as it was pulled into his lungs made him cough, just as it always did. It was inevitable for a relatively new smoker but a downside he was willing to tolerate. Twenty-four was a strange age to pick up the habit, Clemons realised. But he had found that, for all the Surgeon General's warnings, it calmed him down.

And right now he needed that more than he needed his long-term health.

The terminal behind Clemons was typical of the small international airports that were dotted across the United States. Larger than it had any right to be in a place as relatively out of the way as Allentown, it was still minuscule when compared to Philadelphia International, seventy miles south.

Small enough that Kenny Brooks could see exactly what Scott Turner was doing inside.

That visibility explained why Brooks was fixed to the spot, his eyes never leaving the scene that was playing out behind the glass. His attention seemed absolute, drinking in every detail as

Turner hired the car that would take them the final forty miles of their journey to Summit Hill.

Clemons did not question why Brooks was so interested in such a mundane task. He had wasted enough time trying to understand Brooks' irrational mind. But what did concern him was the man's expression.

Brooks was smiling. And that was not normal.

Clemons inhaled another deep lungful of smoke, blew it back out and then risked the only question that was now in his mind.

'What's got you so happy?'

The older man took a second or two to respond, but finally he looked away from his view over Clemons' shoulder and focused on the question. He seemed surprised that Clemons had spoken at all, as if he had forgotten that the other man was even there. Even so, the smile stayed fixed.

'What else?' Brooks asked. 'This thing, it's nearly done. We're nearly home.'

'You miss the camp that much?'

'I miss what don't happen there. I miss not taking orders from a goddamned Limey schoolboy. But he's all over now, ain't he? Least he will be once we get to Summit Hill.'

Clemons' eyes narrowed. Something about Brooks' tone. Something about the way he said the word 'over' . . .

'What do you mean by that?'

'I mean once Peyton's back with us, that's Turner's purpose served.'

'I don't follow, Kenny.'

'I mean he ain't useful no more, is he? Not once Peyton's there. Whatever Cam might have thought, there's nothing Turner can do that Peyton can't. Means that once we're all back at camp and the boss is back with us, everything that made him useful – everything that made him important to Cam – it's gone. It's over.'

Clemons dropped his cigarette and ground it out under his boot. Its calming effect no longer seemed to be working. Not with what Brooks was saying. Not with what he seemed to mean.

'But he's still one of us,' Clemons said. 'He's still a part of the team, even if he's not giving orders any more.'

'Is he? You really think that college boy in there believes in the same stuff we do? You really think he's your friend? He ain't one of us, Cliff. He ain't never been one of us. He's here for his own reasons and they sure as hell ain't the cause. Why do you think I've never liked the sonofabitch?'

'How can you know that?'

'Cam told me. Before we ever headed down to Florida. Told me I had to keep my eye on the kid. Make sure he didn't waiver, because he wasn't really a soldier and he wasn't really a believer. Cam's words, son. Not mine. Are they good enough for you?'

Clemons did not answer. What Brooks was saying, it made some sense. If he was honest, he had himself thought it strange that someone as . . . different as Scott Turner should be a part of Liberation. But he had gotten past that doubt months ago.

And what did it matter now, anyway? Now that Clemons was wracked with his own doubts? He had only ever really sympathised with the broadest elements of what Brooks called 'the cause'. For him it had started with masks and vaccines and his right to choose. And he had been a lost soul in search of a home and that's what Cam Arnold had offered, in exchange for the labour of a big, strong man with physicality that made him useful.

But after what Clemons had seen in the last few days?

If it wasn't for Scott, maybe I'd have been gone myself.

Still, it begged the question: if Brooks was right, then why had Arnold put so much trust and faith in Turner? In fact, why was Turner on the team at all?

'He's coming.' Brooks' warning interrupted Clemons' thought process. 'Not a word of this, Cliff. You got that?'

'What would I even say? I don't know what to believe.'

'You'll know it's the truth soon enough. Soon as we get back to camp.'

'And what happens to Scott when we get there?'

'That'll be up to the boss. I'm sure Peyton's gonna have some ideas on the subject, don't you?'

'But—'

'No buts and no questions. You're either with us or you're against us on this. Prove it's the better one by keeping your head down and your mouth shut. You got that?'

Clemons was unsure of what to say. He turned and looked into the terminal. Through the sheer window wall he could see that Turner was barely ten paces away from the building's sliding glass doors.

'I asked if you got that,' Brooks repeated.

Without looking, Clemons nodded his head in return. He knew now that he had no choice.

'I've got it, yeah.' The words felt like a betrayal even as he said them. 'I won't say a word.'

SEVENTY

11.40 a.m. EDT

Dempsey felt the C-17 bank to the left as he made his way to the front of the cargo compartment. He could see Grace and Joshua straight ahead, with Grace seemingly seven or eight feet higher than the man across from her. The difference told Dempsey the extent of the aircraft's turn as it prepared for its final descent.

'We're seven minutes out of Andrews Air Force Base.'

Dempsey noticed from their reaction that neither Grace nor Joshua had heard him approach. They had been deep in conversation, which was not a development he had anticipated. The last thing he wanted was Grace warming to the man who had been to Dempsey what he now was for her: a mentor, a 'senior partner' and a friend.

Dempsey knew only too well how Joshua could manipulate those who liked him. The man was a scorpion. And like a scorpion, it was only a matter of time before he struck.

He avoided the urge to ask about their conversation as he lowered himself onto the bench next to Grace, just as the plane levelled out and began to descend.

'You two didn't sleep?'

'I got an hour,' Grace answered. She moved along to make room.

'And you?'

'I've slept enough the last four years,' Joshua replied. 'I'm as rested as I need to be.'

'Let's hope that's true. So when do I get an address?'

'Once we've touched down and my arse is on the car seat next to yours. I'm not giving you any chance to leave me behind. That's not the deal.'

'I know the terms. You're coming with us whatever happens. You don't need to hold back the detail to ensure that.'

'And yet that's exactly what I plan to do. Forgive me if I don't take you at your word. Got a bad history with doing that sort of thing.'

'Right. Because you're the one who's been betrayed again and again.' Dempsey did not hide the sarcasm in his answer. 'If you're going to rewrite history, Jim, maybe use something a bit more sophisticated than a crayon.'

'You want to talk about betrayal?' Joshua's voice gave him away. He was irritated. 'Which of us was it that put three bullets in the other's chest? Which of us threw the other in that shithole of a prison? Eh?'

'I didn't know that prison even existed until today. Or that you were alive, for Christ's sake. As for the bullets, you asked for those, Jim. And I'd do *that* again in a heartbeat. Though what any of that has to do with trust or betrayal is beyond me.'

'We were friends.'

'I was friends with the man you pretended to be. That ended in Columbia, when you left me for dead.'

'Fucking shame you pulled through.'

'I could say the same to you about Ireland. Makes us even, I guess.'

Joshua opened his mouth to answer. A reply that would no doubt heighten the ever-increasing animosity of the exchange. And so Grace beat him to it.

'For God's sake, guys. Come on. This isn't helping anyone. You two have to work together here. It's been sixty seconds and you're already at each other's throats. This is bigger than your egos or your history. Just calm it, OK?'

Neither Dempsey nor Joshua said a word in reply. For Dempsey it was because he knew that Grace was right. They *would* have to remember how to cooperate. To at least tolerate each other. Besides, if Joshua was correct then it would be barely hours.

He nodded his head in agreement and looked down, his eyes now fixed on the floor. There was little he could say. And even less that he wanted to. At least to the man who had once been his closest friend.

Joshua, though, dealt with the situation differently.

'So what happened to the DDS?'

Dempsey looked up.

'What do you mean?'

'This ISB thing. United Nations and all that. It sounds like a great gig but I don't see you leaving the Department of Domestic Security to join it. Not a good British patriot like you. So what happened to it?'

'Haversume happened,' Dempsey answered. 'After him, no more DDS.'

'How's that? There was no way Haversume was winning that fight after I was out of the picture. You stopped him.

Whatever bullshit story they told on TV, you killed him. Which means you won.'

'It was a score draw at best, what with everything we lost. But yeah, it was me that killed him.'

'Glad to hear it. I wish I could have had the pleasure myself. But that doesn't answer my question, does it? If you took him out of the picture then how did he bring down the DDS?'

'Because what he was doing before Wicklow – what he had *you* do for him – it wasn't just the two of you. There was a bigger operation behind the whole thing. And as part of that, Haversume had corrupted senior men in intelligence. That included the director of the DDS.'

Joshua seemed to think for a moment.

'You mean Callum McGregor? That massive Scottish fella you were always pally with? You're kidding, right?'

'I'm not kidding, no. Why would I?'

'McGregor was a traitor?'

'He didn't think so, but yeah. He was.'

Joshua shook his head, a look of surprise on his face.

'Fuck me, Galahad. You don't half pick your friends, do you? First me, then Big Callum.' He pointed towards Grace. 'You might want to do a background check on her, mate. On your form she's probably working for ISIS.'

Dempsey said nothing. Joshua's attempt at humour was not welcome. Not on this subject. And he seemed to get that. When he spoke again, his tone was serious.

'So what happened to McGregor?'

Again Dempsey did not reply. Instead he just met Joshua's gaze, an unspoken message passing between them. And so he could see the realisation in his former friend's eyes as Joshua gleaned the truth.

'Fuck, Joe. Tell me they didn't.' There was genuine regret in his voice. 'They made *you* do it. They made you kill him.'

'No one made me do anything. Callum left with me no choice.'

'Christ. It really doesn't pay to be your friend, does it? First me. Then McGregor.'

'Wrong way round,' Dempsey replied. 'How'd you think I found you in Wicklow?'

'You're kidding? So what, *both* of us? In one day?'

Dempsey nodded his head. As he did, Joshua let out a long breath.

'You really are a ruthless bastard.' Dempsey could tell from Joshua's tone that he was genuinely impressed by what he had just been told. 'Honestly, I will never know where they made you.'

'Exactly the same place they made you. Like you said a long time ago, we're no different.'

For a moment Joshua said nothing. Instead he shifted uncomfortably in his seat as his gaze swept from Dempsey to Grace, a knowing look in his eyes.

'You know, you shouldn't think that,' he finally said, his focus now returned to Dempsey. 'We *are* different, you and me. We're not the same.'

'Maybe. Maybe not.'

'There's no maybe about it. If McGregor was working with Haversume then that was a clean kill. And so was I, if you'd managed to kill me. But then the subject gets raised four years down the line and suddenly you're questioning your own humanity about it. You're comparing yourself to someone like me. Let me tell you this, Galahad: I wouldn't have given McGregor a second thought. And if it had been you who'd been left dying in Wicklow, I wouldn't have let that bother me either. Same as I didn't in Bogotá. So listen to me on this and stop beating yourself up. You and me, we're very, *very* different.'

Dempsey did not respond. What Joshua was saying – if it was true that he really could kill those close to him with no thought and no regret – then it did prove his point. They *were* different. But that mere fact did not make Dempsey feel better. Justified or not, he had to live with what he had done.

Not just with the killing of his friend but with so many other deaths on top of that.

And before this day was over, Dempsey was sure, he would have to live with even more.

SEVENTY-ONE

11.51 a.m. EDT

The air on the runway of Andrews Air Force Base was typical of Washington DC in July. Hot and humid, it made Dempsey's all-black operational outfit feel immediately damp against his skin. He could only imagine how Grace's identical clothing must have felt. Unlike Dempsey, she had seen action since pulling it on at Fort Pierce and so she'd had real reason to sweat already.

For now that discomfort had to be ignored. There was work to be done and little time in which to do it. Which was exactly why Dempsey had brought in some help.

Just as there had been at Vandeveer, a number of black Suburbans were waiting a short stroll from where the C-17 had come to a halt. There were three this time instead of five and the vehicles' occupants were out and on the tarmac, awaiting the arrival of their colleagues.

Shui Dai was standing at the head of the group, the natural position for its leader in Dempsey's absence. Just behind but towering over her five-foot-one frame was Salvatore Gallo, the team's six-foot-six Sardinian 'muscle'. Next to him, as he always seemed to be, was Dempsey's lean Appalachian sharpshooter

Dylan Wrixon. And across from those three – standing together at the hood of the second Suburban, their statuesque physiques every bit as complimentary as their skin colour was different – were Kate Silver and Adama Jabari.

Along with Dempsey and Grace, the five agents made up the elite multinational unit that was referred to within the ISB as Alpha Team. Each had been selected over the course of the past four years by Dempsey himself, with their already impressive levels of skill and expertise then supplemented by his own intense training regime. It had made far more than the sum of their already formidable parts; Dempsey had taken independently brilliant individuals and turned them into a tight, peerless team.

They were the very best the Bureau had to offer and a living nightmare for the likes of Peyton Travis and Liberation. And that made them exactly what Dempsey needed today.

Two armed Homeland Security agents passed him as he headed straight for Dai, their weapons raised as they entered the C-17 in order to escort Joshua out. Even when restrained and motivated to stay onside, the man's fearsome reputation demanded that no chances be taken. Dempsey was happy to see the precaution; it allowed him to focus on the task ahead.

'Do we have a target location?'

The question came from Shui Dai. As efficient as always, Dempsey noted.

'Southwest Waterfront,' he replied.

'Address?'

'He won't give it to us until we're close. It's his bargaining chip.'

'How do we prepare?'

'We don't. We go in hard and fast, overwhelming numbers.'

'And those numbers are where?'

'Already arranged through Homeland. They don't take attacks on their people lying down. The secretary has authorised whatever we need.'

'But how can we know what we need, if we don't know the target?'

'We can't. That's why there's ten trucks full of agents in full kit, waiting for us at Washington Navy Yard. That's a hundred bodies, Shui. If we need more than that then we've bitten off way more than we can chew.'

'And the plan, boss?'

It was Dylan Wrixon who had asked the question.

'Simple. We rendezvous with the Homeland force, we get the details we need from Turner and then we go in there and take them out.'

'That easy then?'

'Isn't it always, Dyl?'

'Not the way I remember it.' Wrixon's eyes flitted over Dempsey's shoulder. 'Is that him? Is that Joshua?'

Dempsey turned at the question. With all the noise of the runway, he had not heard Joshua approach. The two Homeland agents were behind, their weapons still raised and trained upon him.

'Yeah. That's him.'

'Shit.' Wrixon's smile was wide. 'I heard a lot about him. He as good as they say?'

'Every bit,' Dempsey replied. 'So be on your guard.'

'He as good as me?'

'At what?'

'Come on, boss. Is he?'

Joshua was coming closer now. Enough that he would be able to hear the conversation. He seemed interested to hear

Dempsey's answer, which suggested that he'd also heard the question.

'Hard to tell. I've seen him make shots most people would say were impossible. But then I've seen you do the same. It'd be a good match-up.'

'Maybe when this is over . . .'

Wrixon was almost speaking to himself when he said the words and so Dempsey did not feel the need to respond. Instead his attention had shifted to Gallo, who had stepped forward to intercept Joshua as he was brought from the C-17 and towards the Suburbans.

Gallo stood himself to his full, imposing height and blocked the path.

Joshua came to a halt and looked up. He had his wrists cuffed together and was giving away at least fifty pounds in muscular bodyweight, yet somehow he seemed unconcerned.

'This is the man who will not speak?' Gallo asked, his thick Italian accent and gruff voice turning the words into a growl. 'You want that I *make* him speak?'

Dempsey did not answer. His focus was now reserved for Joshua, who looked back at him with a smile.

'You recruiting bears now, Joe?'

'If they're good enough with their hands.'

'Is this one?'

'Best I've ever seen,' Dempsey replied. 'I'm pretty sure he could make two of either of us.'

'That supposed to scare me, is it?'

'Not at all. I just thought it was worth you knowing. In case you get any ideas later.'

Joshua nodded his head, his smile undimmed. He looked back up to Gallo, who had not moved an inch.

'Stand down, Baloo. Like I told your boss, now we're here, I'll talk.'

'Pity,' Gallo snorted.

'For both of us,' Joshua replied. 'Could have been a fun few minutes.'

He took a step back and turned to face Dempsey.

'Cato-Centinel Incorporated.'

'What's that?'

'It's what's going to lead us to the correct address at the Waterfront. It's a dormant company that's owned behind the scenes by Travis. Well, it's owned by some corporation that's owned by a corporation that's owned by a corporation . . . you get what I mean.'

'That's it?'

'Trust me. That's all you need. The building owned by Cato-Centinel, it's where you'll find them.'

'What if it owns more than one.'

'It doesn't.'

'How can you be sure?'

'Joe, I've just spent three years in a cell with that arrogant bastard. And he's just done the same with me. That made me the only outlet for his thoughts and his philosophies and all that other shit he needed to spout. And a man like him, a man completely sold on his own genius, he can't keep that stuff to himself. He said more than enough for me to be sure. So like I said: trust me.'

Dempsey watched Joshua intently as he spoke, unhappy with what he was hearing. The revelation that Joshua's knowledge was a name and an area, rather than an exact address, it was unwelcome. But still, the man seemed confident in what he was saying. And he had a point. Three years together *was* a long time. And Joshua was an exceptional study.

If he believed he had read Travis correctly then Dempsey was not going to doubt him. Not least because, of all of them there, it was Joshua who had the most to lose.

'OK. I don't see I have much choice. But you'd better be right about this.'

'I'm right.'

Dempsey turned to Grace.

'Eden, get on to Homeland. We need to know the building we're dealing with and the specs involved. Now.'

SEVENTY-TWO

12.10 p.m. EDT

The hamlet of Summit Hill stood close to the peak of Mount Sharp on the Pisgah Mountain ridgeway, a full fifteen hundred feet above sea level. It was, Scott Turner had discovered, impossible to drive up to the town without the lowering air pressure causing his ears to pop.

He felt that sensation again now as the rented Ford Explorer skirted the centre and headed towards the encampment that Cam Arnold had built nearby. But for once he hardly noticed it. Right now, there was just a single thought in his mind.

Dad.

The encampment was a little over a quarter of a mile away from the town hub and a lot less than that from its limits, and yet the surrounding geography made it completely distinct from Summit Hill itself. A single makeshift road was all that allowed passage through the thick, tree-lined, almost sheer hill that formed a natural barrier between the two.

Originally a mining encampment first built in 1791 and focused on the excavation of anthracite coal, Summit Hill had been dominated by the mining industry for most of its history. As the former home of the Lehigh Coal Mining Company, it had grown in importance and in size, reaching its peak in 1940 with a population of almost six thousand. Times had changed since then and the severe decline in the coal industry had seen the town take a hit. Before the arrival of Cam Arnold, the population had shrunk to a little over three thousand, with many of those struggling to make a living as the final mines closed all around them.

Liberation, through Arnold and with the near unlimited funds provided by Travis, had done a lot to change that. While careful to attract as little attention as possible, Arnold had paid for the gradual regeneration of the town at the same time as he had built his encampment. That philanthropy had made him a local hero, a status Arnold had maintained by keeping his political opinions to himself. As well as gratitude, that generosity had also purchased Arnold something far more important than adulation. It had bought the loyalty, and so the silence, of the townsfolk.

With the local population grateful to their new benefactor, they asked few questions about Arnold's intent or his activities. And they stayed well clear of the growing facility that he had constructed nearby and which he had, much more recently, started to fill with men.

Even with that grateful cooperation, it had become impossible in the last year to keep the nature of Liberation completely unknown to the people of Summit Hill. The pandemic had played its part in that; by the very nature of their beliefs, Arnold's men were unlikely to adhere to the rules of lockdown and social distancing. Combined with that was the fact that many of the wives and even the families of Arnold's recent recruits had moved into the town itself, swelling its population back to almost five and a half thousand.

With Arnold's strict control over his people, the increasing interaction between them and the townsfolk had not proved problematic. With the public name of Arnold's organisation and the more extreme of their views and ambitions remaining a secret, Liberation had managed to portray themselves as a group of like-minded survivalists who simply wanted a place of their own.

To the people of Summit Hill, such beliefs and ambitions may have seemed strange. But Arnold's men were too disciplined to seem dangerous. And so it was that almost no one in the town realised the true nature of the viper they had invited into their nest.

Scott Turner had marvelled at this over the two years he had spent with Cam Arnold and Liberation. How Arnold's planning and his control of the situation had hidden the massive growth of a militia now capable of causing havoc on an epic level.

It had been a very different place back when Turner had first been approached by Arnold. And Turner had been a very different man: an MIT PhD candidate with a talent for nuclear physics and a brilliant future ahead of him. And yet it had taken Arnold just moments to change Turner's life completely. Just three documents and a picture that proved two things beyond any doubt: that Turner's father was not dead and that he was being held without trial in an illegal, unconstitutional US government prison facility. With that information, and the promise that Liberation could secure his freedom, it hadn't taken much persuasion for Turner to abandon the life he knew and join Arnold's few followers on a mission that was now just moments from its end.

Turner's father had always been his weak spot. The Achilles heel of a son starved of approval and attention by a man who was usually absent. Arnold had used that weakness to play him; Turner had realised that from the beginning. But then he had played Arnold in turn, to achieve the one thing that he wanted above all else.

The return of his father.

Turner had made a decision from the beginning which, two years on and with the group having swelled in size, now proved to be the smartest of his life. Because as simple as it would have been to pretend that he was sold on the beliefs of Arnold and his followers, Turner had refused to do that. He knew that he was playing a long game and that a simple lie can become a dead weight over time. And so he had been honest. He had made the basis of his involvement clear, at least to Arnold.

Turner was here to free his father. Nothing more.

That honesty had stood him in good stead with the Liberation leader. It had persuaded Arnold to trust him, a trust that had turned to respect. Even, Turner had to admit, something close to a friendship. There would always be aspects of Cam Arnold that Turner found repellent, but Cam had often kept his more extreme views to himself when they were together. And so, overall, Turner kind of liked him.

Or at least he had. Right up until the trail of dead bodies the man had left in his wake since yesterday.

That had never been the plan. Or more likely it had *always* been the plan and Cam Arnold had just not trusted him as much as Turner had thought. Had he known this would happen – that innocent lives were at risk – then Turner would not have thrown his lot in with Liberation.

He would have played no part in any of this.

And yet, as true as that was, there was something he had to admit to himself.

Without Arnold's plan – without those deaths – Turner would not be where he was today. He would not be mere minutes from meeting the father he had believed dead.

He would not be within touching distance of the end of his mission.

The road to the encampment was wide enough for a full-sized Mack truck, with the surrounding tree-tops offering a dark canopy that made even the midday sun seem dark. It was also short – less than a quarter mile – and so Turner felt his stomach begin to churn with anticipation as the Explorer hurtled towards the daylight he could already see at its end.

'You in some sort of hurry?'

Turner ignored Brooks' question. They were less than a minute from parting company and so he was through with the pleasantries. He pressed a little harder on the gas.

'Slow the fuck down,' Brooks demanded. 'I ain't planning on dying right when things are getting interesting.'

Turner said nothing as they exited the canopy into the bright sunlight of the encampment. He decelerated as he moved into the open, towards the security checkpoint that provided the only way through the fence that surrounded the camp's tree- and rock-lined perimeter.

The barrier was up and the gate unmanned.

'Where's the guard?' Clemons asked.

The same question had occurred to Turner, but he had spotted the answer immediately. He pointed it out to Clemons, through the windscreen of the Explorer.

'I imagine he's over there, Cliff.' A metallic grey Airbus H155 was sat in the clearing three hundred yards ahead of them. 'It's got to be them. They've got to be here.'

'You think?'

'Who else is going to fly into this place in one of *those*? That's a fifteen-million-dollar helicopter.'

'Seriously?'

'Seriously.'

Turner kept the big SUV moving as they spoke, cutting the distance between them, the chopper and – he realised as he grew closer – the crowd of maybe one hundred Liberation followers who had gathered around it. There could only be one reason for the huddle, Turner concluded. Even with the helicopter's massive rotors already stationary.

They've just arrived.

He slowed the Explorer to a stop ten yards behind the crowd and stepped out. Without the sound of the car's engine, he could hear a voice. It was American. Clipped and, from what Turner could hear, well-educated. He stepped forward, into the tightly packed crowd. From here he could see nothing. But with the audience in rapt silence, he could hear every word.

'. . . because *they* think they hold the power. *They* think they have us under their boot. *They* think that the people are defeated. And why do they think these things? Why? I will tell you why. They believe that because, until today, they were *right*.'

The speaker – Peyton Travis, Turner confidently assumed – paused for far longer than seemed necessary. It struck Turner as a strange speaking technique and yet it had the desired effect. Not a single man there broke that silence as they awaited the next word.

'Until today, there was no one who was willing to stand up and say "NO"!'

Travis shouted the final word. The effect on the crowd was electric.

'Until today, there was no one who was willing to stand up and FIGHT BACK!'

The same shout. The same surge of energy.

'Until today, THEY. WERE. WINNING.'

Another pause. Another ten seconds of utter silence.

'But today is *not* just another day. Today is the *first* day. Today is *your* day. Today is *our* day.'

Travis's words were coming out faster now, his tone energised, his voice growing louder with each sentence.

'Today is the day that we say "NO"! Today is the day that we say "ENOUGH". Today is the day that we begin to take back this country. Because today ... TODAY THE WAR BEGINS!!!'

The last words were bellowed, their delivery perfect and their effect exactly as Travis would have intended it. The crowd, entirely male and made up of nothing but Liberation fanatics, was practically designed to receive a Peyton Travis speech with enthusiasm. But that alone did not explain the rapturous reception they gave.

The cheers and the shouts were deafening as Travis finished his call to arms. And it was more than a little confusing. Perhaps it was because Turner had missed most of the speech. He could appreciate Travis's expert delivery in what little he had heard but, without the context of more, the madness around him still seemed over the top.

I guess it makes some sense, he rationalised to himself. *I guess this is what they've been waiting for all this time. It's like someone's finally fired the starting pistol.*

Turner stepped back, away from the still cheering crowd. The power Travis had over them disturbed him; it reminded him of too many rallies seen in too many history classes as a kid.

457

He wanted no part of it and, thankfully for him, it did seem as if Travis was done. At least for now.

It provided a breathing space in which, he hoped, he would get the chance to reach his father.

He turned to Clemons and Brooks.

'I'm going to walk around the side, get in front of the crowd,' he explained. 'They're going to want a debrief from us, no doubt. Are you coming?'

'Sure as hell am.' Brooks gave Turner a nasty smile as he replied. It looked . . . wrong, somehow. Turner ignored it and looked to Clemons. 'You coming, Cliff?'

Clemons hesitated. He seemed to want to say something then think better of it as he finally shook his head.

'No. No, I'll hang back. You two go.'

'You sure?'

'I'm sure. Too many cooks.' He took a stride back. 'Good luck, Scott.'

Turner hesitated for just a moment. There was something about Clemons' tone. A finality, as if they would not see one another again. Turner almost asked but instead he forced the curiosity down.

Now was no time for paranoia. Not when his father was so close.

He turned back to Brooks.

'So I guess it's just us.'

'I guess it is.'

SEVENTY-THREE

12.18 p.m. EDT

'Does this look right to you?'

Dempsey was standing at the hood of the first Suburban, with Joshua on one side of him, Grace and Dai on the other. They had driven the twelve miles from Andrews to Washington Navy Yard in a little over twenty-five minutes. Good time through the midday DC traffic and exactly on time for their rendezvous with the Homeland Security force.

Ray McMillan had been as good as his word. Waiting for Alpha Team within one of the open disused industrial spaces that dotted the area were ten Lenco BearCat armoured personnel carriers, each with ten fully equipped Homeland tactical specialists in the back. One hundred men plus drivers, all under the command of a Homeland legend.

Special Agent Harry Murphy.

It had been Murphy and his team who, ten years earlier, had smashed Liberation and brought down Peyton Travis. Back then, a violent attack on Capitol Hill was the height of domestic terrorism. An unheard-of assault on democracy in the heart of government. Murphy had made his reputation on that bust and now here he was again.

Same bad guys. Same target. But a world apart in terms of scale.

Murphy was standing next to Joshua, oblivious, Dempsey assumed, of Joshua's identity but no doubt intrigued by the cuffs that were still around his wrists. Not that Murphy gave any indication of that. Right now even curiosity was an irrelevance. Like Dai and Grace, his attention seemed laser-focused on the large map of DC's Southwest Waterfront that Dempsey had spread across the front of the truck's hood.

'This one here, I mean,' Dempsey continued. He was pointing to what seemed to be a full block on the scaled plan of the city centre. 'A warehouse, by the looks of it.'

'Is it registered to Cato-Centinel?' Joshua asked.

'It's the only one in the whole district that is,' Dempsey replied.

'Then that's the one. It's perfect for what Travis described.'

'Which is what?' The question came from Murphy. 'What are we facing in there?'

Joshua turned. The first time the two men had interacted.

'Manpower?' he asked. 'That's hard to say. Last time Travis talked numbers, he said there were nearly one thousand active members of Liberation. That might be accurate. Or he might have been exaggerating. Or it might have grown even bigger since then. Who knows.'

'So how does that help us?'

'It doesn't. All it means is that he's not short of bodies, but that doesn't really matter, does it? Because there's just no way they'd use anything like that number for a task like this.'

'Why not?'

'Totally impractical for the job,' Dempsey answered.

'Numbers like that, they'd be as much a danger to themselves and to each other as they would be an effective line of defence.'

'And besides,' Joshua added, 'they won't all be in one place anyway. From what Travis said, they've got a lot of ground to cover on this.'

Murphy furrowed his brow at the comment but Grace beat him to the question.

'What does that mean? What ground?'

'Nature of the plan, Eden,'

Joshua's use of Grace's first name made Dempsey uncomfortable but he did not interrupt. Now was not the time to worry about the man's influence. Joshua tapped the site of the warehouse as he continued.

'This location, it's essential to what they have planned. It'll be the epicentre of the whole thing. But it's not even close to being the only place they've got manned right now.'

'Surely this will be the focus though?'

'It will, but the way this weapon system of his works—'

'System?' The term had shocked Dempsey. 'You didn't say anything about a weapons system.'

'Maybe the wrong use of words. Let me explain.' Joshua brought his cuffed hands back to the map. 'The weapon Travis designed ten years ago – the one he'd made before he was thrown into the Facility – it's a new form of dirty bomb. Much, much more powerful than a traditional version, because it's not just a conventional bomb with some radioactive material strapped on. The device, it has a blast zone of over a mile in every direction. Sheer devastation. From this point here, it's more than enough to both tear apart Capitol Hill and irradiate the place for God knows how long. But that's not all.'

'What do you mean that's not all?' The question came from Murphy.

'This is where the system part comes in. In twenty locations, all positioned in pretty much every direction fanning out from the bomb and all just under a mile from the epicentre, Travis has further stores of ammonium nitrate. Hundreds of tons of the stuff at every site. They're all laced with caesium or whatever radioactive shit it is that he's using as well. All of them just waiting to be set off by the main explosion and multiplying the damage even the big one can do by God knows how much.'

'You mean he's set up a chain reaction?'

Joshua nodded his head.

'Enough to wipe out everything recognisable in the centre of this city. Probably a shitload beyond that, too.'

Dempsey stepped back from the Suburban. He brought a callused hand to his brow and wiped away the sweat that had accumulated there in the hot sun. He took a deep breath as he moved, giving himself time to think.

'You sure about all of this?' he finally asked.

'Yes.' Joshua nodded.

Murphy turned to Dempsey.

'And what? We're just taking this guy's word on this? Jesus, I didn't realise we were relying on some convict. How the hell—'

'I'm vouching for him,' Dempsey said. He had no time for this debate. 'That was good enough for the president. You disagree, take it up with him.'

He turned back to Joshua.

'So what are we looking at here? What do we actually *know*? Some percentage of a thousand men – God knows how many that will be – all spread out over multiple locations across the city. Only one of which we've identified.'

'Yeah. But that's the only one we *need* to identify, isn't it? Because without the main device going off, nothing else goes bang.'

'We hope.'

'Well, yeah. We hope. But when did we ever do more than that?'

'Every single time, as I remember it. This one's a bloody Hail Mary.'

Both men went silent as they considered those odds, until interrupted by the return of Grace.

'I pulled up the schematics.' She placed her tablet onto the Suburban's hood as she spoke. On-screen were the blueprints for the Cato-Centinel building. 'So we could get a better idea.'

Joshua took one look.

'Well, we're not looking at a hundred men, that's for sure.'

'Fifty, absolute maximum,' Dempsey agreed. 'No operational use for more than that in that space.'

'But the place looks huge?' Murphy questioned.

'That building will be full to the brim with ammonium nitrate,' Dempsey explained. 'Enough to increase the blast power on the first device as much as possible.'

'How can you be sure of that?'

'Because it's what we'd do,' Joshua replied. 'Who'd waste that chance? It's not like they're short of the stuff and it's pretty clear Travis has some military brains working with him. He'll do everything he can to maximise the destruction. And he'll know the same thing we know: that holding a place like this doesn't need more than fifty men. For a building that size, fifty's an army.'

'This all sounds . . . it all sounds so . . . I don't know, big. Huge. How the hell could this all be in place, all across the centre of DC, without us knowing? The logistics involved, how could we have missed it?'

Dempsey looked away from the table and towards Murphy.

'You missed it for the same reason we don't notice grass growing. This has been done over years. A decade. Just a small delivery here and there, that's all it takes when you have the advantage of time. The attack that led you to Travis, you thought it was just the failed insurgence. You caught him for something he'd already done, not knowing what he was *planning* to do, even then.

'By putting him away, their plans were interrupted, delayed, but in the end all it did was give him and Arnold a valuable commodity. Time. Ten years to set this whole thing up. To have it ready and waiting, so Travis could just step out of that prison and press go.'

'I should have killed him when I had the chance ten years ago,' Murphy said angrily.

'Perhaps.' Dempsey shrugged. 'And maybe Jim should have killed him in their cell. Or I should have trusted my gut and put a bullet in the bastard the first time I saw him in Texas. But none of that happened, did it? And the way I see it, this day's not done yet. We've all got time to make up for our mistakes. So how about we go and do exactly that?'

SEVENTY-FOUR

12.28 p.m. EDT

Scott Turner felt his heart race as he looked around the cabin's main reception room. The mix of hopeful expectation and the fear of disappointment had been heavily weighted one way – the right way – for the last few hours. Now, as he saw no sign of his father amongst the men who surrounded Peyton Travis, that balance was fast moving in the wrong direction.

The spot from which Travis had made his speech was a bare thirty yards from the front of the cabin, yet it had taken him longer to cover that distance than it had for Turner and Brooks to make their way around the crowd. This had given Turner the chance to get a clear view of the man. And, more importantly, of the people around him.

A group that, he now realised, did *not* include James Turner.

The absence of his father had concerned him but Turner had rationalised it. Why would his dad wait to watch the speech, he had asked himself. James Turner shared no beliefs with Peyton Travis or with any man who followed him, so chances were he had already made his way into the cabin.

Turner had held on to this hope in the minutes that Travis had remained outside, where he had milked the adulation from the assembled ranks of Liberation. But once through the doors he could lie to himself no longer. Turner's father was not here. Not in the main reception room, anyway. And since this was where everyone else seemed to be and where Travis and his team were looking likely to settle, it begged just one question.

Where the hell is he?

A few steps closer and Turner could hear what Travis and the men closest to him were discussing.

'You think he's spoken to them? That he's told them?'

Turner did not recognise the voice and could only see the speaker from behind.

'Of course he has,' Travis replied. 'Now he knows he's not getting what he wants, he'll try to help them. He'll do whatever he can to stop us.'

'And he knows the details?'

'All of them.'

'What sort of time frame does that leave?'

'Enough. But like I keep saying, to be safe we have to do this now. Today. That was always the plan.'

'But what if they know more than we think? What if they—'

'Almost everything is in place. Just one more chess piece and we strike. And that one's down to me, so you can trust it'll be done. Believe me on this, if we do it now, as soon as it's ready, then there's nothing they can do to stop us.'

Turner was still trying to work out what they were talking about when he noticed Brooks step forward and approach Travis. He was taking advantage of the momentary lull in conversation, Turner realised.

Travis took a second to consider the newcomer before deciding on the appropriate greeting. When it finally came it took the form of a forced smile as he reached out with an open hand.

'We haven't met, soldier. I'm Peyton Travis.'

Turner could only see Brooks' back but he would have made a large bet that the man's face was already a deep shade of red. This moment was, Turner knew, one of which Brooks had quite literally dreamed.

'I . . . I . . . you don't . . .' Brooks stammered, his hand tight around Travis's own. 'I know who *you* are, sir.'

'Then you're one ahead of me, son. What's your name?'

'Brooks, Mr Travis. Kenny Brooks.'

'It's a pleasure to meet you, Kenny. Now tell me, what brings you—'

Travis stopped speaking before the question was out. His eyes had flitted away from Brooks, over his shoulder, and they had fallen on Turner. It was enough to stop the man in his tracks.

'Well, holy shit.' Travis let go of Brooks' hand and stepped past him without so much as a final glance. 'There's no need for me to ask who *you* are, is there?'

Turner said nothing. He could feel every eye in the room now boring into him. It was . . . uncomfortable.

Travis stepped closer, just feet away, and for a few moments he seemed to be studying Turner.

'That apple didn't fall far from the tree.'

Again Turner said nothing. He was unused to being the focus of a room. It left him uncertain of what to say or how to act. Besides, he was not interested in small talk. There was only one thing he wanted to know.

'I mean you look just like your dad, son,' Travis continued. If he was irritated by the silence he did not show it. He gripped

Turner's wrist, lifted his right arm and lightly slapped his ribs and then his upper left tricep. He seemed like a farmer examining potential stock. 'Thinner in the shoulders, definitely softer in the hands. But your mother would have needed no paternity test, that's for sure.'

Turner forced down his nerves. The way Travis had manhandled him, combined with the explicit mention of his father? It had emboldened him. If Travis was willing to raise the subject then maybe he had nothing to worry about after all.

'Where is he?' He could hear the nerves in his own voice as he spoke.

'Where's who?'

'My father, Mr Travis. He's supposed to be here. He's supposed to be with you.'

'Says who?'

'Says you, sir. That's what Cam told me. That your plan, it meant you both coming out together.'

'Is that right?'

Travis smirked as he said the words, a combination that caused a cold chill to run up Turner's spine. Somehow, somewhere deep down, he realised he had expected this. And so he was more ready for his own reaction than he could have hoped.

The controlled anger that now seemed to surge through his veins banished all traces of his earlier uncertainty.

'Where the fuck is my father?'

The arrogant grin remained on Travis's face, even as four of the large men behind him stepped forward to put themselves between him and Turner. Travis halted them with a raised hand, his eyes never leaving those of the younger man.

'Your father is exactly where I want him to be. And that's not here.'

'The deal was—'

'The deal is whatever I say it is. The deal is whatever it needs to be for the cause. Look around you, boy. You think we built all this to satisfy your need to see your daddy? You think Liberation exists to serve you?'

'Fuck Liberation. And fuck you. Arnold made a deal. You need to honour it.'

'I need to do one thing and one thing only. Bringing down this government, *that's* what I need to do. Your father, what part does he play in that? What value does he have to the cause? None. He brings nothing to the table, son. So, as far as I'm concerned, he can rot.'

Turner opened his mouth to speak but, as hard as he tried, he just could not find the words. The fury that was brewing within him, it was like nothing he had ever experienced. It had somehow rendered him speechless.

Travis had no such issue.

'Do you have any idea what's about to happen here?' The smirk was gone. Replaced by the look of cold fanaticism. 'Do you have any idea of the blow we're about to strike? Ten years of planning. Ten years of preparation. All of it for today. All of it to bring down the symbol of the betrayal of the American people. To wipe the stain of this republic – of this Union – off the face of the Earth. And you think I'm going to take my focus off of that? For your father?'

Turner could not quite believe what he was hearing. Even through his anger, he could recognise the irrationality of what Travis was saying. As he looked in Travis's eyes and listened to the man articulate both his devastating goals and the actions he would take to achieve them, he could have no doubt:

Peyton Travis was as crazy as the rest of them.

And a million times more dangerous.

'You're a madman.'

'No. I am a man with sight. Here to lead those who see the same evils out of darkness. And if that means that the blind, the likes of you and your father, are not a part of that solution? Then that makes you part of the problem. In fact, just what the hell are you even doing here?'

Travis looked around, at the men who surrounded them. When he spoke again his tone had changed, from megalomaniacal tyrant to something closer to a disgruntled diner.

'Can someone answer that? Why the hell is this outsider still here, now he's served his purpose?'

'Cam's orders, Mr Travis.' The answer came from Brooks. He sounded desperate to please his new master. 'He thought you might need help with things. He figured ten years is a long time away from a lab and that Turner might be some use to you. Bring you up to speed on the new stuff, that kind of thing.'

'Some use?' Travis looked genuinely offended. 'He thought what, I'd need to relearn my trade from a damn college dropout? Jesus Christ, for a smart man Cam really could be dumb as shit.'

'In his defence, Mr Travis—'

'What are you, his fucking lawyer? Fuck his defence. I don't need any help from anyone, and I sure as hell don't need it from some kid. Fucking Cam Arnold.'

Turner felt his blood pump harder as he watched the exchange drift away from the subject of his father. It was as if he and the reason he was even here were just a distraction, to be forgotten as soon as a new topic came up. It was a final insult that Turner just could not handle and it caused a surge of uncontrollable fury.

'WHERE THE FUCK IS MY DAD?'

Turner lunged forward as he demanded his answer, his hands thrust towards Travis's throat, which was chest height to the taller, younger man. Had they been alone, he had no doubt that they would have found their target. And that Travis, for all his bravado and arrogance, would have been no match for the murderous rage that Turner had never before experienced.

Had they been alone, Turner would have killed Travis where he stood.

They were *not* alone.

Turner had moved less than a foot before he was hit from the side. His head spun from the force of the blow, making him stagger forward. As he did he found himself gripped hard on both upper arms by two of Travis's entourage.

Unable to move further, Turner shook off the effects of the first blow. His head was still groggy but he could see enough now to watch Travis step away, his back turned on the violence that was about to take place.

And he could see enough to watch as Brooks stepped forward, his own back slapped encouragingly by Travis as he passed.

A dark, sadistic grin spread across Brooks' face as he approached the helpless man . . .

SEVENTY-FIVE

12.39 p.m. EDT

'A re you seriously taking me in there with these fucking things on my wrists?'

Joshua held up his cuffs as he spoke, his angry question directed at Dempsey.

'The deal was you come with me. The deal was *not* that I free you and arm you to do God knows what. If this isn't good enough, you can always head back to the car.'

'You really are a prick, you know that?'

'I've been called worse.' Dempsey smiled as he spoke. 'Mostly by you, come to think of it.'

'Come on. At least take these off. Give me a fighting chance.'

'For what? You're not needed in there. The only reason you're coming at all is that we made a deal.'

'And if Scott's in there? If someone makes a move his way?'

'We'll be in there to stop it. You *and* me.'

'Jesus, man. Come on.'

'This is as good as it gets, Jim. Take it or leave it.'

Joshua shook his head. His pleas were having no effect on Dempsey and he seemed to realise that. This time he did not ask again.

Dempsey turned away, towards Kate Silver and Dylan Wrixon who were just behind him. Like Dempsey and Joshua, both were now dressed in practical black combat gear under Kevlar mesh vests. And all of them but Joshua were heavily armed, each having been issued with an M4A1 assault rifle by Homeland Security, to add to the Glock pistols they routinely carried.

The other half of Alpha Team – Grace, Dai, Gallo and Jabari – were in an alleyway adjacent to but a block across from the one in which Dempsey and his unit now stood. Both were two buildings down from their target, with each alley leading to one of the two side exits from the Cato-Centinel warehouse.

Exits which, in the circumstances, would work just as well as a way *in*.

The task given to both halves of Alpha Team was to clear a path for the mass of Homeland agents who would follow. The one-hundred-strong team would divide into three to hit the building: one third through the warehouse front door, then a third each to the two alleyway exits. It was a simple, blunt approach, but to achieve it they would first need to locate and nullify any security countermeasures in the alley paths that two of the three units would take.

It was a safe assumption, with what was inside the building, that there would at least be a sophisticated camera and alarm network to provide the Liberation guards early warning of a raid. A warning that could lead to the device being activated before a single government agent was even inside. Before anyone was in place to stop it.

Dempsey could not risk that happening and so it was down to him and to his team to make sure that it did not. Only then, once the security was neutralised and the possibility of an early detonation removed, would the warehouse be hit by the sheer overwhelming numbers that Homeland could bring to bear.

'Either of you see anything obvious?' Dempsey asked. They had so far moved the length of one building.

'Nothing,' Wrixon replied. As Alpha Team's resident marksman, if anyone was going to spot what they were looking for it was probably him. 'Nothing obvious and nothing out of the ordinary.'

'Kate?'

'Same,' Silver replied. 'That strike you as unusual, boss?'

Dempsey nodded.

'I'd have thought we'd have encountered something by now.'

Dempsey lifted his comms mic to his mouth.

'Alpha to Bravo, over.'

'Bravo, over.' The response was immediate. Shui Dai's voice came through clearly.

'Anything your way? Over.'

'Nothing. What about yours? Over.'

'Not a sausage.' Dempsey remembered who he was speaking to and rethought the answer. 'No, nothing. Over.'

'Thoughts? Over.'

'I don't know. Let's keep moving. Over.'

'Check. Out.'

Dempsey waved his hand forward. An instruction for his half of the team – and for Joshua – to move. They did as ordered, four sets of eyes scanning every inch of the path ahead and every visible spot of the tall, featureless buildings that surrounded them. Their attention was absolute, looking for anything that could be a hidden security measure.

A camera.

A motion detector.

An underfoot panel.

Even a hidden laser projector.

Anything that could warn Liberation that they were coming. Anything that could lead to the instant destruction of the heart of America's capital.

They moved slowly. They moved with care.

And they found absolutely nothing.

It took them five more minutes to move the length of two buildings, until they were outside of the exit door. Long enough – slow enough – that Dempsey was certain of the absence of not just any hi-tech security but also of the most rudimentary equipment. Even here, where the most basic warehouse would be expected to at least have a single camera trained upon the doorway, there was nothing.

The outcome concerned Dempsey. It made no sense.

He backed away from the door and retreated ten yards down the alleyway, to a point where he was less likely to be overheard. Joshua, Wrixon and Silver had waited while Dempsey made the final approach and they would already know from the way he was shaking his head that the final short leg of their search had been negative.

'Alpha to Bravo. Over'

'Bravo. Over.'

'Anything? Over.'

'Nothing. Not even a camera. Over.'

'Same here. What do you think? Over.'

'No security, nothing to secure. Over.'

'My thoughts too. Get ready anyway. Over.'

Dempsey looked directly at Joshua.

'You still sure?'

'I'm still sure of what I was told. And I'm sure this is the only place anywhere near here that meets the criteria. This is where it should be.'

'You heard Dai. You agree with her?'

'I can't say I don't. But it makes no sense. This *is* where it should be.'

'You better not be playing me, Jim.'

'I'm the one with a son at risk. Why the fuck would I play you?'

Dempsey nodded his head. It was about as compelling an argument as anyone could make. Despite everything, he still did not doubt Joshua's honesty on this one. He just doubted that Joshua was right.

They would all find out soon enough.

He switched his comms mic to the open channel and held it to his mouth.

'Alpha Team to Tidal Wave. Over.'

'Receiving. Over.'

Joshua recognised Murphy's voice. From his tone, he could tell that the Homeland man was bored with waiting.

'The path's clear,' Dempsey said. 'Send them in.'

SEVENTY-SIX

1 p.m. EDT

Cliff Clemons shuddered as the metal cage around them shook. He was stood shoulder to shoulder with Kenny Brooks, another three men ahead of them and a fourth to Brooks' right. It was, it seemed, the maximum number that the lift could comfortably carry as it descended ever lower into the mineshaft around which the Liberation encampment had been built.

Clemons had never been underground before. As far as he could recall, he had never even been inside a cave. Everything about what was happening was alien to him. He'd had no idea that there even was a mine accessible from the camp.

And he still did not know what use Peyton Travis had for it.

All Clemons understood was that he, Brooks and their four companions had been told that the newly arrived leader of Liberation would be waiting for them three hundred feet below the surface. It was not an instruction he was about to refuse.

The sheer darkness of the shaft seemed unnatural as the lift passed two hundred feet. At this depth Clemons could feel himself becoming disorientated. Despite being on his own two feet, without sight he was finding himself unsure of what was up and what was down. A strange sensation but a fleeting one, as light from below gradually began to break through the black.

A few seconds more and Clemons could see clearly again. Whatever was at the bottom of the shaft – now just fifty feet below – must be heavily illuminated; the closer the lift came to the end of its journey, the more light was finding its way into the cage. By the time they came to a halt, it was nearly as bright as daylight. That fact seemed as strange to Clemons as the darkness.

The cage door was opened the moment the lift stopped moving, with all six occupants being ushered out. They moved as one, herded together and all no doubt as nervous as each other. Even Brooks, normally so dismissive of danger, seemed hesitant. The sight gave Clemons just a little pleasure, while at the same time making him even more fearful.

Because if Brooks is nervous . . .

If Clemons had had the time, his thought process could have spiralled out of control. The very thought of being three hundred feet down was bad enough. But he also had no idea why he was down here, and when he considered the nature of some of the men he was with, the danger was self-evident.

But as it was, he did not have that time.

Not with Travis waiting.

Not with Travis and . . . whatever the hell that is.

Clemons had only seen Travis at a distance, from the very back of the crowd when he, Brooks and Turner had arrived at camp earlier today. This was his first sight up close and he had to admit, it was disappointing.

Travis was stood next to a machine that Clemons did not recognise, the sleeves of his unsuitable white shirt rolled up and his large, protruding stomach sticking out far enough to be touching the metal. He seemed to be out of breath as he worked on the device, tired out by what seemed to be minimal exertion.

He was, Clemons noted, far from a prime example of any kind of master race. But then perhaps Clemons was not the best judge right now. His opinion of not just Travis but of Cam Arnold and maybe of Liberation itself had taken a hit. What had happened to Scott Turner – *what I think has happened to Scott*, he corrected himself – had left him shaken. Almost as much as it had left him ashamed.

Clemons could have warned him, he knew. He *should* have warned him. He should have stood up for his friend. He should have said no. He had done none of those things and it had left him disgusted with himself.

And that, in turn, had made his doubts in the cause grow even more.

Those thoughts were interrupted as Travis turned to face them, giving the impression that he had now noticed them for the first time. That could not be right, Clemons realised; Travis could not possibly have missed the sound of the lift. That one action alone told him something new about Peyton Travis.

The man's a performer.

'My best men.' Travis stepped forward, closing the distance between him and the group. 'My number-one team.'

Clemons was unsure of how to react. The two statements seemed strange; deliberately flattering and the crudest kind of manipulation. He looked at the men around him for some guidance. To see if they felt the same. He could read nothing on their blank faces to suggest that they did.

'You six,' Travis continued. 'I've been told that I can rely on you six as I would rely on my own sons. Is that true?'

'Yes, sir.' The six men spoke as one, including Clemons. It

was an automatic response, drilled into them by Cam Arnold over months of training. Ask the right question and they would all give that same answer, regardless of their own thoughts and feelings.

'That is heartening to hear, because today I'm going to entrust you all with the most important task that will ever be asked of any man in this movement.' Travis began to pace along the line as he spoke. 'Today, I'm going to entrust you with the responsibility to bring down this filthy excuse for a republic. Will you accept the honour that I offer to you?'

'Yes, sir.' The six again, only this time Clemons did not join in because it had been drilled into him. This time he joined in because any other response might end with him never seeing daylight again.

Travis smiled.

'Exactly what I was told to expect from you.'

Travis stepped forward and greeted the first man in line, shaking his hand enthusiastically as they spoke in low voices. It reminded Clemons of the one thing that it should not: a presidential audience, where the commander-in-chief works a line of guests and makes each of them feel like the only person in the room.

It was not a welcome thought and so he tried to distract himself by looking around the mine. What he saw surprised him. Clemons had seen enough movies to have at least an idea of what a coal mine would look like and it sure as hell was not *this*. The roof was low – six and a half feet at the most – but in every other way it had been renovated to resemble a sterile workplace rather than the dark, dank underground cavern it really was.

Only the darkness that stretched off into the distance reminded him of the reality of this room.

'And your name, soldier?'

The question snapped Clemons back to the moment. Fourth in line, Travis had now reached him. He grabbed Clemons' hand and gripped it hard, the same broad, fake smile on his face as Clemons had seen him use on the first man.

'Clemons, sir.'

'And how long have you been with us?'

'Ten months, sir.'

Clemons looked down, into Travis's eyes. He would never forgive himself if he did not ask the question that was now bothering him. And right now he could not deal with more regrets.

'Sir, can we . . . could you tell us what this role is? What it is that you need from us?'

'Of course.'

Travis turned and walked back to the machine he had been working on. It was roughly square, around five feet tall and probably the same around. Travis patted it with his right hand before returning his attention to Clemons.

'This machine is the weapon that will bring down this government and give us the freedom we were born to enjoy. Your job, soldier – the job of you all – will be to transport this to a specified location. You will see that it arrives there safely and you will ensure that all is in place for its use. And then you will all get the hell out of there.'

Travis's manic smile returned as he uttered the final sentence. Clemons chose to ignore it.

'What sort of a weapon, sir?'

The smile disappeared. Travis had evidentially not expected any follow-up questions.

'This is a bomb, Clemons. A new kind of bomb. Well,

not that new. I first designed and constructed it ten years ago. Since then it's been guarded by Cam Arnold and by those who supported him in my absence. But now I'm back and this is almost ready. By the end of today, it will be primed to rip through the home of the republic. And you six, you will have the honour of its delivery.'

Clemons looked around, at the five men stood with him. All of them were emotionless, staring forward. All of them, he realised, carbon copies of Kenny Brooks. And so all of them willing to do exactly what Travis was instructing.

In other words, they were the exact opposite of Cliff Clemons.

He had no intention of saying so now because he wanted to leave this place in one piece, but mass murder was not why Clemons had joined Liberation. That was not the movement that had been sold to him. That was not the mission as Cam Arnold had described it.

Sure, Clemons had heard Cam go off the deep end from time to time. But the plan, certainly as it had been explained to him, had always been ransom. To convince the government that Liberation had these kinds of weapons and that they would use them, all to force Washington DC into making concessions. To force them to change things. To break the hold of the woke elite.

Never for a moment did Clemons think that the movement actually *had* bombs like this.

And never for a moment did he think they would *use* them.

'Is there something you want to say, soldier?'

Clemons realised that he had been staring at Travis while he was thinking. It left him just a heartbeat to think of an answer.

'Just . . . just . . . that your escape. That was today. This morning. Surely security's gonna be increased, with you out? If we push ahead today, are we not asking to fail?'

'That's smart, Mr Clemons,' Travis replied. 'I'll need to keep an eye on you, soldier. That's the kind of thinking we need here. But no, I'm not concerned. I made arrangements before I came here. Before I left my cell, in fact. I seeded an idea in a mind. An idea that guarantees all eyes will be on Washington DC, while you'll be at the home of the ultimate betrayal. Thanks to that idea, soldier, where you're going is as safe today as it will ever be.'

'And where is that, sir?'

'I've already told you. The place where this entire bastardisation of a democracy began. You're taking this device to Philadelphia.'

SEVENTY-SEVEN

1.05 p.m. EDT

Harry Murphy pulled off his black ballistic helmet and threw it angrily across the empty space of the warehouse. With so much distance to cover and with literally nothing to obstruct its flight, the helmet hit the floor before it came close to the building's far wall.

He turned towards Dempsey, standing just a few feet away.

'What the hell happened here? Where the hell . . . what the hell . . .'

He seemed unable to finish his sentence. And Dempsey understood why. Not only had they wasted over one hundred highly trained personnel on bad intelligence, they had done so when − if Joshua was right about anything − there was still a weapon of mass destruction out there.

A weapon on which they now had no leads.

In the circumstances, Dempsey could understand both the urge to throw things and the inability to form a coherent question.

'Where the hell are they, Agent Dempsey?' Murphy finally managed. 'Where the hell is the goddamned bomb?'

Dempsey shook his head. What he had to say, he already knew it was not enough. He glanced at Joshua before he spoke.

Even without asking, he knew that his former friend had reached the same conclusion.

Dempsey turned back to the Homeland agent.

'I think we've been played.'

'You *think*?' Murphy indicated to the massive empty space in which they now stood. 'I'd have said that was a given, wouldn't you? Unless they've somehow hidden a few hundred tons of ammonium nitrate in a deserted building?'

'OK. You've got a point. We *have* been played.'

'So what does that mean? Just how wild *is* this goose chase? Is the bomb real and we've been sent to the wrong building? Or is the whole thing bullshit?'

'The bomb's real.' The answer came from Joshua. His tone right now, if Dempsey had to describe it, was best termed as 'pissed'. 'I'm the one who's been played here. That fat little fuck, he was dripping this stuff into my ear for three years. All that time when I thought I was filing away information that could hurt him, all that time, it was *him* setting *me* up.'

'And who the hell asked you to speak?' Murphy took a step closer to Joshua, his anger and his frustration as evident as they had ever been. 'Do you really think we're gonna keep listening to you? After *this*? Your credibility is shot, buddy. You're going back to the shithole they dug you out of.'

Dempsey could see how Joshua wanted to react to Murphy's words. And cuffed or not, that would not end well for the Homeland agent. Dempsey acted first, to prevent an escalation. He placed the back of his hand gently on Murphy's chest and guided him a few steps back. Then he stepped in between the men and faced Joshua himself.

'Why?'

'Why what?'

'Why would he play you like this?'

'Are you really going to buy into this shit?' The question came from Murphy.

'I'm not buying into anything,' Dempsey said, speaking to Murphy from over his own shoulder. 'But I'm not writing anything off, either. We need to get to the bottom of this.'

'The bottom of this is that you've put your trust in a convict and now it's come back and bitten you in the ass. So how about we don't make the same mistake twice, huh?'

Dempsey turned to face him. This time it was his turn to be irritated. And he made no attempt to hide it.

'Agent Murphy, if you've got a better idea on how to deal with all this then why don't you go and do you, eh? And I'll stay right here and do me. We'll both get a lot further if we're not in each other's way, don't you think?'

Murphy seemed uncertain of how to react. Dempsey's message was clear; his tone and body language left no doubt that his question was not really a question at all. Murphy, it seemed, was unused to taking that kind of instruction. It took his brain a few moments to catch up with his basic survival instincts before he stalked away without another word. Back towards his own team.

Dempsey did not watch him go. His attention was already back on Joshua.

'What's your theory? Why did he send us here?'

'Because the bomb's somewhere else.' Joshua's answer was matter-of-fact. As if he did not quite understand Dempsey's question.

'That's not what I meant. Without you, we wouldn't even know an attack was imminent. And he didn't have to tell you that it was. So why say anything at all?'

Joshua took a moment to think. The answer came quick.

'To take you off his tail.'

'Me?'

'You or whoever else was leading this thing. To make sure there was no way you could connect the dots of his real plan.'

'But we still could.'

'Yeah, but how long will that take now? If he really does intend an attack today, this little distraction? You're now so far off the pace you'll never find him in time.'

Dempsey nodded his head. Joshua's reasoning matched his own.

'So you think the attack is going to be today?'

'Is there any point in this red herring if it isn't? This doesn't buy him forever. It doesn't even buy him that long. But it buys him today.'

'And he could be anywhere.'

'Well, we know he's not in DC. He wouldn't bring us to the city where it's really going to happen. All that does is increase the chances that we stumble on something we shouldn't.'

'Agreed. So where does that leave us?'

'It leaves us nowhere. We have no idea where it's going to happen. No idea at all.'

Dempsey shook his head.

'And there was me hoping you were going to pull a rabbit out of the hat for me.'

'Miracles were always your forte, Galahad.'

'Right now I'd settle for a parlour trick.'

'Sorry, kid.' Joshua held up his cuffs. 'My sleight of hand's a bit compromised today.'

Dempsey mustered a small, defeated smile.

'We're not finding this bastard, are we?'

'I don't see how. Not now. Not in time, anyway.' Joshua took a long look around the empty warehouse. 'He really is one clever little shit, isn't he?'

'Smarter than you. And that's not the insult it seems. I've never seen anyone capable of playing you before. A hand of poker was all I could ever manage and even that was one time out of ten. Travis? He did it for nearly three years.'

'Speaks to the level of planning of this, too, doesn't it? If he was that careful over that long, what are the odds that he's going to slip up on anything else?'

'Thanks for that.' Dempsey's grim smile returned. 'That's really perked me up about our chances.'

'Realism. Never was your strong point.'

'Realism gets in the way. I find hopeless optimism presents more opportunities.'

'You're talking to a man who's slept in a cell for the past four years, surrounded by bastards who want to kill him. Optimism isn't something I have a lot of these days.'

Dempsey took a step back. For a moment his mind conjured images of the Facility and thoughts of the life Joshua lived inside its walls. It almost made him sympathetic for the man he had unknowingly put there.

Almost.

He banished the mental picture as quickly as it arrived, sucked in a deep breath and forced away the negativity. They had taken a hit. A bad one. But as long as the attack had not yet happened, they still had a chance. No matter how small.

And yes, the odds *were* against them. But when weren't they?

'Enough of this,' Dempsey announced. 'You're bringing us down. I've got a job to do and you've got a son to save. So let's stop feeling sorry for ourselves and work out what the hell we do next.'

Joshua smiled. But unlike Dempsey's, it was not grim.

'Now I remember *that* Joe Dempsey,' he said. 'Never say die, eh?'

'When did either one of us ever do that?'

'I guess so. You have any kind of a plan?'

'No kind at all. Other than we keep moving forward. Let's go.'

Dempsey walked past Joshua without another word, towards the main entrance of the warehouse. The raised full-length shutters were wide enough to accommodate the Lenco BearCats five abreast, and so the front of the building was now lit by intense sunlight.

The contrast made near silhouettes of the figures on whom the sunlight fell but still Dempsey could make out Murphy. Even without his facial features being visible, it was impossible to miss the figure now aggressively directing the withdrawal of the Homeland.

'He's still not happy.'

'And then some,' Dempsey replied.

'I don't think he'll be too keen to help you again, if you need him.'

'Lucky he has no choice, then.'

Dempsey had not taken his eyes off of Murphy as he and Joshua spoke, and so he noticed as a figure brushed past the Homeland agent and made a beeline in their direction. A few more steps out of the sun and he could see who that figure was.

Against all the odds, Eden Grace looked excited.

'Boss, you're not going to believe this. We've found Scott Turner.'

SEVENTY-EIGHT

2.03 p.m. EDT

'What do we know?'

Dempsey asked the question as he took his seat on the C-17, next to Joshua and Harry Murphy. Grace and Dai were sat on the bench against the opposite wall.

'It's definitely the place, by my reckoning,' Grace confirmed. 'An encampment on the Pisgah Mountain ridgeway in Pennsylvania. Just outside a town called Summit Hill.'

'The address Scott Turner gave on the car hire agreement at Allentown Airport,' Dempsey said.

'Exactly. Once we had that address we looked into any intelligence on that particular area. There wasn't much and there wasn't anything that related directly to Liberation, but there was enough to make us take a closer look.'

'Such as what?'

'Just a few reports,' Grace replied. 'Mainly during the lockdown. Relations between the camp and the town seem to have been pretty good in general. But when the pandemic was at its height there were a few complaints from Summit Hill residents that were passed up the chain about people from the camp breaching lockdown rules when they came into town. We looked into them and their statements contained some pretty casual references to a militia and to the patriot movement. As if those things were just everyday facts of life.'

'And no one followed this up at the time?' Dempsey asked.

'I guess there was a whole lot going on last year, boss. There was nothing threatening in any of the reports. No suggestion that these people were a danger or that they were violent. Not like some of the other groups who sprung up during the pandemic. It just made it clear that they were a group of like-minded non-conformists. Chances are someone would have gotten around to checking them out in due course. Just not yet.'

Dempsey nodded. The explanation made sense and Grace was right. The past eighteen months of unprecedented lockdowns and regulations had seen a massive rise in far-right, anti-authoritarian groups. An increase that had caught the attention of the country's various intelligence agencies.

But with so many to observe, it was no surprise that a minor group with no hint of violent revolt fell way down the list for investigation. And it was equally no surprise that someone as astute as Cam Arnold could make Liberation seem to be exactly that: benign and harmless, instead of the biggest threat on American soil.

'But how can you be sure this *is* Liberation?' The question came from Murphy. He was determined that this would not be another mistake, Dempsey realised. 'If there is nothing in the reports to connect them?'

'The connection to Scott Turner is fairly definitive,' Grace replied. 'He and two other men – a Kenneth Brooks and a Clifford Clemons – boarded a plane this morning in North Carolina. Looking at the distances and time elapsed, Fayetteville Airport was just about as far north as they could be by that time, assuming they had departed Key West after the murder of Ricardo Garcia. That was the final piece of the puzzle to confirm something we already believed we knew: that Scott Turner was with Cam Arnold when Mr Garcia was killed.

'That ticket purchase flagged up on the ISB system, thanks to Agent Dempsey's tag on Scott Turner's name. Same reason the Bureau became involved in this whole thing in the first place. We looked at the ticket and that took us to Allentown. Once we got there, we checked with the airport's only car rental service and that's brought us to here.'

'Does this not seem a little convenient?'

'How?'

'Scott Turner is on your watch list and suddenly he's boarding a plane under his own name. After what happened here today, does that not raise some questions?'

'It did. Which is why we contacted the NSA and secured these satellite pictures of the encampment.'

Shui Dai opened a thick folder she had rested on her lap, stood up and passed out bundles of photographs to Dempsey, Murphy and to Joshua. She handed the last to Grace herself and, still standing, she took over the explanation.

'What the pictures show, no doubt this is a quasi-military facility.'

Dai pointed to a detail visible on the first photograph, which was an overview of the entire camp.

'Weapons storage,' she said. She pointed to another detail. 'Armoured vehicles.' Another. 'Firing range. And this is on the widest view. When the satellite zoomed in, we saw more. It is in the pictures. You can look at your leisure, but it is enough. This facility, it is *not* peaceful.'

'And it's not empty, either, if that's what you were worried about.' Grace was looking directly at Murphy. 'You'll see from the pictures further in, there are a lot of bodies present. One hundred and twenty-eight at our count. Maybe more within the various buildings. Add these pictures to the presence of Scott Turner in Summit Hill and it all becomes undeniable. This *is* Liberation. This *is* where we need to go.'

Dempsey nodded his head. Grace had sold him already, before they had ever boarded the plane. He turned to Murphy.

'Is that good enough for you?'

'I guess it's going to have to be. It's not like we have a whole lot of time here, is it?'

'Not if we're correct, no,' Dempsey replied. 'Are you happy to board your men?'

'Yeah. Yeah, I am.'

Murphy stood up as he spoke and walked away when he was done, towards the open back of the plane. His team were outside, all one hundred of them, waiting on the tarmac for their orders. In just moments they would begin to board and, for the first time that day, the C-17 would have a load that justified its massive size.

Dempsey considered none of this. His attention was already back on Grace.

'Contact Henry. We're going to need some resources waiting for us.'

Grace had expected the order. As ever when Dempsey was thinking outside of the box, it was the logistical skills of Henry Garrett back at the ISB who would make those thoughts a reality.

'What are you thinking?'

Dempsey looked again at the satellite photos. The size of the encampment, the way it was set up and the lack of good access points for any sizeable force. It left them few options.

'Bombers,' he finally replied. 'We need four bombers, primed and ready to fly.'

'You need what?'

Dempsey looked around at the sound of Joshua's voice. He was unsurprised to see the horror in the man's eyes.

'Joe, Scott's in there. You can't—'

'We've got no choice. With this set-up, we're not taking that camp in a frontal attack. Arnold designed this thing specifically to make that unviable. It's hemmed in between cliff faces and densely packed woods, making a side assault impossible. We don't have time for a siege. The only way we stop them in the window we have is from the air.'

'But Scott—'

'Scott won't be in there. Not when the bombs come.'

'How can you be sure of that?'

'Because we're going in there to get him, Jim. You and me.'

SEVENTY-NINE

2.41 p.m. EDT

Scott Turner looked around the bare wooden room and tried to shake the sluggish confusion that ached in his head. He had no idea of where he was or how he had got here, but right now those two questions were secondary.

What mattered more was why the hell every inch of his body hurt.

He rolled slowly in his bunk, trying to shift from his back onto his side. The movement was as slow as he had ever managed and yet still the effort was too much. He was barely halfway when his right side gave way, forcing him to fall backwards onto the thin, dirty mattress that was beneath him.

The impact was agony, felt all through his upper body. But it was also useful. The movement hit his broken left hand and his broken ribs, and the searing pain that both sent shooting through his nervous system somehow cleared the fog that was clouding Turner's mind.

The image of a ranting, rabid Peyton Travis returned with a clarity Turner had rarely experienced. His own fury at Travis's betrayal had been a shock. Turner had never been that angry in his life and so he had never known how focused and keen his mind could become when fuelled by emotional adrenaline. He figured that it must be an inheritance from his father. A genetic predisposition to think clearly when most would be losing their heads.

It was even more surprising now as he realised just how accurate it made his memory. Every blow. Every kick. Every stamp. It was not the kind of thing Turner wanted to remember, but he nonetheless found himself fascinated by the fact that he could.

Not that he needed that memory to know where his injuries were. The pain told him that. And he found, for the first time in his life, that this was not an entirely bad thing. Awareness of where he was hurt allowed him to tailor his movement up from the bunk, relying on only his uninjured limbs to pull him to his feet without having to suffer the agony and the strength-sapping that would come from testing which parts of his body were useless to him. The process still took longer than it should and much more effort than was normal, but it worked. After a few minutes, his feet were on the floor and, but for the help of the bedhead, they were taking his full weight.

Now standing, Turner assessed his surroundings. He squinted as he did so, to keep out the bright sunlight that was beating through the narrow, high window that seemed to encircle the four walls. The pain of doing just that was intense – he remembered now the efforts that had been made to stamp on his left cheek, not all of them unsuccessful – but Turner pushed through.

He wanted to understand where he was. And he needed to know how to get out.

The room, like all of the cabins in the encampment, was a basic wooden structure. But unlike the various offices and barracks and storerooms and everything else in the camp, it seemed to be a lone, one-room structure. The window that ran along the top of each wall was proof of that.

He wracked his brain for a corresponding structure. Looking around the cabin, it was no more than ten feet by ten. Ironically, a building that small should stand out when the norm was a pattern of much larger cabins. And yet as far as Turner could recall, he had never seen one anywhere in the encampment.

He dismissed the thought for a moment. It was getting him nowhere. Instead he studied the room itself.

The only source of light, other than an open bulb hanging from the ceiling, was the strip window that surrounded the structure. Not an option for escape, Turner immediately realised. Even if his body had not been too broken to contemplate a climb, there was no way he could fit through an opening that slim.

And that's assuming the bloody thing even opens, he thought.

The rest of the four walls, other than the doorway, were featureless. No windows. No air conditioning grate. No gaps of any sort. Just thick, perfectly planed logs that intersected to create a building so solid that – barring fire or demolition – it would certainly outlast Turner himself.

And that left just the door.

Turner had no doubt that it would be locked. He was a prisoner. The chances that he would be held captive in a room with a single unsecured door were practically non-existent. But what other option did he have?

He moved towards it, slowly and with care. Each and every step was agony, sending jolts of pain up through his ribs and damaged neck, but he pushed himself on. He kept shuffling. He kept moving forward. And ultimately he made it to the door.

Locked.

If he was honest with himself, Turner was not even disappointed. He had known that the exercise was futile. He gave the handle one last try, to confirm what he already knew, and then turned to face the room. And with what little energy he had now used up, he rested his back against the door and let his body slide downwards.

'Scott. Scott, can you hear me?'

Turner opened his eyes. For just a moment he was still in his own sleeping mind, watching as the Alsatian dog his father had buried thirteen years earlier called out his name across Times Square. An instant earlier and the dream scenario had made perfect sense. Now he saw it for what it was. A dream, where the dog he had relied on to protect him and his mother during his father's many absences had come to rescue him.

He tried to physically shake off the dream. A mistake, he quickly realised, as he remembered the extent of his injuries.

'Scott.'

The voice was whispered but still it cut through Turner's pain. For a moment he was unsure. Had he really, had he . . .

'Scott, can you hear me?'

Turner sat bolt upright, ignoring the new thunderbolts of agony that the movement caused. He had heard a voice. A voice he recognised.

He slowly turned his body towards the door.

'Cliff . . . is that . . . is that . . . you?'

The words came out slowly, shallow breaths taken between them, his broken ribs making each one agony. Even Turner had not realised how hurt he would sound.

'Jesus, Scott. Are you OK?'

'No. No, I'm not. I ... I ... need to ... get out of ... out of here.'

You and me both,' Clemons replied. 'Can you travel?'

'I can do ... whatever ... I have to.'

Turner was not confident in his own answer, but he would not tell Clemons that. If he stayed here then he had no doubt that he would die here. He could not let that happen. He had to at least try.

'OK. Look, I'm getting out of here. Within the hour, Scott. I'm running. And I'm taking you with me, buddy. Can you do that?'

'Like I ... said. Whatever I ... whatever I have to.'

'I'm gonna need to get through this door. I'll see if I can find a key somewhere. Get yourself comfortable and I'll be back, OK? As soon as I can.'

'OK.'

The sound of footsteps told Turner that Clemons was moving away. It was his own signal to allow himself to fall, his back hitting the door once again. He did not try to prevent himself from sliding back to the floor. If he did have any energy left – and he was not confident that he did – he would need that when Clemons came back.

Until then, he would sleep.

EIGHTY

3.06 p.m. EDT

Dempsey spread the largest of the NSA's satellite images across the floor of the Huey that had flown Alpha Team from Allentown Airport to the peak of Sharp Mountain. The image was pin-sharp. Hard to believe that it had been taken from literally miles above. It showed the full Liberation encampment, with every detail that was not under cover visible in precise form.

The Huey had set down less than a mile from the target location. It was closer than Dempsey would have liked but, like everything else today, circumstances demanded that he cut corners. The clock was against him; he knew that for sure, even though he did not know by how much. And so today he lacked time to do things the right way.

Luckily for Dempsey – luckily for them all – the geography between the two points made the spot on Sharp Mountain safer than it would usually be. The populated pockets of the surrounding area had grown from a collection of mining encampments, holes blasted into the mountains and peaks to access the then precious coal hundreds of feet beneath the surface. Those same peaks now provided the visual and sound cover that the team had needed for their approach. Short of radar, there was no way for the camp to be aware of their arrival. And even if Liberation *did* have that detection system, a single chopper would not concern them.

The same would not have been true of a fleet, which was what it would have taken to bring Murphy and his full Homeland Security force by the same route. This was why Dempsey had insisted that they travel by road. It would inevitably slow their journey to Summit Hill, but they would still cover that forty miles quickly.

And so they would, Dempsey was sure, be ready and in position within the next fifteen minutes.

Just in time to mop up after the jets.

'OK, one more time.'

Dempsey had been through the plan three times already; years in the field had taught him the efficacy of repetition. Using the photos for reference, he pointed to the small portion of fence that seemed closest to the woodland that surrounded the parts of the camp not bordered by rock face.

'Jim and I will enter at this point. I want a pair of eyes on us the whole time, so Dyl, you find the best spot you can for a bird's-eye view of this entry point and then of the camp in general.'

'Got it.'

'Any direct threat to us, you take it out. But only when you're sure. If you can avoid it, avoid it.'

'No problem.'

Dempsey turned to the rest of the team.

'Everyone else, you know where I want you. Up high and covering the compass points. Divide the grid up between you and study your sector until you find Scott Turner. The moment you spot him, you call it in and you guide us to him. Understood?'

Every member of Alpha Team nodded.

Each of them knew their instructions but they could no doubt understand the care Dempsey was taking. He and Joshua were about to enter a camp of well over one hundred armed men, all of them, they had to presume, willing to kill. As skilled as the two former soldiers were, those were not good odds.

It was a knife edge: either this plan worked perfectly or it ended in disaster.

Dempsey continued.

'Best-case scenario, this whole thing plays out without a shot. That's the goal, OK? That Jim and I go in, get Scott and get the hell out before anyone sees us. And well before the bombs start dropping. But if it doesn't go that way – if Dyl has no choice but to fire – then I don't want a single one of you to hesitate. The instant *he* takes a shot, you *all* take a shot. And if that happens, I want that camp turned into a shooting gallery. I want them cowering from you and not looking for us. Is that clear?'

'It is clear.' The answer came from Shui Dai.

'One more thing.' Everyone, Dempsey included, turned to face Joshua as he spoke. 'You all know what my son looks like. If things go south and the shooting starts, just make sure there are no accidents. If there are, you'll have me to answer to.'

None of Alpha Team said a word, but Dempsey could feel the irritation that now bristled between them.

'That's helpful,' he commented.

'What's that mean?'

'Just that it might be better to stay onside with the people about to keep us alive.'

'I'd say it's better to be honest.' Joshua shrugged, and appeared unconcerned.

Dempsey shook his head. He was wasting his breath. He turned to Grace.

'Eden, the moment Jim and I are in that camp, that's when you call down the strike.'

'You're sure it's long enough?' Grace had asked the question twice already.

'I've told you already, it's exactly fifteen minutes between the call and the strike. If that's not enough time to find Scott then we're not finding him.'

'Are you—'

'I'm sure, Eden.'

Dempsey stepped back from the chopper and away from the satellite pictures. His team did the same.

'I'm counting on you all, now.' He indicated to Joshua. For the first time, the older man was un-cuffed and armed. A vision from Dempsey's past. 'We both are.'

EIGHTY-ONE

3.11 p.m. EDT

Joshua reached the fence first, just a few strides ahead of Dempsey. True to their deal, they had stayed shoulder to shoulder as they'd moved through the forest coverage that led from the chopper to the camp. Less than a mile in distance, the uneven ground and the need to beware of any security measures had barely slowed them.

It was only as the selected section of the fence came in to view that Joshua had pulled ahead.

Proving he hasn't slowed with age, Dempsey thought.

The perimeter was barely three feet from the thick line of trees it bordered and so they had no trouble maintaining their camouflage against the wooded backdrop. They had selected this spot for a reason. As the only point that was not either butted up against sheer rock or with a no man's land of space between the fence and the wood, it was the only suitable place to breach the fence undetected.

Combined with the cabin that had been built on the other side of the chain-link, it was a clear security flaw in the design of the encampment. The only one, Dempsey had noted. An anomaly in an otherwise solid design.

Dempsey surveyed the fence itself. At eighteen feet in height, it was far too tall for them to scale without being seen;

even the poorly placed cabin ahead of them would only cover the first nine or ten feet. It left them only one option.

He touched his hand to his ear and activated his comms receiver.

'You see us, Dyl?'

'Barely, but I've got you.'

'How's it looking?'

'No movement visible through the cabin windows and no one outside within one hundred and fifty yards. If you're going, you should go now.'

'Agreed.'

He turned to Joshua.

'You ready for this, old man?'

'Don't insult me. I was doing this while you were in school.'

'We both know that's not true.'

'Sound's good, though, don't it?'

'Let's just get on with this.'

Dempsey had removed the wire cutters from inside his Kevlar mesh vest as he spoke and he now stepped forward. A few seconds later and the fence was breached. A hole wide enough for both men to slip through with ease.

A moment more and they had done just that. Now on the other side, they flattened their backs against the wooden building that was less than two feet from the fence. It gave them little room to manoeuvre but it also gave them cover. It was an advantage that strongly outweighed the restriction on their movement.

Based on its size, they had assumed the building to be the camp's main barracks. A conclusion that Wrixon had already confirmed. It was the one disadvantage of their chosen access point; if the barracks were manned and their breach was observed, there was just no way that Dempsey or Joshua could have fought their way out of the thin rathole they were now in.

Lucky for them, then, that Wrixon had also confirmed the barracks to be near empty.

Dempsey held his M4A1 rifle in one hand, at his side and aimed towards the floor. Joshua was doing the same, but using the opposite hand. It was far from ideal for either of them but that simple fact still gave Dempsey confidence. Joshua had made the decision to switch gun hands without discussion and by doing so had ensured that – as a pair – they could at least fire one-handed in either direction if they were discovered.

It confirmed the one thing that had concerned Dempsey as they'd moved ahead with the mission. However much the four years in the Facility had impacted on Joshua's skills, it had not dampened his natural instincts.

Dempsey put the comms mic to his lips.

'Which way, Dyl? Left or right?'

'Right,' Wrixon replied. 'Small building across from the barracks. Thirty-yard distance, no one else within one hundred, no one facing your way.'

'OK. We're about to move. Grace?'

'Boss?'

'Time to call in the strike.'

'On your mark.'

'This *is* my mark.'

'Fifteen minutes takes us to 3.28 p.m., Boss. You're sure that's enough time?'

'Call it, Eden. Now.'

Dempsey lowered his arm to his chest and set the timer on his watch to fifteen minutes. Joshua did the same, then looked up to find that Dempsey's eyes were already on him.

'Let's go get your boy.'

EIGHTY-TWO

3.14 p.m. EDT

The impact of the door on his back woke Scott Turner with an agonising jolt. It was opened hard, forcing him forward with a thud. Turner cried out as the pain from his injuries, dormant when he was unconscious, once again shot through his body.

'Jeez, Scott, are you OK?'

The look of concern on Clemons' face only increased as Turner climbed to his hands and knees and looked up. He had given no thought to how the damage inflicted upon him would look. Now he did not need to ask. Clemons looked distraught as he knelt down, placed an arm around Turner and physically lifted him to his feet.

'Come on. We gotta get going, buddy.'

The pain of movement – even involuntary movement, powered by someone else – was excruciating, but Turner was determined to make no more sound. This was his way out of here. His one chance at survival. He owed that to Clemons; he would not make this any harder for the man than it already was.

'I can walk, Cliff.' He noticed that his words were coming out easier. As if the short rest had done him some good, however meagre. 'I just need some support is all.'

'I'm sure you can.' Clemons threw Turner's right arm across his shoulder as he spoke and gripped him hard around the waist, making Turner wince. 'But we ain't got time to get you limber right now. They're gonna be looking for me.'

Turner did not ask who 'they' were. Clemons had somehow found and used the key that had been used to lock Turner in the small cabin. That was a serious offence, enough to see him beaten and locked in here, too. Maybe worse. Maybe much worse. And so Turner understood his haste.

'How far?'

'The truck's right outside and the gate's still unmanned. If we hurry, we're out of here before they know we're gone.'

Turner tried to force a smile. His damaged cheekbone would not allow it. He settled for just nodding his head.

'Thank you, Cliff. Thank you.'

'Don't thank me yet.'

Clemons began to move as he spoke. Turner did his best to help, trying to take as much of his own weight as he could. As they shuffled forward, Clemons spoke again.

'I should have done this much earlier. I'm sorry, Scott.'

Turner did not waste his breath by asking Clemons' meaning. If there was something to discuss then they would do that later. Right now, what little energy he had was focused on staying upright and moving forward.

They were through the door in seconds and then stumbling across the cabin's short porch, towards the rented Ford Explorer that had brought them here. The driver's door was open and the engine was running.

There really was no time to lose.

The realisation made Turner's heart beat even faster. On any normal day that would have made him quicker and stronger, at least for a few moments. But with the injuries he had sustained, Turner's body did not react in the usual way. Instead, the renewed adrenaline made his legs give way, just as they reached the first of the three steps that went down from the porch to the dirt floor below.

The sudden stumble almost sent them both to the ground. Somehow Clemons avoided that. Steadying first himself and then Turner, he kept them both on their feet. A display of sheer physical strength that would have surprised Turner if only his mind had been in any place to note it.

'I thought you could walk?' Clemons said, a nervous smile on his face.

'I thought . . . I thought you could . . . carry me,' Turner almost laughed, his mind sharp again in that moment; the injection of pain that had shot through his body as he fell had also cleared his head, however temporarily. It was an instant of humour he regretted, banished immediately by the agony of his broken face.

Clemons clearly noticed his pain. His concerned expression returned.

'Come on. We're nearly there.'

Renewing his grip, he took Turner's full weight before shifting around to take a next careful step.

A step that he would never complete.

Turner saw Kenny Brooks' grinning face a heartbeat before he heard the sound. Even in his once again clouding mind, he felt the horror of what was about to happen.

A single gunshot, fired from barely feet away.

How Brooks had come so close without them seeing him or hearing him was a mystery, but it was also a question that changed nothing. With no chance to avoid the bullet, Clemons was propelled backwards by the impact while Turner, his support gone, slumped helplessly to the floor.

EIGHTY-THREE

3.17 p.m. EDT

'Who the hell was that?' Dempsey barked the question into his comms mic. 'Who fired that shot?'

Dempsey and Joshua were still inside the first cabin. Checking it had taken longer than expected, despite them knowing quickly that their search was a bust. The building had no sign of Scott Turner. What it *did* have were six large members of Liberation, all sat around a table in the middle of the room, playing poker.

Determined not to attract outside attention on their very first cabin, Dempsey and Joshua had resorted to the only silent way to deal with that many targets: the Ka-Bar combat knives they had been issued by Murphy's team before leaving DC.

It made for messy work and it took longer than a few bursts of their rifles would have done, but it was a price worth paying to keep their presence under wraps. Dempsey and Joshua needed as little obstruction as they could get if they were going to do what needed to be done in the next . . .

Dempsey checked his watch.

Under eleven minutes.

'It *was* gunfire but it wasn't any of us.' Grace's answer came directly to Dempsey's ear. 'It was someone else.'

'Have we got a problem?'

'Yes and no, boss.'

'What does that mean?'

'It means we've found Scott Turner. But we've also found Peyton Travis. And boss?'

'What?'

'I think we've found the bomb.'

EIGHTY-FOUR

3.18 p.m. EDT

Dempsey pushed the door of the cabin ajar by barely an inch but he already knew that the effort was fruitless. Thanks to the angle and the need to keep the gap narrow to avoid detection, the view it would give him was going to be inadequate.

He was quickly proved correct. While he could just about see in the direction Grace had given him, his field of vision was too restricted.

'It's no use.' He spoke into his comms mic as he stepped back inside, pulling the door fully closed behind him. 'I can't get a good view. You need to talk me through it.'

'Where's Scott?' Joshua asked the question into his own mic.

'He's heading towards Travis right now,' Grace answered.

'By himself? Where? Can we intercept him?'

'Not safely. And no, he's not alone. In fact, he's not even moving under his own steam.'

'What the hell does that mean?'

'He seems injured. From the state of his face and the way he's moving, he's taken a beating.'

'Is he OK?'

'Hard to say. He's basically being dragged across the encampment ground, towards Travis.'

'He's a fucking dead man.'

Joshua began to rise as he spoke, his pale skin reddening in anger. Dempsey reached out his hand and placed it on Joshua's shoulder, to prevent him climbing all the way to his feet.

'He will be. But not yet. We need to know more.'

Joshua looked at Dempsey, their eyes fixed. For a moment he seemed ready to argue, which would take time they did not have. Dempsey was relieved, then, when he indicated his agreement with a nod of the head.

It allowed Dempsey to return focus to where it was needed.

'OK, Grace. Travis and the bomb. Where are they?'

'We don't know for sure that it's the bomb. It just—'

'Let's assume it's the bomb. Where is it? And where are they?'

'It's fifty or sixty yards up from the cabin you're in. Out the door, go right and hug the fence. Eventually you'll hit what looks to be the opening of a mineshaft.'

'A mineshaft? That wasn't on the images.'

'The area's full of them, boss, but we didn't see this one from up here, either. Not until it was opened and . . . whatever that thing is was wheeled out.'

'You mean the bomb?'

'Yeah. They must have been storing it in there.'

'Makes sense if it is the bomb. If it's something Travis made ten years ago. They had to keep it somewhere.'

Dempsey looked at his watch.

Less than nine minutes.

'How many men with Travis?'

'Twelve. But there's an open cargo van waiting right next to them. I can't guarantee no one's in there.'

'How many with Scott?'

'Just one.'

'And how far is he?'

'Two hundred yards from Travis and closing. Directly to your left if you were hugging that fence.'

'And everyone else? Any significant numbers nearby?'

'Small groupings here and there, as you'd expect. No single mass of men and the small groups are dispersed all over the camp.'

'How many in total?'

'Hundred and twenty or so, give or take.'

Dempsey turned to Joshua.

'What's going to happen if the air strike hits that bomb?'

'No idea,' Joshua replied. 'If it was a military nuke then nothing. But it's not, is it? So we have to assume it goes bang.'

'Which means either we get it back into that mine opening or we have to call off the strike.'

'We aren't getting out of here alive if there's no air strike, Joe. Me, you *or* Scott. Your team, they can only pin a hundred and twenty men down for so long.'

'Then we have to move quick. You as fast as you were?'

'Are you?'

'Everyone, this is happening now. Leave Travis and his men to us. Same goes for Scott. We need you to keep every other bastard off of our backs for as long as you can. On my first shot, cause havoc.'

Dempsey lifted his rifle to his shoulder and looked his former friend in the eye.

'Let's go find out.'

EIGHTY-FIVE

3.21 p.m. EDT

Dempsey turned right out of the door and broke into an immediate run. He did not doubt for a moment that Joshua would be at his shoulder. Moving fast, he put some distance between himself and the cabin.

'Boss, Travis is to your right. Where are you going?'

He ignored Grace's voice. Dempsey had already selected his first target. He knew that he could not take Travis and his men alone. He needed a fully focused Joshua, and he would not have *that* until Scott Turner was safe.

From what Dempsey could see, Turner was being manhandled. Dragged and pushed and pulled against his will by a meathead twice his width. Poor odds at the best of times, but worse when the boy was so obviously hurt. The sight made Dempsey angry. He could only imagine what it was doing to the man behind him.

Turner and his captor were now less than a hundred yards from the cargo van that was parked closed to Travis's location. But they were less than thirty from the fast-approaching Dempsey.

The meathead spotted them a moment later. At first he

did not seem to register the sight. Why would he, Dempsey realised; who would expect to see two gunmen taking on an encampment of this size?

A second later and he was going for his gun. Just one more and he was dead, courtesy of a hole in his chest and another in his head.

One from Dempsey.

And one from Joshua.

Neither man had slowed at all as they'd fired and so the final few yards took Joshua just seconds to cover. Dempsey veered off to the left and stopped as Joshua passed him. He listened to the sniper fire that was now raining from the hills around them, as Joshua fell to his knees next to his injured son, cupped his bloody head in his left hand and used his right to pat him down for any sign of a bullet wound.

'Are you hurt?'

Scott seemed unaware of where he was or even of who was holding him. His tearful eyes were widened in shock and in pain and he seemed on the cusp of unconsciousness.

'Son, are you OK?'

Scott still said nothing. Wherever his mind now was, it was not here.

'Jim. We've got less than seven minutes. We need to do this.'

Dempsey turned a full three hundred and sixty degrees as he spoke. Checking every detail he could see from where he stood. In the few seconds of gunfire, the effect had been exactly as he had planned. All around the camp, Liberation men were running for cover. It was precisely the effect Dempsey had wanted. While Travis's men were avoiding death from the hills, they were not protecting Travis.

He turned back to Joshua and saw that he now had his son's

injured cheek resting in his large, rough hand. Scott was not moving, other than the deep rise and fall of his chest. It told Dempsey all he needed to know.

He's hurt. But he's alive.

'If you want any of us to live through this then it has to happen now.'

Joshua said nothing. Instead he took his hand away from his son's cheek and stood up, his expression grim.

'Let's end it.'

Dempsey had almost forgotten how well he and Joshua complimented one another in the field. Both were dangerous when working alone but together they had been nothing short of lethal. He now discovered that the years they had spent apart had not changed that at all.

They moved in perfect unison as they first reached and then passed the cargo van. Operating in a near-dance of sweeping rifle barrels and back-to-back cover, the speed and the effortlessness with which they took out first the driver and then the three armed men in the back almost surprised Dempsey.

The efficiency of their expert movements was an art in and of itself. They moved ever forward, an inevitable tide of death, with every step taking them closer to Travis.

And Travis knew it.

At first his attention had been caught by what seemed to be an attack from the hills. He had reacted as anyone would, diving for cover from the sniper fire and ordering his entourage to do the same. But behind that cover he had finally seen the real danger that was coming for him.

Dempsey had seen the moment where Travis had laid

eyes on Joshua and he had watched the fear spread across his arrogant face. What he had also seen, though, was the effect that fear seemed to have. Instead of cowering, Travis had rushed to his device. For cover, Dempsey had first assumed. But as they came ever closer, working their way through Travis's men as he ordered them to face his two would-be killers, Dempsey was no longer so sure.

Not that he had time to focus on what Travis might be doing. With the man's full entourage now set upon them, Dempsey's attention – like Joshua's – had to be on the task at hand. One slip up and they would never reach Travis at all, Dempsey knew, and so he allowed for no distraction. With Joshua at his side, every threat was neutralised the moment it arose. Single shot after single shot, the bodies mounting with every step.

Until, finally, there was only one man left.

'Did you really think I wouldn't come for you, Travis? You really thought you'd get away with what you did to my son?'

Travis said nothing. Instead he just smiled. Dempsey noted that he had one hand rested on the side of the device. A part that neither he nor Joshua could see. His instincts were suddenly screaming. Something was very wrong.

'What have you done?'

'I'm not going back there.' Travis's voice was calm as he answered Dempsey's question. 'I won't be silenced again.'

'WHAT DID YOU DO?'

'You know what I've done.'

Joshua stepped forward.

'Is that what I think it is?'

Travis's eyes flicked away from Dempsey and settled on his former cellmate.

'I told you enough about it. You'd think you'd know.'

'*You* can't do that Peyton. That thing, it'll kill everyone in Summit Hill too.'

'It's done. Nothing's going to stop that now. Nothing can.'

'You can. You don't need to do this.'

'I'm not getting out of here alive, anyway. I knew that the moment I saw you. So if this is the only message I get to send, well, it's not the one I wanted. It's not Philadelphia. But it's better than nothing.'

'But they're *your* people, you lunatic. You'll be killing your own people.'

'Fuck them. They're a means to an end.'

Dempsey stepped forward, lifted the tip of his rifle's barrel and pressed it to Travis's head.

'How long?'

'Four-minute warning, Agent Dempsey.' He smiled as he spoke. The threat of the rifle meant nothing.

'Turn it off.'

'Fuck you.'

'Turn it off now.'

'Or what? You kill me?'

Dempsey looked at his watch.

Three minutes until the strike.

'Turn it off. Now.'

'Not a chance.' Travis's smile grew as he answered, his eyes fixed on Joshua. 'You know what makes this OK? At least I get to take you with me. You and that fucking snivelling kid of yours. At least—'

Travis would never complete his sentence. It was cut short by a burst of bullets, fired into his face by Joshua from barely five feet away. The impact shattered his head, exit wounds splattering the ground behind him with the contents of his skull.

Joshua had dropped his rifle and was moving forward before the body even hit the ground. He rammed his shoulder into Travis's device and began to push.

'Come on,' he shouted at Dempsey. 'Help me with this.'

Dempsey hesitated. Joshua's execution of Travis had taken him by surprise.

'We didn't have time for his bullshit,' Joshua explained. 'But we do have time to get this thing underground. If I get it far enough in, maybe you all walk away from this.'

Dempsey understood, and it made his stomach drop. He stared at his old friend-turned-enemy for just a heartbeat as the words sank in. He knew that Joshua was right; that for any of them to survive this, someone had to stay behind. The realisation hit him hard, but there was no time for debate. No time for delay.

Instead he rammed his shoulder into the spot next to Joshua's and together they pushed Travis's bomb back the way it had come. Towards the mine lift that was, Dempsey now saw, sitting open at the top of the shaft.

Straining every ounce of strength in both their bodies, it took them thirty seconds to force the device back towards and then into the lift.

Joshua climbed in beside it, then turned to face Dempsey.

'You're sure?'

'The shaft probably won't be enough. To be safe, this needs to go *into* the mine.'

'Jim—'

'I came here to save him, Joe.'

Dempsey nodded in understanding, swallowing hard.

'You sure you can push it alone? When you get to the bottom.'

'I guess we'll find out. Now go get my son out of here.'

'I will.'

'And look after him for me. OK?'

Dempsey could not bring himself to answer, no more than he could hide the tears that now began to fill his eyes.

'He's a good kid, Joe.'

'I know.'

'He's not like me. You make sure he stays that way.'

Joshua slammed the cage door without another word and hit the button that would send it down.

Dempsey could spare no time to watch him go.

Within ten seconds he was in the cargo van. The vehicle's keys were in the ignition, saving him the time it would otherwise take to hot-wire the thing. It took another twenty seconds to drive the truck to where Scott Turner was lying unconscious on the ground and to physically lift him into the passenger seat.

He risked one last glance.

Sixty seconds to the strike. Maybe a hundred to the bomb.

Shifting the transmission into drive, Dempsey hit the gas as he turned the wheel hard, spinning the truck to face the right direction and accelerating towards the open gate at the far end of the camp.

The vehicle was not built for speed but it was still fast enough for Dempsey's purpose, killing the distance quickly so that they were already through the gate and motoring along the dirt road to Summit Hill as the US Air Force jet bombers passed overhead.

Dempsey kept his foot on the gas until they had cleared the canopy of overhead trees that lined the road, conscious of the thunderous sounds of destruction that were shaking the ground behind them. Only once he was clear of the dirt road and on the highway back to the nearby town did he pull the handbrake and bring the van to a sharp sideways stop.

From here he could see the plumes of fire exploding upwards as the bombs hit and the jets banked to take their next run. The four bombers had been given one brief. To wipe out the Liberation encampment. Even from this distance, Dempsey had no doubt that they were doing exactly that.

He looked at his timer. Travis's four-minute warning had come and it had gone.

There was no way for Dempsey to tell which of the explosions had been Travis's device, detonated deep within the mine. With so many conventional bombs being dropped above ground, the sound of the weapon that would have killed them all was simply lost in the mix.

The barrage continued for over a minute more. Enough to guarantee the end of all life in the Liberation camp, and with it the end of Liberation itself. A threat to the very existence of the United States, wiped out while still nothing more than a name from the past.

For Dempsey, the victory was more personal. He had done what he had set out to do. He had protected the boy.

Scott Turner was only a few years younger than his father had been when Joshua and Dempsey had first met. And yet, as Dempsey looked over at him now, unconscious on the seat next to his own, all he could see was the boy he had once known.

The son his friend had loved.

And, in that moment, he could understand Joshua's sacrifice.

15 JULY
2021

EIGHTY-SIX

11.34a.m. EDT

'How's he doing?'

Dempsey turned in response to the question and smiled as Grace walked down the corridor towards him in the intensive care unit at Thomas Jefferson University Hospital.

'He's doing OK,' he replied. 'He woke about an hour ago. In and out since then, but it looks like he's out of the woods.'

Grace took a look through the window that was beside them, into the private room beyond. The bed was occupied by a figure too heavily bandaged to identify by sight, but she already knew it was Scott Turner.

'What did the doctors say?'

'That he took a hell of a beating but that hopefully it's nothing that won't fix itself. It's his brain they're monitoring now. He had a pretty severe concussion. But even that seems to be improving.'

'Is he staying in the ICU?'

Dempsey smiled again. Like him, Grace knew that the best test of what a medic really thought was how long they allowed a patient to take up valuable critical care time. It was exactly why he had asked the same question himself just thirty minutes earlier.

'They're moving him today.'

'Good news, then.'

'Yeah. Good news.'

Dempsey looked back into the room. Grace was right, it *was* good news. The boy was going to be fine. Sore, but fine. His recovery, though, was not what now concerned Dempsey. His mind was on something that would be far more painful.

'Have you seen him yet?'

'No.'

'Any reason for that?'

Dempsey turned to face Grace.

'You know the reason. What am I supposed to tell him?'

'The truth.'

'The whole truth?'

'That's up to you. How much can you live with?'

Dempsey had been asking himself that question for the best part of two days. He still did not know the answer. Telling Scott about his father's death – both the fact of it and the detail – was inevitable; the young man had a right to know what his dad had done for him.

But what about the rest? What about where his father had been for the past four years?

And what about who put him there?

'You think he's even going to remember who I am?' he asked.

'You were basically his uncle for three years, right? When you and his dad were stationed together?'

'A little more. But he was young. It was a long time ago.'

'He'll know exactly who you are. Trust me. You're a pretty damned memorable uncle.'

'That makes it worse, surely?'

'What?'

'What I did to his father. Jim Turner was my closest friend, Grace. As close as you are now. And look what I did to him. Where I put him. How's the kid going to see that as anything but a betrayal?'

'Where you put him? Jesus, you do guilt like no one I've ever met. You didn't put him anywhere. You didn't even know that place existed before two days ago. None of this is your fault. That guy in that room, Dempsey, he's alive because of you.'

'What if he doesn't see it that way?'

'Who gives a shit? If he doesn't then he doesn't, and all that'll mean is that he's not worth your time. But if he does, well, after what he's put himself through in the past two years, he's going to need a friend.'

Dempsey said nothing, because there was nothing to say. Grace knew him too well; enough to cut to the heart of the thing in just moments. There was no room for debate on this one.

As hard as it would be, he had no choice. With Joshua gone, it was his duty to step up.

'You coming in with me?' he asked.

'Not my place.'

'Then why are you here?'

'Thought someone should bring you up to speed. You've been AWOL in this place since Tuesday.'

'AWOL? Technically I'm on leave, remember.'

'Oh, yeah. This is your vacation, isn't it? How's that going?'

Dempsey laughed. The first time in two days. It felt good.

'So what do I need to know?' he asked

'Just what you'd expect. Homeland mopped up what was left of Liberation in Summit Hill. Which wasn't a whole hell of a lot once the bombers were done.'

'And the bomb system in Philadelphia? The other locations?'

'Not ideal, to be truthful. When we wiped out the camp, we wiped out the plans. So we didn't have the site references for a series of fast strikes. It took them three hours to find the first and thirty to find them all. Not one of them was manned.'

'You think the message got out? That the big one had been taken down?'

'Got to be. Every single building we hit had been abandoned in a hurry.'

'That means there's God knows how many of Travis and Arnold's disciples still out there.'

'Like I said, it's not ideal. But look how long it took them to regroup last time. And that was without Homeland laser-focused on them. They'll turn up. In the meantime they're no real threat we know of.'

'That we know of. We didn't know about this one.'

'Or a hundred others. There are always threats, Dempsey. That's why we exist. But this one's done. They're Homeland's responsibility now.'

Dempsey nodded his head. Once again Grace had a point.

'Speaking of Homeland, how's O'Rourke?'

'Worse off than your friend in there, but she'll live. It's going to be a hard hill for her to climb but it could be worse.'

Dempsey was happy to hear that the Homeland agent had made it. He had quickly grown to like and respect her. It made the forced retirement that must lie ahead for her all the more disappointing.

'And Arnold? How'd he take it all?'

'Badly. All that arrogance and bullshit, once he knew Travis wasn't coming for him, that disappeared like smoke. McMillan threatened him with a spot in the Facility and he crumbled. He gave up banking details, company info, political supporters, everything. Most important for you, he also gave us what we needed to know on Scott. He confirmed Scott was never a part of Liberation. That they'd manipulated him with promises about his father.'

'What did that buy him?'

'Absolutely nothing. Colonel Walker's already got his room made up and waiting for him in Texas, and no doubt there's half a prison worth of inmates itching to meet a diehard Liberation man who's not protected by Joshua.'

Dempsey would not allow himself to smile at the news. He still hated the idea of the Facility. The idea that anyone should be imprisoned for life without trial. But in Cam Arnold's case, with all that man had done . . . Dempsey wouldn't be losing any sleep.

'And what about Scott?' he finally asked. The question he had been avoiding. 'Did you do what I said?'

'Of course I did. He's free. There'll be no record of any involvement from him in any of this.'

'Thank you.'

'You need to thank someone a lot higher up the tree than me. You realise this is your one "no questions asked" favour used up, right?'

Dempsey nodded his head in understanding. Grace's access to the president of the United States was always valuable, but Dempsey had never before asked her to use it for personal reasons. John Knowles owed him more than he owed any man on Earth, and yet Dempsey had refused to call it. Until now.

Until Scott Turner.

'I hope he's worth this,' Grace said.

'So do I. But even if he's not, I had a promise to keep.'

'You've got more than one of those. You know you have to be in London in two days, right? For the baptism?'

'I know. My flight's in a few hours.'

'You need a ride?'

'Yeah, that'd be good.' Dempsey looked back into the small room. From the movement in the bed, he could tell that Scott Turner was awake again. 'I'll meet you at the car.'

He turned without another word, took a deep breath and opened the door to the room.

ACKNOWLEDGEMENTS

As ever, this book could not have been written without the help of a great many people, a fact which is especially true this time around. Until February 2020 the fourth book in the Dempsey/Devlin series was about a race to stop a weaponised virus that threatened a pandemic in the United States. By March 2020 that was no longer a viable story — at least not for now — and so I had to come up with a new thriller for my 2021 release.

No Way to Die is that new thriller, based on a single-line idea and written without preparation time, all during a global lockdown. These were the strangest writing conditions I have ever experienced and, for all of our sakes, I hope not to encounter them again. That this book now exists despite them is thanks in no small part to the following people.

To Pippa Crane, senior editor at Elliott & Thompson and my ongoing lifeline to the world of books. In the last few months Pippa and I have spoken a lot about how painless this book's edit has been; how, four books in, we seem to have found our synch and our rhythm in turning a first draft into the book readers will find on the shelf; I hope that this is evident when you read *No Way to Die*. What Pippa has tactfully not mentioned, however, is her management of my writing through 2020 and some of 2021. Of pushed backed deadlines and no doubt exasperation at failed promises of 'next week'. Pippa, it cannot have been easy. Thank you for bearing with me.

To Donna, my copy editor. After four books with Donna, too, the process has become a pleasure. I sincerely hope it's not just me who thinks that.

To the rest of the Elliott & Thompson team: to Sarah, to Marianne and Jennie, and to Lorne. I feel as lucky with my fourth book as I did with my first, and as I am sure I will with my eighth (and beyond?). To have the support of such an amazing team behind me makes even the harder times effortless. Thank you all for your dedication, your expertise and above all your friendship. It is important to work with people you like and in that respect I am very lucky indeed.

To the rest of the team: to Gill and her sales maestros; to the marketing guru Andrew and to my publicist Emma. Without you guys this book would be nowhere to be found and no one would have heard of it anyway. Thank you all for the invaluable jobs you do.

To everyone at Ewing Law and particularly to Scott Ewing, to Nicola Mitchell and to Rebecca Ireland. Without your unquestioning support there is simply no way I could juggle my day job with this whole writing thing! I've said it before and it bears repetition: you guys are the difference between doing this and not doing this. As ever, I cannot thank you all enough.

To my friends within the book world whose advice and encouragement and often just deeply inappropriate humour keep me on track and typing even when I'd rather be doing something else.

To everyone whose name I 'borrowed' for this book, whether I realised it or not (all except Dylan Wrixon, who doesn't deserve thanks because he demanded inclusion). And particularly to Bambi O'Rourke, whose very generous husband donated to charity for her name to feature in *No Way to Die*, and who in doing so gave me perhaps my favourite character name in any of my books so far.

To my sister Kate and my friend Grant: my beta readers. Both enthusiastically honest and brutal when needs be, your always genuine reactions to the plot and the overall pace of the story are my essential barometer to know if I'm getting it right. You probably don't realise it but your regular three-word-text demands for 'any more book' are all the encouragement I need to get back at the screen for the next lot.

To my readers. Whether you be bloggers, reviewers, dedicated thriller fans or just holidaymakers who picked up a book that looked suited to a beach. You are the reason we write and your engagement with my books – whether it's the act of buying and reading them, or whether it's coming to festivals and/or events, or interaction on social media – is one of the most pleasurable parts of this whole process. For those of you who have read my previous thrillers before this one, thank you. For those who haven't, I hope you don't stop at *No Way to Die*. Taking time out to enjoy a book is one of the best things you can do for yourself and recommending one you love is one of the best things you can do for others. Never stop reading, never stop reviewing and never hesitate to get in touch.

To my mum. My original fan. You had to listen to a lot less than you usually do as I mulled over the plot on this one; lack of any thinking time whatsoever *and* the distraction of a global pandemic will do that, I guess. But still, once you got your first half of the first draft it was back to action stations and long, meandering conversations about characters who – let's be honest – we both now think are real. Regular readers of my books will by this point be getting bored with my always lengthy acknowledgements, I'm sure, but if they can just indulge me one last time I will say it again: you are as responsible for these books as I am.

And finally to my wife and to my son.

Victoria, you are the greatest cheerleader, the most enthusiastic fan, the most diplomatic beta reader and the most effective cracker of the anti-procrastination whip. How you manage all of that while also being the perfect wife and mother is frankly beyond me, and that's before we consider that you have a career of your own. Our life is made possible by you and there is literally nothing I could do to repay you for all that you do and all that you are. That rainy night when you said 'yes' on Waterloo Bridge seems luckier by the day . . .

And Joseph? What can I say? You are my greatest and happiest distraction. Love you, son.

ALSO BY TONY KENT

Power Play

A nation under attack. A web of corruption. But who is pulling the strings?

When a plane explodes over the Atlantic Ocean, killing US presidential candidate Dale Victor along with hundreds of other passengers, it appears to be a clear-cut case of terrorism. But as criminal barrister Michael Devlin and intelligence agent Joe Dempsey are about to discover, everything is not as it seems.

But who would have wanted this potential new president out of the way – and was willing to commit mass murder to do it? As the mounting evidence starts to point all the way to the top of the US government, together they must find a way to free the White House from the deadly grip that has taken hold of power. But someone is determined to stop Dempsey and Devlin from discovering the truth. At any cost.

RRP: £8.99 | ISBN: 978-1-78396-491-8

Marked For Death

A Richard and Judy Book Club pick

A deadly secret. A chilling game. A past you can't escape.

When London's legal establishment is shaken to its foundation by the grisly death of a retired judge, Detective Chief Inspector Joelle Levy is tasked with finding his killer. But with fifty years of potential enemies to choose from, it's no easy challenge.

News reporter Sarah Truman sets out to investigate on her own, not suspecting that the trail will lead straight back to her own front door and her fiancé Michael Devlin when tragedy strikes close to home.

Struggling with his grief and guilt, and now caught up in a madman's terrible quest for revenge, Michael must race to bring the killer to justice – before it's too late.

RRP: £7.99 | ISBN: 978-1-78396-449-9

Killer Intent

A Zoe Ball Book Club Choice

An assassin's bullet. A deadly conspiracy. But who is calling the shots?

When an attempted assassination sparks a chain reaction of explosive events across London, Britain elite security forces seem powerless to stop the chaos threatening to overwhelm the government.

As the dark and deadly conspiracy unfolds, three strangers find their fates entwined: Joe Dempsey, a deadly military intelligence officer; Sarah Truman, a CNN reporter determined to get her headline; and Michael Devlin, a Belfast-born criminal barrister with a secret past.

As the circle of those they can trust grows ever smaller, Dempsey, Devlin and Truman are forced to work in the shadows, caught in a life-or-death race against the clock, before the terrible plot can consume them all.

RRP: £7.99 | ISBN: 978-1-78396-382-9

To hear all the latest news about Tony,
his writing and his events, visit **www.tonykent.net**
or follow him on Twitter: **@TonyKent_writes**,
Instagram: **tonykent_writes**,
Facebook: **Tony Kent – Author**
and YouTube: **Tony Kent Writes**